"I want my babe back. I never agreed
that you should have him!"

Jehan held out her arms to Roger, the cloak falling
back to reveal her softly rounded figure. De Mortimer
rose from his chair and shook his head, his dark eyes
cold and hard. "You forget that although I fathered
your bastard, I've plans for myself which don't include
old loves. If you persist in this nonsense, I would fear
for you."

The menace in his voice was not lost on Jehan.
She unlaced the ties of her shift, whispering through
her tears, "Then slay me now, Roger, for I don't wish
to live. You're hard, selfish and cruel . . ."

She picked up his dagger, drawing it from its sheath
and thrust it into his hand, pressing it against her bared
breast. He threw the dagger to the floor, furious with
her, and gave her face a resounding slap. "Jehan . . ."
he murmured softly, coming to stand close behind her.
"Give up this insane quest for the boy. Let him be and
know that he is well cared for."

Shaking her head stubbornly, she leaned her head
back weakly against him as she felt his hands slide over
her shoulders, caressing her throat and slipping inside
her unlaced shift. Was this what she had wanted from
him and why she had sought him out, she thought with
surprise as she gazed at his dark passionate face and
found his mouth taking possession of hers? She twined
her arms tightly about his neck, remembering nothing
and knowing only that Roger was claiming her again . . .

A Banner
Red and Gold

by *Annelise Kamada*

The quiet mind is richer than a crown.
Robert Greene (1560–92)

WARNER BOOKS

A Warner Communications Company

WARNER BOOKS EDITION

Cover art by Elaine Duillo

Warner Books, Inc., 75 Rockefeller Plaza, New York, N.Y. 10019

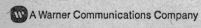 A Warner Communications Company

Printed in the United States of America

First Printing: August, 1980

10 9 8 7 6 5 4 3 2 1

To my dear friends,

David Christmas, for his faith, encouragement,
and persistence; and
Carl Johnes, who believed in me

Main Characters

GLAIRN CASTLE

JAMES KILBURN, Earl of Glairn
GILLIAN KILBURN, his wife
ALAIN KILBURN, their eldest son
MISTRESS NON, Kilburn's nurse
GRAEME, her son, Kilburn's former squire
SIR SIMON JARDINE, castle constable
HAL JARDINE, his grandson and Kilburn's squire
MASTER BRASSARD, physician
AGNES BRASSARD, his daughter
FATHER GODFREY, priest
SIR THOMAS FITZHUGH, knight
EILYS FITZHUGH, his wife

THE BARONS OF ENGLAND

AYMER DE VALENCE, Earl of Pembroke
THOMAS PLANTAGENET, Earl of Lancaster
HENRY PLANTAGENET, Earl of Leicester, his brother
EDMUND FITZALAN, Earl of Arundel
JOHN DE WARENNE, Earl of Surrey
HUMPHREY DE BOHUN, Earl of Hereford
ROGER DE MORTIMER, Baron of Wigmore, later Earl
  of March
ROGER DE MORTIMER, Baron of Chirk, his uncle

THE ROYAL COURT

EDWARD II, King of England

ISABELLA, his queen

PRINCE EDWARD (NED), heir to the throne and Duke of Aquitaine

THOMAS OF BROTHERTON, Earl of Norfolk

EDMUND OF WOODSTOCK, Earl of Kent

} half brothers to the king

HUGH DESPENSER, the elder, later Earl of Winchester

HUGH DESPENSER, the younger, his son ("Nephew Hugh")

OTHERS

CHARLES IV, King of France, Isabella's brother

ROBERT, Duke of Artois, her cousin

ADAM ORLETON, Bishop of Hereford

WALTER STAPLEDON, Bishop of Exeter

ROBERT DE HELAND, Constable of Nottingham Castle

GERALD DE ALSPAYE, Sub-lieutenant of the Tower

EMRYS, Welsh harper, squire to Wigmore

SIR RALPH DE MAUDLEY, knight

JEHAN DE MAUDLEY, his wife

SIR POWYS AP RHYS, Welsh knight

BLEDDYN AP RHYS, illegitimate son of Jehan and Roger de Mortimer

LIONEL PORCHER, wool merchant, Kilburn's uncle

GEOFFREY HARRON, Gillian's brother, secretary to the earl of Pembroke

ROBERT HARRON, Lord Kestwick, Gillian's brother

ELIZABETH D'UMFRAVILLE HARRON, his wife

ALIANOR FITZALAN, daughter of the Earl of Arundel

Author's Note

The historical events, as chronicled in this novel, are as accurate as I have been able to portray them within the context of the story itself. Where a point of history is in dispute, the one which best enhanced the dramatic force of the happenings of the day was chosen. Although James and Gillian Kilburn, their families, Glairn, Alianor Fitz-alan, Jehan de Maudley, Sir Powys ap Rhys and Bleddyn (pronounced "Blethin"), Pen-yr-bryn and the manor house near Shrewsbury are fictitious, King Edward II, Queen Isabella, Roger de Mortimer, Aymer de Valence, and the other earls all lived, and while the curtain of time may have obscured or warped their true likenesses, they are shown through my eyes, as I would have wished them to be.

For their kind assistance in my research, I would like to thank Anne Cotton of Harvard University and Mrs. Hannah Lewin of the New York City Club of the Women's Welsh Clubs of America, who introduced me to the medieval Welsh saga, "The Mabynogion," in which I found the wolf's cub, Bleddyn; but most of all, to Raphael Holinshed whose Chronicles, written in 1577, are so wonderfully filled with historical trivia.

The tapestry of history is an endless one, and the silken threads of Edward's reign have not yet been woven into a completed pattern. Only partially are the figures in the foreground filled in, while some will join those already in the fabric of that which is the past. Still others hover, shadowlike, in the background, waiting for their time to come.

Prologue
1316

As the seagulls circled and wheeled about the large ship moving slowly into the tidal current of the channel, their plaintive cries shattered the stillness of the gray morning. Bristol lay hours behind the voyagers, and the empty, barren land, sloping darkly toward the water's edge, became visible to them now and again as the eerie white mist was shredded by a stiffening east wind. Soon the channel would broaden and the restless, turbulent expanse of the Irish Sea would surround them.

Jehan de Maudley stood in the stern of the ship, her face to the wind, tendrils of red hair tangling wildly against the hood of her cloak which had slipped back, revealing its soft brown fur lining. She seemed oblivious to the activity about her, and so bitter was her expression that none dared to approach her. She stared at the receding shoreline where an occasional flash of russet and gold gave a hint of the autumn which lay over a weary earth. A cold smile twisted her mouth as she raised her green eyes toward the dark, rain-laden clouds scudding low across the dismal sky.

'Tis fitting! she thought. 'Tis right that the weather weeps, for I've no tears left.

She had not always felt so empty. An unbidden remembrance of strong arms holding her and a hard mouth moving against hers flooded her mind.

De Broze is dead and lies in a nameless grave. The words echoed within her. He was never mine, she told herself. All he cared for was his wife, and his desire for her destroyed him. But the knowledge gave her no comfort.

She had seen her lover's widow in York that dreadful winter following his death in battle at Bannockburn when her own grief was near to hysteria. Gillian de Broze was already large with James Kilburn's second child and quickly wed thereafter. Now she was the countess of Glairn. Aye, she's done well for herself, Jehan thought spitefully, remembering how Kilburn's hazel eyes had blazed with hatred at Tynemouth while he humiliated her for being Arnaut's mistress. Her thin hands tightened their hold on the wooden rail.

Why had they not let her die! She had chosen death; the empty vial was still clutched in her hand when she was found. The queen's physicians had wrested her from the dark, peaceful oblivion into which she had fallen, returning her to the living pain of her memories.

Jehan shivered and wrapped the woolen cloak tightly about her slender body. Ugly! She had grown ugly—gaunt and bloodless—in the months following her return to the Welsh Marches. She caught a glimpse of a squat stone tower looming out of the fog on the distant shore, dark and brooding, keeping watch over a coast totally bereft of humanity. And then it, too, was lost to sight.

"Arnaut, I bid you farewell," she whispered brokenly. "I cannot mourn you any longer . . . I cannot." With an effort she turned her thoughts to her husband, who had come to York after her vain attempt at suicide and carried what remained of the beautiful, vibrant, and sensual girl he had wed home to his small holding near Wigmore. For the first time in their indifferent marriage, Ralph de Maudley had remained with his lady, seeing that she received the best care possible.

Now the gray-haired knight came out on the deck, his eyes quickly finding the small figure of his wife as she stood by the ship's rail watching the coastline fall away. A solidly built man of fifty-odd years with thinning hair and quiet, pleasant features, he stayed where he was, fearing to disturb her. In the weeks following their return from York, he had blamed himself for her state. As liegeman to the young baron of Wigmore, he had followed his lord on the endless Welsh campaigns. While privy to Roger de Mortimer's schemes and ambitions, he had never questioned the often near-treasonable actions of the high-born nobleman. Nor had de Maudley realized until too late that he had allowed his wild and headstrong young wife too much freedom. He could only guess what manner of perverse pleasures and passions she had found at the royal court as one of Queen Isabella's ladies.

As he looked with mute love at the pale profile of his lady, he found the purity of her heart-shaped face with its sharply defined cheekbones and the graceful line of her throat more compelling than the soft roundness of her girlhood. Dark brows swept winglike above slanted green eyes and her mouth had lost none of its sensual fullness. Lord de Maudley was pleased that Jehan had consented to accompany him to Ireland when Roger de Mortimer had summoned him, for he feared leaving her.

Had he known his wife's thoughts, Sir Ralph would have been startled, for her mind had suddenly returned to her girlhood . . . and Roger de Mortimer . . . and the pain. A wordless cry escaped her as she struggled to forget what had been forbidden her to remember.

It began to rain as the ship swung around the headland into the choppy gray waters of the Irish Sea. Jehan lifted her face, feeling the rain fall on her cold skin and mingle with the sudden stinging tears that welled into her eyes.

So there are still tears left! she realized with wonder and not a little fear at the thought of meeting Roger de Mortimer again.

PART ONE
1316

Chapter 1

The Great Hall echoed with laughter and gleeful cries, and the delicious and mouthwatering aroma of roasting meat permeated the air. Huge spits near the enormous hearths were tended by young serving boys who turned the carcasses of three boars the hunters had brought in the night before. They basted the crackling skins with juices which dripped into the trough pans beneath the heavy metal spits as the meat roasted to a crisp golden brown. Whole baked geese, eel pies, platters of vegetable fritters surrounded by hard-boiled eggs glazed with honey, and huge game pies covered with flaky crusts were placed before the members of the household seated at the long trestle tables flanking the dais where the earl and his lady sat beneath the red and gold canopy. Large trenchers of bread and smaller pieces used for sops were passed around while flagons of wine and the new October ale stood on the boards within easy reach of all, should the retainers overlook an empty cup. Not for many a month had Glairn's household beheld such an abundance of food, and they fell with appetite on this harvest feast.

The people deserved a celebration, James Kilburn reflected as he watched his assembled household enter into the spirit of the occasion. Outside, on the large meadow before the castle, huge bonfires were being lit as the autumn day began to fade. Glairn's villeins and serfs would soon be dancing to the accompaniment of pipes and tabors and drinking their fill from large casks of ale set up for them by their lord. For these humble folk, too, oxen roasted on outdoor spits, and the castle kitchens had provided great quantities of mouth-watering pasties stuffed to bursting with all manner of minced meats, raisins, and nuts. On the morrow all would kneel to thank God for having brought them his largesse once more.

"I think Hal Jardine has had more than his fill of wine," Gillian said, breaking into Kilburn's thoughts, while she laughed at the antics of his squire. Hal, in the midst of the younger knights, was unusually animated, even for so lively a youth. His cheeks were flushed and his eyes glittered with mischief as his companions teased him unmercifully about the physician's pretty daughter Agnes, who sat shyly by one of the earl's staunchest knights, Thomas Fitzhugh, and his wife, her dark eyes cast demurely down to her food. At the first sounds of Hal's dulcimer, she looked at the auburn-haired young man quickly, a becoming flush rising to her cheeks as he played a lilting melody directly at her. It was obvious to Kilburn that she was still unused to such attention, but Hal meant no harm with his youthful wooing.

"Young Agnes is an uncommonly pretty young maid," he remarked to his lady, who looked at him with eyes glowing brightly.

"She's that, Jamie, and bears a great affection for Hal..."

"Spare me your matchmaking, lovedy," Kilburn countered with good humor. " 'Tis to Master Brassard and Hal's grandfather you should direct your words, not to me. Whatever they decide, I will agree to, so long as you assure me of peace and harmony. I value the friendship of both my physician and my constable too highly to risk either one's displeasure!"

Gillian's pale cheeks flushed pink and the corners of her red mouth turned up in a delighted smile as she gazed fully at him. As always, the impact of her luminous dark blue eyes stirred the flame that flickered deep within him whenever he was with her.

How little she's changed, he thought with pleasure, studying her as she leaned gracefully toward him to drink from his goblet. How well he knew the texture of the glossy dark hair caught and smoothed by the jeweled gold fillets on either side of her well-shaped head. How often had his hands caressed the silken skin and ripe firmness of the body covered now by rich brocade. Fashioned in the new style, her gown fitted snugly over the bosom, from the deep neckline and tight sleeves to its voluminous skirt flaring out to reveal an under-robe of apricot satin. It was an extravagance, but one he did not begrudge her, for she looked as fine as any lady in Edward's court.

It was difficult to remember a time she had not been a part of his life, but there had been those empty, lonely years after he had foolishly allowed her to enter into a disastrous marriage with the brutish Gascon knight who had nearly cost her her life. What havoc Lord Arnaut DeBroze had brought to all their lives until he was slain at Bannockburn!

The earl sat back in his carved chair, swept by turbulent and tortured memories. Bannockburn! Never in the history of England had there been such a total, crushing defeat. The flower of the land's knighthood had fallen in the hidden pits and traps of the boggy earth of Scotland while the king had fled from the battlefield with his guard surrounding him. Edward's kinsman, the earl of Pembroke, had guided him safely to Dunbar where ships waited to carry him to safety. Kilburn sighed, and his long fingers tightened on the stem of his goblet. He had lost his best friend to the thrust of a Scottish sword, and Gillian's father had been swept to his death in the swift current of the Forth. Had it not been for the unselfish actions of his own squire, he would have joined in death his fellow barons whose lives had been forfeited through the self-willed indulgences of their king. Injured himself, Kilburn's loyal Graeme had carried his gravely wounded lord through Scotland, stripping him of all badges which might have revealed his identity. And at what a price, Kilburn thought bitterly, for now his former squire was condemned to a dark and sightless world because no physician could heal the wound he suffered in their flight.

"Jamie, where are your thoughts? You're much too grim. 'Tis not fitting on so joyous an evening!"

Gillian had been watching her husband with concern, for he seemed in an odd mood. The shimmering light of the candles burnished his smooth cap of chestnut hair with a brightness that belied the brooding, inward gaze of his hazel eyes. The finely drawn features were stern and his mouth austere. To what agonizing memory had his mind turned, she wondered. She longed for the evening's end, so that they could be alone. Had it not always been so, she asked herself. She had ever drawn her strength and peace of soul from him. He felt her uneasiness and touched her cheek lightly with a slender hand, his expression still bemused.

"Nay, sweetheart, 'tis just a touch of melancholy brought on by remembering those no longer with us!"

"Oh, Jamie, so many are gone!" she exclaimed in dismay. He smiled at her suddenly troubled face.

"Aye, my love, but I'll not mourn them all tonight, I promise you!"

One good thing had come of the battle, Kilburn thought with a smile, for they had been able to wed, making the son born of their unsanctioned love his legal heir. When Margaret was born in York shortly before Christmas of 1314, the royal approval of their marriage, with Edward's seal affixed, was in their possession. Queen Isabella had herself placed it into Gillian's hands as a gesture of her abiding affection and friendship. During the past two years, life had been hard, not only for those at Glairn, but throughout England. Gillian had remained steadfastly at his side, sharing his worries and his fears, unflinching in fulfilling the demands thrust upon her as chatelaine and countess of Glairn.

Deeply immersed in his private thoughts, Kilburn was not aware at first of the harsh, wild notes of the harp which suddenly echoed through the Great Hall. A small dark minstrel had begged entrance to the castle earlier that evening, offering to pay for his supper by playing for the lord.

"Jamie!" Gillian whispered urgently, breaking into

Kilburn's musing. "I don't like the manner of this minstrel's music. It disturbs me."

The primitive cadences of the harp's voice assaulted her senses, frightening her with the feelings it evoked within her. Kilburn saw her pale, her eyes darken with panic and her mouth tremble with unspoken dread. He stretched out his hand and clasped hers as the music began to coil insidiously about him. Alarmed, he raised his head and stared into the strange, slanted green eyes of Roger de Mortimer's squire.

Damn the man, he thought angrily. How did he get here?

In the hall everyone sat as if hypnotized by the odd little man in the wood-brown tunic and tattered cloak of animal skins. Blind Graeme, sitting in his eternal darkness, recognized the hands stroking the harp strings, and his body stiffened in sudden foreboding. He had not heard the sound of that harp for many years, and it brought back many uneasy memories. If the harper was here, his master was not too distant! And Roger de Mortimer's presence boded no good for Glairn, he was certain.

"Stop this wild playing!" Kilburn commanded loudly, and the harper's hands came to a discordant halt. "If you cannot find a more pleasant and harmonious air for this occasion of harvest celebration, then I must order you removed from the Hall."

The green eyes gleamed slyly, acknowledging the earl's recognition. The fine hands began to stroke and caress the small harp as if it were the body of a beloved woman, and the sensuous strains of a familiar lay drifted over the people. Suddenly the harp changed its mood and sang out joyously, soon joined by Hal's dulcimer and the other instruments from the musicians' gallery. Kilburn relaxed as his knights sang out the words lustily. Only the white, blind face of Graeme remained strained as he groped his way toward the dais, allowing the boy who tended to him to lead him to Kilburn.

"My lord, the harper . . . !" he called out. A hand grasped his arm with warm strength.

"I know, Graeme, 'tis de Mortimer's squire." Kilburn reassured him.

23

"Beware of him," his former squire said urgently. "He bodes trouble."

Guiding Graeme to a chair near his own, Kilburn thrust a cup of wine into the thin hand.

"Come, Graeme, let us drink together. 'Tis seldom that we meet anymore." He looked anxiously at the gaunt man seated uncertainly beside him, trying to find the childhood companion and the strong, seemingly invulnerable man who had stood at his side through so many battles. Life had dealt most unkindly with his Scottish-born squire. Bowing to Graeme's wishes, the earl had allowed him to work in the falcon mews where the hooded birds, as chained to their dark world as he was, seemed fitting companions. How greatly the squire had failed since his return from York. The paralysis the physicians predicted had not yet manifested itself, but he obviously was weakening.

"I must find out what the harper wants." Kilburn spoke softly so that only the blind man heard him. "He has not appeared here just to satisfy his hunger. As far as I know, my lord de Mortimer is still in Ireland. I'd not heard of his recall."

Graeme shook his head. "Emrys has ever been Wigmore's messenger and tool, and totally loyal to his master."

He did not need to speak of the days in Tynemouth when they had been in pursuit of the king, before the death of Piers Gaveston, and Emrys had been shunned by all. He knew Kilburn recalled the dark talk of necromancy, potions, and spells. Displaying that rare intuition so much a part of him, Kilburn assured his old companion that he would take care.

"He's not the black magician you fear, Graeme. He's just a small, twisted soul with hands that can make his harp speak and utter faith in the master he serves."

But Graeme could not be dissuaded from his belief. He emptied his wine cup and the boy placed it on the table. Kilburn gazed once more into the sightless face with its dim blue eyes framed by short, colorless lashes and the straw-colored hair that fell over the deep scar on his forehead, and he watched every step of his slow progress back to his seat.

Motioning the harper to approach as the music ended in a whisper of molten gold, Kilburn ordered his steward, Master de Blount, to give him some coins. From his place at Kilburn's feet, Emrys thrust a folded piece of parchment into the earl's hand. Glancing at it briefly, Kilburn nodded almost imperceptibly, and the small Welshman murmured barely intelligible words of thanks, bent low before the seated lord and scuttled away quickly. The torches flared brightly and the light of the many candles shimmered in the smoke and heat of the Hall as Kilburn ordered his goblet refilled. Although the tempo of the fete was once more renewed, Gillian noticed that Kilburn remained in a reflective, constrained mood.

So our newfound peace and prosperity are not to be allowed us, Kilburn thought sadly, his somber gaze sweeping over the familiar faces of those people who were a part of his own special world. Their unwavering loyalty to Glairn and its lord had brought them all safely through the turmoil and unspeakable horrors of the year following Bannockburn.

Returning to Glairn early in the previous year, he had found mute evidence of the ravages inflicted by raiders emboldened by England's politically impotent king and a Parliament more interested in bringing him to his knees than strengthening their defenses. Geoffrey Harron, Gillian's younger brother, on a rare visit to Glairn, reported that the Welsh had risen in rebellion, seizing much of their land which had been taken from them centuries before and held by the English barons as spoils of war. As personal secretary to Aymer de Valence, the earl of Pembroke, he told them how the earl had struggled to retain his hold on the vast estates in Wales which he had inherited from his father.

As the Scots raided ever deeper within England, the border lords battled hard to keep their holdings safe against the marauders. The red and gold banner flew high above the turrets of Glairn constantly and the earl remained on his land, seeing to the plowing and sowing of the fields in company with his steward and the village reeves. As the seeds began to send tender shoots through the brown earth, warming beneath the soft breath of spring, the first rains fell. But the kind, gentle, life-giving rain turned into an unceasing deluge and gradually devastated the land. The crops rotted in the ground; the low-lying regions of the realm turned into seemingly endless lakes. Fruit failed to ripen on the trees and quietly flowing streams suddenly became roaring torrents as the rain continued relentlessly. Kilburn's uncle, Lionel Porcher, stopping at Glairn while traveling through Northumberland in his quest for wool, reported seeing bloated carcasses of cattle and sheep swept up against the fallen trees that dammed the swiftly running waters. Serfs made homeless by the encroaching floods, soldiers cast out by impoverished liege lords unable to support them, infested the vast stretches of forest land, preying on lonely travelers journeying along the king's roads. Rotting corpses hanging from trees used as gibbets became common sights but did little to deter the robbery and murder which mounted as famine stalked the land. Glairn, despite its filled storehouses, was careful in doling out enough provender to keep its folk fed and its cattle alive. Kilburn ordered his knights and mounted men-at-arms to keep a strict vigil throughout Glairn's forests to prevent outsiders from invading its preserves. Inevitably pestilence followed famine, and the people stayed behind their locked and barred doors, fearful of the invisible death that stalked the ravaged land. Through it all, the second Edward and his court continued to pursue their extravagant pleasures, and feelings ran high against his callous indifference to the plight of his people, who now felt that God's hand had wreaked retribution on the king's people for having brought England's pride low through their defeat at Bannockburn.

As the months passed and winter gripped the land once more, Glairn and its folk settled down to the grim task of surviving. As in previous years when the harvest had been poor, the storehouses were opened and food was carefully distributed so that no one would starve. There was neither Yuletide fest nor Twelfth Night reveling, and while the castle household fared slightly better than the villagers and other manor folk, the board was simple, and prayers were offered by Father Godfrey in the castle chapel and village church that the famine would end when the next year's crops were harvested.

More than once Kilburn thanked the good fortune which had allowed Master Brassard to join his household, for the former royal physician had labored to keep Glairn's folk free of the diseases which beset so many of the holdings. With his daughter and Gillian beside him, he ministered to the old, the sickly, and the children who needed his skills. They became a familiar sight, the tall, spare man with the long gray beard, dark robes, and red physician's cap, flanked by the small, dark, winsome maid who spoke but rarely and the countess with her gentle voice and soothing touch. Though darkness fell, their lanterns still flickered in the cold air as they continued to tend those who needed them.

With the new year, it was evident that the evil tide had turned. Spring arrived with its gently falling rain and the summer was hot and dry. The fields greened and turned to gold as the crops ripened and the livestock grazed on pastures once more lush with grass. Three weeks after news was received that the queen at Eltham had presented her people with another prince, Gillian was brought to bed for the birth of her second son. It was an easy birth with no complications, for the ghosts which had haunted her other two pregnancies had long been laid to rest and she welcomed her babe's arrival with joy. The child had Gillian's dark hair and fair skin, but his father's features, and was named Hugh after the friend Kilburn had lost at Bannockburn. From his first strong cry, Hugh gave every promise of being lusty and healthy.

As his mind dwelled fondly on his newest son Kilburn's face relaxed and he impulsively grasped Gillian's hand and raised it to his lips.

"Who was that strange harper?" she asked quietly, pleased that Kilburn's attention had returned to her.

"No one you need concern yourself with, lovedy. The matter is well in hand, although I fear we may have to entertain an unexpected guest."

In answer to her unspoken question, he said in a low voice, " 'Tis Roger de Mortimer, Gillian, and he wishes to see me most urgently. I know little of the reasons or manner of his arrival myself, but I trust the stay will not be a long one."

"The baron of Wigmore? But you've not seen him since Tynemouth!" Gillian frowned, disturbed at the prospect of the sudden unexplained visit.

"Roger was always one to choose the dramatic above the sensible way of doing things. He's overly ambitious to attain the power he feels he is destined to wield, and that is what has ever made me distrust him."

Fighting an odd feeling of fear, Gillian rose from her chair.

"I'll leave you then," she murmured to him. "You can instruct Master de Blount as to the needs of your guest." She hesitated, standing before him, and a scent of sandalwood drifted over him sensuously. "I hope you'll find your way to bed before dawn."

Her large eyes sought his as he returned her gaze gravely. The long, dark-lashed hazel eyes told her what she wanted to know, and her pulses started to pound as she felt a blush rise to her face. Nothing had changed. Words were still unnecessary between them.

"Have you lost your senses totally, Roger?" Kilburn's tone was harsh. "Why did you not ride through the front gate? Your feeling for the dramatic is not to my liking."

He looked at the gaunt, bedraggled figure standing by the hearth, warming himself. Kilburn threw his cloak over a chair with an impatient gesture, and seated himself in his usual place by the hearth. Several of the earl's dogs had followed their master into his study when he had brought de Mortimer into the castle. They stretched themselves out at his feet, enjoying the chamber's warmth. Waiting at the hidden postern gate leading into the kitchen gardens for Thomas Fitzhugh to bring the Marcher lord to Glairn, Kilburn had been beset by doubts as to the wisdom of having anything to do with his reckless friend.

" 'Tis not what you think, James." The musical voice still held the familiar undertone of sardonic amusement. The tall, dark man looked totally exhausted. No badge revealed his identity, although his tunic was well cut and his torn cloak and the hose covering the long, strong legs were of the finest quality cloth. One leather boot was slit and a rough bandage wrapped about his ankle. His sword, leaning against the side of the hearth, glittered sharply in the firelight.

"God's blood, but the night has turned cold," he said, gratefully accepting a cup of wine handed to him by Thomas Fitzhugh, who stood mutely by Kilburn's chair, liking de Mortimer as little as he had four years before in Tynemouth.

"For God's sake, Roger, sit down. Let Tom look at your leg, and tell me what all this intrigue is about. Your squire delivered your message quite successfully. Since you seemed to need assistance I sent Tom along to bring you in. How could you have ridden your mount into the ground? Will you never learn temperance?"

The younger man threw his head back and laughed mockingly, white teeth flashing in his dark face.

"You have ever sat in judgment of me, James. Nay, stop frowning, I'll sit down. And this is not a game that I play."

He hobbled to the chair opposite Kilburn, stretching out his injured leg gingerly. As Thomas drew the boot carefully from the swollen foot, Roger's face blanched with sudden pain. "When that damn nag foundered, I went right over its head into some bushes."

"A physician should tend to you."

"Nay! No one must know I'm here, James." The dark eyes burned with determination. "I must find Pembroke, and try to reach the king through him. I've sent messenger after messenger but have had no reply."

"That doesn't warrant your presence here," Kilburn remarked dryly, knowing there was more to the tale than his guest had revealed so far. Out of the corner of his eye he glimpsed Emrys huddled in a corner of the study, his thin arms clutching the harp to him. He poured a cup of wine and offered it to the Welshman. The small man did not move, his strange eyes fastened on his master.

"Oh, take the damn wine, you miserable Welsh cur . . . I suppose you've earned it," de Mortimer said irritably, and the harper took the cup from Kilburn. Beads of sweat sprang up on the young baron's forehead as Tom's fingers prodded the red, puffy flesh of his injured leg.

"Take a care, damn you!" he muttered, and Tom placed the leg carefully on a stool set before his chair. As he rose to get warm water and clean cloths, de Mortimer asked him to bring back some food also. Kilburn gestured agreement, and Tom nodded his understanding as he disappeared through the door, making certain that it was closed securely behind him.

"Of course, Roger. You look famished. How long has it been since you've eaten last?"

De Mortimer shrugged and closed his eyes for a moment against the painful throbbing in his leg. He suddenly felt chilled, despite the heat of the fire.

" 'Twill be simple fare . . . particularly since no one is to know of your presence," Kilburn told him. He was irritated and mystified by de Mortimer's sudden appearance. His attitude smacked of flight and he had no great desire to be drawn into any intrigue in which Wigmore might have embroiled himself.

"Edward Bruce, obviously sent by his brother, sits in Ireland with a large army and is claiming all of the territory for Scotland. We've not half enough men or equipment to withstand him, James. I faced him at Kells, and it was an utter disaster. We've been driven back to Dublin because I've not been able to throw more fighting men into the field. We need archers and good stout spearsmen to send Bruce back to Scotland. I've called for reinforcements, but none have come."

"Does that give you the right then to leave your post and your responsibilities and skulk about northern England in search of Pembroke?" Kilburn said sharply, his hazel eyes narrowing as he looked with disbelief at de Mortimer. "Nay, Roger, your tale does not do your fertile imagination credit!"

De Mortimer ran a grimy hand through his unkempt hair, eyes glinting with sudden laughter, his pain forgotten for the moment.

"Well, what with creditors hounding me night and day, 'twas becoming impossible for me to remain much longer in Dublin. Edward Bruce is in Ulster and the latest whispers were that he's to be made king of Ireland."

"I'm sure the Irish will relish that." Kilburn's tone was heavy with sarcasm. "What else happened?"

His guest looked at him innocently.

"Damn it, Roger, stop this play-acting and tell me everything if you expect to receive any assistance from me."

The younger man held up a hand in surrender. How unfortunate that Lord Kilburn had so little patience with the dramatic aspects of life, he thought, for he relished what he had to tell.

"A great piece of luck, as a matter of fact. Those wild, lawless de Lacy relations of my wife's tried to have me killed."

Seeing that Kilburn was mystified by this piece of news, he explained, "My wife's grandmother was heiress to half the de Lacy lands in Meath, and Joan inherited them through her."

As Kilburn turned away impatiently, de Mortimer cried, "Wait 'tis all part of what happened. For years that damn tribe of them in Ireland have been crazy with jealousy over the power that came to me when I wed Joan de Gineville. They've refused to part with any of their lands. When it came to my ears that some mischief was afoot to murder me, I put the grand lord in irons in Dublin Castle, ran the whole damn lot from the holdings, and took possession of the estates in her name once and for all. Of course, they still hold Meath, but I vow 'twill not be for long." The dark eyes glowed with the sheer adventure of it as he recalled the satisfaction he felt as Lord de Lacy knelt before him, chained and shackled. The old man had raised red-rimmed eyes and spat at him, cursing him blackly.

" 'Tis true, James, but the de Lacys are an old family in Ireland and my methods of subduing them were not received with a great deal of admiration . . . so I needed to leave Ireland for a while—at least till tempers cool. But I am totally in earnest when I say the king must move in Ireland. I must speak to him, or to my fellow Lords Ordainers, if needs be."

The humor and lighthearted manner had fallen from him abruptly as he spoke, and Kilburn saw the desperation and passion which had brought this strange, satanic-natured man to the situation he was now in.

"I dared not land in Bristol, or Caernarvon—my enemies are waiting for me there—so I went north, lying off the coast near Burgh until I was able to come ashore just before daylight a week ago with Emrys. I managed to buy two horses from an innkeeper near Carlisle." His mouth twisted wryly. "Good gold for those spavined creatures . . . ! Hearing that Pembroke was in Berwick, we rode eastward."

"The city fell to Robert Bruce some time past. And if you must speak to anyone, it would be Lancaster."

"That twin-headed ass? He's as incompetent as his royal cousin, and ten times more stupid! Has he indeed grasped the scepter then?" De Mortimer was incredulous. "Where is Pembroke?" he asked as Kilburn smiled bitterly.

"There was little choice after Bannockburn. The barons, led by the Lords Ordainers, are now totally in power—particularly those barons most loyal to Thomas of Lancaster. The rules laid down by the Lords Ordainer so long ago are once more in effect, but with even more restrictions upon the king. Edward seems little concerned, so long as he is given enough freedom to pursue his pleasures. He's turned against Pembroke, too, for haranguing him overlong on his misdeeds and follies. 'Tis a thankless position to be the king's conscience."

For the first time since he had known de Mortimer, Kilburn saw him utterly dismayed. Never had his fortunes been so low; he had fled Ireland without permission, deeply in debt, leaving a trail of violence and probably murder behind him. The reckless face looked grim. Perhaps because he was exhausted and in pain, he seemed totally adrift.

"James, what can I do?" he asked in a low voice.

"Get your leg tended to and rest. We'll both sleep on it."

So engrossed were they in de Mortimer's dilemma that neither man heard the door open softly.

"My lord, I feared something ill had happened!"

They stared at Gillian standing uncertainly before them, suddenly flustered as neither man spoke, unaware of the effect she had on them with her sleep-drenched eyes and tousled hair.

She had awakened in the darkness of the curtained bed to find herself alone. Slipping down from the bed, she observed the chamber was still bathed in night, and disquieting fears had gripped her, for Kilburn had not yet come to bed. Sliding her feet into soft felt slippers, she donned her chamber robe and quietly opened the door. The corridor outside the bedchamber was silent, dimly lit by the flickering torches thrust into wall sconces spaced wide apart. Her shadow preceded her as she descended the short, winding stone stairs to the small hallway leading to Kilburn's study. A murmur of voices reached her ears as she lifted the latch to the door.

Seeing Gillian appear before him so suddenly, Kilburn sprang to his feet. He saw her eyes turn from him to de Mortimer's perplexed face and then become aware of her own state of dress.

"My lord . . ." she said again in a low voice as Kilburn grasped her hand and drew her to his side.

"Lord Roger de Mortimer, may I present my wife, Lady Gillian Kilburn."

The handsome-visaged man acknowledged her presence, and Gillian felt an uncomfortable warmth steal through her as his glowing dark eyes swept boldly over her as if knowing what the soft velvet cloth of her robe concealed. Only when he flashed a sudden smile in apology for not rising did she notice the exhaustion and pain in the tense line of his mouth and tightly stretched skin over the high cheekbones and beneath his eyes. She saw the leg stretched out before him, the torn boot and rent hose.

"My lord, you've been hurt!"

She sank down beside him, her shyness forgotten in her desire to ease the stranger's pain. Light, deft fingers prodded the bruised leg gently, but she heard him gasp as she touched the ragged gash that showed white against the angry red flesh surrounding it. Gillian stared at it for a moment and then raised troubled eyes to Kilburn.

"Jamie, Master Brassard should see this. It has a look to it that I care not for."

A hand clamped her wrist with fingers of steel as de Mortimer leaned over her with unexpected urgency.

"Nay, my lady, you shall tend me—no other must know of my presence here."

He fell back, white-lipped with the sudden pain which flooded through him at his abrupt movements. Kilburn felt a sharp stab of anger at the imperious manner in which de Mortimer had spoken to Gillian until he realized the desperation which motivated it.

"How can we possibly keep his presence secret, short of placing him in the dungeon?" Gillian asked Kilburn, studying the young baron anxiously. He watched her warily, for he sensed her instinctive withdrawal although she scarce had spoken to him.

"In the robing chamber! It has a small cot and can be bolted from within. The other door leads to our bed-chamber, and it will be easy for you to tend his leg."

Gillian nodded reluctantly. "Aye, and I can say that I am unwell and wish to remain in my chamber to rest. I can also take my meals there, and should Eilys or Master Brassard come, the door to the robing chamber will remain bolted. 'Twill only be for a few days . . ."

Kilburn was pleased at the ease with which the problem had been resolved and took no notice of Gillian's unhappy face. It was not in his nature to turn an old friend away, even when there was something conspiratorial in his sudden appearance at Glairn.

Thomas returned with hot water and clean cloths which Gillian used to clean the wound while de Mortimer devoured the meat pie and large wedge of cheese the young knight had found in the castle kitchen larder. He washed down the food with wine poured from a leather flagon Tom had brought to replenish that which had already been drunk. A short time later de Mortimer, fortified with another cup of wine to ease the pain, hobbled up the stairs and down the hallway to the robing chamber aided by Kilburn and Thomas, each holding an arm. Followed by Emrys, who bolted the door leading to the hall, they laid the injured man on the cot. While Tom was sent for the salves and powders Gillian needed, Kilburn and Emrys drew de Mortimer's travel-stained clothes from him. He fell into a restless sleep while Gillian bound his leg with strips of cloth Tom had brought. Touching his forehead, she found it clammy and abnormally warm.

"I fear that he is becoming feverish, Jamie. All we can hope for is that the salve I have spread on the wound will prevent infection."

"You've done your best, sweetheart. Emrys can see to him now. I've put two braziers near Roger for warmth."

Cautioning the Welshman to keep his master quiet, he drew Gillian into their chamber. He begged her patience and understanding for allowing de Mortimer to remain hidden in Glairn, for he knew how she despised deception.

"I don't like him, Jamie. He brings misfortune with him."

She shivered in the chamber's chill air. Kilburn looked at her with surprise as he unfastened his tunic and drew it from his weary body. The first faint glow of dawn reflected on Gillian's troubled face. There won't be much sleep this night, he thought as he unbuttoned his linen chainse.

"How can you say that?" he challenged her. "You don't know him!"

" 'Tis an aura about him and something in his face . . ."

She stopped speaking, puzzled by her own words. Kilburn smiled as he reached out to draw her into his arms, feeling her body press against his for comfort. The desire to lose himself in her rose strongly within him and he slid his hand over the satin skin of her throat and shoulder for a moment.

"Don't brood about Roger, my love. He's hurt and desperate to find Pembroke. As soon as he's able to sit a horse, he'll be gone and that accursed Welsh shadow with him. Young Wigmore is like a cat—he'll always land on his feet safely, no matter how outrageous his behavior."

He tilted her face up and brushed the ruffled hair from her brow.

"Tend him well, lovely, so that he can be gone from here soon," he murmured against her soft mouth. But even as he felt her relax in his arms, he heard Pembroke's voice from an earlier time cautioning him to heed Gillian's instincts, and his troubled eyes lingered on the closed door to the robing chamber.

"And how do you find my leg today?"

The question was asked in a low, teasing voice as Gillian gently applied more salve to the healing wound. She kept her eyes lowered, for if she looked at de Mortimer, she knew that his dark, burning eyes would try to draw the soul from her body. For two days he had lain in the robing chamber drifting in and out of a fevered sleep. She had taken turns with Emrys bathing the flushed face and restless body with cool water until the fever had broken. A strange bond had been formed between the small Welshman and the young countess, and she marveled that she had ever feared him. Watching the sensitive hands bathe his master's face with gentle care and hold him still while she changed the dressing on his leg, she realized that he loved the young man in his odd, wild way. He was grateful to her for ministering to his master although he sensed the shrinking dread within her whenever she came near him. Emrys spoke rarely, and his speech was difficult to follow, for he was used to a different tongue, but Gillian understood him well enough as he tried to explain de Mortimer's behavior to her. She understood, but it did little to allay her fear of him.

In his slumber, Roger de Mortimer seemed younger than his thirty years. The reckless arrogance was erased from the dark face with its arched black eyebrows, straight nose, and firm, rather sensual mouth. The heavy, almost black hair lay in a loose tangle about his forehead and fell over one high cheekbone, hiding his eyes. He wore one of Kilburn's chainses and she saw the glint of a gold chain against the smooth skin exposed by the unlaced cloth. Asleep, the demon in him seemed to have fled, and Gillian hoped he would not awaken until she was finished.

"You wish me gone, my lady. I'm aware of it."

His words startled her, but she replied in a calm voice, "You're almost healed, my lord. I would say by tomorrow you could safely sit a horse without too much discomfort."

He had studied her face at length, pretending sleep, drawn by her shy, gentle manner almost as much as by the beauty which had insinuated itself into his senses even in his fevered state. He had been aware of the silken, fragrant hair brushing his face and had caught a glimpse of the warm curve of a soft full breast pressed against him as she leaned over him. Once he had suddenly stared into large, dark blue eyes, contemplating him with concern, and a familiar ache had risen within him. It returned now and grew stronger as his eyes swept over the lovely young face, coming to rest on the red-lipped, sensuous mouth. Oh James, he thought, but you're a clever man to have snared this prize.

Gillian felt herself redden, for his expression revealed de Mortimer's thoughts. She prepared to leave, but he grasped her arm, keeping her by him.

"Don't go just yet, my lady. Stay and talk to me. It gets cursedly lonely here, lying for hours by myself save for Emrys's silent presence."

He noticed suddenly that they were alone.

"Where the devil has he disappeared to?"

"My lord sent him with Thomas Fitzhugh to find out where the earl of Pembroke is. We heard that Lord de Valence is somewhere near Newcastle."

"Thomas Fitzhugh?" De Mortimer tried to place him and suddenly laughed. "Ah yes, the flaxen-haired knight who tended to me so painfully."

Gillian looked down at her hands, aware that he still held her arm.

"Your lord was with me when he received the tidings of his son's birth," the young man said softly, willing her to look at him. "I'd never seen a man so moved at the news."

She turned to him then, dimples deep as she smiled.

"He loves his children well," Gillian said in a low voice.

37

For a moment de Mortimer's face clouded over.

"As I do mine, my lady, although I see them but rarely. My wife tends to them, for they must be raised to fulfill the roles they were born to play."

His face grew grim and the black eyes glittered with a dangerous fire as he was reminded of his life beyond the walls of Glairn.

She sounded shocked at his words, forgetting her fear of him.

"Our children will do as they wish within the bounds of our way of life. But I would not dream to use them as if pawns in a game of chess."

"And how many have you?" He sounded amused at her reprimand.

"Three. Our eldest son is now four, some six months older than the crown prince. Our daughter was born just before Yule two years ago, and our youngest son is but three months old."

"I warrant he'll not be the last."

De Mortimer's hand slid up the soft inner part of her arm in a caressing motion, and Gillian felt him pull her toward him. She blanched at his temerity and broke free of him.

"My lord de Mortimer, you presume too much," she said coldly. She was furious at his manner and the fact that he lay back on his pillow looking at her with mocking eyes, a sardonic smile on his dark, handsome face.

"A thousand pardons, my lady. Perhaps my fever has not left me as we had thought."

He watched her run into her bedchamber and heard the bolt lock the door against him from the other side. Sweet Jesu, but she can stir a man's blood, he thought and suddenly remembered another woman whose almond shaped blue eyes gleamed in a white heart-shaped face framed by pale golden hair. She would not run from me, he mused, reliving his brief glimpse of the queen when she had so defiantly faced the barons at Tynemouth, and the passion he had felt lie dormant within her as their eyes met.

At daybreak, Tom and Emrys returned with the news that Pembroke would be in Newcastle within two days.

"If you leave tonight and travel straight for Newcastle, you should still find him there."

Kilburn had brought a tray of food and some wine for his friend, to discover de Mortimer standing for the first time by himself. To his delight, the younger man found the leg did not pain him too greatly. He was eager to leave, but Kilburn urged caution.

"In the meantime, try to exercise that leg by walking about." He gazed down at the wild face staring moodily into the wine cup. "Roger, once you've seen Pembroke, what will you do?"

De Mortimer selected a tart from the platter set near him and bit into the flaky pastry, tasting the almond milk in the creamy custard filled with bits of candied fruit and raisins. It gave him an opportunity to frame a careful reply.

"If I can convince the Lords Ordainers of the danger we're in should Scotland gain a foothold in Ireland, I can take back an army to send Edward Bruce to hell. If not, the Welsh coast will have to be heavily fortified." He sighed. "I wish it possible to see my uncle of Chirk." The black eyes bored into Kilburn's hazel ones. "What have you heard of the Despensers? My uncle feels there's a great danger to the Marcher barons in their ascendancy."

" 'Tis true, and each year they manage to worm their way closer to the king, although Lancaster has managed to slow their progress somewhat. But I should think your uncle would be more able to give you information. I fear we live in a border backwater here."

"Damn you, Glairn, you should be in the midst of the fray where you belong, if not beside me then beside Pembroke! All your instincts tell you so. And yet you stay within your own walls. Does your wife's body beckon so passionately that you cannot leave her bed?"

He had flung the wine cup from him in a paroxysm of sudden anger as he spat out the words. It infuriated him to see a man of such rare intelligence and capabilities waste himself when he should carve a place for himself through wealth and the power it could buy. That Kilburn's principles would play a deciding role in any decisions held little meaning for him.

Kilburn grew white with fury at de Mortimer's mention of Gillian, and his eyes blazed as he regarded him with unconcealed distaste. He contained himself with difficulty, for he would not allow himself to be baited into any rashness.

"Your lack of understanding of my position reveals your callous stupidity and total arrogance, Roger. I need not explain my reasons for withdrawing from the court to you or anyone else. As for your remarks regarding my wife, I find them insulting and insufferably cruel. Rather brand me coward and traitor as all the others have! You've gone too far this time in overstepping the bounds of my hospitality. Were you not injured and my guest, I swear I would fight it out with you. Since that cannot be, all that is left is for you to go. I am as anxious to see the last of you as you are to leave." He found his hands shaking as he rose. "You have embroiled not only me but Gillian in your arrogant ambitions and headstrong actions, but no longer."

"James . . . you're right. It was wrong of me to speak so. I have ever spoken out of turn and without thought."

De Mortimer reached out a hand, conscious of the earl's stormy eyes and closed face. The passion which had raged through him was spent. Apologies were difficult for him, for his arrogance forbore admitting he was capable of making mistakes.

" 'Twill be better when I'm gone. Confined to these narrow walls, I feel caged. I need to see the sky and feel the wind. Your lady's scent is seductive, but surrounded as I've been by it these past days, 'tis beginning to stifle me."

He laughed awkwardly and to his relief saw the anger begin to fade from Kilburn's lean face.

"My words cannot be forgiven—I understand that, but perhaps the circumstances can." His voice was husky with emotion for in that moment he truly felt remorse. "I hold the Lady Gillian in the highest esteem, James, and am grateful for her ministrations . . ."

"Enough, Roger, enough. I understand your meaning." Kilburn sighed. "I'll instruct Tom to accompany you as far as the king's road tonight. There'll be no need for further speech between us until you leave."

And indeed it was not until later that night that Kilburn returned to the robing chamber and found de Mortimer dressed for his journey in some of the earl's clothing as well as a hauberk and helm from Glairn's armory. Kilburn nodded in satisfaction at his appearance, advising him that all was in readiness below. Leaving de Mortimer to fasten his sword belt, he strode through the empty bedchamber and descended the tower stairs, wondering idly where Gillian disappeared to. The castle lay deep in sleep as the moon rode full and bright in the night sky.

"My lord de Mortimer," Gillian called softly, peering into the small chamber. "Are you still here?"

"Yes, and struggling with this damn clasp. Where did Emrys get to now?" de Mortimer snarled impatiently.

"Gently, Sir Roger. I've done this many times for my lord." Her deft fingers engaged the clasps of the broad belt about the slender waist. She picked up a small sack and handed it to him.

"I went down to the larder for some food for you to take with you on your journey. 'Tis simple fare, but will do until you find an inn."

"'Twas thoughtful of you, my lady. I have much to thank you for," he told her, laying the sack by his helm for Emrys to carry down. He followed her into the dimly lit bedchamber and was close behind her as she turned to wish him well. He lifted her hand to his lips and at his touch she drew back as if scalded. She felt his hand on her hair for a moment and found herself trapped against him.

"Nay!" she cried softly, struggling to escape his hands.

"Oh, Gillian, I can't leave without having tasted that seductive mouth. You would not be so cruel as to deny me that."

His hand was on her jaw, forcing her face to lift to his. She caught a glimpse of his bold black eyes gleaming with excitement before she closed her own. His mouth covered hers, hard and bruising, taking everything from her and giving nothing until she felt a faintness steal over her. He was suffocating her with the force of his attack. His kiss was as he was, passionate, reckless, selfish, and totally without love. One hand caressed her neck and found the gentle curve of her breast beneath the silken cloth of her robe as, with a strength she had not known she possessed, she renewed her battle to escape. Even Arnaut de Broze had not frightened her as did this cruel, satanic man.

To de Mortimer she was like a small bird caught in a snare which would be released only when he willed it. He would have her someday, he promised himself as his head lowered to find her mouth again. A strangled snarl reached his ears and he found two blazing green eyes staring at him from the narrow dark face of his squire Emrys.

"Arglwydd, 'tis time to leave." The words were low, but Roger sensed the anger in his squire's voice as he used the Welsh term for lord while addressing him. Damn that sneaking Welsh devil! The passionate outrage on the small man's face cooled his ardor and filled him with amusement. He released Gillian, stroking her cheek gently with a slender finger.

"Forgive my lack of courtly manners, my lady, but it was worth the struggle. You're a rare woman."

His voice was gentle and kind, but Gillian could scarce trust the abrupt change in him. She turned away, refusing to look at him, and, with a feeling of relief, heard him stride through the door.

Emrys stood near her, watching her with concern. She had been ever kind and too gentle to endure his master's rough amorality. Was there no sense of decency or humanity left in his lord at all, he asked himself sadly. The image of stricken green eyes staring tearfully from a white, pinched face rose unbidden into his mind. The red-haired maid so many years ago had also been a victim to his lord's willful passions. Did he ever think of her, the Welshman wondered, a wave of hatred against de Mortimer washing over him for a moment. Hesitating, he crept forward and quietly kissed Gillian's hand before hurrying after his young master.

When Kilburn returned, Gillian was standing by the windows, staring out into the darkness, her soft hair loose and unbound about her shoulders. The chamber looked as it always did, serene and welcoming, bathed in the golden light cast by the fire roaring in the large hearth. The rich colors of the tapestries glowed warmly against the gray stone walls while the great bed with its velvet counterpane and drawn-back curtains beckoned invitingly. He noticed a piece of sewing lying forgotten on the wooden settle by the hearth opposite his large padded chair with its comfortable cushions and high carved back. The small door to the robing chamber stood ajar.

"He's gone, lovedy, and we can go back to our life. I only hope he finds what he's searching for."

He stood behind her and she leaned her head against him, feeling the secure warmth of his arms encircling her.

"Death, Jamie, 'Tis what he seeks and 'tis what he'll find. Death, treachery, and murder. They ride with him wherever he goes."

Her voice sounded strange, bemused. As he turned her to face him, he saw that the dark blue eyes were shadowed, haunted by a vision he could not see. There were still traces of tears on her cheeks, as if she had wept.

"Gillian," he said quietly. "Sweetheart, 'tis over," and he kissed her gently until the large eyes closed and the soft red mouth opened beneath his.

"Oh my darling, promise me you'll never heed his call," she murmured.

"Aye, lovedy, I promise."

He was disturbed by her obviously fearful concentration on de Mortimer. Knowing how unprincipled and reckless the younger man was, he began to wonder what had happened between them during those hours Gillian had been alone with him. It was then that he saw the faint marks on her cheek where de Mortimer's fingers had bruised her. A blinding rage shook him as he realized why she had wept. Why had he not suspected it earlier! Had Roger ever been able to stay away from any woman?

That unholy bastard! he thought furiously. I'll kill him for having touched her. Red-hot jealousy coursed through him as he imagined Gillian in de Mortimer's arms. Why had he not heeded her words when Wigmore first arrived at Glairn?

Although he pressed her, she would say nothing of what had happened. What difference would it make, she reasoned. De Mortimer was gone and had not really harmed her, save for a few bruises, which would soon disappear.

"Truly, sweetheart, I'm all right. Emrys came in and naught occured to warrant your anger. Let him be. He is his own destroyer."

Drawing him to their settle by the hearth, she showed him the gift Emrys had pressed into her hand as he was leaving. Turning the mantle brooch over in his hand, Kilburn saw that it was made of heavy silver enameled red and fashioned into the shape of a dragon. Its eye winked brightly in the firelight. Rubies! He looked at it with awakening interest, recognizing it as the badge of the Llewellyn family, the hereditary chieftains of Wales. What connection did the strange little man have with the Llewellyns, he wondered for a moment, and then remembered that a long-dead de Mortimer had wed a Llewellyn daughter. Gillian stared at him in surprise as he began to laugh. God's wounds, what a joke it all was—the futility of all their mad maneuvers and tactical moves on life's chessboard. His reluctance to be drawn into England's politics, de Mortimer's insane ambitions, and now the gift to Gillian of a dead Welsh prince's mantle brooch. Was it all a part of some grand heavenly scheme? As if it would all matter in a hundred years!

Still amused, he drew Gillian into his arms and rested his cheek against her hair. "Aye, what did it really matter," he thought. As far as he was concerned, he had seen the last of de Mortimer and his harper. Could Gillian be right—would death truly be his destiny?

The sound of Gillian's muted cries woke him to the unaccustomed sight of a chamber suffused with the cold light of a gray dawn. He remembered then that the bed curtains had not been drawn and were still tied back by their tasseled cords. Turning toward Gillian, James saw

44

that she was asleep, caught in the tangle of bedclothes and trying vainly to free herself. When he touched her, he found her drenched with icy perspiration, the dark hair lying wetly about her face. Bending over her, he attempted to waken her, for she seemed trapped in a nightmare. She fought him wildly as he tried to take her into his arms and her blind panic at his nearness washed over him in scalding waves.

De Mortimer had followed Gillian into her dreams, and she tried desperately to evade his hard, unloving hands as his mouth moved against hers, insistent and rapacious. She struggled vainly to escape him and saw the black hypnotic eyes change, burning suddenly with a familiar cold fire. Sweet Jesù, she sobbed, 'tis Arnaut . . . he's returned from his grave! The snarling lips drew back over sharp white teeth and the fear which he had instilled deep within her during their brief marriage through his cruel perversions and bestiality swept over her. How could she have forgotten the agonizing pain that had knifed through her time and time again as he assaulted her body grown cold as marble. Never again, she had promised. Jamie! Her mind screamed his name. Jamie! He alone could save her from Arnaut. She wept, knowing that her tears were useless against her dead lord's vindictive hatred.

"Gillian . . ." The voice was far away, but she sensed its urgency.

"Gillian . . . wake up!"

Her eyes opened, enormous and dark with a nameless dread, meeting James's steady, concerned gaze.

"You were dreaming, lovedy. But such a frightening dream!"

His husky voice murmured softly to her as her body shook, still snared in the dream.

"Love me, Jamie—love me—please . . ."

She lifted her mouth eagerly to him, and he held her close, fearing to let her go. In the growing light of dawn, she saw his eyes burn with the hunger she always evoked in him. The familiar weight of his body against hers blotted out all memories of de Mortimer and Lord De-Broze as a consuming fire swept over her. She came to life in his arms, answering his body as she always had, clinging to him when she felt herself drowning in their shared passion.

"Jamie . . ." she called softly, and he bent over her, his lips gentle on hers.

"Aye, my darling. I'm here. I'll always be here. I promise you."

He held her in his arms, his heart full of the overwhelming love he held for her. Gillian lay quietly, at peace, her phantoms once more defeated by the only man she had ever loved. James rested his cheek against her soft hair, remembering her suddenly as the small girl of nine whose pain he had so unexpectedly shared at the funeral of her mother. Fourteen years had passed since that day, he thought, realizing that at thirty-six, he was still awed and mystified at the strange bond between them that allowed their very souls to merge and become one.

The days following de Mortimer's secret departure through the postern gate flowed into quiet weeks. To Gillian it sometimes seemed that Glairn was an island of tranquillity surrounded by the turbulent ocean that was England, but she knew that the serenity was false and that before long Jamie would be drawn into the web of baronial intrigue despite his efforts to remain clear of its entanglements. The outside world would once more encroach upon their private domain.

Early in December, as the frost lay softly on the cold earth, a messenger, clad in the green and gold house livery of the baron of Wigmore, rode up the stone causeway and demanded entry at the massive front gate of Glairn. De Mortimer wrote that he had been successful in convincing Pembroke of the danger in Ireland, and together they had gone to Edward to petition for reinforcement of the fighting force facing the massed might of Edward Bruce. The Lords Ordainers, through Parliament, had also concurred and de Mortimer felt confident that the Scots would be driven from Ireland as soon as his campaign began. The message was terse and matter-of-fact, and Kilburn watched it burn brightly in the study hearth with a sense of satisfaction.

Christmas and Twelfth Night passed uneventfully.

Master Porcher sent a chest loaded with toys, trinkets, and sweetmeats, but was unable to come himself. He was no longer young, he explained in his letter, and the winter's journey from York was becoming increasingly difficult for him, but he assured them that he would miss being with his family.

For Gillian the best hours were those spent in the solar on the long winter afternoons, sitting by the windows to catch the fading light, the embroidery spilling over her wool-clad lap in bright cascades. She listened distractedly to the chattering of her ladies clustered about the tapestry which seemed never to be finished. The constable's wife, Lady Jardine, her white hair barely visible beneath a dark veil, presided over the needlework, watching that the pattern was copied perfectly. Agnes Brassard, her dark hair braided neatly into two heavy plaits, bent dutifully over her piece of canvas. The deep blue velvet of her robe emphasized the translucent pallor of her small, delicate face, her concentration accentuated by the tip of a red tongue visible between sweetly curved lips. Her betrothal to Hal Jardine had been celebrated at Twelfth Night, and their wedding was to take place the week following Easter. Lady Jardine was well pleased with her grandson's choice, for the young girl was gracious, charming, and well trained to take her place as wife of the knight-squire to the earl of Glairn.

The needlework of Eilys Fitzhugh, Gillian's tiring woman, had improved exceedingly in the years since Gillian's arrival at Glairn, and she kept the chamber ringing gaily with her laughter. Her child was due quite soon and Eilys was convinced that she would present Thomas with a son. Her awkward body did not prevent her small felt-clad foot from tapping to the strains of a pretty song being played by Gillian's young page. Not as adept at the dulcimer as the boy Hal had been, young Arthur d' Umfraville still was able to keep his mistress amused. A nephew of Elizabeth Harron, the child had been accepted into service under the patronage of Glairn a year past, and had settled down to the rugged training which would culminate in knighthood.

Gillian's eyes turned to the hearth, where Non, the

old nurse, sat nodding in the fire's warmth, her gnarled hands at rest in her ample lap. Margaret's golden hair glinted in the light as she sat on a small stool beside her, playing with a tattered, much-loved doll. The heart-shaped face with its large blue eyes was a merry one, for she was a child blessed with a happy disposition. Gillian felt her heart contract as she gazed at her daughter with love. How close they had come to losing her, she thought, thanking the blessed Virgin for allowing her to remain with them. Gillian rose, leaving her embroidery in a crumpled heap on the chair seat. The baby stirred and, before he could disturb Non, she had him in her arms, feeling his sweet breath warm on her neck as she held him against her. He tried to grasp her jeweled circlet, reaching out a dimpled hand, his eyes intent on the glittering stones. Gillian studied the rosy face, marveling again at the perfection of his features. If only Hugh could have seen his namesake, she mused wistfully, and tightened her embrace. It had seemed so natural to her when Jamie had suggested calling the babe Hugh. She kissed his silken cheek and small fingers until he smiled in delight, the long blue eyes with their dark thick lashes laughing at her.

A gust of cold air rushed through the chamber as the door opened and Alain flew in a few steps ahead of his father. Tall for his age, he gave every indication of becoming a mirror image of James. Returning Hugh to his cradle, Gillian was nearly overcome by the violence of her oldest son's embrace; and as his arms encircled her waist tightly, she felt him tremble. She noticed traces of tears on the handsome face now flushed with emotion, and she looked at James questioningly.

"Young Master Alain fell from his pony twice, and twice was returned to his mount's back. I fear 'twas not to his liking. Nay, lovedy, he's all right—'tis just his pride that's been bruised."

Kilburn suddenly swung the small form onto his shoulder and walked to the windowseat to deposit the child with a sweet cake in each hand to ease his embarrassment. Gillian poured her husband a goblet of wine and joined him by the hearth.

"I see Non is still napping!" he observed dryly, drawing Gillian to sit beside him. "Henry de Percy stopped by today en route to Alnwick Castle. He had but time for a cup of wine before he continued his journey."

Fingers stopped their work and all eyes were on him, burningly intent, for a visit from without the castle augured news.

"De Percy spent Twelfth Night at the court in Windsor, and said the king celebrated with great pomp and splendor."

" 'Tis sae shameful when puir folk hang on the gate watchin' the lairds disport themselves," Non snapped, now wide awake.

Kilburn smiled thinly without replying to her remark. Because she had been at Glairn all his life and had been his nurse, she could take liberties others did not dare to, but she irritated him when she abused the freedom he allowed her. Feeling his unspoken disapproval, she gathered up her charges, allowing Gillian to kiss both children before hurrying them from the chamber.

Alain remained quietly on the windowseat, munching his cakes and wishing desperately that he could climb onto his mother's lap and bury himself in her softness. She would kiss him and tell him that it didn't matter that he had fallen from his pony. But she was with his father, who would not approve of such childish behavior, so he hugged his misery to himself. On his fourth birthday, Alain had been given over to the care of a tutor, much to his dismay, and he had not yet resigned himself to the change.

Kilburn looked after Non's retreating figure moodily, remarking that she was too old to tend the baby. Besides the wet nurse, Gillian should find another nurse to tend him.

"Oh, Jamie, it would break her heart to give up her nursling. 'Tis all she lives for since you took Alain away from her, and her own son refuses her help."

It was the wrong thing to say, she realized as she saw Kilburn's eyes darken. He did not like to be reminded of Graeme, who sat in the falcon mews amid the captive birds and dreamed of the days when his eyes were as sharp as theirs. Unable to use his hands now for more than lifting food to his mouth, and embittered by the increasing loss of his mobility, Non's son had retreated into his own black universe and wanted no part of the outside world.

Gillian asked if there was news of Ireland, trying to turn his mind elsewhere. He shook his head and stretched out slender hands toward the fire's warmth.

"Nay, 'tis too soon. But Henry told me that there's great unrest among the barons again. Lancaster is mounting a campaign against the Scots as soon as the snows are gone and he's calling for support."

At Gillian's exclamation he smiled slightly, for he knew what lay in her heart.

"I will remain at Glairn, lovedy. I want no part of Lancaster. Nor do I want any part of the Despensers. De Percy told me they grow stronger by the hour, tying the king ever closer to them. He has finally sanctioned the Clare holdings in Wales to go to Hugh Despenser, and the de Mortimer family is incensed over it. Even Pembroke was heard to complain, for the younger Despenser is already one of the greatest landowners in Wales. 'Tis felt that the Welsh are restless and must be watched, should rebellion flare, and now is not the time for dissension among the Marcher barons."

Kilburn sighed, shifting uneasily in his chair. He glanced at Gillian's pale face beneath the gold circlet and brushed a strand of dark hair back behind her ear. She was with child again, and he wondered if it perhaps was not too soon after little Hugh's birth. Headstrong and determined to bear him children, Gillian welcomed this pregnancy as she had the others. But he feared it was taking too much of a toll of her emotional strength. Usually tranquil and patient, Gillian was becoming increasingly restless, sharply reprimanding children and servants alike. It was totally unlike her and disturbed him, for it seemed to have begun with de Mortimer's stay. He sighed, staring moodily into his goblet.

Pressing white fingers to her temples, Gillian closed her eyes. Too much was happening about her, and de Mortimer's attempt to make love to her had shaken her more than she had admitted to Jamie. Where had the months gone to? It seemed that scarcely any time had passed since they had heard of Aunt Constance's death at Kestwick. She had slipped quietly from life, lingering just long enough to see Robert's son brought to her in his father's arms. Gillian had not been able to go to Kestwick for the funeral, for Hugh had been born the day the news of Constance's demise had arrived. Aunt Constance—her father's only sister. The aunt who had taken care of Robert and Geoffrey after their mother's death while she herself had been sent to live at Baillendel Castle. Aunt Constance who had so wanted Gillian's marriage to Arnaut De Broze. She had been a second mother to them, despite her own sorrow at the untimely loss of a husband deeply loved. Her death had been long in coming and it seemed she had welcomed it, but she was sorely missed.

Not so the earl of Warwick, Gillian thought, suppressing a shudder. News of his horrible death had come, with the ugly details: his gasping for breath, his face mottled and purple. No one had talked of anything else for weeks. It was whispered that the king had exacted revenge on him for his part in the murder of the king's beloved Gascon on Blacklow Hill, but naught could be proven that the death was anything but a natural one brought about by the earl's own notoriously unbridled temper. Gillian pitied his heir—a mere child no older than Alain. Even while she prayed that he be guided wisely into maturity, she knew better, for he was already betrothed to Katherine de Mortimer. As the father of the small girl who was even younger than her fiancé, Thomas de Beauchamp, Roger de Mortimer had been named guardian of the Warwick heir and administrator of his fortune until the young earl reached his majority. How much would be left, Gillian wondered with a cynicism alien to her gentle nature, when that day arrived. She suppressed a shudder, remembering for a fleeting moment Roger's hungry, demanding mouth on her own.

"Will the intrigue ever end, Jamie?" she asked shakily.

He smiled at her question, but he had no reassuring answer to give her.

Chapter 2

The ships were sighted while they were still well off the coast. When the news was brought to Lord de Bermingham in the castle that the fleet was expected to enter the mouth of the Liffey within hours, he ordered the river cleared of all traffic.

It was a great relief to him to know that Roger de Mortimer, the baron of Wigmore, was to take charge of English matters in Ireland once more. The months since de Mortimer's hasty departure for England had been difficult ones for the English forces and their Irish allies. Although he, together with William de Burgh, the loyal son of the captive earl of Ulster, had won a victory over their common enemy at Athenry in Connaught, there had been heavy losses on both sides. Weary but triumphant, the English had returned to a besieged Dublin. They found many of the city's churches torn down and the stones reused to erect high walls around the huddle of timbered and stone houses on all the land sides, from the flat, low land of the north and west to the south where the foothills of the Wicklow mountains pushed undulating fingers toward the coast. Taking up arms again, and with the aid of the city's citizenry, the English beat back the Scots, and the countryside was able to settle down. The uneasy quiet was broken now and again, however, by devastating Scottish forays into the territory they had not been able to conquer. Now that spring lay over the torn land, the raids had been increasing both in scope and ferocity.

Well into the afternoon when the first ships were moored at the large quay by the riverside, the others sent down their anchors to lie in the dark waters of the river to unload their cargo into the tenders beginning to swarm about them. The castle walls were alive with people watching as the baron of Wigmore rode through the huge gates of the fortress at the head of a large body of knights. The pale golden light of a late spring day shimmered over the riders, their open helms revealing faces still white and drawn from the ravages of the rough journey across the storm-laden sea. Knights and horses were the first to disembark on the soil of Ireland, but it would take many hours yet to unload all the men and sorely needed equipment from the ships and transport them to the castle and the waiting fields beyond the walled city.

Jehan de Maudley stood on the walkway atop the massive gate with several other ladies who had accompanied their lords to Ireland. With mounting excitement, they watched the long line of riders clatter over the roughly paved causeway amid the welcoming cheers of the castle folk. But Jehan's mind was not on the bright banners snapping in the soft breeze, nor did she notice the light dancing on the horses' bridles and the riders' plumed helms. All she could think of was that her waiting time was over . . . de Mortimer was here.

On their arrival in Dublin, Sir Ralph de Maudley had been suprised to learn of his liege lord's sudden disappearance from Ireland, but Jehan was not. She shrewdly surmised that personal arrogance had played a larger role in his flight than political urgency. The winter months had dragged on endlessly, broken only by the Scottish siege. Unpleasant and frightening as it was, she had at least felt useful, herding her panic-stricken companions to the chapel hastily turned into a hospital. There, amidst the stench of blood and the moans of wounded men, she had been able to forget what still lay before her, for a confrontation with Roger de Mortimer was inevitable. Smiling wryly to herself, she believed she would welcome it.

Now, with a suddenly racing heart she saw the yellow and green de Mortimer banner flare out defiantly in the rising wind. And then the tall, slender baron passed through the gate followed by his squire. The young woman's eyes narrowed with dormant hatred at the sight of the small Welshman riding close behind his master, his harp slung behind his back. Seeming to sense the black virulence directed at him, he looked up and caught a glimpse of green eyes blazing in a white face and the glimmer of red hair beneath a veil. Jehan. He shook his head in disbelief and looked again. Nothing. Perhaps he had been mistaken, Emrys thought, although the emotional force of hatred that had surrounded him without warning left him shaken.

Jehan leaned weakly against the wall of the tower leading to the cobbled courtyard where she had fled in sudden panic. Sweet Jesù, the sight of Roger's squire had awakened feelings long forgotten. She closed her eyes against the light pouring through the doorway, following the high steps winding downward. The bright sunlight had no place in the darkness of her emotions. Her nails clawed at the cold stones as she fought to regain control of herself. How many years had it been? If the sight of the harper could affect her so violently, how would she react to his master when she came face to face with him? Wild thoughts raced through her mind as she fought the desire to weep. Nay, she would not give either of them the satisfaction of her tears. She stood without moving, as still as the stones which supported her. The violence of her feelings ebbed, replaced by an icy determination to discover a way of repaying both of them for her years of futile pain. As though from a distance she heard her name called. Looking up toward the tower entrance she saw the laughing face of Marie de Chillon, the wife of one of Lord de Bermingham's lieutenants.

"My lady, we missed you! Come quickly . . . 'tis all so exciting."

Eyes shining, the young woman thrilled to the sound

of the trumpets and drums as knights, horses, and equipment continued to pour into the castle in brilliant array. The smile Jehan presented to Marie as she mounted the stairs and stepped out onto the sunlit walkway once more did not reach her eyes. The anger settling within her was reflected there in cold green fire.

The Great Hall was aglow with the light of huge candles held by the many tall iron holders placed about and between the long trestle tables and the glitter of jeweled headdresses and robes elaborately embroidered with gold and silver thread and set with precious stones and pearls worn by the revelers crowded into the immense chamber. The torches, in sconces set high up on the stone walls, flared and flamed wildly in the drafts which crept through the narrow slitted windows, illuminating the upper reaches of the smoke-blackened wooden-raftered ceiling where several doves looked down in panic at the teeming mass of humanity. The tremendous hearths, where sides of beef roasted on the revolving spits, roared loudly as the fires sent billowing smoke and sparks upward through the huge flues. Involved in their wild revelry, the diners scarce took heed, neither of the scorching heat nor the dogs snapping and snarling over remnants of food and discarded bones already half-buried in the rush-covered floor. Although the food prepared that night by the castle kitchens was rough, simple fare, it was plentiful, for the baron of Wigmore included in the fleet several ships laden with provender. Cattle, sheep, and swine had been driven from the docked ships, while crates of poultry, too, were unloaded and transported to the castle as the half-starved citizens of Dublin watched in sullen silence. The English soldiery had been quartered in the city for a long time and what the countryside had had to offer had long been foraged and pillaged, if not by them, then by the marauders from the north.

When the young baron entered the Hall, all rose and lustily cheered his triumphant return. Hopes were renewed that now at last a move could be made against the Scotts and their recently crowned king of Ireland. The Anglo-Irish nobles and knights had scarce given Roger de

Mortimer time to divest himself of his armor before they began to petition him to mount the greatly desired northern campaign. For two days he had been closeted with one group after another, his handsome face blank and unreadable, adroitly managing to avoid a firm commitment to any of them. The banquet had already commenced when the seductive sound of music floating faintly through the silent corridors reminded him of the revels planned for that evening.

As he drew on an amber-colored surcoat trimmed with dark fur over his knee-length velvet tunic, he frowned and said roughly to his squire, "Has Lady de Maudley spoken to you at all?"

Emrys, fastening the wide gold belt about the baron's narrow waist, shook his head.

"I've not seen her since her lord presented her to you on the day of our arrival."

Roger fell silent, unable to conquer the uneasiness which he had felt since seeing Jehan again. What a shock to have looked into those green eyes after so many years. He had never imagined that Ralph de Maudley would bring his lady to Dublin. After all, it was common knowledge that their marriage was a travesty and that they scarcely saw each other. He tried to remember the stories. There had been a lover from the king's circle—even for a court such as Edward's it had been quite a scandalous affair . . . He had accepted the introduction to her formally, giving no hint of his inner agitation. She had seemed composed as she curtsied to him until he raised her with one extended hand and felt her arm tremble.

"My lord, why bother yourself over something which happened so long ago. Had she wanted to, Lady Jehan could have driven you to ground years ere now . . ."

The squire's voice faltered as de Mortimer turned abruptly. Although his face was black with sudden anger, he said coldly, "Mind your tongue, Welshman! No one drives Wigmore to ground, and 'tis better not forgotten. That little bitch had best take care. I have no patience with a troublesome woman."

His dark eyes hardened suddenly. The last thing he needed was to be reminded of the past. There were enough problems pursuing him . . . the old de Lacy lord still languished in the castle's dungeons while his two misbe-gotten kinsmen, Hugh and Walter de Lacy, were serving at Edward Bruce's side. That afternoon he had signed a proclamation outlawing both of them. He smiled grimly to himself . . . before he was finished, half of Ireland would be his as legal claimant to the de Lacy lands.

Looking about the almost spartan bedchamber, he said, "Get a few of my personal belongings in here for comfort's sake. The chamber smacks too much of this barbaric land. The coffers brought up yesterday contain some of the gold plate, and a few velvet cushions and new bed hangings would not be amiss either."

Emrys bowed low as the tall, dark man strode to the door. He scuttled quickly after the baron, lifting the latch before he received a cuff for his slowness. De Morti-mer turned and stared at his squire, who stood with eyes averted.

"Bring your harp . . . I have need of some of your soul's music to sweeten the bitterness in mine."

The small Welshman gazed with amazement at his master's retreating back and wondered once more whether he would ever understand him.

For two days Jehan had waited to speak to Roger de Mortimer, but she had not even seen him. She was furious at his pretense of not knowing her. When her lord had brought her before his liege lord and she raised uncertain eyes to the face she had long ago tried to forget, it was as if nothing were changed. He was older, yes, but the rather long face with its high cheekbones, straight nose, and sen-sual mouth were the same. For a moment she thought she had detected a brief light in the bold black eyes, but they were so quickly veiled that she could not be sure. He had bowed calmly, indifferently acknowledging the introduc-tion as she curtsied before him.

How dare he not remember! Rage suffused her as she sat at the long table, squeezed between her husband and a heavyset, drunken knight whose arm brushed against her breast every time he reached for the platters of food and pitchers of wine and ale. His velvet-clad thigh pressed hers, demanding an answer she had no intention of giving him. Deep in thought, she sat crumbling the trencher of bread before her with nervous fingers. She had no appetite for the large slice of roasted beef Sir Ralph had laid on the trencher, although it was just as she loved it, pink and juicy with the edges crisp and brown. The aroma rising from the food made her stomach lurch and nausea shook her. She looked at the dais where de Mortimer sat beneath the yellow and green canopy, deep in conversation with Lord de Bermingham, while the fair-haired Lord de Burgh, seated at his right, listened attentively.

He's ignoring me, she thought angrily, emptying her wine cup in one draft. The potent liquid left a warm path through her vitals, and she watched silently as a serving man refilled the cup from a silver flagon.

"You see, my lord, we drink from silver cups, while Lord de Mortimer's goblets are made of gold and crystal," Jehan told her husband.

" 'Tis fitting, my love, since he's the lord and I but his liege man and you my lady."

Ralph de Maudley had no illusions about his social status nor ambitions to rise above it. He was aware of Jehan's disappointment and knew she thought little enough of him, but he loved her. Smiling indulgently at his young wife, he saw that her green eyes were sharp with envy and her usually pale face was flushed. The heavy red hair was swept back from her broad forehead and lay coiled about her ears in gold fillets set with pearls. She had regained some weight since he had brought her to Ireland, and it gave her a softer, less gaunt look. The dark green velvet robe she wore accentuated the clear white skin, and her breasts swelled enticingly above its low neckline. He noticed that more than a few admiring glances were directed toward her. The long, full sleeves swept back to reveal the tight yellow silk of her undergown. Green and yellow . . . the de Mortimer colors. She had chosen them deliberately, hoping to bring attention to herself by annoying Roger, but, for him, she seemed not to exist at all.

The rising heat of the torches and roaring hearths was beginning to take its toll of her. Jehan felt a trickle of perspiration roll down her back and another one find its way between her breasts. Taking a silken handkerchief from the intricately wrought girdle about her slender waist, she delicately patted her face and bosom.

"My lord." Her words were short as she pushed back abruptly from the table, sending the besotted knight sprawling across the table with the vehemence of her action. "I feel quite faint . . . 'tis the heat and the noise. I beg your pardon, but I must have some air." She bent down and picked up her cloak from the bench.

Gray eyes full of concern, Sir Ralph helped her to her feet, offering to go with her, but she assured him it was not necessary. All she wanted was to escape from the Hall, from the heat and the press of folk about her, but most of all, from the presence of the man who refused to even acknowledge her existence. Tears stung her eyes as she fled through the huge doors into the courtyard, empty save for the guards. Crossing the hard-packed earth, she climbed the stone steps leading to the top of the inner curtain wall. The light of a flaring lantern shone briefly in her face as a guard stepped out of a tower doorway. Recognizing her, he closed the lantern's shield and turned back toward the outer edge of the wall.

Jehan breathed in the chill, penetrating air, clearing her head of the wine fumes. She leaned against the wall while tears of frustration streamed unheeded down her cheeks. Bastard! Betrayer! She vilified de Mortimer, spitting out one curse after another, venting her rage in the inky blackness of a starless night. Slowly she began to feel calmer as she stood looking out over the fields where she could make out the fires of the encampments glimmering in the darkness like stars that had forsaken the sky and fallen to earth. She was unaware of the passing of time as she stood there alone with her thoughts.

"Jehan . . ."

The remembered voice made her spin around with a gasp. Tall, his face hidden in the darkness, de Mortimer stood before her, a cloak thrown carelessly about him.

"My lord," she murmured as she bowed down politely before him. He raised her to her feet, his hand warm on hers.

"I was checking the watch . . . 'tis a habit I have. I find it keeps the men alert to wonder when I'll appear."

"We're most grateful that your mission to seek Edward's aid was successful."

Her voice sounded strange to her, forced and strained. They walked silently along the wall, halting finally near the side of a round tower, protected against the wind. The flickering light of a flaring torch fell over them, and he saw the white, heart-shaped face turned to him, framed by red hair shining dimly through the glittering gold netting. Her tongue nervously moistened the full lower lip of a mouth he remembered well.

"How have you been, Jehan?" he asked softly, wondering at his question. Did it truly matter to him?

"Fair, my lord. The time lies heavy on my hands with little to do but remember the past. 'Tis the fate of women whose men wage ceaseless war and are less than protectors of their own."

In went the small barb, and her eyes sparkled with satisfaction. All England knew of his shamefully neglected wife who had brought him her vast inheritance and been given his name and an endless string of children in return.

"Then you should have stayed at home and tended to your husband's holdings." It was said indifferently, de Mortimer's mind already dismissing her.

He was taken by surprise as she suddenly stepped close to him, a small white hand grasping his arm, holding him back.

"Where is my child, Roger?" The question was asked in a tense, strained voice.

"Your child, Jehan? You have no child." If she had thought to catch him unawares, she had failed, forgetting that he was like a cat in his ability to land on his feet. He sounded amused.

"You lie . . . he was mine and you took him from me!"

"Nay, foolish one, your father gave him to me to do with as I wished." He would say no more.

"I want my son!"

The anguished memory forbidden her so long broke through the wall she had built about it, and the pain was unbearable. She threw herself against him, beating her hands against him and shrieking wildly until he clamped a hand over her mouth. "Jehan, get control of yourself! 'Tis unseemly and common to act as you do."

His voice lashed out at her, hard and low-pitched. Her cloak fell back and he glimpsed the pure line of her throat and the flawless porcelain skin above the green robe. For a moment she yielded to the temptation of feeling his body against hers. He lifted a hand to touch the soft hair while a familiar scent of roses drifted into his senses. Full breasts and soft thighs pressed against him as she raised her face to him, the slanted green eyes full of tears.

"Please, Roger, tell me where my son is."

And she was standing alone, staring in astonishment as de Mortimer threw back his head and laughed.

"Very good, Lady de Maudley! You've not lost your ability to use all your weapons to dissemble."

"You whoreson!" she screamed furiously.

"Truly spoken. That's the Jehan I remember, with the instincts of a foul-mouthed harlot," de Mortimer said, still greatly amused. His dark eyes burned with a sudden hot flame, giving the reckless face a satanic look. Reaching out, he pulled her toward him, finding her mouth with his, and forced her lips to part under his unexpected attack. She struggled to escape him as his tongue ravished her mouth. He was treating her like the common strumpet he had named her . . . sweet Jesu, how she loathed him.

"Green and yellow indeed . . . your subtlety is to be applauded, my lady." He released her so suddenly that she staggered back. "And you're as seductive as you ever were, my lovely Jehan—perhaps even more so."

With another arrogant laugh, he was gone, leaving her alone with her rage.

"Lecherous bastard," she screamed after him. Trembling uncontrollably, she supported herself against the wall, weeping tears of pain and anger. She had lost the first joust. He had told her nothing but made an assault on her senses as he alone could do.

Next time, Roger, you'll not find such an easy victory, she vowed, still feeling the pressure of his mouth against hers. Merciful Virgin, what door had she opened in her desire for vengeance.

As spring took a firm hold over the land, preparations went on to mount a serious campaign against Edward Bruce and his Irish supporters. The baron of Wigmore allowed his men time to recover from their sea voyage, judging that a delay of a few weeks would make little difference to the campaign schedule despite the pressures placed on him by those Anglo-Irish lords who had the most to gain by driving the Scots from their land. Too often had he seen a battle lost because of the poor physical condition of foot soldiers and archers, so he remained adamant in the face of the lords' impatience.

Black eyes flashing angrily, he stood tall and slim before them, dressed simply in a short, dark red velvet tunic trimmed with black leather and soft suede boots, coldly reminding them that he had been named Justiciar of Ireland by Edward and, as such, the decision lay within his power alone. Muttering their disapproval, the lords had little choice but to accept his decree. As they turned to leave the council chamber, de Mortimer told them that they, too, should turn their attentions toward their men, preparing them for the long march northward, and he smiled grimly as they bristled in resentment at his less than gracious comments on their inadequacies.

Bending over the map which Emrys had unrolled across the top of the massive, elaborately carved table, de Mortimer pointed a slender finger to the great central plain of Ireland stretching down to the coast.

"The first order of business will be to secure Meath and rid myself of the Lacys once and for all."

"But, my lord, I thought we were to proceed directly to Ulster! 'Tis what you promised our barons and the Irish leaders," his chief lieutenant protested.

"Don't be as naive as the damn fools who have just left me, Ralph. 'Twill all be taken care of in good time, but I'll have no peace with that wretched tribe loose to do me mischief."

De Mortimer looked with annoyance at Ralph de Maudley. Perhaps he's been with me too long, he thought, seeing the shock on the older knight's face. They had shared many years of campaigning together. Sir Ralph de Maudley had sworn fealty to Wigmore when the young baron, while still under age, had finally won his legal release from Piers Gaveston's guardianship. De Mortimer realized that de Maudley had also shared his ambitions, following him without question until now. Running a hand through his thick black hair, he observed the aging man closely. For the first time since his arrival, he noticed new lines in the pleasant face and a worried expression in the steady gray eyes. Ralph had lost weight, too, judging from the way his tunic hung from his broad shoulders.

"Are you well, Ralph? There's a look to you which gives me unease."

Surprised, Sir Ralph laughed abruptly, assuring him that he was quite well, but that like all the baron's knights, he had been much beset prior to his return.

"Yes, that I can understand. And I fear 'twill continue to be so. What do you think of sending the ladies back to England when the ships sail? With the army gone, Dublin will be vulnerable if the enemy should break through."

The knight shook his head.

"I can't speak for the others, my lord, but I know my lady will battle to remain. Besides, there's little for her to go back to." His voice was bitter, and for a moment an anguished look crossed his face. "She's still young and has never learned prudence."

He hesitated, surprising an unexpected attentiveness in de Mortimer's attitude. Uncertain as to how much he should divulge, he sighed and said sadly, "You see, my Jehan tried to take her life while at the queen's court. Her lover was slain at Bannockburn." At de Mortimer's raised eyebrows, he shrugged. "Yes, I knew about it. Who didn't? She made no secret of it. Arnaut de Broze was his name—a Gascon knight whose own lady had fled from his abusive treatment of her. What Jehan saw in him remains her own secret."

Ah, now I remember, de Mortimer thought, only half listening to Sir Ralph's rambling account of his wife's rash deed and her slow recovery. He was Gillian Kilburn's first lord and it had been expected that James Kilburn would face him on the field of honor, but the earl of Pembroke forbade it. He would have laughed, for the tangled affair delighted his sardonic sense of humor, but Ralph's pale, stricken face made him restrain himself.

" 'Twas my fault . . . I allowed her too much freedom, but she's always been as one possessed, even from the day we wed . . ." He suddenly remembered that he was speaking to his liege lord and apologized.

" 'Tis no concern of yours, my lord, and I beg your pardon for having spoken as I did."

"Nonsense, Ralph, if this is what's troubling you, I want to know. We'll speak no more of sending Lady Jehan away."

He dismissed the matter abruptly and turned back to the map once more. But Emrys noticed that his master's hand trembled slightly as he began to point out possible routes of march. So he's not quite forgotten his part as much as he believes, the harper thought, hearing in his mind a young girl's heartbroken cry as her child was torn from her arms. He closed his eyes for a moment. Never would he forget her tears, for they had burned his hands with their agony. ·

It was already late when de Mortimer was able to at last find himself alone in his chamber. After his conversation with Ralph de Maudley, he had ridden out to the encampment and accepted Lord de Bermingham's invitation to share the evening meal with him. Now, finally, all his knights and retainers who usually crowded the antechamber were dismissed, leaving only Emrys on guard. De Mortimer stretched, feeling an uncommon weariness of spirit. Stripped down to naught but his linen chainse, he settled down comfortably near the hearth, leaning his head against the padded back of the chair and smiled with grim satisfaction at the knowledge that even more soldiers were on their way to Ireland. It was a point of information he had withheld from even his own lieutenants. Their arrival would be quite a surprise! Particularly for the informers he was positive were among his own people. Pembroke had done his task well, de Mortimer thought, for King Edward was not easy to convince when the peril was not directly before him. He toyed idly with his sheathed dagger and then threw it down on a small table drawn near to his chair.

Damn Edward and his extravagant ways! He'd lose his kingdom rather than discomfit himself! Sweet Jesù, how he despised him.

He held out his graceful hands toward the fire's warmth and stared moodily into its dancing depths. He supposed that he owed some of his successful mission to James Kilburn. He could not help admiring the man's high principles and sense of integrity while deploring his lack of ambition for himself. And then, of course, there was the fact that he had risked all he possessed, including his very life, for a woman who had belonged to another. By all that was holy, what kind of sorcery did she use to so tie him to her by passion and need that he turned his back on his rightful place among the highest lords of the realm. He felt a surprising pang of envy as he thought of his own quiet docile wife who had never once tried to become a part of his life, save to bear his children. The memory of Gillian Kilburn in his arms was difficult to erase, for she had drawn him in a strange, hypnotic way. Tenderness, compassion, and the gentler emotions were alien to his nature, and there was a strong compulsion in him to destroy utterly that which he did not understand.

The fire's glow threw his strong wild face into an eerie study of light and shadow, while a fringe of shining black hair fell over his forehead, hiding dark eyes suddenly narrowed in thought. What odd premonition had made him visit Powys ap Rhys just before he left for Ireland? That fierce lordling sitting in his castle in the mountain fastness of the vast de Mortimer holdings in Radnor had been less than pleased to see him. Pen-yr-bryn Castle was isolated, and it was easy for the Welshman to forget that he still was liegeman to the baron of Wigmore. Had Emrys not guided him up the winding, hidden road, de Mortimer never would have seen the small castle clinging to the crest of the hill. The castle was as forbidding as its lord, dark and dank, despite the hearths which roared ceaselessly, trying to banish the chill drafts which swept through its stone walls. He had stared curiously at the child brought to him, meeting green eyes gazing steadily and defiantly from a pale thin face topped by an unruly thatch of dark red hair. The boy, called Bleddyn, was tall for his age and, his uncle claimed, wild as the mountain valleys he ranged over on his pony. The boy had not liked the baron and was not afraid to show it. De Mortimer chuckled to himself. He'd shown courage. He'd grant him that.

A knock on the door brought his reveries to an end and he looked up as Emrys entered.

"My lord, you have a visitor who wishes to see you most urgently . . ."

Before he could say more, Jehan pushed him aside impatiently.

"I must speak with you, my lord."

De Mortimer remained seated, contemplating her with rising annoyance.

" 'Tis very flattering that you come to see me at this time of night, but, my dear Jehan, 'tis late and I'm weary and ready to retire."

He dismissed her with a gesture, but she came and stood before him, ignoring his order.

"I will speak with you now, for I daren't think when you'll allow me this chance. My husband told me you wished to send me back to England!"

"For your own safety. You and all the other English wives. The castle will be no place for you once we take to the field."

"Nonsense . . . 'tis just an excuse to rid yourself of a guilty memory." Her voice lashed out sharply at him, her red hair falling in a gleaming mass over slim shoulders and a back stiff with defiance.

"Jehan, I will not tell you where the child is. 'Tis no use to ask. Go back to your lord's bed and leave me in peace."

"Nay, I'll not! You play with me as a cat plays with a mouse that it refuses to kill. It gives you pleasure to taunt me. All these years I've kept the knowledge of my child locked away, forbidden to me. But I carried him, Roger. I had the pain of giving him birth, not you and not my father who knew only the outrage of my betrayal of his ambitions. It mattered naught to either of you that he was part of me. 'Twas my arms which longed to hold him and my breasts which ached to suckle him."

She blazed her wild anger at him with impassioned words until he had heard enough.

"Stop this ridiculous tirade, Jehan. You make a mockery out of motherhood. I'm not the only man whose bed you've shared. Your husband should have given you children to make you forget instead of allowing you the freedom to make a fool of yourself at court. Or is it possible that you fell in love with one of your lovers?"

His words died as she swayed in front of him, white and drained, her slanted green eyes glittering with tears.

"Don't mock me, Roger. Why can't you ever take me seriously! You've always treated me like some half-witted child who couldn't help doing what was wrong. If I'm governed by my passions, that is what I am and I'll not change. The babe was mine and I want him back. I never agreed to giving him to you."

She held out her arms to him, the cloak falling back to reveal her softly rounded figure clad in a short-sleeved silken shift. De Mortimer rose from his chair and shook his head.

" 'Tis sheer foolishness from a pampered and spoiled young woman. How would you explain the boy to Sir Ralph? Even he could not be so understanding as to accept him without question. And after all these years?" He leaned over her, his dark eyes suddenly cold and hard. "You forget that although I fathered your bastard, I've plans for myself which don't include old loves. As for this bastard—well, that's my business, and if you persist in this nonsense, I would fear for you."

The menace in his voice was not lost on Jehan. She unlaced the ties of her shift, whispering through her tears, "Then slay me now, Roger, for I don't wish to live. You're hard, selfish, and cruel . . ."

She picked up his dagger, drawing it from its sheath, and thrust it into his hand, pressing it against her bared breast. He threw it to the floor, furious with her, and gave her face a resounding slap. She gasped, turning her back to him, mortified by both their reactions. She should never have come and abased herself as she had. He wasn't worth it, for he cared for no one but himself.

"Jehan . . ." he murmured softly, coming to stand close behind her. "Give up this insane quest for the boy. Leave him be and know that he is well cared for. Let that knowledge be enough."

Shaking her head stubbornly, she leaned back weakly against him as she felt his hands slide over her shoulders, caressing her throat and slipping inside the unlaced shift. She groaned, despising herself at her body's betrayal beneath his touch. He turned her toward him and unclasped her cloak, which fell unheeded to the floor. Her hands glided over his linen chainse, feeling the smooth muscles tense beneath her fingers, and she pressed herself against his hardness, sensing the hunger for her rise within him. Was this what she had wanted from him and why she had sought him out, she thought with surprise as she gazed at the dark, passionate face and found his mouth taking possession of hers. She twined her arms tightly about his neck, suddenly remembering nothing and knowing only that Roger was claiming her again as he had done so many years before. He lifted her into his arms, asking, "And what about your lord, Jehan? Won't he miss you beside him?"

As he laid her on the bed, she replied, " 'Tis his night to serve as captain of the watch. His bed is empty . . ." and knew only the pleasure she craved from him .

A coverlet wrapped carelessly about her nakedness, Jehan crouched by the hearth, warming a flagon of wine. Her body felt totally sated and her movements were languid. It had been a long time since she had given herself so completely to any man. Her eyes were bemused.

"Roger . . ." she said softly, "what makes a woman so faithful to one man that even her husband means naught to her?"

De Mortimer, propped up on one elbow in bed, looked with malicious amusement at her earnest face.

"Whatever it is, Jehan, 'twill never involve you, for I fancy 'tis a quality totally lacking in you!"

She was startled at his words, having expected neither his reaction nor his observation. Shaking her head she said, "Nay, you mistake my meaning . . ."

"I understand your meaning all too well, my love. 'Tis Gillian Kilburn you meant. Do you still hate her so much?"

Jehan reddened, for he had caught her out. She had not dreamt he knew of her involvement with Arnaut de Broze.

"My dear Jehan, don't tell me you still mourn that piece of Gascon filth you gave your wanton heart to!"

He watched as she carefully poured the heated wine into two gold goblets heavily encrusted with precious stones. Picking them up, she carried them to the bed, the coverlet slipping to reveal a firm, coral-tipped white breast to his appreciative gaze. Jehan nestled against de Mortimer's lean, smooth body as they lay back together against the large, plump pillows. Sipping her wine and touching the jeweled goblet admiringly, she said, "He was privy to the king's council and stood high in Edward's favor!"

"Being in Edward's favor bespeaks virtue to you?" Roger was incredulous.

"Arnaut was proud, ambitious, and brave. He was also good to look upon . . ."

"And perverse, judging from some of the things you must have learned from him in bed."

Jehan leaped up as if stung, spilling some of the wine. Seeing the glint of laughter in de Mortimer's eyes, she bristled with indignation.

"You didn't seem to object, my dearest lord. Surely you didn't expect me to be the docile, untried maid you took so long ago."

He laughed and twined a strand of red hair about his finger. It was darker than when he had first known her, but it had lost none of its flaming, lustrous beauty.

"Untried, yes, but neither docile nor a maid, my sweet. That treasure you had yielded up to another before I ever made love to you."

"You never loved me, but neither did Lord de Broze. Gillian held him in thrall even beyond death." The green eyes hardened. "What is there about her that men cannot

70

forget? He always believed he would have her back, and Lord Kilburn was obsessed by hatred for him because Arnaut possessed her first."

"How can you know that? Have you ever met the earl of Glairn? Or his lady?" The questions were asked casually, but she felt his body tense against hers. "A woman such as Gillian Kilburn is born to be possessed." He spoke as if to himself.

You too, she thought, and suddenly felt resentful, refusing to answer him. Try to find that out, my love. Leaning over him, her green eyes met his bold, black gaze and she kissed him deliberately, pressing her softness against him. With a stifled oath, he cast his goblet to the floor and twisted his hand in her long cloud of hair, forcing her back against the pillows.

"Damn you," he said angrily, hearing the laughter which bubbled from her at his reaction. "You are indeed a wanton, perverse bitch."

Accepting his opinion of her, she proceeded to prove it to him.

The days passed quickly as the activity in and about the castle rose to a fever pitch. There was much traffic between the castle and the encampments, and the gates stood open for the messengers and wagons to pass through. Guards were doubled, and travelers entering the city were searched, for it was common knowledge that Edward Bruce and his Irish allies had spies scattered throughout the countryside. The baron of Wigmore had ordained that no one was above suspicion, and all who were accused were sent into the castle's dungeons. Everyone was pressed into service to prepare for the coming campaign. Even those wives who had chosen to remain with their lords were ordered to supervise the packing of linens, blankets, spare clothing, and other goods into the strong wooden coffers banded with iron which were placed in wagons drawn up in the outer bailey. Other wagons were piled high with sacks of dried beans, peas, flour, rice and sugar, smoked hams, large wheels of cheese, and barrels of dried and smoked fish. The forges glowed red through the night as the powerful destriers were shod, and swords, battle axes, and knives sharpened to a keen edge. The encampments beyond the city's walls were not spared, and the forges there too rang with the sound of busy anvils. Fletchers made additional supplies of arrows while the Welsh archers stretched and tautened their bows, testing their accuracy on targets set out on the surrounding fields. Men practiced their arts of war on the broad meadows, the thousands of feet and hooves turning them into muddy, barren wastes.

Nearly all was in readiness, and still de Mortimer refused to give the order to march. He seemed to be waiting. But for what, the other lords asked angrily, chafing at the delay. Most of the ships had returned to England, slipping silently from the Liffey into the bay as the sky began to pale in the east. Only the knights whose wives were returning to England stood on the castle's battlements high above the city and watched the ships' sails catch the morning breeze.

Ralph de Maudley, as the baron's most trusted officer, was placed in charge of administering the encampments and found little time to spend with Jehan. Away from the castle for days at a time, he worried constantly that she might become restless and discontented. She assured him that she understood—there was also much for her to do— and smiled warmly at him as her tiring woman coiled the long braid of hair tightly at the nape of her neck before covering it with a white linen headcloth.

"The wimple gives you an unfamiliar look, my darling," Sir Ralph remarked fondly, grateful for the short time they could spend together. The deep green color of the sturdy woolen gown she wore made her enchantingly tilted eyes sparkle, and there was a glow to her beautiful white skin he had never seen before. In the months she had been with him in Ireland, he had developed a deep and passionate love for her whose intensity disturbed him. Sadly he would chide himself, forcing himself to remember the disparity in their ages. Yet, the wistful hope that she might someday return his love would not be quenched. He relaxed in the comfortable chair she had ordered drawn close to the fire for him. The warmth of the hearth felt good to a body too long in the saddle.

"I have been ordered to the storehouse to assist in seeing what must be kept here in case of another siege."

She stared at her image in the silver-edged mirror on the small dressing table. He was right, she thought. But 'twas not the wimple which made her look different, she reminded herself smugly. Jehan blew a kiss at the unsuspecting knight and rose to leave. He caught her hand, drawing her close to him.

"I never see you any more," he murmured, gently stroking her softly rounded cheek. Green eyes looked at him in innocent astonishment.

"My lord, 'tis you who are never here. Bid your liege lord release you from your duties so that you may spend more time with your lady. I'm sure he will agree!"

Sir Ralph smiled as Jehan laughed at her absurd sally. Impulsively she threw her arms about him and kissed him with unexpected tenderness. He was taken by surprise, for she rarely showed any affection toward him.

"Jehan . . ." he said thickly, his eyes clouding with emotion, but she moved away from him, her mind already far from her husband. He marveled at the change in her, for in the years of their marriage, she had never been interested in attending to her duties as chatelaine of his manor. Perhaps when they returned to England, things would be different between them. He wondered whether a child would make her more content to stay with him. He yawned and stretched stiffly, gazing about the empty chamber strewn untidily with Jehan's things. God's blood, he was tired! Ruefully he admitted that he was too old for all the responsibilities which were being placed on him by Lord de Mortimer. Lying down with a grateful sigh on the unmade bed, he felt the weariness creep through his body, and buried his face in a pillow redolent with the scent of roses.

"Jehan . . ." he murmured as he sank into an exhausted sleep.

The courtyard echoed with the sounds of men loading the high wagons with sacks from a large pile stacked outside the storehouse. Dogs whined and yelped, straining at their chains, eager to be released, while horses stood un-

73

easily between the wagon shafts. The shrieking of wheels rolling over the rough stones of the cobbled yard added to the mounting din. Roger de Mortimer, accompanied by Emrys and two of his younger knights, stood in the center of the busy yard watching the activity with a critical eye. Bareheaded and clad in a short tunic, hose, and high boots, he had been up since dawn and had just returned from outside the city walls. The castle steward came to him with his account book under his arm and a harassed look on his lined face.

"Well, Ned, how go the preparations?" Roger asked. The heavyset man sweated profusely in a heavy brown tunic fashioned of a roughly woven woolen cloth. A large ring of keys dangled from the wide belt about his ample waist. "Will there be aught left in the storehouses when everything is loaded on the wagons?" de Mortimer wondered.

The steward laughed darkly, pointing to the small figure emerging from the dark entry of the stone building.

"Lady de Maudley has made sure of that. She's fought me over every sack of flour and sugar I've ordered placed on the wagons. My lord, I pity her husband, for she's a very determined, strong-minded, and sharp-tongued wench."

A frown settled over the baron's face.

"Is she really? I would have deemed so fair a face betokened a milder disposition," de Mortimer remarked blandly.

The steward smirked, a lewd expression in his eyes. "But she's red-headed, my lord, and 'tis known that red-headed wenches are——"

"To be sure, Ned, to be sure." De Mortimer interrupted the steward impatiently, not wishing to continue the subject of Lady de Maudley. She was too much on his mind as it was. He felt increasingly uneasy about the relationship into which they had plunged, for her passionate sensuality was beginning to drug his senses more than he had intended. He had forgotten how well she matched him temperamentally and physically, but he could ill afford to allow himself to become ensnared in the emotional web she was weaving about him.

74

He looked up at the pale blue sky above the battlements, watching the clouds drift overhead. His banner fluttered in the rising wind from the central tower, and he saw the white wings of seagulls as they glided through the air. Emrys followed his gaze.

"The wind blows from the east. Perhaps soon there'll be some news."

"What news?" Roger asked sharply. "At what door have you been listening . . . or are you privy to my personal papers now?"

The harper's dark face reddened in confusion and he turned away.

"Nay, Emrys, stay," the baron said in a milder tone. "I should know by now that you can read my private thoughts, and I am grateful for your loyalty, though I show it but little."

Bowing low before de Mortimer, Emrys accepted the rare apology in good grace. Looking down gloomily at the shaggy black hair which obscured the sly, all-seeing eyes of his squire, Roger could scarce remember when the Welshman had not been beside him, knowing him first as a youth some ten years older than himself. Through the years, Emrys had shared his master's fortunes and misfortunes, enduring the cuffs, kicks, and impatient curses with stoic silence. Because of his solitary nature and strange ways, most men shrank from Emrys in fear, endowing him unfairly with supernatural powers. De Mortimer fostered the belief, for it suited him to have the devil's familiar as his shadow. How he must hate me, he thought and found the idea amusing. Leaving the two knights with the steward to assist in sorting out the problems in the storehouse, he crossed the yard toward the archway leading to the stables. Jehan ran after him, holding her long skirts up to avoid tripping over them on the uneven, filthy ground littered with straw, rotting garbage, and steaming offal left by the draft horses.

"My lord . . . please."

Roger turned at the sound of her voice, amused by the sight of her angry face. A strand of red hair had escaped the confines of the headcloth and lay damply over her pale forehead.

"Your steward finds it difficult to realize that some of the food must be left back for the castle folk. He tells me you've given him leave to empty the storehouses completely."

Her eyes met his, surprising an odd look in them for a moment, but he only said, "Then he misheard my instructions. Rest your fears, my lady, I'll not leave the castle without provender. Besides, I'm sure that he was just making sport of you."

She bristled angrily at first and then smiled her relief, but he remained serious, asking whether Sir Ralph had returned to the city. When she told him that he had indeed arrived that morning, totally exhausted after an absence of several days and was probably sleeping, de Mortimer sighed, almost reluctant to make the decision, and then sent Emrys to call him.

" 'Twill be necessary for your lord to be captain of the watch tonight. There's no one else available."

They stood together in the archway, for the moment out of earshot of everyone. He looked down at the heart-shaped face framed by the white wimple and noticed a smudge of dirt on her chin. She gazed at him questioningly and he shook his head.

"Nay, Jehan, I'm not doing it deliberately. I do have need of your husband. He's of too great value to me for such selfish abuse." De Mortimer wiped the dirt from her chin with a gauntleted hand.

"Roger, shall I come to you tonight?" she whispered, her heart hammering so loudly she was sure he would hear it. Waiting for his reply, she caught the same strange look in his dark eyes that she had seen before. When he nodded almost imperceptibly, Jehan realized that for the present, Roger was as trapped by what lay between them as she was. She watched him stride rapidly with that easy, catlike tread through the passage toward the stables, and wondered how long it would take before he tired of her. She must find a way to be useful to him so that he would not send her away.

It was quiet in the chamber save for the crackling of the fire still burning in the hearth. In the wide bed placed

76

beside a tapestry-covered wall, de Mortimer was awake, propped up against several pillows. Jehan lay close beside him, resting her pale cheek childlike on both her hands. He could feel the warmth of her even breathing against his bare skin. She had come to him during the night, moving into his arms without hesitation, her hunger for him naked in her eyes. Involved in their need for each other, they had not even bothered to draw the velvet curtains about the bed, neither giving any thought to the privacy of darkness. There had been a desperation in her submission to him that had taken him by surprise.

Later, he had at first been amused and then caught by her astute and shrewd observations of the men surrounding him as she lay in his arms whispering to him in the dim light of the things they had confessed to her. 'Twas true, he admitted, that unless one was very careful, the beautiful Lady Jehan had a way of making a man bare his soul to her.

He smoothed the tumbled hair from about her face, wondering again at the turn of fate which had brought her back to him.

How very young and spoiled she had been when she had first given herself to him capriciously—Lady Jehan Gouland, the only daughter of an enormously wealthy and ambitious Marcher baron. She was betrothed at that time to the young heir of Lord Thomas de Brasney, a match her father had worked hard to achieve. The de Brasneys were an old and distinguished family, and she would bring to the marriage a great fortune in exchange for their power and prestige. But Jehan, though just fifteen, had even then been guided by her emotions and a body that craved love. De Mortimer remembered how captivated he had been by her flamboyant beauty and high spirits and then found himself entangled in a relationship which had amazed him in its physical fulfillment. Young himself and already bored with his gentle, obedient wife, he had allowed his desire for Jehan to rule him for a short while, but he had been rudely awakened by the reality of the child conceived through their madness.

Lord Gouland was furious when he discovered that he was with child. Although she swore later that she had not told him, he had somehow ferreted out the truth. How she must have fought her father, de Mortimer thought, for she had borne her babe in her father's home.

Roger stared up at the velvet canopy embroidered with small golden stars. It all seemed so long ago, and to him had meant so little save the annoyance of having to face the existence of a bastard in whose veins ran some of the best blood in the realm. His face hardened. Too much was at stake to jeopardize his plans by allowing a headstrong woman to claim a child who for now best remained unknown. Nay, she would not win her game, no matter how hard she dissembled. And yet, he thought, running a hand lightly over her warm, sleeping body, she was an exciting and sensual creature. Jehan stirred under his touch. She raised her head, meeting eyes fathomless in their blackness.

"Roger . . ." she murmured, reaching up a white hand to draw his head down to hers. He drew her closer, feeling the taut-nippled fullness of her breasts press against him as she moved eagerly into his arms.

They both froze as the sound of loud, excited voices in the antechamber was heard through the closed door. Emrys's angry voice was protesting, the words tripping over themselves in his agitation while another's deep, rumbling tones continued to insist. Without warning, the door opened and Emrys's small figure was outlined briefly in the light streaming in from the other chamber, barring the man who finally succeeded in gaining entrance.

"My lord, forgive my intrusion but I bring important news . . ." He fell to one knee before the bed as de Mortimer threw back the covers and sat up.

Horror-struck and unable to move, Jehan stared at her lord whose eyes slowly focused on the sight of his wife beside de Mortimer, her wild mass of unbound hair gleaming brightly in the firelight the only covering to hide her nakedness. The passion which had risen within her still suffused her pale features and Sir Ralph felt a shaft of sickening pain drive through him.

"Why have you come? What news is there?" De Mortimer's voice cut through his shock sharply, bringing him back to the agonizing reality of his lord's bedchamber.

"Uh . . . my lord . . . news . . ." The elderly man shook his head, dazed, unwilling to believe what was before his eyes. Roger stood by him now, a long velvet robe banded with fur hastily thrown over his tall body, dark eyes glowing with a mixture of annoyance, anger, and impatience.

"Yes, Ralph, news. You come into my bedchamber unannounced—what did you expect?" He motioned to Jehan to stay where she was, although she had not moved at all.

Gray eyes staring over de Mortimer's shoulder, Sir Ralph cleared his throat, trying desperately to remember his reason for coming. The messenger—that was it! A messenger had just arrived . . .

"Ships, Lord de Mortimer, English ships have been sighted off the coast . . ."

A triumphant laugh rang through the chamber and both Jehan and Sir Ralph stared at Roger in surprise. He shouted with sudden glee.

"So they've come at last! Did you hear, Emrys? Now we can begin . . . Ralph, rouse the castle at once. We move out at first light to meet the ships in two days' time."

All else forgotten for the moment, he called loudly for his clothes, striding impatiently about the chamber before remembering Jehan's husband. Emrys silently helped the shaken knight to his feet as de Mortimer sobered in the face of the older man's obvious humiliation.

"My lord, let me explain . . ." Jehan's voice was hesitant as it broke through the thickening silence. Roger shook his head, giving her a warning look.

"Nay, Roger, let me be," she whispered. And de Mortimer, angry at the position in which de Maudley's unthinking intrusion had placed him, and out of patience with what he knew was to follow, strode from the bedchamber to call his lieutenants together. Already the sounds of a stirring castle reached their ears, for Emrys had wasted no time in calling out the guard.

"Cover yourself, my lady. 'Tis indecent to show yourself so," was all Sir Ralph could say in a voice scarce his own, as she hastily drew the coverlet high about her shoulders.

"And now you know, my lord. So it has ever been with me. Did you think that in all the years I was at court, I remained faithful and true to you? The very circumstances of our marriage should have warned you what sort of woman you had agreed to wed." She sounded defiant, resentful at having been found out.

"Nay, Jehan, you are mistaken," the elderly man said sadly. "Your father told me of your foolish act and how the de Brasney family withdrew from the betrothal contract. There were few illusions left to me after my first wife died. I had loved her well and mourned her deeply, but you needed someone to give you the protection of a name and care for you." He sighed, shifting his gaze away from her white face. "So I agreed to wed you, knowing full well that you had wantonly given your virginity to a mere page."

He was startled by her bitter laugh.

"Is that what you were told? And you believed it? You fool! I'll not allow you any illusions at all, my dearest lord. Yes, the nameless, faceless page was first, but 'twas Roger de Mortimer I loved and wanted and could not have. And I wanted to die then, but my father stopped me and forced me to marry you. There was naught else for me." Jehan saw his stricken face and tried to hold the words back, but it was as if a door had opened which could not be shut. "To me you were old. You meant nothing to me—nothing! And even worse, you were liege man to the baron of Wigmore. Yet, how indulgent you were—it even seemed that you were glad to be rid of me when I bade you allow me to leave."

Jehan was sitting on the edge of the bed, clutching the covers to her. At last she was able to tell him all that she had kept from him, and in an odd way, she delighted in the pain she was inflicting upon him by her cruelty. "You never suspected how desperate I was to get away. But then all you seemed to care for was to follow Wigmore wherever he led you. Simpleton! How little you knew either of us!" Her voice rose, lashing out at him contemptuously. "Had I stayed with you, I would have killed myself rather than be so close to Roger and not have him, for he had no thoughts for me anymore. Who was I to him but . . ." She caught herself in time. "So I escaped to court."

"And were quickly consoled," he murmured, wishing he had the strength to leave. Her words tore at his soul, flaying him with the truth of her feelings. How cruel she was!

" 'Twas not as you believe. The Gascon knight and I—we were both caught in a trap. He loved his wife in the twisted, insane depths of his soul and I . . . I mourned my lost lover who had forgotten me and tried to replace him with another. That was what held us together, that and what finally grew between us."

She began to weep, remembering de Broze and the agony she had felt at his death. What had been left to her?

"And it almost killed you!" The words were blurted out from deep within him. Why had he allowed her to come to Ireland. He did not want to hear her confessions any longer, but she suddenly stood before him, wrapped in the coverlet, stretching out her hand to him. Her voice softened.

"I never meant to hurt you, my lord. What do I truly know of you? One gives pain to those one loves, and did we matter to each other in all these years? I know that you've been ever good and kind to me and I've given you naught in return. But my wanting was too great . . . and my fear."

Tears streamed down Jehan's pale face as she spoke to him, but as she wept, his features became cold and hard. He longed to forgive her, but not once had she asked for his forgiveness, nor did she seem ashamed for what she had done. All these weeks she had lain with de Mortimer, and he had never suspected it. How they must have laughed at his innocent trust.

"And the child you bore? Do you ever remember it?"

His questions were torn from him. Jehan's weeping ceased abruptly as she stared at him in sheer terror, her eyes dark in a face devoid of all color.

"You knew?" she whispered hoarsely.

"Yes, I knew, but till now I had thought it sired by the page. Your betrayed father!" He laughed in derision, goaded beyond endurance. "By the Virgin, I was betrayed even in my act of charity. You wanton bitch . . . 'twas Wigmore's whelp!"

Ralph shook off her trembling grasp as the chamber spun before his eyes. How could he have been so blind to the truth. Her father, too, had lied to him, pretending fawning gratitude for his kindness and understanding, pressing a large settlement upon him for his debauched daughter. Yes, and you took the gold gladly, a small voice told him. What did that matter when the truth had been kept from me, he replied silently in defense of his shame. Jehan and de Mortimer! Why had he not sensed it? He knew her not at all. His ears rang and he shook his head, blind rage coursing through him at last. From a distance he heard Jehan speak to him, a pleading note to her voice.

"My lord, please . . . promise me you'll never mention your knowledge of the child to Lord de Mortimer . . . promise me, please!"

What was she babbling about, he thought. The child had been stillborn . . . Oh sweet heavenly Jesù! The truth broke over him in an icy deluge. White-faced and expressionless, he pushed Jehan away from him, refusing to answer her. Never would she be a part of his life again, he vowed . . . he could not bear it. And his love for her twisted and writhed within him with unbearable agony.

His gray eyes looked out from a face suddenly old, seeing her as if for the first time. How many faceless men had enjoyed her sensuality and passion . . . had slaked their desire in that soft white body, he wondered, torturing himself with images best driven off.

"Please, Ralph, don't mention the babe to Roger. Swear it!"

But he was beyond listening to her. Holding a metal-banded gauntlet in his hand, he struck her face and shoulders until she fell back, screaming with pain.

"Filthy slut!" His voice shook with anger as he spat out the words. "Whore!"

Letting the gauntlet slip from suddenly nerveless fingers, he stumbled blindly from the chamber. Emrys turned his eyes away from the knight's twisted, tortured face. Buckling the leather strap about a large wooden coffer holding his master's personal papers, he once again felt a wave of hatred rise in him toward de Mortimer. Why did he persist in betraying the few human souls who allowed themselves to love him?

"The day is ours!"

Still wearing his hauberk beneath a surcoat stained with blood, John de Bermingham pulled back the flap of the green and yellow striped pavilion, a triumphant smile on his weary face. De Mortimer had returned to the encampment some time earlier and sat motionless in a camp chair strewn with velvet cushions. A wine cup, its contents untouched, was held loosely in his hand and gleamed dully in the light from an oil lamp suspended from the ceiling of the tent. He looked up moodily, not responding to the other man's greeting. It had indeed been a victory, but a battle hard won, for the Irish force they had come upon without warning had fought desperately, falling back toward the marshy ground they alone knew well. Remembering the disastrous results of Bannockburn, he had sent a company of men to flank them on either side, driving them together. The tactics had worked, for thinking themselves trapped, the main body of men, comprised of mostly spear-wielding foot soldiers belonging to the O'Neall, along with a small band of mounted Scottish knights astride sturdy highland horses, had made their stand facing a formidable enemy. The sheer lunacy of their allowing themselves to be cut down one by one had angered and sickened him. Where had been that greatly lauded military acumen he had experienced at Kells when he was driven from the field by Edward Bruce?

"This was no battle, de Bermingham. 'Twas mere slaughter of leaderless sheep and the senseless slaying of our own men." His voice was bitter as he slammed down his cup with an impatient gesture, spilling the contents over the small wooden stand.

He could hear the sounds of men riding past the tent, the musical jingling of the horses' bridles in sharp contrast with the fatigue in their muted voices.

"Has de Burgh returned yet with the roll of our losses?" Roger asked, motioning Emrys to draw a chair near for Lord de Bermingham. Handing his belt and sword to the squire, the baron's general sat down heavily, stretching out legs still covered by armored guards spattered with mud. He drank deeply from the wine cup that the Welshman handed him.

"I've not seen him yet, although his master of arms rode past a few minutes ago."

They sat together silently, each busy with his own thoughts, while Emrys crouched against the tent wall behind his master's chair, his thoughts turned inward. De Mortimer had angrily thrown his stained surcoat into a corner, furious that Walter de Lacy had apparently slipped through his hands again. Word had come during the night from an informant that he was near, but he had been reported close to their line of march all through Meath and northward toward Ulster. Greedy for the reward placed on the fugitive's head by the baron of Wigmore, many had been eager to reveal his hiding place, but each time he had managed to elude his tracker. Roger smiled darkly at the knowledge that Meath at least was his, seized in the name of the crown. However, he had no intention of allowing it to pass out of his own possession.

The past weeks had been grueling, marching the large army of men and equipment over barely passable roads under skies leaden with low gray clouds. When the rain was not pouring down on them, they would find themselves wading ankle deep in mud while thick curtains of silent white fog surrounded them, distorting even the most familiar shapes and sounds. The relief force from England was placed at the end of the long line, adding the necessary thrust for the expedition which the Lord de Mortimer had hoped would effectively break the Scottish influence in Ireland. To his surprise, several Irish lords, appalled at the devastation and savage destruction of their land by the Scots, had begun to add their support to England's side.

A steady drumming on the pavilion's ceiling brought Roger's mind back to the present. The strong, primitive smell of wet earth pervaded the tent and a damp chill settled into the air. He called for braziers to be lit and placed on the carpeted ground. Servants hastened to obey, and one entered with a large ewer of steaming hot water, which he placed near a stand holding a shallow brass bowl.

"This accursed climate—'tis only fit for the people who breed here," Roger growled as he pulled off his tunic and sweat-soaked chainse. Stripped naked, he proceeded to scrub the stains of the day's battle from his body, using finely milled soap which covered his skin with a soft lather. Refilling the bowl with fresh, cool water, the servant waited with a thick towel as his master immersed his head. Soon the taut-featured face glistened clean of grime and wet strands of black hair hung thickly to below his ears.

De Bermingham watched the ablutions uneasily. Aware of his own filthy state, he longed to retire to his tent, but his lord had not yet dismissed him. While he did not fear de Mortimer, he avoided antagonizing him by challenging the authority he used with such overbearing arrogance. Looking at de Mortimer dispassionately, he wondered not for the first time what sort of thoughts passed through his sharp and clever mind. Even when he acted for the crown, as he did now in his capacity as Justiciar and Warden of Ireland, he seemed rather to be acting in his own interests. The handsome baron would have an enemy killed without one thought as to the morality or legality of the deed. He watched as de Mortimer drew on fresh hose, a clean white chainse, and a dark red woolen tunic which reached to his knees, and Emrys helped him pull on soft black leather boots and clasped the wide belt set with stones about his waist. A heavy signet ring sparkled in the light as his slim hand smoothed down the still-damp hair.

A gust of rain-laden air streamed in as William de Burgh entered, shaking the wetness from his sodden cloak. Doffing his helm, he reached into the pouch suspended from his shoulder. Drawing out a roll of parchment, he handed it wordlessly to de Mortimer. Scanning the list of English casualties rapidly, his eyes came to rest on one name, and he looked quickly at his squire. Before he had a chance to speak, Lord De Burgh drew back the tent flap, saying, "My lord, I think this will be of interest to you."

Curious, Roger stepped to the entrance of the pavilion as a mounted lancer pushed the burden slung before him on the saddle to the ground. The body of a man, clad in battle dress, sprawled at his feet and he turned him onto his back with the toe of an extended boot. A torch flared, illuminating the dark, bearded face of the corpse. Walter de Lacy! De Mortimer stared at his enemy, scarce believing that he was dead. The de Lacy arms were prominently displayed on the blood-soaked surcoat. How had he missed being seen, he wondered, exulting nonetheless at the sight of the lifeless face.

"Where was he found?" de Mortimer asked the young lord. De Burgh smiled grimly, his fair hair dripping into his face as the now-steady rain beat down on him.

"He was found on the battlefield, slain by a fortunate sword thrust through a weak spot in his mailed shirt. He must have fought like a demon, for the ground was littered with our men."

"Good," de Mortimer said, a devil's grin breaking over his even features. "Then the reward need not be awarded!" He pushed the body once more with his booted foot. "Throw this offal to the wayside," he said coldly. " 'Twill be an example to those who oppose my will."

Donning the long mantle Emrys had brought, he threw the wide hood over his head and strode into the teeming darkness of the encampment, past dimly lit tents and hastily raised tarpaulins shielding open cooking fires from the relentless rain.

"Should I be needed, look for me at the de Maudley camp," de Mortimer called back to Lord de Bermingham and young de Burgh, who still stood in the rain beside Walter de Lacy's crumpled corpse.

A fiery red sea of searing pain carried Ralph de Maudley into the darkness, but there was no peace there for him. Sharp talons dug into his torn flesh, causing new waves of agony to wash over him until he heard himself cry aloud. He prayed for death, but it had so far been denied him.

Facing the enemy in battle had eased the anguish which gnawed at his soul since that terrible night in Dublin Castle. Although it was not easy, he had managed to avoid the baron of Wigmore as much as possible. Seated with the lords at de Mortimer's conferences, he had presented an expressionless facade which belied his inner turmoil. In the recesses of his mind he relived the scene with Jehan over and over again, asking himself why he had been so angered by her behavior. He had known of her infidelities at court. The knowledge of her affair with Lord de Broze was bearable because he had convinced himself that the guilt was his for neglecting her through his allegiance to Wigmore. He had believed himself too old for love and then had been ensnared by it. And now it has slain me, he thought, feeling tears trickling down his cheeks. Why had de Mortimer denied the existence of the child when he finally had mentioned it to him? As liegeman to Wigmore, he could not call him out, nor even accuse him publicly for his adulterous behavior. De Mortimer's friendliness and attitude of reliance despite all that had happened infuriated him and he had used the only weapon he possessed against a man no longer his friend.

His chest was on fire, the flames licking deep into his vitals with unrelenting fury. So intent had he been this morning on wielding his sword to either side of his advancing destrier that he had seen the mace whirling down on him too late to deflect it with his shield. As the spiked ball smashed and ripped through his hauberk to gouge into his body, he caught a glimpse of the green and yellow badge on the unknown knight's surcoat. Wrenched from his mount's back by the force of the blow, he had fallen between the feet of his attacker's horse, thrusting upward with his sword. But it had been futile, for horse and rider were lost amid the tangle of battling men, while he began to sink into a pain-filled void.

"Ralph . . . can you hear me?"

The voice was faint and he struggled to rise above his agony. A face swam dimly before his vision. De Mortimer's dark eyes burned into his.

"My lord . . ." De Maudley's words were barely audible. "Why, my lord? Why did you order my death?"

De Mortimer looked down at Ralph de Maudley's broken and mangled body covered now by a blanket dark with blood that could not be staunched. When he had entered the tent, the rasping, rattling sound of breathing greeted him. A twisted tangle of chain mail lay in a corner with other torn clothing, and Jehan's husband was stretched out on his camp bed, a mass of bruised and lacerated flesh where the mace had dug and torn into his body. The surgeon, probing the gaping wound across the stricken man's chest, had shaken his head at Roger's unspoken question.

"I didn't order your death," de Mortimer told de Maudley quietly, kneeling beside the low cot. "I read your name listed on de Burgh's roll and came to see if you had need of anything."

With closed eyes, Sir Ralph murmured, "Death is what I need to deliver me from this misbegotten world. Why, my lord . . . and don't pretend innocence . . . 'tis over for me."

Opening his eyes again, he saw that the surgeon was gone. Perhaps to tend a living man, he thought wearily. He gritted his teeth as the pain clawed at him again. De Mortimer wiped the dying man's face with a damp cloth. He leaned over him, asking urgently, "What did Jehan tell you?"

"Naught. I guessed rightly . . . and you've slain me for it." He stared suddenly into Roger's face. "Why do you fear this child, my lord? Surely there are many bastards about who could claim you sire!"

"Serfs' brats? Children bred off serving sluts and yeomen's daughters?" Roger shook his head. "They're of no importance . . . they've no claim to me nor I to them. But this child, Ralph . . . did you know that Jehan's grandmother was of Angoulème . . . kinswoman to old King John's queen?"

De Maudley's eyes glazed with pain and a moan escaped him. What did Jehan's grandmother matter? But de Mortimer's voice was insistent, eager now to share the fruit of his folly with his betrayed friend, forgetting what he himself had done to him.

"This child carries the blood of Llewellyn in his veins, as well as that of England's kings and their noble cousins, Pembroke and de Warenne. His blood is as fine as that of my own heir! Think, Ralph, of what that means . . . how he can be used, if it be necessary. He will belong to me, do my bidding alone, and none will know that I control him." His tone hardened, remembering. "You fool! 'Twas the weapon of your own destruction you held in your hand."

"Jehan . . . don't harm her, my lord . . ."

A curious sense of peace began to steal over him as the words slipped from lips suddenly soft and moist. The pain was easing, and Sir Ralph felt himself slowly drift into the warm, beckoning darkness. He no longer felt menaced by his lord's presence. The anger and hatred which had become such a part of him during the past weeks vanished, for naught mattered to him now. Instead, a feeling of pity stirred within him briefly. He smiled as he thought of the turmoil and human passions he was leaving behind forever and delivered himself gratefully into nothingness.

Motionless and brooding, Roger remained at Sir Ralph's bedside. Emrys was the first to realize that the labored breathing had ceased. He swung the small harp from his back, cradling it for a moment in his arms. Crouching by the dead man's feet, his hands stroked the strings until they quivered to life beneath his touch. The wild, mournful melody that filled the silent tent and spilled out into the black stormy night held unshed tears and splintering sorrow for all those who had that day ceased to be. And as he emptied his soul into that of his harp, the Welshman's green eyes turned toward his master, seeing all that de Mortimer refused to admit lay within him. Grief tore through him for the loyal knight who had been naught but a pawn in de Mortimer's game of chess with fate. And he lowered his dark head against the lamenting harp and wept.

"Your husband is dead, Jehan!" De Mortimer's voice was flat and expressionless. "Do you understand what I'm saying to you? Have you no words?"

Jehan stared blankly at Roger. He stood by the hearth in the council chamber, still clad in his hauberk and travel-stained surcoat, its yellow and green stripes spattered with the road's mud. Why couldn't she feel anything, she wondered, as a numbness settled over her. When she had answered de Mortimer's summons, there had been no time to realize that her husband had not been among those who rode so triumphantly up the causeway to the castle's doors, opened wide to receive them. While the castle folk lined the walkways of the battlements and parapets, she had stayed in the chamber once shared with her lord and now shorn of all his possessions. He had left nothing of himself behind, and there were many times in the weeks following his departure that she prayed fervently to the blessed Virgin for understanding. He was gone from her life—angry and hurt, shamed by his wife and his liege lord. But when she slept, it was of Roger that she dreamed.

Entering the council chamber, she found William de Burgh and John de Bermingham in lively conversation with Roger, sharing a goblet of his best claret. They had greeted her politely as she curtsied low before them, knowing that she looked well in her dark blue gown intricately patterned with gold embroidery. Her hair, glowing like flames, hung in two long plaits over her rounded bosom. The bruises from the blows her lord had given her were completely gone and her skin was once more unblemished. Quickly finishing their wine, the two lords had taken their leave, and de Mortimer bluntly told her of Sir Ralph's death. She waited for some kind of feeling to come to her—of sorrow or guilt or even pity—but oddly, all she noticed was a dent in the gold cup Lord de Burgh had placed on the council table and the sound of Roger's mailed feet on the stone floor as, made restless by her silence, he walked toward her.

"Did he provide for you?"

He looks very weary, Jehan thought, not answering his question. There were lines about his eyes and mouth that had not been there before. His thick black hair fell damply over his forehead and he pushed it back with an impatient hand.

"You killed him," she said calmly, without surprise.

De Mortimer shrugged, neither admitting nor denying her words.

"And now I suppose you'll find some way to eliminate me from your life as well!" A small flame of fear flickered in her mind. "I never told him of our son." Her voice rose slightly in the face of his reaction.

He sighed and tried to push back a feeling of annoyance at having to explain his actions to her.

"Jehan, he was mortally wounded in a battle with the O'Neall's men. He was still alive when they brought him to his tent."

Her green eyes turned fully on him, trying to read the truth in his face.

"He guessed rightly, Roger. I begged him not to tell you of it, but he was so angry with me. He must have revealed his knowledge to you for reasons he alone could know. Perhaps others are aware of our secret as well. Will you slay them too, trying to deny our son's existence?"

He flushed as she continued to accuse him in the same quiet tones. Jehan had resigned herself to share her lord's fate in the moment when she realized what Roger had done. She leaned against the heavy wooden table, feeling the edge of it bite into her hip. Bowing her head, she murmured, "There's naught left for me! Whenever I've loved or cared, 'twas shattered or torn from me."

Her white finger moved lightly over the glossy table top, absently weaving intricate patterns with a long, rosy nail.

"My father cast me out, you stole my child from me, Arnaut de Broze lies in a nameless grave, and now my lord has been taken from me."

Despite her resolve not to display any emotion, her lips quivered and a tear slowly rolled down her pale cheek. De Mortimer stared intently at her as she spoke and finally stifled the amusement which grew in him. This time he would not mock her, for she truly believed all she was saying.

"His last thoughts were of you, Jehan, and he swore that you had not told him of the child. He loved you well, my lady. Better than you deserve."

Roger reached out his hand and touched her white throat, circling it easily. She suppressed a shudder as his hand tightened for a moment. How simple it would be to snap that slender neck, he thought, and the look of sudden terror which crossed her face brought him back from his idle musing. So the little dove still clings to life, in spite of her words! And his dark eyes peered closely into hers.

"What's to become of you? Did your lord provide for you?" he asked again. She nodded her head, knowing a sweet sense of relief at his questions. In spite of his threatening gesture, Jehan knew that for the present, de Mortimer would not harm her.

"My husband told me that he had arranged an annual sum for my maintenance, should he be taken from me. 'Tis all in a parchment he once showed me. He said . . ." Her voice faltered and her eyes flew to his face. "He said you held a copy and would see to it, should the need arise."

Roger's expression was one of surprise. He had forgotten having been entrusted with the undertaking.

"Perhaps I could return to the queen," she added as an afterthought. De Mortimer did not reply, and Jehan saw that he was deep in thought. Had he heard her at all? Seeing her hover uncertainly before him, he said brusquely, "Leave me, Jehan. There are matters which must be attended to that are of more importance than what to do with you."

His words were curt and she recoiled at the sudden coldness of his voice.

"I've not asked for your aid, Roger. Rest assured that I will manage somehow to sustain my life," Jehan replied stiffly. The green eyes flashed suddenly. "Besides, I'm still young and you've said yourself I've always been generous with my favors. Virtue has never provided a roof over my head!" she spat out defiantly.

"Jehan . . ." Resentment rose in him as he watched her, without leave, sweep angrily from the chamber; but as the door slammed behind her, he realized that he had wounded her with his callousness. A strange, unfamiliar stab of jealousy shot through him at the thought of her offering herself to another man. He smiled bleakly at the knowledge that he had not yet been able to shed himself of the physical and emotional need which shackled him to her.

He remained in the council chamber until late in the night, taking time only to allow Emrys to divest him of his armor. A long, simple tunic covering his chainse, he sat at the long table, poring over the documents which

92

had arrived from England during his absence. His scribe sat beside him, jotting down his replies and making notes on work which would keep him at his writing the entire night.

When de Mortimer finally permitted himself the luxury of sitting in the large chair drawn close to the hearth, he was amazed that midnight had long passed. A silver platter of meat tarts sat at his elbow, and he ate one wearily as Emrys poured more wine into his emptied goblet.

"So it seems we will soon return to England," he told his squire with satisfaction. What a triumph that would be, he thought smugly. How different from the last time when he and Emrys had landed secretly near Carlisle under cover of darkness. He could safely leave Lord de Bermingham to finish clearing Edward Bruce from Ulster. If the present trend of defection by the Irish clans to the English side continued, it would take little to secure Ireland against the Scots.

His stay in Ireland had been an eventful one, he mused, staring into the leaping flames of the hearth. It had done no harm to his reputation as a loyal baron, and his purse was richer now than when he had arrived. As for the de Lacy claim . . . Roger stifled a smile. Meath was his and, added to the other lands he held in Ireland, a substantial amount of the country now was claimed by the de Mortimers. That most of it had been brought to him in his wife's dower held no importance for him. The means were insignificant compared to the achieving of a goal.

Closing his eyes, Roger leaned his head against the padded back of the chair and allowed his mind to run free. Jehan! For the past hours he had forgotten her. Human life held little value for him, and when it threatened his plans for the future, he could order it be ended with no sense of wrongdoing, but Jehan was different, Roger admitted to himself. She was the mother of his son . . . one he would have given much to have acknowledged as his own. The bloodlines were as good as those of his legitimate sons and daughters. Nay, he would allow no harm to come to her, he decided. He owed her that much at least, for her father's cruelty had proven even too much for him.

A log fell in the hearth, sending up a shower of sparks as he recalled the curt message that had been waiting for him at Wigmore when he had returned from one of the king's ill-fated military campaigns. Taking only Emrys with him, he had ridden through a late winter snowfall, determined to defy whatever Lord Gouland wanted of him. He could still see the widening stain of wetness his sodden boots and cloak had made on the flagged stones of the floor as the older man indulged in a monumental display of parental and baronial rage.

"You goddamned son of Satan," he had spat out at de Mortimer. "I warned you last year to stay away from my daughter!"

His heavy-jowled face was flushed with anger and the knuckles were white as his hands gripped the arms of his massive chair. Had he dared, he would have whipped the knight within an inch of his life, but the high social standing, wealth, and power of the de Mortimer family made him cautious in his approach.

"Yes, my lord, you did that," Roger admitted, his mouth twisting in wry amusement. "But did you tell your daughter the same?"

At the other's strangled oath, he laughed. Had the older man known his true thoughts, he would have been less hesitant, for the young man was not a little anxious. Instead, Gouland had taken him to where Jehan and her child were being kept. Emrys followed silently as the two men climbed dark, narrow stairs winding upward to a tower room. He had never forgotten Jehan's white, frightened face as they entered the chamber.

The scene that followed had been unbelievably cruel for Lord Gouland was determined that his daughter would not keep her child. The de Brasney family, having heard continuous rumors of Jehan's amoral ways, had finally broken the betrothal contract, and the old man was near mad with shame and humiliation.

She held the child in her arms and Roger saw the firelight gleam golden on the downy head as one small rosy hand grasped the soft cloth of her robe. He still felt sick when he remembered how she had pleaded with them while her father ordered him to take his son from her. Enraged by the man's imperiousness, he had refused, denying any responsibility until the babe's very life was threatened, for Jehan's father swore to cast it out rather than allow it to remain where it would forever be a reminder of his daughter's deceit.

Hysterical with fear and grief, Jehan screamed and fought him as he tried to talk to her. Finally he had ordered Emrys to take the child from her, leaving her nothing but an empty blanket which she held in trembling hands.

Her wild shrieks followed them as her father had said with finality, "So, my lord, he's yours to do with what you will. 'Tis your spawn—two months old, nameless and unwanted. Perhaps you can take it to your lady and explain it to her."

And he had closed the chamber door in Roger's face. Before leaving, Roger brought the babe into Lord Gouland's small hall, holding him for a time in his own arms. Studying him in the light of the fire, de Mortimer saw that he was truly a beautiful child, strong and well formed, with features remarkably like Jehan's. He had felt a pang of regret that the babe had not been borne by his own wife. Taking a fur cover from one of the chairs, he had wrapped the child in it and returned it to Emrys.

"Find a wet nurse for him among the women in the village and take them both to where you wish to leave him," he ordered his squire. "But it must be a home befitting a son of the de Mortimers."

And it was not until he had gone to Wales to see Powys ap Rhys that he knew where his son was, for Emrys, doing what he was bidden to do, had never mentioned the child to his master.

Jehan could be forgiven for wanting her son, for she shared his memories of that terrible night. Roger shielded his eyes with his hand for a moment. They both could never forget the child they had created between them, but he would not allow her to wield his existence as a weapon against him—as her dead lord had tried to do.

The fire dimmed and became naught but glowing

embers before de Mortimer stirred. Rising stiffly from the chair, he left the silent chamber, his decision made.

Jehan's chamber lay in darkness save for a faint shaft of light which fell from a narrow window over the floor and across the bed. She lay huddled against the bolster, still clad in her blue velvet robe. The bed curtains were drawn back, held by their tasseled cords, and the hearth was cold, for no one had come to light a fire. Although the air was damp and chill, she felt nothing. Her mind tried to fasten on Roger's words, but images of Sir Ralph continued to intrude. She had accused Roger of killing her husband, but she knew that had it not been for her, he would still be alive. She remembered the sick humiliation in his kind gray eyes and felt a momentary shame for the things she had said to him. Nothing in the years of their marriage had given her the right to castigate him as she had. The anger which finally was kindled in him had been justified. She gripped the coverlet tightly as the dead man's furious accusations washed over her. She stared dry-eyed into the darkness about her. How long had she lain here, Jehan wondered. She had sent her tiring woman away when she came to prepare her for bed, and the servants who had come to turn back the bed and light the candles. She wanted to see no one, for they would say kind, meaningless things to her to ease her grief. How could her grief be eased when she felt none? Her thoughts ran wildly through the corridors of her weary mind, seeking some sort of feeling toward her dead lord.

"Jehan . . ." Her name was murmured softly as a hand gently touched her shoulder. Roger—she had not even heard him enter, yet as she allowed him to turn her toward him, she saw that he was seated on the bed, his white chainse gleaming where it showed through his loosened tunic. He placed a lighted candle on the small stand, and in its dim, wavering glow, Jehan saw his dark eyes gaze at her somberly. His hand stroked her cold, pale cheek softly, brushing wayward strands of hair from her face.

"Jehan, I've thought deeply this night on what to do with you . . ."

At his words, she tensed and tried to draw away from him, but he clasped her cold hands in his.

"Nay, 'tis not what you fear. I've been remembering the past, and I've no cause to be proud of what befell you. But you must understand once and for all that your child—our child—is lost to you. I cannot allow you access to him, nor can I allow his existence to be made known."

"But why, Roger?" she asked pleadingly. "Other lords have sired children out of wedlock. John de Warenne . . . certainly everyone knows of his affair with Lord Holland's daughter and the children she has borne him. Yet no one cares—not even his wife. And the king's own cousin, Lancaster, occupies another bed each night while his wife tries to escape him. Why should this be different, Roger?"

Her green eyes glittered as she whispered urgently to him, but he shook his head, refusing to accept her argument.

"I've told you before, Jehan, that my ambitions and plans are more important than anyone who stands in their way. I'll not hesitate to destroy anything which imperils the dream I've striven for all my life."

He drew her stiff, resisting body into his arms.

"I give you no other reason for ordering you to forget our son. Yet you bore him, and for that alone, I'd not harm you. Besides, my sweet Jehan, you give me far more than even you realize."

His lips moved lightly over her neck to the silken softness behind her ear.

"I'll keep you with me for now," he murmured, and she felt his fingers unfasten the small gold buttons of her robe. "And when I return to England, you'll join me in Bristol."

His hand closed over her breast, feeling the chilled velvet skin warm under his touch, and then his searching mouth was on hers while she fought him weakly.

"Nay, Roger, 'tis unseemly. Ralph is dead . . . I should mourn him . . . I should!"

"Yes, my love, you should, but for now, I have need of you and what you alone give me."

All thoughts of Ralph de Maudley flew out of Jehan's

mind as she returned Roger's kisses feverishly, her natural sensuality sweeping all else before it. Nothing mattered save de Mortimer's desire for her. A sense of power surged through her as she realized that this arrogant, self-assured man was no different from any other in his lustful appetite for her. As long as she could keep that hunger for her alive, she would be safe. She felt his hands uncover her as he pressed her back against the velvet coverlet, his body warming her as she lay beneath him. She smiled in the gray darkness of dawn as she gave herself to him with the passion that was such a part of her.

PART TWO
1317

Chapter 3

Glairn

"I shall never understand why my lord Pembroke did not choose to return to England from Avignon with the others. Indeed, they tried to persuade him to return with them, but he claimed there was some personal business for him to see to. It seemed to be connected with the countess's family—I don't know what . . . 'tis not important. He had sent me ahead, to Calais, to arrange passage for the journey home."

Geoffrey Harron's voice was hoarse with emotion as he spoke of the mission to the Papal Court at Avignon. Together with Lord Badlesmere and the bishops of Norwich and Ely, the earl of Pembroke had spent several months attempting to persuade Pope John XXII to intervene in the increasingly dangerous political atmosphere created by the animosity between England's king and his cousin, the earl of Lancaster. Through his unmatched talent for diplomacy, the earl of Pembroke had convinced the pope of the tragic consequences of a civil war, not only in England, but abroad as well. When the royal envoys finally left the papal court, it was with assurances that the church would lend its assistance to prevent a direct confrontation between the two factions. Young Geoffrey threw himself down upon the wide bench, his gaunt white face gleaming eerily in the darkening chamber.

"I waited for him nearly a week before I discovered

what had happened. He was abducted between Orleans and Paris, so 'tis believed. Had the messenger not sought me out, I'd not know the little I do."

"At least now he's safe once more, Geoff. You must be thankful for that."

Sitting close beside her younger brother, Gillian looked anxiously at him. Geoffrey had arrived an hour earlier, his horse covered with lather, sides heaving from the pace his rider set. Accompanied by a servant and two men-at-arms, Pembroke's secretary had ridden steadily from Windsor, taking time only to change horses and for the barest of rest. Without preamble, he launched into his tale of the earl's kidnapping as if trying to convince himself of the fact that it had happened at all, almost incoherent in his relief that his lord had finally been released. Kilburn leaned over grimly and touched him on his sleeve. Geoffrey's arm felt like a coiled spring.

"Easy, lad, easy. If you allow your health to break, you'll be of no use to the earl—and he'll certainly need you when he returns to England."

Geoffrey strode to the window, looking out at the waning day.

"I'm all right, Jamie . . . 'tis just that I've lived with this for weeks, and everyone seems to have a different tale to tell. The king has said very little about the reasons for my lord's capture, but 'tis rumored that it was the work of a Burgundian knight called Jean de la Morliere—a mercenary who claimed that services he performed for the king had not been paid. Apparently by seizing the earl, the Burgundian saw his chance to force the king to acknowledge his debt." He turned and looked at Kilburn eagerly. "My lord expects to return within the month and the countess bids me ask whether you could meet him in Calais and accompany him back to England."

Gillian was appalled at the suggestion, sure that it had come from Geoffrey rather than Lady Beatrice. It was an outrageous request. Jamie had enough responsibility in seeing that all his holdings were in good order. The earl of Pembroke certainly was capable of returning safely without the presence of James Kilburn! Geoffrey leaned toward his brother-in-law, gray eyes burning in his thin, pinched face.

"Can you be ready to leave in two days' time? Lady Beatrice should have word by the time we arrive as to when he expects to reach Calais. She fears trouble and 'twould be best if aid were near, should it be needed."

Gillian would have spoken, but Kilburn motioned her to keep still. It was no use to protest. Geoffrey was much too agitated to take any sort of opposition calmly.

"You are to go to bed and rest, Geoffrey. That's the only place for you now. You need sleep—after that we will discuss my possibly going to Calais."

Kilburn's tone was firm. He saw that Geoffrey was on the verge of hysterical collapse and, aware of the instability of his nature, told Gillian to stay with him. Wordlessly, she rose and drew Geoffrey gently from the chamber.

" 'Twill be all right, Geoff . . . I'm sure of it." Gillian's soft voice soothed her brother, and he clung to her hand as he had done in their childhood.

Jamie is wrong, Gillian thought as she looked at her brother's taut features. 'Tis not only rest he needs, but peace of spirit. They walked slowly through the dim corridor, descending a winding staircase and stepping through an archway into the small garden Gillian had claimed as her private sanctuary when she first came to Glairn. Sitting with Geoffrey in the lovely bower where only the sound of a small fountain broke the stillness, and surrounded by the soft blue twilight of the summer evening, Gillian spoke of mundane things—how tall Alain had grown, of the other two children, and of their brother Robert's visit at Eastertide. She told him of Hal Jardine's wedding to Master Brassard's daughter and saw Geoffrey's tortured eyes turn to her at last. He gazed at his sister's pale face, barely discernible in the growing darkness. He touched her silken cheek, and for a moment was transported to an earlier time when Gillian had been his only refuge. She smiled.

"You've not yet seen our new daughter. We've named her Jennifer and she's . . ."

"Jillie . . . ! His cry was anguished. " 'Tis more than

103

I can bear. I feel so guilty . . . I keep thinking that had I been with him, I might somehow have prevented it from happening."

Geoffrey reached out for her and she held him as his tears burned her skin. "My foolish little brother . . . naught would have been changed. Try to see the truth of it and stop tormenting yourself needlessly."

Rocking him gently, she stroked his heavy dark hair. Poor Geoffrey! Gillian did not try to fathom the reasons for his overwhelming misery, for her younger brother had always walked apart from other men. Fleeing from his law studies at the new university in Cambridge because of the humiliation caused by her scandalous love for Jamie, he had entered Pembroke's service at an age when boys were still searching for heroes. Geoffrey had found a hero of such stature in the earl that all men paled in comparison. He was fortunate that Pembroke treated his monkish and worshipful young secretary with understanding and patient good humor. The Harrons were a warrior family, and denying his birthright by choosing a pedant's life over that of knighthood had brought naught but confusion to Geoffrey. His brilliant mind and frighteningly ascetic soul still refused to acknowledge the existence of the fierce and passionate side of his nature.

Brother and sister sat in the garden for a long time, Geoffrey's head heavy on his sister's breast, drawing comfort from her warm softness. Tightening her arms about his gaunt body, Gillian's heart wept for all the lost years of his young life.

It was nearly twilight as the riders made their way through the narrow streets of the port. The huge fortification that was Dover Castle looked down grimly on the houses huddled below it, with the high chalk cliffs stretching out on either side glowing whitely in the June dusk.

Gillian felt numb from fatigue, and it seemed to her that the little mare followed Kilburn's stallion down the hilly street through sheer instinct. Hampered by the pilgrims crowding the road on their way to Canterbury and St. Thomas à Becket's shrine, their progress had been slower than Kilburn would have wished. They had found shelter at a wayside inn for a few hours' sorely needed rest, sitting in the common room while the landlord bustled about, providing them with hot food and drink. After that they had pressed on urgently, hoping to reach Dover before nightfall.

A breeze drifted toward Gillian, bringing the sea's salty tang to her nostrils, and she could hear the shrill cries of the gulls. It was a sound she had not heard in many years—not since the days she had spent with the court at Corfe Castle, she thought with a shiver. Masts could be seen dimly in the fading light and she was grateful that it was only a short distance further to the house of the harbor master and royal collector of customs. That good sir had extended the hospitality of his home when word reached him that the earl of Glairn was embarking at the end of the week for Calais to meet the king's own cousin, Pembroke. Looking upward at the forbidding stones of the castle, Gillian was glad that Kilburn had declined to stay there, preferring the relative comfort of a dwelling closer to the quay.

Her mind blurred with fatigue, she was not aware that they had ridden through the stone gateway almost at the end of the street into an outer courtyard where grooms waited to lead their mounts away.

"Lovedy, you're dreaming again!" Kilburn's husky voice murmured in her ear as he lifted her down from the gray mare's back. She saw his hazel eyes glint with laughter.

"You've caught me again, my lord. Must I pay a penalty?" she said lightly, and felt his arms tighten about her.

"Later, my love, I shall exact your punishment," he replied, releasing her as their tall, gray-haired host hurried from the house to greet them.

While Hal and Geoffrey supervised the unloading of their baggage, Agnes followed her mistress to the chamber prepared for them. Gillian sank gratefully on to the large, comfortable bed hung with dark green curtains that dominated the chamber. Robert Harron's laughing face appeared in the doorway. "I see your chamber is more spacious than the small one I share with Geoffrey and the other knights. I fancy 'tis our host's when not occupied by visiting nobility."

Without being bidden, he sat on the bed beside his sister. Agnes began to unpack the coffer containing Gillian's clothes. "I doubt that 'tis necessary to unpack too much—we won't be here that long," he said.

Gillian opened her eyes, sitting up in dismay. She had almost forgotten!

"That's right! Jamie told me that they would sail tomorrow if the weather holds . . . and 'tis an early tide. Robbie, he'll be all right, won't he?" she asked anxiously, not for the first time.

He laughed at her fears.

"Sweeting, Jamie is not alone. He's brought four of his young knights, and Hal will be with him, as will several retainers, not to mention the two knights Lady Pembroke has sent along. Besides, Jamie is a very capable man and quite able to fend for himself. You are a goose!"

Wrenching her heavy veil and circlet irritably from her head, Gillian lay down again, her mind whirling. She had insisted on traveling south with James and Geoffrey, taking the opportunity to visit her brother Robert and his wife, who had themselves come down from the north a few weeks earlier. The manor house at Hurley, a dower gift to Elizabeth from her father, Lord d'Umfraville, lay close to Windsor, where the court was presently residing. Kilburn had ridden on with Geoffrey to see Lady Beatrice while she remained at Hurley. Shrinking from the thought of seeing Windsor again, Gillian had begged Kilburn's understanding that the nightmarish memories of her life there would prove too painful to bear. Even after seven years she feared that ghostly voices and the mute cry of her stillborn child might still echo through the familiar corridors and chambers of the rambling palace. Kilburn listened to her, studying the pale face and pleading eyes. Would those wounds never heal, he wondered, sharing her remembered agony. But he said nothing, silently placing her in Robert's care.

When he returned, he was accompanied by the countess of Pembroke, looking drawn and wan. A normally dig-

106

nified and self-possessed woman, she was tearful in her gratitude for Kilburn's agreeing to meet her husband in Calais. Gillian was astonished at the passion the older woman displayed, revealing for the first time the depth of the love and devotion she held for her remarkable lord.

Lying on the bed in the darkened chamber, Gillian drifted in and out of sleep. Her mind a jumble of fevered images, she did not know whether it was a memory or that she dreamed of the secret glade hidden deep in Glairn's forests. Known only to Gillian and her lord, it waited to enfold them. She heard the waterfall singing its siren's song, cutting them off from the harsh realities of the forth-coming journey and even of Glairn itself. Thoughts of the castle, of the children, even of her newest babe with its large eyes so like her own, faded from Gillian's mind as the water's spray cascaded into the dark pool, sparkling in the morning sunlight and turning the grass into a green velvet carpet.

Gillian stirred and felt a gentle hand stroke her hair. Kilburn's breath was warm on her cheek.

"Lovedy, wake up. 'Tis time to change. We must not disappoint our host tonight."

Kilburn kissed her lightly as the dark blue eyes opened reluctantly. The vision of their glade faded slowly and a nameless dread rose within her as she remembered where they were. Pushing it from her, she told herself all would be well, for Jamie had made his decision and there was naught to be done about it.

The dinner was pleasant, for their host had put forth every effort to entertain his distinguished guests. Unfortunately the journey had taken its toll and the atmosphere in the hall was subdued. Gillian dwelled miserably on the leavetaking from Jamie the next day, and one look at Agnes revealed similar thoughts. Hal, too, felt reluctant at leaving his new bride, but the coming channel crossing beckoned to him strongly. Foremost in Geoffrey's mind was the worry that time was growing short.

Although Lady Beatrice had accompanied them to Dover, Kilburn adamantly refused her request to be allowed to go with him. She was not a robust woman, and the past months had been difficult for her. If aught were to befall her on the crossing, the earl of Pembroke would never forgive himself or Kilburn for having risked her health.

Deep in conversation with his host, Kilburn had little time to examine his own feelings. The harbormaster, a veteran of many channel crossings, was only too pleased to offer gladly accepted advice to the earl.

Robert sensed Gillian's inner agitation and was filled with a rising feeling of unease. She was overly disturbed by Kilburn's simple mission, and he wondered if Jamie too had recognized the signs of her withdrawal. It had been so at Hurley and later at Cairven following her illness at Windsor, when she had taken refuge in her dreams. Looking at Gillian's remote expression, he was glad that she would wait at Hurley for Jamie's return rather than travel back to Glairn alone. He and Elizabeth would see to it that she remained too busy to brood. His handsome face, so similar to his sister's, lightened as he smiled at the prospect of having her with him again.

Gillian woke with a start, confused by the milky light suffusing the chamber and shimmering over the bed. The curtains had been pulled back to allow what coolness there was in the air to reach them. Kilburn lay stretched out asleep beside her, with only a sheet covering him, for the chamber was stifling. Slipping on her bedrobe, she padded barefoot to the casement and pushed the small window open. A cool breeze swirled the fog in great white clouds all about her, sending ghostly streamers pouring over the casement sill into the quiet chamber behind her. Although she could hear the muted murmur of the channel waters not too distant, she could see nothing. It was an eerie silvery world, and somewhere quite close on the other side of the water lay France. Never before had it held such meaning for her. The air smelled damp and salty from the sea and she felt the fog's ghostly fingers begin to clutch at her chilling flesh. She stood by the window, letting her robe slip to the floor. Her eyes closed as she gave herself up to the silent white tendrils creeping through the open casement, twining and coiling sinuously over her naked form. Bemused and removed from reality, Gillian gasped as she felt a gentle touch on her throat and shoulders, gliding lightly over the smooth skin to linger sensuously for a moment on her breasts, taut-nippled from the fog's embrace, before moving downward over the soft curves of her body. Where phantom hands caressed her trembling flesh, a burning ache began to grow and silently she allowed herself to be turned by Jamie from the window. His lips, tracing a path from her brow down her cheek, intruded but little into her private world.

Waking from an uneasy sleep, Kilburn had found her gone from his side. Seeing her stand transfixed before the open window, he approached her quietly. The sight of the spectral fog licking at the silvered beauty of her body unleashed a desire for her which stunned him with its suddenness. His searing, searching mouth found her own salty from the fog's kiss and while she responded to him, he saw that the night still held her in thrall. His mouth and hands grew less gentle as the craving to rouse her to his need began to overtake him in its urgency.

"You are a maddeningly fanciful creature, Gillian," Jamie muttered thickly as he laid her on the bed, "but, God help me, I never have enough of you." His pulses quickened as she stirred under his touch.

Still caught in her reverie, her eyes remained shut, and it seemed to her that it was the fog lying over her, caressing her with Jamie's hands, kissing her with Jamie's mouth until her dreams swirled wildly all about her, crystallizing finally in her own abiding passion and hunger for him. His love was her only reality, and returning to him at last, Gillian took fire in his arms.

Peering out of the small window set into the thick, whitewashed wall of the low-ceilinged, cramped chamber, Pembroke caught glimpses of a deceptively placid channel glinting gray and white in the ghostly luminescence of early dawn. Beyond the inn, the road ran along the coast until it turned toward the dark, dreary walls of the not-too-distant town of Calais. From the courtyard below he heard a cock crow loudly for the second time, and somewhere a door creaked. The air coming through the open window still retained its biting night chill and he took a deep breath before turning away. His men lay sprawled about the chamber floor on pallets, still sleeping soundly, as was Lord Badlesmere, with whom he had shared the only bed.

He moved quietly about the chamber, drawing on the tunic discarded the night before. He finally found his boots and managed to pull them on without too much trouble. Every bone ached with weariness, for they had set themselves a demon's pace since his release. He had slept badly despite his fatigue. He tried to push the last weeks from his mind. They were over and it was best not to dwell upon them. He smiled suddenly in the darkness, remembering his surprise the evening before at the sight of James Kilburn striding toward him across the hard-packed earth of the courtyard as his party had clattered through the inn's open gate. Bartholomew Badlesmere had been disturbed by his appearance, perhaps fearing a royal conspiracy, but he need not have worried. Bartholomew has always had a suspicious nature where Edward is concerned, Pembroke thought as he unlatched the door quietly, grateful that his companion had remained in Paris until his release had been achieved.

The earl found Kilburn in the large common room, seated at a long table with his back to the wall. The wide chamber was almost empty, for it was still very early, but pleasant aromas stole in from the nearby kitchens. Pembroke sat down wearily beside Kilburn, who looked up from his bowl of broth, amazed to see him up so early.

"Have some of this excellent soup, my lord. 'Twill prepare you for the day."

The older man motioned to a serving girl as Kilburn pushed a wooden dish laden with slabs of freshly baked bread toward him. In minutes a steaming bowl of rich broth was placed before him with sops of chicken and vegetables floating in it. He inhaled its fragrance with pleasure, discovering an unexpected hunger within himself.

"You'll find the fare excellent here," Kilburn commented casually. For a while they applied themselves to their food as several other early-rising guests appeared to take seats at the long, highly scrubbed and polished oaken tables.

He seems well enough, Kilburn thought, noting that while he looked older than his forty-seven years, the tall, overly slender Aymer de Valance still bore himself with pride and dignity. His once black hair, though now liberally streaked with white, swept back vigorously from the high forehead and fell smoothly to below his ears, and his fine dark eyes were clear as they beamed at Kilburn.

"James, what can I say to thank you for meeting me here . . . it has certainly lightened my spirits, for there were days I thought I would never taste freedom again."

"Nay, my lord, don't thank me. 'Twas my chance to make a gesture of repayment to you for all the support and aid you've given me since we first met . . . for your understanding and the protection you extended to my son before Bannockburn. 'Twas but a small way."

"Small way? Don't be an ass, James. I know only too well what it meant for you to climb down from the heights of your beloved Northumberland and cross the channel in order to meet me. But 'tis good to see you, lad."

Pembroke leaned back in his chair, his bowl empty. Almost shyly, he asked, "Have you seen my lady? How did she fare through all this?"

"Frantically, my lord. 'Tis she who bade that I accompany you home. She came with us as far as Dover, as did my lady, so she was not alone. So fearful was the countess that your release be an unfounded rumor, I had difficulty persuading her not to come with me to Calais. To make things easier for her, I insisted Geoffrey remain with her to see to her well-being."

"My dearest Beatrice," the earl murmured, his eyes suddenly moist. "She was ever my closest friend. I cannot imagine my life without her love and strength." He sighed, speaking as if to himself. "Her years with me have not been easy—none of our children survived infancy, and yet she faces each day as it would come. Beatrice . . . our times together have been so few, I sometimes marvel that her love abides."

His voice was low and wistful. Kilburn looked at him in surprise, for never had he revealed his inner feelings so clearly. So Aymer de Valence too knows the bonds of love! No wonder he understood so well and refused to condemn Gillian and me when all others had, Kilburn thought. The silence between them grew, as each man pursued his own memories.

Crumbling bits of bread between thin, restless fingers, Pembroke asked after the king's health.

"He's well and anxious for your return. I'm told he made every effort to effect your release through diplomatic channels."

"So Lord Badlesmere advised me. I'm surprised that Edward is capable of such prompt action—but thankful as well."

"You are of great value to him, Aymer, as you are to all of England."

Pembroke took note of Kilburn's familiar use of his Christian name and was pleased, although his companion seemed unaware of it. It had taken James a long time to overcome his formality of manner which was so much an ingrained part of him. Kilburn's repeated question brought him abruptly back to the present.

"Will the French lord accompany us to England?"

The earl could not conceal a smile. Already James was planning the journey back, and he was suddenly grateful that he had not been asked too many questions regarding the subject of his imprisonment. That was something he was not prepared to talk about, if ever. He frowned, remembering.

"The count of Aumale has been sent as an escort for me . . . to assure my safe return." Pembroke's lean, dark hawk's face relaxed as he watched Kilburn. "I take it Geoffrey unburdened his guilt to you."

Kilburn nodded, his eyes somber. "He takes life too hard. 'Tis all so painful for him, Aymer. I've known him since he was a child—in many ways he's a child still—and finely wrought."

"I know, James and understand all too well."

A shaft of sunlight suddenly penetrated the chamber's dim interior and both men were startled to see that it was fully day.

"I've lost all track of time," Pembroke remarked, idly observing the serving maid as she carried away their empty bowls. She placed a large pitcher of frothy beer on the table before them, but neither man felt a desire for it.

"God's blood, I nearly forgot," Kilburn said with a start. "A messenger came from Arundel just before you came down . . ."

"Arundel? Don't tell me he's here as well!" Pembroke said with amazement.

"Aye, he is—but 'tis pure co-incidence. A personal matter brought him to France and he is in Calais en route home. He heard that you had arrived, and has decided to travel with us. We're to join him on the ship in a few hours and wait for the tide."

"All I long for is to lie down again upstairs and sleep. I'm sure a few hours' delay won't matter."

Kilburn was firm in his refusal.

"Nay, Aymer, although I beg your pardon for refusing. 'Tis better we set our backs on France as soon as possible. I'll have no peace till our own coast is sighted."

Pembroke gazed with amusement at the man sitting opposite him. He was indeed a man more deeply rooted in the soil of England than any of his peers, most of whose loyalties were as strongly bound to the continent of Europe as they were to the land which had bred them. He found he could not read Kilburn's finely drawn, handsome face, locked away from him in some private thought. Between the two of them, Kilburn and Arundel had matters well arranged, and they expected naught from him but compliance to their plans. It would not surprise him if Bartholomew Badlesmere was also party to their arrangements. He felt suddenly old and somehow useless. Sweet Jesù, he was tired of the endless battle to survive this life.

That's how you feel now, he told himself. But wait until you've stepped on England's soil once more. Then will the old fires and ambitious pride begin to overwhelm all else. He knew himself well and never deceived himself. Pembroke startled Kilburn with his chuckle.

" 'Tis naught, James," he reassured him, "I've just experienced a self-revelation. 'Tis good for the soul, lad, 'tis certainly good for the soul!"

Although Pembroke, Badlesmere, and the other members of his party accompanied Kilburn into the port of

Calais a few hours later, their plans to sail with the tide were soon shattered, for bad weather settled over the channel and no amount of persuasion would move the captain from his safe mooring within the harbor.

Already on board the sturdy vessel, Edmund Fitzalan, earl of Arundel, had greeted Kilburn effusively. They met but rarely, much to their mutual disappointment, for a strong friendship had sprung up between the two earls at their first meeting in Tynemouth seven years earlier. Both had survived Bannockburn, and Arundel nursed as vast a grievance against the Scots as did the northern lord. For a while it seemed that the young earl's allegiance had shifted to Thomas of Lancaster, the king's cousin, who had lost no time in gathering the disgruntled barons to his side following Edward's disgrace for the disastrous battle and total rout of the English following it. But Arundel had at last chosen to support Pembroke's moderate stand between the king and his cousin. The deep admiration and sincere affection Kilburn felt for Aymer de Valence were equally shared by Edmund Fitzalan.

It took little time for the two friends to resume their easy relationship. Even Pembroke allowed his inherently serious nature to lighten at Edmund's continued high spirits. Young Arundel's good humor and sunny disposition were infectious, and it was a greatly relaxed party of lords who waited for the storm to subside before attempting the channel crossing.

By the next morning, the storm had spent itself sufficiently for the captain to agree to sail with the early tide. He cautioned his passengers that there still would be rough seas, and, true to his words, barely an hour out of port, the ship began to pitch in a most disquieting fashion, sending most of the men below with seasickness. The seas continued to run high, and the sight of the gray, lowering sky made even those who did not feel the effects of the unstable channel waters grow anxious. Kilburn went down to where the horses were kept to assure himself that all was in good order. He had little faith in the handlers, doubting that many of them were even well enough to care for their animals. He was surprised to find Pembroke there, calming the restless animals who were frightened by the sudden pitching of the ship.

"Ah, James, come to tend your four-footed companion?" Pembroke called out, as a white-nosed bay gelding nudged him gently. The earl scratched the animal soothingly between its eyes.

"The weather is worsening and I thought it best to see to him . . . he's not as world-wise as his sire was, and the ostlers do not always suit him." Kilburn reached for the stallion's bridle. The black horse whickered softly at the sight of his master, his blind fear calmed by the comforting presence. Kilburn could have left him in England, buying a mount once he had arrived, but not knowing what might face him once he had landed, he preferred the company of an animal he understood and trusted.

"I detest any sort of sea voyage," Pembroke admitted, grasping a post as the ship gave a sickening lurch. "I think I'll lie down till the seas quieten. Bartholomew is praying for death to deliver him—perhaps I'll be forced to do the same." Pausing in the doorway, he turned back to Kilburn. "Edmund was looking for you. He seems to have something on his mind."

Kilburn caught a gleam in Pembroke's eyes as he slowly ascended the ladder leading to the upper deck. A short time later, wrapped in his cloak against the weather's chill, Kilburn stepped out on the deck to find Arundel watching spellbound as the restless waves hurled themselves increasingly at the ship's prow. His light brown hair blew wildly in the wind and he smiled as he watched Kilburn slowly and carefully cross the heaving deck toward him.

"I can see you're not a sea-faring man," he shouted over the sound of the wind caught in the sails and the creaking of the ropes. Kilburn laughed, wiping spray from his face.

"You'll see a happy man when we come in sight of land."

"Yes, the sea is not for every man. My squire is below, green and retching miserably. But there's a cleanness about the open water I never find on land."

He turned his face into the wind, his blue eyes mere slits as the gusts hurled the sea over the open deck. For a few minutes the two friends stood side by side, wordlessly contemplating the wild scene. When Arundel spoke, his words were torn from him by the uncontrollable wind.

"Do you remember Lord Bardestour, James?"

He looked at Kilburn, who turned puzzled eyes toward his friend. Lord Bardestour . . . the name sounded familiar but he was unable to place him.

"Think, man. John Deveron . . . he was with us at Bannockburn and at York Castle when Edward singled you out for his ill-timed reprimand."

The king's nasty comments had told all present that Glairn's feud with one of Edward's beloved Gascons was not forgiven. Kilburn shrugged with indifference at the memory. He had long since ceased to mind Edward's childish outbursts. John Deveron. Of course! He was the slightly built man with pleasant features and a quiet manner whose eyes had revealed anger at the court's intrigues.

"The Deveron family is an old one with great holdings in East Anglia," Arundel told him as James began to nod. "He's also on our side!"

"And which side is that, Edmund? Against Lancaster or against the king?" Kilburn smiled and grasped the wooden rail, preparing himself for a shower from the wave which had just broken over the ship's prow.

"On Pembroke's side, James. He's the only one who can bring any order and peace to England, for he alone has the ability to draw the moderate barons into a position between those two incompetents." Arundel had scarcely noticed the drenching wave.

"Aye, I can see your reasoning," Kilburn replied, relieved to see Edmund serious for once. "But what has that to do with Lord Bardestour?"

Arundel laughed and tightened his hold on a line as the ship, having ridden the crest of a wave, began to descend once more into a trough of the turbulent channel waters.

"Naught save that he's asked me to speak with you about your eldest daughter."

"Margaret?" Kilburn was distracted as a sailor moved

past him and started to climb up the rigging of the main mast.

"God's blood, James! For an intelligent man you are remarkably dense. John Deveron would like to propose a match between his son and your Margaret. The boy is about Alain's age and is John's only child."

Kilburn was disturbed by Arundel's words. Golden-haired Margaret—already sought out because of her status as a Glairn daughter! It was not the first time Arundel had spoken to him of marriage contracts. When Edmund approached him in York the winter following Bannockburn to propose a match between Glairn's heir and an Arundel daughter, Kilburn had been startled. It had taken little thought to realize that a marriage between the two influential houses would further strengthen their alliance, and he had readily agreed. Since Alianor Fitzalan was now but four and her future lord a child of six, it was decided that the actual marriage would not take place until they were both deemed of the proper age for such a union. Although both children knew of their future marriage, it mattered naught to either of them, and as yet they had not even met.

Remembering Gillian's hysterical reaction to his announcement of Alain's betrothal to Alianor Fitzalan, he hesitated. It had upset her beyond reason to think of losing Alain in a marriage about which she had not even been consulted. What would she say to this contract, James wondered, knowing the truth of it already in his heart.

"Young Walter Deveron will inherit all the Deveron holdings, James. There's also a good chance he will become baron of Kenniston since his mother's brother has no other heirs. 'Tis a fine match . . . had I another daughter, I would have pressed for it myself."

Hazel eyes narrowed in thought and, his chestnut hair tossed wildly by the sea wind, the tall, austere-featured earl stood silently beside Arundel. Enveloped in his dark blue woolen cloak, he seemed turned to stone. Edmund noticed that the knuckles of the slender hand clutching the rail were white with tension.

"I've already discussed the matter with Aymer, and

he too believes it to be an excellent merging. Why do you hesitate?"

Arundel was puzzled, for he had been certain that Kilburn would be pleased by Lord Bardestour's overtures. There had been no such hesitation on the occasion of the betrothal between Kilburn's son and his own daughter. James's tense expression suddenly eased into a smile.

"Edmund, where can I find John Deveron? I would want to speak with him myself." The words were tossed about by the wind, but Arundel let out a great bellow.

"He's in London, waiting for us."

Although James would continue to be cautious and refuse to commit himself too soon, his friend knew that the betrothal would take place. Edmund threw an arm about Kilburn's shoulder and drew him toward the door leading below deck.

" 'Tis time for a cup of wine, friend James." Arundel laughed, blue eyes sparkling with merriment. "Despite my passion for the sea, I must confess I'm near frozen to the bone by this infernal wind."

And they were so engrossed in their mutual laughter that neither man noticed the gray-white chalk cliffs of England become visible on the horizon.

Chapter 4

Bristol

Jehan looked with dismay at the ruined de Mortimer coat of arms as a small drop of blood made a scarlet stain on the square of white velvet. Disgusted with her clumsy attempt at embroidery she threw the half-finished purse down on the settle. Sucking her finger where the needle had pricked it, she wandered over to the square casement window. Kneeling on the upholstered seat within the recess, Jehan stared through the small leaded glass panes into the garden where the storm bent a young pear tree to its will in the gathering darkness. The wind-driven rain, drumming against the window, hammered at her nerves. In the three days of almost ceaseless rain, the dampness had begun to creep unbearably through the low-ceilinged chambers. The fire Jehan ordered to be lit in the simple hearth warmed the small bedchamber with a cheerful glow—yet its flickering cast shadows against the dark-timbered ceiling that somehow increased her feeling of isolation.

Bristol! Jehan sighed, remembering that it was nearly a year past that she had sailed from here with her lord. Leaning her cheek against the cold sill, she closed her eyes, struggling with herself not to dwell on the past. Sweet Jesù, she was lonely and bored! De Mortimer had sent her back to England in midsummer with no explanation other than that she was too great a distraction to him. She told herself that he was right. The Scots were still battling desperately to regain their foothold in Ireland and he needed all his resources to hold the Anglo-Irish lords in line to prevent another Scottish victory, but the knowledge was small comfort to her. His solicitor, Master Barnet, a tall, emaciated bag of bones, had greeted her without curiosity when the ship from Ireland docked. He had taken her immediately to the house which de Mortimer had ordered be provided for her. No word had she had from her lover since leaving Dublin, and were money not provided each month for the household, she would have believed herself forgotten.

She missed the excitement of Dublin Castle, the noise and tumult of an army ready to take the field and the attentions of men drawn to her by the sensuality she could not conceal. In Bristol she rarely saw anyone save the servants and her own tiring woman. Berthe Lowndes, the widow of one of Sir Ralph's knights, had been with her since her days with the queen. She was her sole companion, for no other ladies had accompanied her from Ireland. The household steward, engaged by Master Barnet, saw to the running of the house while Jehan wandered aimlessly through the small chambers trying to occupy the long hours. She spent most of her time in the solar, working on a tapestry she knew would never be completed, while Berthe chattered idly of the exciting days at Isabella's court. When the weather allowed it, she would stroll in the ill-kept garden feeling the crisp air of approaching autumn against her skin. Once she had been able to take a brief ride along the riverside beyond the city walls accompanied by a young serving boy, but glimpsing a ship set sail into the channel had brought back guilt-ridden memories of her lord, and she did not venture out again.

"Roger, where are you?" Jehan whispered against the stones and felt a tear trickle down her cheek. He was back in England . . . the first to tell her had been a young lieutenant of Lord de Bermingham's. John de Chillon, looking for the baron of Wigmore, had called on her. Admiration for her showed in his wide blue eyes as the stocky knight sat in a high-backed chair near her own, telling of his stormy crossing from Dublin. She had successfully masked her ignorance of Roger's whereabouts, inquired after de

Chillon's lady wife, given him a cup of wine, and when the door closed behind the unsuspecting knight, indulged herself in a towering temper tantrum. Several times after that she had entertained other visitors seeking the baron and each time she sank deeper into despair.

Jehan refused to delude herself any longer. As long as she was with Roger, she was able to hold him with her passion, her willing body, and her quick wit, but de Mortimer was mercurial, and it was a rare woman who could hold him for long.

"My lady . . ." The servant's tone was fearful and hesitant, for Jehan was demanding and difficult to please. Several times he had knocked at the chamber door, but she had not heard.

"Go away," Jehan said coldly, not moving from the window. "And should it be someone asking for my lord de Mortimer, say . . . say I have no knowledge of him."

"I think you do, my lady!" The familiar voice brought her to her feet.

"Roger?" The name burst from her as she looked unbelieving at the tall dark man standing by the door, his cloak hanging in sodden folds about him.

The look of joy which blazed suddenly in the slanted green eyes startled him, for he had not expected so naked a reaction from her. She threw herself into his arms, forgetting her decision to remain aloof and disdainful. All she cared about was that he had come to her. He had not forgotten her! Her fears dissolved in the reality of his lips pressed hard against hers, his hands drawing her into himself. All else faded and was washed away by the storm which had entered the house in his person.

Seated on the settle by the hearth, Jehan watched as Emrys, his own mantle still dripping from rain, unclasped his master's cloak and unbuckled de Mortimer's sword, leaning it carefully against the wall by the bed. Gathering up the cloak, he bowed and left the chamber, leaving the baron to the ministrations of his bodyservant. While the elderly servant stripped Roger of his wet garments, Jehan's eyes grew puzzled, for she suddenly realized that he had worn neither hauberk nor light armor. She wondered how short a distance he had travelled that he had

121

no need of armor, but thrust the unbidden thought from her guiltily. The Welshman returned silently with servants bearing ewers of steaming hot water and trays laden with food. Soon all was in readiness and de Mortimer, washed and clad in a fresh chainse, turned his attention to Jehan.

"Come join me, my lady," Roger said to her, holding out his hand. Her robe of blue silk whispered softly as she moved toward him, and he murmured, "How beautiful you are."

At his words, Jehan flushed and lowered her gaze, suspicious that he might be mocking her. He smiled at her confusion and cupped her chin in a slender hand, tilting her face to his.

" 'Tis truly good to see you . . ." Roger's black eyes studied her intently, seeing the smudges beneath her eyes and the stain of recent tears. There was a withdrawn quality to her which was new. She's not a woman to live alone, he realized, feeling the familiar quickening of his blood at her nearness.

Sitting quietly opposite him while he ate, Jehan toyed with her wine goblet, her fingers as restless as her mind. There were questions she burned to ask, but spoke instead of mundane, everyday matters. He offered no information of himself as he downed with appetite the cold roast fowl, jellied eels, and a large dish of custard baked with glazed fruit. At last he sat back and allowed the servants to remove the small table and the empty dishes. At a final impatient gesture from de Mortimer, the servants vanished, leaving them alone.

The candles burned low in their holders and flickered feebly as he chose a nut from a silver dish placed at his elbow. The walnut was fresh, its shell light brown and easily opened. With a feeling of unreality, Jehan watched Roger carefully peel the beige skin from the succulent and sweet nutmeat. Concentrating on its delicate taste, he chewed silently while his eyes rested on the woman opposite him. Neither spoke and Jehan grew pale beneath de Mortimer's scrutiny. She was still as he remembered, the heart-shaped face with its piquant features and a mouth so ripe for kissing. He stirred, following the cascade of her dark red hair over the blue silk robe that outlined the body he could not forget. Suddenly impatient, he reached out his hands and drew her toward him. The familiar scent of roses surrounded him, drugging him.

"You've been a long time coming, Roger. I'd begun to think you had forgotten me." She was still wary of him.

"Not yet, Jehan." He kissed her wrist where a pulse throbbed wildly. "When that time comes, I will tell you." He laughed as she pulled back from him, hurt by his bluntness. His grip tightened and he pulled her down beside him in the large chair.

"You've missed me," he murmured, brushing his lips lightly over hers.

"Nay, I've not," Jehan replied, her mouth trembling as his kisses deepened. His hands caressed her until he felt her body soften and begin to yield to him.

"Liar! Your mouth and body betray you." He laughed softly. Sweet heavenly Virgin, she still can draw the soul from a man, he thought, and tangled his hand in her hair, pulling her head back.

"Admit you still want me," he demanded thickly, but her eyes glittered stormily at his words.

"Nay, I shan't admit to anything! There are times I despise you!" she told him stubbornly, trying to break his hold. He was treating her like a common strumpet, possessing her mouth with his kisses and caressing her with a touch that turned her blood to fire. It was not fair! Did he think that she had sat quietly waiting for him all these months so that within minutes of his arrival she would fall panting into his arms and allow him to bed her? Did he truly believe it was all she wanted from him?

Angered by his behavior, she told him what she thought. Startled, he stared at her defiant face for a moment and then began to laugh. He picked her up unceremoniously and dumped her roughly on the bed, sitting down beside her.

"Jehan my love, I had no idea that you knew how a strumpet is treated." His smile was dark and the black eyes smoldered. "You are mine for now, you know. You've allowed yourself to be paid for, and if I find that you've had aught to do with anyone else, I'll kill you." He dropped his sardonic laughter and Jehan felt herself grow cold, for this was the Roger she feared the most.

"No words of protest, my dove?"

He began to kiss her, harsh, savage kisses, his mouth and hands demanding a response she could not deny him, and Jehan wept, furious that he had once more mastered her. It was futile for her to fight him, for cruel, selfish, and arrogant though he was, he was with her once more, and he gave her what she yearned for most. Although she did not know it, her answer to his passion and overpowering desire was what held him to her, that and her quicksilver temperament which, despite his mockery, so enchanted him. Holding her in his arms, he knew that he could never exorcise her from his soul, no matter where fate and his ambitions would lead him.

"Jehan?" De Mortimer's voice was blurred with sleep as he peered through the loosely hung bed curtains into the dim chamber. He could see her small figure curled upon the windowseat, a coverlet wrapped about her.

"I'm here."

Jehan stared out at the garden gleaming gray and green in the growing light. The rain had ceased, but storm clouds hung low in the slowly brightening sky. The stone casement felt damp and cold to her touch and she shivered. Waking in the darkness of the bed, Jehan had felt Roger's presence beside her, warm and vital, and fear surged through her—fear of Roger, of that driving ambition which permitted no deviation from the course he had set for himself. She knew then that he would destroy her if she allowed herself to be manipulated by him. His words to her had made it all quite clear. He considered her a possession, bought and paid for, and when he had no further need for her, she would be cut from his life, leaving no trace. The worst of it was that she was snared in her own trap.

"Are you mad, Jehan?" His tone, impatient and irritated, broke into her thoughts and she looked up to see him standing before her. "What possesses you to huddle here by the window in the chill of dawn? The fire's burned out and 'tis damn cold."

He reached out a hand to her. She did not stir but gazed wordlessly at him with veiled eyes. Surrendering to her strange silence, Roger turned and strode back to the comfort of the bed. Reluctantly, Jehan followed him, torn by the revelation of her thoughts yet knowing that she could not bear to lose him. Slipping beneath the warm covers, she let herself be drawn into his arms. With a sigh, she relaxed against him, letting the heat of his body flow into hers, and felt his hand stroke her hair.

"Now, my love," he said softly, "tell me who has inquired for me . . . you sounded so angry when I came."

"I was angry because you had not come," Jehan replied. "How long have you been in England?"

"Three weeks," His voice was expressionless. "I fear that my fortunes in Ireland have turned against me for the moment, but I'll return."

"Where were you all this time?" Why had she asked —did she truly want to know?

"At Wigmore, to be with my wife."

Jealousy knifed through her—damn him! She wished it did not matter to her.

"I have another son."

A moan escaped her. She could not bear hearing of the wife he would always return to or of his children whom he loved above all else save his own ambition. What manner of man was he? Even while she had pleaded for her own child in Dublin and he had possessed her once more with all the ardor of their youthful loving, he had known that his lady carried his child. Did any woman mean aught to him, she wondered, stifling a sudden desire to weep.

Roger felt her stiffen and draw away from him, but when she spoke, her voice was cool and indifferent. She told him of Lord de Bermingham's lieutenant and the others who had come seeking him. He listened quietly, knowing that he had hurt her, and caressed her soft skin, soothing her.

"I found Lord de Maudley's will at Wigmore and took it to Master Barnet," de Mortimer said. "Your lord provided well for you—you need never want for aught, Jehan. 'Tis a large sum in gold."

"Sweet Jesu, 'tis probably the gold my father gave

him to wed me," Jehan remarked, and laughed bitterly. "My bride price was high, and 'twould be like Ralph to return it to me!"

"Then look upon it as your reward, Jehan."

"I wish I didn't need it, for I wanted naught from him," she said with a belated feeling of guilt, having no desire to be haunted by her dead husband.

"You don't need it, for I too spoke to Master Barnet on your behalf. I've signed over a small manor house near Shrewsbury to you. The house is yours and what rents you get from the land and its people are yours as well. 'Tis little enough and a gesture I've made rarely in my life, but too much has grown between us." It was the closest to his true feelings toward her he would ever allow himself to admit.

Jehan was stunned. She dared not think of her lost child, but she knew it was for him that de Mortimer had made her the gift. Her jealousy was forgotten and she twined her arms about his neck, pressing herself against him. She whispered her thanks against his mouth, but he pushed her away.

" 'Tis enough, Jehan. Sentiment becomes neither of us—'tis not in our natures." He slapped her bare buttocks and threw back the coverlet, for the morning light peered through the bed curtains. Jehan knelt before him, her white skin gleaming through the silken mass of red hair.

"I nearly forgot to tell you," she said, "a Welsh lord came to see you a few days ago and seemed upset that you were not here."

"A Welsh lord? How would he know where to find me?" De Mortimer was puzzled.

Jehan smiled and pushed back her hair. "He said he had been to see Master Barnet. Sir Powys told me that his lady was ailing and he had brought her to Bristol to see a proper physician."

She stared at Roger in amazement as the dark brows drew together in sudden anger and he grasped her arms tightly.

"Sir Powys was here? Powys ap Rhys?"

Jehan nodded. "He mentioned something about needing a higher payment." Green eyes looked at him slyly. So the Welsh lord had the power to upset him! Jehan tucked the thought far back in her mind. It was an interesting bit of knowledge that Roger had allowed to slip past his guard. "He seems a pleasant man, if a trifle rough in manner and speech."

"He's impossible," Roger said, but the anger wracking him disappeared as Jehan said, "Sir Powys was accompanied by his nephew—an absolute horror! A pretty child but he refused to speak aught save their ridiculous tongue and threw a cup of wine to the floor in a fit of temper."

Laughter rumbled deep inside Roger. It was unbelievable . . . her son had stood before her and Jehan had not known him . . . had noticed neither the slanted green eyes so like her own, the red hair, nor the similarity of features.

"What's wrong, my lord?" Jehan asked in alarm, seeing only the glittering black eyes and the wolf's grin on the dark face.

"Naught, my love! 'Tis life's joke played on us all!"

He caught her in his arms, tumbling her down to the pillows as she joined him in laughter, innocent of the ironic humor which seized him.

" 'Tis truly a lovely view!" The words burst from her as Jehan drank in the sight of the rolling hills of the Welsh Marches glowing with all the brilliance of an early fall. Turning her face toward the west, she knew where the broad meadowlands of Clun thrust upward toward the sun. Although too far away to be sighted, the memory of the undulating heights, purple with heather, would always be a part of her, for it was there she had been born. The great wooded stretches spread their verdant growth many leagues westward, reaching even into Wales, and she remembered the tales told of the blood spilled in savage battles through the border forests to keep the Marches safe. For a moment the quiet scene swam before her eyes as she realized that never again would she see the dark stones of Gouland Castle rise strong and invulnerable above the familiar trees. If her father had ever been inclined to forgive her past indiscretions, the discovery of the illicit liaison between his daughter and the detested baron of Wigmore would harden his resolve to totally obliterate Jehan's existence from his life.

A hunting horn sounding in the distance broke into her reveries. She turned a smiling face to her companion who sat tall and graceful astride a powerful bay gelding. The afternoon sun shone brightly on his thick dark hair and sparkled on the metal tip of the spear which he rested on his stirrup. Bareheaded and clad in a russet-colored woolen tunic, Roger refused to wear a helm or any sort of armor for the hunt claiming that it hampered his mobility. His dagger, in its jeweled scabbard, was strapped to the broad leather belt circling his narrow waist, and a small triangular shield hung from the high cantled saddle. Jehan pushed back the hood of her mantle and felt the light breeze against her face with a sigh of pleasurable relief. Her full-skirted kirtle was fashioned of too heavy a cloth for the unexpected warmth of the sun, and she could feel it cling damply to her body. The small black mare she rode was young and spirited, moving nervously away from the other horse as Roger extended a gauntleted hand to point out the small stone manor house partially hidden by a large stand of pines. It was well fortified with recent crenellations running the length of its high roof where the de Mortimer standard now fluttered yellow and green in the gentle breeze, and she caught a glimpse of the water shimmering placidly in the encircling moat.

"How charming the old manor looks from here," Jehan exclaimed.

"I've always liked this small holding," Roger said softly, pleased at her response. "It was a dower gift to my mother, and it became mine when I took possession of my lands." Jehan started to speak, but her words were cut short, for the horn sounded again, closer this time, joined by a chorus of dogs' voices, shrill with excitement.

"Where is Emrys?" Roger asked with annoyance, looking about for his squire, but they were alone on the small hill's crest. Damn him, he thought with irritation. He's wandered off again. He was needed close at hand, for he carried his master's other weapons. Listening to the sounds of the approaching hunting party, he said with sudden wild urgency, "The dogs have found a scent!"

He wheeled his horse around, pulling hard on the bridle, and disappeared into the trees, the joy of the chase racing hotly through his veins. Jehan followed him, urging her mount to quicken its pace. Although the hunt held little interest for her, she had no desire to be left behind to lose her way in a still unknown forest. Galloping between the large trees, her horse pounded over the sun-dappled earth. She felt branches tear at her hair and snatch at the cloak streaming behind her. An excellent rider, she easily kept her seat as the mare jumped a fallen log. The horn rang out again and Jehan turned her mount's head toward what she thought was the direction of the hunting party. It was a foolish move, for she had veered sharply from the path before realizing that Roger had disappeared. As she entered a small glade, her horse reared without warning, screaming wildly in sudden fright. Startled, Jehan lost the reins as the mare refused to be calmed. She clutched its mane in a desperate attempt to stay in the saddle while the animal flailed out with its hooves, totally out of control. Her knees pressed tightly against her mount's sides, she fought to stay on its back when, with a bucking motion, it stiffened its front legs and Jehan found herself catapulted over its head. Pain shot through her arm as she put out a hand to cushion her fall, and she struck the ground with a sickening thud, still hearing the horse's terrified cries. Stunned, she lay where she had fallen until her head cleared. Slowly opening her eyes she stifled a cry, for she was covered with blood. The horse was down, blood pouring from its body. The long slender legs quivered and a terrible rasping sound issued from its throat. Still dazed from the fall, she tried to get up, but a snuffling, grunting sound made her freeze. Despite the icy fear which gripped her, she lifted her gaze and looked into the fiery, maddened eyes of an enormous black boar, its sharp tusks red from the mare's blood, spittle dripping wetly from the long snout. She could make out bits of caked mud and leaves clinging to its heaving flanks. Its short legs moved restlessly while the beast waited indecisively for the terrified woman to stir, giving it cause to attack.

Panic swept her as she shrank from the boar's presence, for it was loathsome in its ugliness.

"Stay where you are! Don't move!"

De Mortimer gave the order quietly as he entered the glade. He had been unaware that Jehan was not behind him until he heard her mare scream. Following the sound he had seen Jehan thrown by the mortally wounded animal. Although the boar was not visible from where he silently dismounted, he assumed that the beast, flushed out by the hunters and driven into the glade, was now threatening her. It was sheer madness to face a frightened, cornered boar on foot, but he gave no thought to any peril to himself in that moment, knowing only that Jehan was in danger.

Treading carefully, his booted footsteps muffled by the covering of leaves on the soft earth, he held his spear ready in his right hand and his dagger clutched in the other. The boar had not yet seen him, its attention still focused on the blood-spattered figure of the young woman crouched beside the dying horse.

"Are you hurt?" he asked in a low voice, coming nearer.

"I—I don't know . . ." she whispered between lips gone as dry as her throat. It was oddly silent in the glade. The sounds of the hunt, which had seemed to surround them moments before, had vanished. She heard a bird chatter on a nearby branch and the wind gently rustle through the treetops. Light filtered fitfully through the thick foliage as the sun emerged from behind a cloud. She saw two mushrooms growing fat and round by a bush near her foot. The boar still watched her and she could feel her heart beat painfully as panic returned to grip her. Roger's tunic blended with the autumn foliage as he slowly circled the animal, taking care not to startle it. And then he stood before her as the boar, its decision made, lowered its head. Looking upward, she saw Roger's knees bend slightly, prepared for the beast's attack. Although his leg muscles tensed, the spear, raised to strike, did not tremble as with wild, bellowing snorts, the animal charged, its tiny eyes furiously intent on its prey. Roger threw the spear with a forward thrust of his body and buried its head deep within the boar. Jehan screamed as the glade exploded into sound. She glimpsed the glitter of the dagger's blade as it seemed to leap into Roger's right hand. His excited cries mingled with those of the boar's. The black body hurtled toward them as it tried to shed the spear, maddened by the pain which spread outward from where the barbed point had penetrated its vitals. Both man and beast crashed to the ground, the spear's shaft splintering with the impact, while Jehan became almost mindless with terror. She could smell the boar's fetid breath and saw the sharp ends of the tusks shiny with new blood.

"Roger . . ." she shrieked and closed her eyes, certain the boar had slain him. Tears streamed down her bloodstained cheeks as she waited for her own death. Instead she felt urgent hands touch her, running over her body with light, deft fingers.

"Stop that ridiculous screaming," Roger said, satisfied that she had not been badly hurt. She opened her eyes to see him kneeling beside her, his eyes still full of death. She winced with pain when he touched her wrist. It was swelling rapidly and he took the kerchief from her girdle to bind it.

"I thought you were slain," she sobbed, still crouched on the ground, submitting blindly to his ministrations.

"Nay, my lady, it takes more than an enraged boar to do that." De Mortimer laughed shortly. He helped Jehan to her feet and, feeling her tremble, held her close for a moment. Her ashen face was smudged with dirt and blood, the frightened eyes bright with tears. She felt his hand pick out bits of grass and dried leaves from her hair, which tumbled wildly down her back. She clung to him, her terror slowly subsiding.

"Sweet Jesu, the poor mare . . ." she whispered brokenly, catching a brief glimpse of her horse, its belly ripped open by the boar's tusks, lying in its own blood, terror held captive in the glazed eyes. Roger turned her from the sight.

"There's naught we can do for her, Jehan." He disengaged himself from her clasp, bending down to draw his knife from the boar's body.

As he straightened, cleaning its blade with leaves, Jehan cried out, "You've been wounded!" She stared in horror at his thigh where the torn cloth exposed a nasty gash which curved inward as if the boar had tried to impale him with its tusks. The blood was beginning to ooze from the jagged wound. "We must stop the bleeding," she told him, beginning to weep again.

Roger caught the hand she reached out to touch him, saying harshly, " 'Tis but a scratch . . . I allowed the boar to come too close." When she began to protest, he shook his head in warning. " 'Twill be attended to, Jehan. Now leave me be with your hysteria."

His tone was cold and short, leaving no room for pity or concern. She realized that he was angry and upset over what had happened, and fell silent. His mood darkened even more as Emrys rode into the glade. Before the squire could dismount, de Mortimer pulled the small man from his horse, cuffing him roughly.

"You damned accursed whoreson," his lord snarled. "Where did you disappear to? Did you hope I would be slain?" He struck him a stinging blow across the face.

White-faced, the Welshman cowered under his master's fury.

"Arglwydd, nay . . . I followed you, but you disappeared among the trees. The horns came from every side! I could not find you . . ."

" 'Tis true, my lord," Jehan screamed, clinging to Roger's arm, holding him back, for she feared he would severely harm his squire in his blind rage. De Mortimer was in a towering fury, finding a release of the tension and fear within himself by lashing out at Emrys.

"And where by the wounds of Christ are the others? There was enough din in this glade to awake Satan himself!" Roger swayed for a moment, the gash in his leg starting to throb painfully.

"Emrys, your master has been wounded by the boar," Jehan sobbed, her arms flung about Roger's waist.

Furious with Jehan's behavior, Roger tried to free himself from her embrace and ordered Emrys to call the

132

hunting party together. Fearful of Roger's wound, Jehan insisted that they return to the manor house and, surprisingly, he offered no objections. The first of the baron's knights appeared, crashing heedlessly through the underbrush, followed by several retainers holding back the dogs. Catching sight of the dead boar, they snapped and snarled in their eagerness to reach the carcass. Other knights rode in, bringing de Mortimer's horse with them. Suddenly the glade swarmed with people, all curious to know what had happened. A huntsman pulled the splintered remains of the spear from the boar and had the carcass lashed to a long pole. As de Mortimer carefully mounted his horse, he ordered the huntsman to signal the end of the hunt. He was beginning to feel lightheaded from loss of blood and gritted his teeth to keep from grimacing with pain. He knew that he should not be riding, but the thought of being carried in a litter was intolerable.

Jehan watched him struggle to keep his seat, fighting a rising nausea as the tumult about her increased.

"My lord will be all right, Lady Jehan. He's endured worse wounds in his life." The Welshman spoke in quiet tones, allaying her fears. She felt his arms support her as he lifted her on to his mount's saddle and swung up behind her. She wondered at the unexpected gentleness he had shown her and allowed it to sustain her as the subdued hunting party returned to the manor.

"The queen's messenger be damned . . . 'tis barely dawn!" de Mortimer snarled, slamming the door in the face of the startled servant. His healing wound stretched painfully and he stifled a groan as he returned to the bed. Jehan turned her head on the soft pillow and opened her eyes to find him leaning over her.

She smiled, parting her lips to his kiss. For nearly two weeks Roger had remained with her on the small holding. The wound had kept him in bed for a week while he fumed and fretted at his inactivity. Fortunately the gash had not festered, due partly to the poultices Jehan applied to it, drawing out the bad humors. She tended him herself, her wrenched wrist forgotten in her concern for the man who had saved her life. Only Emrys did she allow near him the first few days, permitting him to wash and shave his master. She had never been happier, for Roger allowed her to tend him without his usual sarcasm and comments which could cut her to the heart. For the first time in her life she knew what it was to be totally involved and committed to another human being. She realized a love for de Mortimer she had not dreamt existed, knowing too that she could never tell him of it. At night Jehan lay in her lover's arms, listening to his quiet breathing as he slept, secure in the knowledge that he would still be with her when morning came.

Now he was on his feet once more, favoring his wounded leg only slightly. A man whose nature lacked capacity for idleness, he kept himself busy inspecting the manor and its lands, seeing that all was in good order. There was little enough for him to do, yet he said naught of leaving. Toward Jehan he was both gentle and kind, which puzzled her, for it was totally unlike him. Rather than probe the causes for the change in him, Jehan chose to accept him as he was, while still wondering uneasily when he would revert to the hard and cruel warrior she knew him to be. She even grew to tolerate Emrys who, because his master willed it, sat by the hearth in their bedchamber while they supped, playing his strange melodies. It seemed to matter little to him that the Lady Jehan listened with no great interest, for he knew that before long his lord would begin to caress her, paying no heed to the presence of the harper. To de Mortimer, the Welshman had less than human status. Yet, while the music flowed sensuously through the chamber, Emrys's sharp eyes would see the young woman's lovely features glow with loving passion, and he ached for her futile devotion to his master. Disturbed and discomfited by their final abandonment before him, he would lay a hand on the harp's strings, stilling its voice, and slip unnoticed from the chamber. So had it been last night, Jehan mused, remembering the consuming hunger for Roger which never seemed to diminish.

"Who was it?" she asked sleepily.

"Naught, my dove," he answered, drawing her into his arms. "Naught save a messenger from the queen."

"The queen's messenger . . . the queen's messenger!

Roger, has a message arrived from the queen?" Jehan sat up abruptly, suddenly fully awake. As she threw back the covers, she shivered in the early morning's chill. De Mortimer gazed at her, the memory of pale golden hair and cool porcelain skin intruding into his contemplation of the passionate mouth and tumbled red hair of the woman before him. He saw Isabella's almond-shaped eyes blazing with an ice-blue fire, peer from Jehan's heart-shaped face.

"Roger?" So intense and burning a look had come over his wild face that Jehan felt a pang of fear, for she sensed that he did not even see her. The fire faded from his eyes and de Mortimer pulled her into his arms, feeling her body smooth and warm against his own. He cupped her face in his hands and kissed her mouth, savoring the velvet texture of her soft lips as they moved against his. The queen's image blurred as he heard Jehan repeat her question.

"Yes, my lady with the fiery locks and bewitching mouth . . ." Roger kissed her again until her head swam, and she twined her arms about his neck. With a sigh, Roger loosened his hold. Sweet Jesù, but the wench was insatiable, he mused, giving no thought at all to the fact that she truly loved him. That emotion had no place in the ambitious dream he was following. The queen had sent a messenger to Jehan. Isabella! Did she too remember their brief encounter in Tynemouth, he wondered.

"Have you a thought why the queen would send a messenger to you?" De Mortimer's voice, lazy and amused, broke into her languid reverie as she leaned into his spare, hard body. She felt him tense, as if her reply would be important to him. Her head was buried in his shoulder, so she did not see his eyes when he asked his question.

"While I waited in Bristol for you to come, I wrote to the queen requesting permission to return to court."

With a suddenness that was almost painful, Jehan found herself faced with the old Roger. She saw that he was annoyed and wondered why. Yet, as he mulled over her answer, a crafty look crossed his face. There was no time to be wasted, he decided. Within minutes he had called Berthe to attend her so that she could receive the royal messenger. He himself was nowhere in sight when the royal equerry, a fresh-faced youth with fair hair and a charming smile, was shown into the solar and presented the folded parchment with the queen's seal affixed to it. Although it was still early, she offered him wine and sweet cakes while she slowly read the contents of the message. Isabella had heard of her lord's tragic death and offered her sympathies in addition to expressing her pleasure at welcoming her back to court. It was all Jehan had hoped for, yet she was disquieted and not a little alarmed at Roger's strange reaction. That at some time they would part, if even for a short while, was something she had tried not to dwell upon during the past weeks, but her instincts told her he would soon leave her. Better to make her own plans since she knew she would not stay on the holding without him.

A nagging fear began to grow within Jehan as she told de Mortimer of the queen's message, for she could not fathom his thoughts. His eyes narrowed in silent contemplation as he listened to her low, silken voice. So now his plans would be taken one step further, he told himself with satisfaction. Jehan did not understand the reasons behind his forcing her to swear that she would tell no one of their relationship and particularly not the queen. Of course she would not tell, Jehan said peevishly, asking slyly if there was aught he would want to know. His eyes flashed in anger and he strode restlessly about the chamber without replying to so obvious a question.

"How soon does she want you with her?"

"When I can come . . ."

"Then you must leave as soon as possible." It was stated flatly, without room for any protests from her. He stood before the hearth of the solar, clad in a short leather tunic, dark hose, and the high boots he always wore for riding about the holding. His body was like that of a panther, poised to spring, while his mind moved rapidly over his planned actions.

"I must go to Warwick . . . the young earl's affairs should be looked into." Jehan raised startled eyes to him as he said smoothly, "Since I'm both his guardian and his future father-in-law, I consider Thomas's interests as my own."

She shuddered suddenly, for this was the Roger she could not control. His black eyes bored into her as he smiled coldly.

"We will meet in London. My factor there will arrange some sort of accommodations for you . . . you will stay there until you leave for court. We can't be seen together any longer . . ."

"Roger, nay!" Jehan cried in protest, rising from her chair. Now it begins, she thought, seeing his mind caught by his ambitious schemes once more.

"My dove . . . 'tis not meet for us to share our quarters, but I'll come to you. Few will know of our continuing association."

"But all in Dublin must have known that I shared your bed."

He reached out a finger and traced the outline of her mouth. His voice softened.

" 'Twas in Dublin . . . a brief passion satisfied and soon forgotten. Of little importance once we parted. You will be busy at court . . . the queen's confidante, as before." He brushed his lips against her temple, below the jeweled band. "And you will listen . . ." Tilting her face to his, he kissed her lightly. "You will be my ears to all that is spoken by the queen and my eyes to all who come to see her."

"You're asking treason of me!" Jehan whispered, her green eyes searching his face for some hint as to his reaction to her shocked protest.

"Of course I am, my lady, and if you remain as clever as we both think you are, only we two will know of it."

De Mortimer watched with amusement as Jehan struggled with the shreds of her conscience and laughed as she threw herself into his arms, capitulating as always to his will. But as Roger's laughter rang in her ears, Jehan resolved to bide her time and tread his road with care, for she knew only too well that where his ambitions were concerned, he held loyalty toward no one but himself.

Handing the reins of his horse to a waiting groom while Emrys and the two men-at-arms accompanying him dismounted, de Mortimer looked about him with interest.

As he stood in the cobbled courtyard, its stones still glistening from the recent rain, he felt a stab of envy that the earl of Pembroke had been able to salvage at least a part of the valuable lands ceded to him by the old king when he had destroyed the power of the Templar knights. Although most of the properties had been lost to Pembroke following the political upheaval among the barons after Bannockburn, he had retained possession of the small palace where he resided when he was in London. Ideally situated on Flete Street, the main thoroughfare west of St. Paul's Cathedral leading directly to Westminster, the building was on the far side of the city wall and easily accessible without the need for keeping to the curfew. The palace was built of stone and kept in excellent repair, Roger noted, observing masons re-facing a small tower set in the corner wing which seemed to house the guards. Hearing the sounds of hammers beating upon anvils, de Mortimer surmised that an archway visible to the right of the entry led to the stables. High stone walls muted the noises from the wide street that was thronged with folk shopping at the stalls crowded together alongside the open sewers which ran the entire length of the roadway.

As de Mortimer strode beneath the stone escutcheon bearing the Pembroke arms and past the massive doors opened to receive him, he was startled by a cheerful voice.

"Good day to you, my lord! I've not seen you since before your successful return to Ireland."

Arundel stood before him, a smile on his pleasant face. His bright blue eyes twinkled with amusement as they rested on the dark-visaged man, who did not bother to hide his annoyance at their meeting. Edmund Fitzalan was well aware that the baron of Wigmore considered him a fool and found it to his advantage to encourage that opinion. He had no desire to be linked with de Mortimer in his ambitious scheming. Too often had they stood on opposite sides in the continuous political disputes among the realm's powerful peers.

Roger returned the greeting with barely concealed scorn. He would have passed Arundel without further conversation, but the earl barred his way.

"Will you be returning to Ireland soon, my lord de

Mortimer? 'Tis said there's still one more de Lacy to conquer," Arundel remarked, drawing on his gauntlets.

"I'm still Warden and Justiciar, Fitzalan, and as such, you need not remind me where my duties lie," de Mortimer replied coldly as a servant unclasped his mantle and placed it on a large wooden coffer standing near the door. The stone entry felt chill, and although it was yet daylight, the candles in circular iron holders suspended on heavy chains from the ceiling were already lit.

"Lord de Mortimer, I am the last one to chide you for lapses of responsibility . . . particularly after the victorious battles you waged against the Scots and their allies. I understand all England lay at your feet in admiration of your great military achievements." Arundel's voice was bland and his face quite devoid of any deviltry, but de Mortimer regarded him with suspicion. As if reading his mind, the young earl laughed.

"Nay, Roger, I did not mean to discredit your achievements. I've only recently returned from France and heard of your return when I landed in Dover."

They stood together, neither one quite trusting the other, until Arundel turned toward his squire who handed him his helm. As he started toward the door, he said, "If you've come to see my lord Pembroke, you're too late. He's gone to Northampton to see the king. There's much to report on his unfortunate kidnapping, and we're all relieved at his safe return. But I'm sure I need not tell you of the affair since you seem to know all that happens, no matter where you are." And with a wave of his hand and a final laugh, Arundel departed, leaving de Mortimer staring after him. A hot ember of bitter hatred began to glow deep within the Marcher baron's soul toward the carefree Arundel whose thoughtless remarks had been interpreted by the arrogant baron in quite a different way from that intended. A retainer's low, servile voice broke into de Mortimer's musings, and he banished the thought of Edmund Fitzalan from his mind as he followed the man up a short flight of worn stone steps.

"Roger, I had not thought to see you in London!" James Kilburn came forward to greet his visitor as he stood in the doorway of the small chamber used by Pembroke as his study. He had been surprised to hear that the baron of Wigmore wished to see him, and not a little curious as to his reasons.

"No more than I had when I heard you were staying with my lord Pembroke."

The two men clasped each other's arms, and de Mortimer noticed the fatigue stamped on Kilburn's taut features. The long hazel eyes were shadowed, but though he smiled in welcome, there was a coolness of manner new to him. Roger was impressed by the fine quality of his host's tunic, made of burgundy velvet banded with marten fur, and the gold chain about his neck was handsomely wrought, being set with matched gemstones. The Glairn ring gleamed on the graceful hand which waved him to the large chair by a table strewn with documents. Kilburn gathered the papers together, placing them into a leather portfolio.

"Lord Arundel and I had business to conclude," he explained briefly as he called for a servant to bring wine for his guest. "I've been staying here at the kind invitation of Lord Pembroke . . . we met in Calais and made the crossing together."

"So I've heard," Roger said, accepting a silver mazer of wine offered by the servant. The shallow drinking bowl bore the Pembroke arms, and he saw that the blue and white stripes and small red martlets were exquisitely enameled in fine detail. "All of England speaks of nothing else but the earl's safe return."

"As they did when you triumphed in Ireland," Kilburn replied, beginning to wonder again at the purpose behind Roger's visit. The Marcher baron needed little prompting to boast of his successes in Ireland, and Kilburn found himself greatly impressed once more by the younger man's cleverness and passion to succeed. Yet the feeling of wariness which always rose within him when he was in Roger's company remained. As they sat together in the comfortable chamber, warmed by the fires burning in large braziers set near them, Roger began to relax in the company of Kilburn, who listened quietly while contributing little to the conversation. De Mortimer's mazer was filled again and again, and his white teeth flashed a devilish smile in his dark face as he described his next campaign.

"This time I'll fight for myself and not the king. Have you heard of the Despensers annexing much of the held land in the Marches and Wales—all with the king's sanction? Well, I'll not stand for it. I'm joining Lancaster in his battle against Edward and his blood-sucking friends."

"Roger, don't be a fool. Lancaster is an incompetent ass and sooner or later will be brought down. Believe me, 'twill happen. Edward is just waiting for the chance to wreak vengeance on him." Kilburn tried to reason with him, but Roger refused to listen.

"You're a fine one to talk, James. How gallant of you to offer to escort the earl of Pembroke back to England! That sly fox managed very well to return just in time to bolster the king's self-assurance."

"You're speaking daft! Pembroke has always been loyal to the crown above all else. He is speaking of creating a new political party to stand between those who follow Lancaster and those who support Edward, and hopes to win the moderate barons to his side. There are more of them than you might think. Besides, it may gain more for all of us if there isn't so much dissension. He has already spoken to Roger d'Amory and Lord Badlesmere, and now Arundel is convinced of the soundness of his views. Of course, I must admit that Aymer despises Lancaster. He's never forgiven him for Gaveston's death . . . nor has the king."

De Mortimer's dark eyes narrowed.

"And neither have you, James. Has it rankled so much all these years?"

"You weren't there, Roger. 'Twas an ugly deed." Kilburn hated to think of that dreadful night, the final terrified shrieks of the murdered Gascon still ringing in his ears.

"So was Warwick's death, James." It was calmly said and Kilburn sensed a change in the surprisingly simply clad man with the familiar green and yellow arms emblazoned on the linen surcoat. De Mortimer slapped a gauntlet lazily against one long leg stretched out comfortably before him and stared at the toe of his black leather boot.

"I would like your oldest son for one of my daughters, James."

Typically said, Kilburn thought, as if a de Mortimer daughter was a greater prize than Glairn's heir. Of course, he'd want another earl to add to his household, since one daughter was already affianced to Warwick's orphaned heir.

De Mortimer's eyes glowed as he contemplated Kilburn, waiting confidently for his assent.

"Well, James, what do you say? Our two houses allied through our children! It sounds formidable."

"But impossible. My son is already betrothed to Edmund Fitzalan's daughter!"

Letting out a surprised gasp, de Mortimer stifled an oath.

"Arundel? James, you have aimed high! I didn't know you and the fickle Edmund were friends—or is it Pembroke's doing?" He sounded wryly amused, masking a shocked anger.

"Stop being snide, Roger. I've known Edmund for several years and have a great liking for him. Besides, from what I hear, your choice of bridegrooms has stepped over partisan lines before this, so don't cast aspersions before taking stock of your own sense of honor. And my oldest daughter, too, is betrothed. 'Tis why I'm in London, to conclude negotiations with Lord Bardestour." Kilburn saw Roger's face darken and warned him not to consider young Hugh nor his infant daughter. " 'Tis not possible between us, Roger. There are other reasons as well why I would refuse, but 'tis not necessary nor wise to discuss them. Besides, I leave London shortly to return to Glairn."

Suddenly James found himself clutching the arms of his chair with fingers tight from anger too long held in. The overbearing arrogance of the man seated opposite him had finally become unbearable. He remembered Gillian's tears and bruised face—the ingratitude shown by Wigmore for Glairn's aiding him in time of trouble. Nay, he thought, he'll get naught from me.

Kilburn's outburst had startled Roger by its vehemence and he pondered the reason for it. In actuality he was sincerely regretful that nothing could be arranged, for an alliance with a powerful northern house would have been extremely advantageous to his schemes. Realizing further talk would be futile, he took his leave, suppressing a desire to ask after Gillian's welfare. Long after he left Glairn he held the memory of her soft mouth and the feel of her body under his hands. Glancing sharply at Kilburn's closed face, Roger wondered whether he knew what had occurred that night. Could that knowledge have made a difference in Kilburn's decision? He felt a sudden chill as he remembered Gillian's large eyes looking as if into his very soul. What had she seen that made her shrink from him? It was a question he had asked himself many times.

Jehan felt like a stranger before Roger. He had come without warning to the small merchant's house near the Guildhall that he had rented for her, mounting the stone stairs built against the outside of the building, in the London manner, to the second floor where her apartments were. Entering the long chamber, which served both as dining hall and solar, he called loudly for wine, and the servants hastened to obey his command. Jehan's words of welcome died on her lips when she saw his fearful black visage. He said nothing to her and threw himself heavily into the wide, low-backed chair she had hastily ordered placed before the fire for him. After the servants brought the wine and several platters piled high with meat pasties, she dismissed them, pouring the wine for him herself, taking care not to spill any of it on the carved table set by his side. She caught a glimpse of the huddled figure of the harper crouched in the corner by the hearth, and, stirred with pity for the little man so often at the mercy of his master's moods, brought him some pasties and a cup of wine. Flashing her a grateful look, he proceeded to wolf down the food.

Seating herself quietly opposite Roger, she observed him cautiously. His mouth was grim, giving the wild face a savage, angry look and she puzzled at his strange mood. She had seen little of him since arriving in London four days earlier. When he did come to her, accompanied only by Emrys, it was after darkness had fallen. At dawn he would leave her, having told her nothing of his activities or his plans. She was aware of a growing restlessness in him and feared each day that he would not return to her.

Twice she cleared her throat and began to address him, until she realized that he had forgotten her presence. She felt a stab of disappointment that he had not even noticed that her hair was unbound, in the manner he preferred, held only with a gold band about her forehead and falling softly about her slender figure to below her knees. Because of his customary impatience, Jehan dressed simply, clad now in a loose robe of amber silk with full, flowing sleeves and soft neckline which accentuated the extraordinarily beautiful skin of her throat and bosom.

With an impatient wave of his left hand, de Mortimer ordered Emrys to play for him, and after a while the soothing voice of the harp filled the chamber with a sense of peace. Roger's body relaxed as he drank the last of the wine in his goblet and unfastened his tunic. He let out a deep sigh as he stretched out his legs toward the fire's warmth, and Jehan was aware of the tension draining gradually from him. She rose quietly, moving gracefully to refill his goblet. Lightly touching the heavy black hair falling about Roger's closed face, she realized with surprise that her hand trembled. How silken and full of life his hair feels, she thought as her fingers smoothed it back from his forehead. He sighed again and reached out for her, drawing her into his arms. Bending his head, his lips found the hollow between her breasts swelling gently above the silken cloth of her robe.

"Roger . . . my dearest lord," Jehan murmured softly, feeling her skin tingle and grow warm at the touch of his blindly searching mouth.

He leaned his cheek against her breast and closed his eyes. The slight weight of her small body cradled in his arms felt good to him. There was a comfort in her presence he found rarely with others, especially his own wife, he thought bitterly—but for how much longer could he afford himself the sensual luxury of their relationship. The image of his wife flashed through his mind . . . she was passably pretty, graciously charming, accomplished, and exceedingly well trained to do him honor as chatelaine to his many holdings. Why could he not love her, he wondered. He knew that she loved him, for she welcomed him eagerly when he visited her. Joan bore him child after child gladly, knowing that their children forged a bond between them he would never break. How willingly had she ceded all her properties to him, bringing him more wealth and power than he had dreamed of—perhaps that had been the catalyst to his ambitions, he thought. But she could not share his vision, nor did she care to. She was dutiful but dull, lacking the sexuality which was so strong within himself. Roger moved his cheek against Jehan's fragrant silken skin, and his heart grew cold as his mind returned to his meeting with James Kilburn.

His plans were not going well. He had truly believed that all was in order, for since leaving the Marches, he had attended to many of his affairs which had been neglected during his stay in Ireland. He was well satisfied with the state of his holdings and had finally gone to Warwick where the young earl, in company with his future countess, had greeted him shyly. Katherine de Mortimer was overjoyed to see her father again, for she sorely missed her parents and the brothers and sisters she had left behind at Wigmore. Barely six years of age, the pretty, dark-haired child had wept when her father told her she would have to stay at Warwick with Thomas. Sitting in the solar with Warwick's constable, a man he knew was loyal to the de Mortimers, and the small earl's tutor, who had been chosen by himself with great care, he watched the two children play together. He found his Kate pale and thin, and for a moment felt a pang of pity, recalling the rosy, merry babe with her bright dark eyes and charming prattle. Katherine's nurse, worried over the child's delicate nature, begged that she be allowed to return to her mother, if only for a short while, but de Mortimer refused. 'Twas best she remain at Warwick, he told the woman who had cared for the little maid since birth. Soon enough would she become the countess of Warwick, and 'twas best she put such childish emotions as homesickness from her, he said bluntly.

Feeling Jehan stir in his arms, he decided that perhaps he could arrange for one of Kate's sisters to come for a

145

visit . . . that would probably allay her feelings of strangeness.

Roger smiled grimly as he thought of the coffers of collected rent monies he had removed from the holding, transferring them to his factor in London for safekeeping. What use did a mere child have for the wealth stored at Warwick when it could be utilized for his own purposes. He had thought himself well satisfied with his affairs, but now—he stifled a groan. He had counted heavily on an alliance with Glairn through the marriage of one of his daughters to Kilburn's heir. Roger was furious at having been refused. What could James have been thinking of, he asked himself, to have allied himself with such a scapegrace lunatic as Arundel and the ineffectual and nondescript Deveron family, however much wealth they possessed! Pembroke, he thought angrily. Of course, it was that fine, high-ranking silver-tongued lord who had brought it all about. Damn him! Damn James Kilburn! Damn them all! And a fiery hatred flamed through him.

His hands tightened and Jehan cried out with sudden pain. She perceived the stricken bleakness on a face suddenly stripped of its usual reckless arrogance. Alarmed by the unexpected change in him, she touched his cheek gently.

"My lord, what is it?" she asked anxiously, seeing his black eyes grow hard with angry hatred. He didn't reply, but she had heard him utter Kilburn's name in his fury.

"Has Lord Kilburn angered you? Take care with him, Roger, for he can be quite mad if he is driven to anger."

His attention caught at last by her warning, Roger thrust her roughly from him, his hands holding her shoulders in an iron grip.

"What do you mean, Jehan? What do you know of James Kilburn?"

"Very little, my lord . . . I met him in Tynemouth when I was with the queen . . ." and she reminded him of the king's flight from Tynemouth Castle to find safety for Piers Gaveston with nearly all of England's barons in pursuit, leaving behind a pregnant, furious Isabella. "You

146

were there . . . I hid from you in the queen's apartments although I saw Ralph briefly before you were sent to York. I heard Lord Pembroke tell the queen that Lord Kilburn had been ordered to guard her . . ."

Everyone knew the scandal of Kilburn's abduction of Gillian from her lord. And Jehan had decided to seduce him. If she could find a flaw or weakness in him, she could place it as a weapon into the hands of Gillian's husband, Arnaut, who was her lover.

"I only thought to help Arnaut, for he hated Lord Kilburn with an insane passion . . ."

Jehan's voice faltered, for she remembered how her body had suddenly quickened in Kilburn's arms as he pretended to make love to her. She had forgotten the molten fire which rose in her veins as his mouth possessed hers . . . De Mortimer saw the green eyes darken with remembered passion and his voice lashed out at her.

"And you gave yourself to him . . . ! God's wounds, I should have known!" The thought of her with Kilburn was surprisingly painful.

"Nay, Roger, I swear that naught happened. He knew somehow that Arnaut was my lover . . . he went mad . . . he exploded with rage and accused Arnaut of having murdered his own child. His eyes—his eyes were like icy green fire—they had no soul . . . By the holy Virgin, Roger, I vow that I feared he would kill me. And all for the passion he held for that whey-faced bitch he wed when Arnaut was scarce cold in his grave!"

Tears poured down her cheeks as she relived those terrible days, and the hatred for Gillian that had lain dormant within her for so many years suddenly erupted with a violence that startled them both.

"'Tis Gillian . . . with her innocent face . . . she deceives all men and bewitches them! How often did I see it when we were girls at Baillendel Castle. And she pretending not to notice . . . Arnaut talked constantly of her like a man possessed. Her spirit shared our bed . . . when he touched me, 'twas Gillian he touched!"

For a moment she paused, knowing that she was as guilty as Arnaut, for her own longing for Roger had never died.

"Lord de Broze swore the child Gillian lost was not his . . . and although she denied it, he believed that she had betrayed him with one of the queen's equerries while he was with Lord Gaveston in Ireland. And all the while . . ." Jehan said wildly, "all the while she coveted James Kilburn. 'Twas her fault that Arnaut was slain at Bannockburn, for he was obsessed beyond reason with killing her lover. And she survived! She triumphed, Roger . . . in York I saw her, great with Kilburn's child, holding the king's sanction of their marriage."

She wrenched herself free from de Mortimer's grasp and stood by the fire like an ancient Fury loosed from her chains. The green eyes glittered wildly as she allowed her hatred full vent, beating her fists futilely against the warm stones of the fireplace. She became incoherent, and de Mortimer could make little sense of her ramblings. He paid little heed to her, letting her unbridled hysteria run its course unchecked. He scarce heard Jehan's jealousy-laden words, for he suddenly remembered the confrontation between Arnaut de Broze and James Kilburn at Carlisle Castle when the Gascon had publicly accused the earl of adultery, and Kilburn's astounding reaction. Had he and Kilburn's friend, Lord Martleigh, not held him back, he would have slain de Broze. Jehan was right, he thought with surprise. James Kilburn could truly be driven to a murderous rage. He looked with renewed interest at Jehan, whose emotions seemed finally to have been spent. Leaning against the mantel, she was sobbing quietly.

"Come, my dove, stop your weeping . . . 'tis all past and the countess of Glairn can cause you no more pain. Her lord keeps her safely in the north and she'll not cross your path again."

"Can you deny that she has stirred your blood as well? That you've felt no desire for her?" Jehan whispered, tears still glistening on her cheeks. She knelt before de Mortimer, demanding a reply from him. He stared at her, seeing the passion and longing on her face.

"Many women stir my blood, my lady . . . I'll not deny that. I'm not a man to remain faithful to any woman and you knew it when you came back to me. I admit to you that you have meant more to me than any of the others, and I do not speak only of our son. We're much alike, and you've crept deeper into my soul than I ever wanted. 'Tis something neither of us could help. Yet never use it as a weapon against me, Jehan," he cautioned. "For the present, I have no wish to end our affair, but . . ." He bent over to lift her from her knees, her face ashen and drawn in the flickering firelight.

"But?" Jehan asked with quivering lips.

"But I return to Ireland in a few weeks, and you will join the queen at Eltham."

And I will join Pembroke's new moderate party, he told himself silently, for they were both Marcher barons with too much at stake, and his political sense told him that for now it would be necessary to unite against their common enemy. He thrust Kilburn's demeaning refusal to unite their families from his mind, although the insult to his arrogant pride festered within him.

Chapter 5

Hurley

The dry leaves swirled wildly in spiraling columns blown by the cold wind, and the riders drew their cloaks more tightly about themselves as they rode along the road leading to Hurley. The trees, half stripped of their autumn foliage, stood like ageless sentinels sharply etched against the pale yellow light of the dying day. Darkness was beginning to overtake them sooner than expected, but Kilburn was anxious to reach the manor, no matter how late the hour. The earl, accompanied by Hal Jardine, several knights, and a goodly number of mounted men-at-arms, had left London long before dawn and, except for brief stops to rest the horses, pressed on in weather that had been steadily becoming rawer as the wind increased. He felt bone-weary beneath the weight of the chain mail, while his thighs and legs ached from the hours astride the huge destrier. His eyes, red-rimmed from fatigue and the road's dust, peered through the open visor of his helm. Turning back, he could see his own exhaustion mirrored in the faces of his men.

The guttering light of the torches burning on either side of the huge gates revealed the approaching company as the herald rode ahead of his lord bearing the Glairn banner with the golden hawk on its red field. With what seemed excruciating slowness to the earl's growing impatience, the gates were swung wide by the manor guards with much screeching of chains and hinges.

Allowing James scarce time to dismount and give over his reins to the waiting groom, Gillian was in his arms, enveloped by his cloak against the evening cold and held close. Handing his helm to Hal, he returned her eager kisses, oblivious to the hysterical greetings by the rest of the household, aware only that she was with him once more. No one had expected the earl's arrival at so late an hour, and while James, Hal, and the other Glairn knights were welcomed into the small entry hall, Elizabeth Harron ordered that sleeping quarters be arranged for their guests, as well as for the men-at-arms who would share the dormitory housing the manor guards. Doors closed tightly against the gusting wind, the hall with its large colorful tapestries seemed warmly welcoming and the men breathed easier as servants deftly divested them of their hauberks, while their arms and other equippage were taken to their sleeping chambers. Too weary to accept the hospitality of the great hall, Kilburn's knights craved permission to seek their beds and were assured by their hostess that food and drink would be brought to them. Hal eagerly went in search of Agnes, whose joy at seeing her young husband again was overshadowed by a sudden shyness.

The earl gladly joined his family in the solar beckoning cheerfully to him. The heat of the roaring fire felt good to him as he stretched out his hands gratefully. Gillian, unable to take her eyes from him, was concerned to see the handsome, austere face so tense and drawn with exhaustion. For weeks she had waited with mounting anxiety for his return, praying in her heart that each day that passed would bring him to her. Holding her close to his side, James joined his brother-in-law in a cup of heated wine, feeling the herbed liquid spread a warming glow through his chilled body. Seated close to the hearth, they all listened raptly to his accounts of his journey to Calais and his reunion with Pembroke. They found his description of Pembroke's reappearance fascinating, but were disappointed by how little he was able to tell them about the earl's imprisonment.

A servant refilled James's empty cup as he stopped for a moment to press a kiss on Gillian's soft hand. He caught the familiar scent of sandalwood which she had made her own, and realized with a surge of regret how long they had been apart. Elizabeth, touched by the weariness on the lean face still covered by the road's dust, ordered that food be brought for him, but he declined it, merely holding out his cup to be once more refilled.

"Too much wine on an empty stomach will make you ill, my lord," Gillian whispered to him. "Perhaps a small meat tartlet would satisfy you."

"Nay, my love, there's a hunger in me that food cannot satisfy," he replied in a tone only she could hear. Her large eyes flew to his face as a blush rose to her pale cheeks.

Robert, impatient to hear all of James's adventures, plied him with so many questions that Elizabeth finally chided her husband in her gentle voice, reminding him of the earl's weariness.

James laughed, assuring her that his fatigue lessened with each cup of wine, and indeed, the solar seemed to glow and sparkle brighter than it had before. Gazing at Elizabeth fondly, he found her delicate, pale beauty and shining hair turned to silvery brilliance by the fire's light pleasing to his eyes. She and Robert suited each other well, James thought, glad suddenly for both of them and grateful for their obvious devotion to Gillian.

"How long have you been back in England?" Robert asked after Kilburn had finished telling them of the rough channel crossing.

"For several weeks . . . I did send word of my safe return," James said evasively, and felt Gillian stiffen slightly.

"Aye, a messenger from my lord Pembroke brought it. It told us little enough!" Gillian said to him, and Robert suddenly felt uneasy. Attuned as he was to his sister's moods, he had noticed her withdrawal at James's words. "We expected to see you each day thereafter." Her voice was low and even, but it was obvious to her brother that her first overwhelming, mindless joy in seeing her lord again was beginning to wane.

James nodded, refusing to notice her hurt tone. He finished his wine and set down the heavy silver cup.

" 'Tis for a very good reason, my lady, that I was delayed in London," and he began to tell them of the betrothal contract drawn up and signed by himself and Lord Bardestour. They had also spent some time visiting that lord's holdings, which were impressive, James said a trifle smugly. He was well pleased with himself, knowing that the betrothal was an excellent alliance. He had forgotten his earlier misgivings, but listening to his voice, slurred from the effects of the potent mulled wine, recount Arundel's role as matchmaker, Gillian felt the blood drain from her heart. The room swam before her eyes suddenly in a haze of colors and for a moment she felt faint. She sat quite still, and the chamber slowly righted itself once more, but a coldness had settled over her which she could not shake off. With a great effort she forced herself to stand, and only Elizabeth seemed to notice the shocking change in her sister-in-law as Robert turned to Kilburn with excited words of congratulations.

"You've further matters to discuss with Robert, I'm sure," Gillian told James, breaking into his conversation. "I shall order a bath prepared for you before you retire . . ." and without another word, she left the solar. Had Robert not placed a restraining hand on his lady's arm, Elizabeth would have followed her. But Robert, too, had recognized the stricken look on Gillian's face.

Standing by the open window in her white silk shift with its wide elbow-length sleeves, Gillian watched as servants brought the high-sided wooden bathtub and large ewers of hot water she had ordered prepared for her lord. Before dismissing Agnes, she had allowed her to divest her of the heavy silk gown with its delicately scattered gold embroidery and small, intricately fashioned buttons. After slipping out of the lighter weight under-robe, Gillian assured the young tiring woman that she would manage quite well herself. Turning toward the darkness beyond the window, she did not feel the chill night air streaming in. Jamie's words echoed over and over in her mind . . . Margaret has been betrothed to Walter Deveron . . . Margaret betrothed . . . Margaret, three years old come

154

Christmastide! Anger began to course through her . . . why had she not sensed that this was happening when Jamie did not come immediately to Hurley after his safe return to England. Margaret, born in York; the babe they had nearly lost—Gillian could almost feel the pain which had wracked her as she had fought the birth, fearing that a force from beyond the grave would snatch the babe from her. Only Jamie's loving strength had sustained her, his strength and the strange bond which existed between them.

She heard the chamber door open and close softly, her lord's footsteps muffled by the carpets covering the floor.

"Oh, lovedy, how I've missed you all these months. 'Tis been so long since I've held you." She felt Jamie's lips against her neck, and she closed her eyes, wanting him despite her bitter hurt and anger. Nay, she reminded herself sharply, he gave no thought to you in this matter.

His hands turned her to him, and in the dim light of the hearth he drank in the remembered loveliness of her pale oval face with its large, hauntingly beautiful dark blue eyes. Twining a hand in the dark, silken hair, he tilted her face to his and kissed her. Gillian remained stiff and unresponsive until he released her, bewildered at her coldness toward him.

"You've done it again!" she whispered between dry lips. "You knew how I felt about it when you arranged Alain's betrothal . . ." Her voice shook as she allowed her anger to break through the wall she had tried to erect against him.

Not accepting her anger, Jamie tried to soothe her. "The alliance with Edmund has turned out very well, Gillian . . . even you have finally admitted it."

"I admitted nothing, Jamie. What choice did I have . . . that deed was done. I truly have no objection to the earl of Arundel, but by the sweet saints of heaven, not one word did you say of it till the contract was signed."

Her eyes glistened with tears as she remembered the bitter words between them in York.

"I've no desire to quarrel with you," Jamie said

wearily, turning from her. She moved to stand before him, her face white with fury.

"Don't walk away from this, Jamie! For weeks I've been sitting here in Hurley, waiting for you . . . wondering why you've been delayed. I've not seen my children for months . . . I ache for them. Have you forgotten that Jennifer was but two months old when we left Glairn! I have no knowledge of her at all . . . but you ordered me to remain here and wait for you."

"Gillian, stop these outrageous accusations!" Jamie's voice rose as his own anger began to grow within him. "I've done naught to give you cause to doubt me. What right have you to question my actions!"

"Right, Jamie? Sweet Jesu, even Geoffrey has been here, assuring us that all was well. He seemed surprised that I had not seen you." she shouted at him.

The earl looked at her in amazement. Never had he seen her so furious, and, angry now himself, he refused to admit the truth of her words. His silence infuriated her even more.

"You've become so enmeshed in the political intrigues of your fellow barons, you care only for advantageous alliances for our children. Had I been a Douglas bride rather than a distant Kilburn cousin, what sort of wonderful marriages could you arrange for our other two children?" she spat out at him.

She was beyond caring what she said, conscious only of a great desire to wound him. Jamie's lips whitened with fury and he grabbed her arms, shaking her until her eyes widened in sudden fear.

"You accused me of this before, Gillian, and I'll not tolerate it. I love you more deeply and passionately now than in those years when I near went out of my mind with wanting you. You are mine . . . as I am yours. Not only your body but your soul belongs to me, as mine do to you, and no one will ever stand between us. No one! But the future of my children is something I alone will decide, unless the matter is such that an instant decision is impossible." His face was grim. "And you can be glad that Alain is betrothed to Alianor Fitzalan."

He released her, the fire slowly fading from the long

hazel eyes. Gillian backed away from him, rubbing her arms where his hands had gripped her. Mutely she watched him pour wine from a fine pewter flagon set on the large carved wooden chest into a crystal mazer she had brought from Glairn. Emptying it in one draught, he refilled it to the brim. She had never seen him drink so much, and an old fear stirred faintly in a corner of her mind, remembering the nightmare nights of her first marriage.

As he held the empty mazer in his hand, Jamie desired above all else to sink into the steaming hot water which stood waiting for him in the large wooden tub before the fireplace. It had been a long, exhausting day and he had no stomach for doing battle with Gillian. He stripped off his clothes, refusing to say another word as he stepped into the soothing bath. Gillian quietly lit candles set into a large round metal stand placed against the wall opposite the hearth and the tall slender tapers suspended in holders on either side of the wide bed. The bright luminous light cast strange flickering shadows on the chamber's walls and Gillian watched with fascination as her ordinary movements took on an eerie grotesqueness.

She finally sat down at the small dressing table and began to brush her hair, afraid to look at Jamie. The mirror reflected her eyes, enormous in a face suddenly pinched and white. She could feel her heart hammering painfully in her breast as she thought of the words they had shouted at each other. Jamie bathed quietly. She could faintly hear the splash of water against the wooden sides of the tub. She put down her brush, struggling with her pride, but deciding to make the first gesture, she rose and went to her lord as he lay with his eyes closed, his weary body immersed in the still steaming water. She knelt by him, disturbed by his weary gauntness. Although his face was turned from her, she could see that his mouth was still set in an angry line. Taking the bar of fresh scented soap from his hand, she began to wash his hair, feeling its softness as her hands touched him. It was a ritual they both usually enjoyed, for he had always refused to have servants aid him with his bathing. Pouring clear water from an ewer over his head, she rinsed out the soap so that his bright hair glistened in the firelight. Some of the water splashed over her shift, but she paid little attention to it, his final words suddenly penetrating her mind.

"Why should I be glad about Alain's betrothal?" she asked tremulously, breaking the silence between them, but was totally unprepared for the blazing eyes turned on her. She shrank from him, for this was a stranger she had never seen before.

"Would you rather I had accepted Roger de Mortimer's offer of a daughter? Aye, you may stare at me . . . I saw Roger in London. He's returned in triumph from Ireland, and all England is at his feet. He's feeling extremely confident and arrogant at the moment. Besides wanting Alain he even entertained the possibility of an alliance with Margaret for one of his sons!"

"Nay, Jamie . . ." The very idea was odious to her.

James continued glaring at her. De Mortimer's visit had left him bitter and uneasy, filling him with a vague suspicion that there was more to Roger's words than he had first thought. He had seen the hard arrogance and selfish ruthlessness as the dangerous qualities Gillian instinctively had recognized in him from the start. In his weariness, resentment against Gillian's sharper perception rose within him.

"Nay, Jamie, never a de Mortimer . . . please."

"Had I not previously accepted Arundel or Bardestour, what could I have said?" he asked her coldly as he rose dripping from the tub. Picking up a large towel from the settle, he dried himself vigorously before the fire.

Gillian walked away from him, her hair hanging about her like a gleaming mantle. Her damp shift clung to her body as she peered out again into the darkness. She gripped the stone casement tightly and pushed the window open wider with her other hand. The night air was cold against her skin. Perhaps I'll catch a chill and die! she thought wildly in her misery.

"Do what you wish—as you told me, 'tis man's business anyway," she said with a cool indifference she did not feel. "Would what I believe or want ever enter into a matter like this? Why should you bother to even ask if the match would please me?"

At her words, Jamie was consumed by a blind rage. Throwing the towel down furiously, he was beside her in two steps, spinning her around roughly.

"Don't ever say that to me again, Gillian. Never has a man been more mindful of his wife than I—and 'tis not natural nor meet for you to even say it."

"Mindful, Jamie? Not where our children are concerned. Ours, Jamie, our children . . . not yours!"

He stifled a sudden urge to strike her, for she had pushed him beyond endurance. She was like ice in his hands, her mind focused on her laughing, carefree children. Why could they have no say in choosing their marriage partners within their own world. Gillian thought of Isabella, married to a man who cared naught for her, lavishing all his royal love and affection on men who were willing to pander themselves to his whims. But Isabella was the daughter of a king, and what choice had she had save what she was told? Had she and Jamie not both suffered because of the horrendous custom of bartering one's sons and daughters for political reasons or financial gain? Their love had been stronger than any convention, and while she regretted nothing, she had no wish to place her children in the same situation. Why could he not have waited until Alain and Margaret were of an age of awareness, Gillian asked herself bitterly. She was filled with angry indignation at Jamie and struggled to free herself. Again she was overcome by the feeling that he was a stranger to her, wondering whether it was all the wine he had drunk that brought out a cruelty and hardness in him she had not thought in his nature. He would not release her, drawing her to him instead.

"Never a de Mortimer, Jamie, do you hear me? 'Tis a family conceived by Satan!"

Seeing the dark blue eyes harden and the mouth with its sensuous curve set into a stubborn line, his fury broke its restraints.

She fought him, remembering de Mortimer with sick loathing. James's grip tightened, frustrating her attempt to escape from his frightening fury. Stinging pain flamed hotly through him as she raked his chest with her nails in desperation. He captured her hands, holding them fast behind her back, aware in spite of his rage of the soft body pressed against his nakedness. The hysterical anger which poured from her kindled a black, mindless desire in him to subdue her. Perhaps it was his weariness from the journey and the tension of the confrontation with de Mortimer or the effects of the mulled wine too copiously and too quickly consumed, but he continued to abuse her unmercifully, denying the wild accusations she flung at him. Never before had he treated her so roughly and the realization shattered her anger, leaving an overpowering fear in its wake. She clawed and kicked at him, defending herself with all the strength she possessed, as he lost himself in a tempest of fury. Her struggles steeled his resolve and he held her now frantic body against his as if his strength would bend her to his will.

"Vixen!" he hissed, seeing the large eyes swamped with panic. Her body twisted in his grasp and he felt the silk cloth of her shift tear beneath his hands. He found her mouth, forcing her lips to part under the unrelenting pressure of his own and tasted blood as she sank her teeth into him, determined not to surrender herself to him. Trying to hold her as she bent back to elude him, his hand closed over a bare breast and the round, pliant softness of the silken flesh with its nipple hardening beneath his fingers released a wild desire for her he could not control. She saw the change in him and renewed her efforts to escape as the edge of the bed pressed against her thighs.

"Nay, Jamie . . . not this way, please . . ." she begged him, for never had he taken her in aught but love. Gillian felt the heat of his aroused body as his mouth renewed its assault on hers, stifling her cries. And still she fought him, slashing him with her nails until his skin bled, wildly praying that the pain would bring him to his senses.

And then he was a part of her, vanquishing her angry disillusionment. Suddenly naught existed for her save the man who was awakening deep within her being a shimmering, consuming passion which in all their years of love she had never experienced. In that one shattering moment, Gillian lost the battle to retain her identity, but it did not matter any longer. She ignited in Jamie's arms, her body opening to his totally, lifting feverishly to him as if attempting to draw the very life from him. She cried out his name over and over while tears streamed down her face in response to her body's ecstatic betrayal. Holding her tightly to him, sanity and sobriety slowly returned as Jamie was brought to the awesome realization of what their mutual rage had done to them. For a moment Gillian's stricken eyes stared into his and then slowly closed as her arms, which had clung so tightly about him, loosened their hold. She never felt the pillow placed beneath her head nor the blanket he drew over her.

The large shaggy wolfhound lifted his head sleepily and watched as Jamie slipped from between the curtains of the bed. The dog had somehow pushed the chamber door ajar during the night and, finding the fire still burning in the hearth, had stretched out before it. When the woman joined him a short time later, he had pressed his head eagerly against her thigh, contemplating her with his large brown eyes. He edged closer to her, wanting to ease the deep sadness he felt surround her. Gillian found a small measure of comfort in stroking the warm gray fur and scratching the animal gently behind his ears. She could not stop trembling as awareness slowly returned to her. Crouching by the hearth, she leaned against its warm stones. Jamie was a stranger . . . the man she loved and had lived for since childhood had been possessed with such an insane rage that she had not known him. The gentle hazel eyes had blazed with a green fire cold as the heart of an emerald. Yet, had she not also responded with a quickening desire for him? Her body had received his with an insatiability which had finally terrified her as her reason once more returned.

Now she felt Jamie's hands move over her wildly tangled hair, and she shrank from him as he knelt by her side. Disturbed, the wolfhound lumbered to the other side of the hearth and settled down, choosing to ignore them. Gillian unconsciously drew the shreds of her torn shift about her as Jamie quietly pulled her into his arms. Fearfully, she raised her eyes to his face, but the frightening stranger had disappeared. The long-lashed eyes beneath their arched dark brows had returned her gaze solemnly.

Gillian started to cry bitterly as he pressed gentle kisses on her face and hands, filled with remorse for what had happened between them.

"Whatever you fear about de Mortimer, my darling, I promise you that Glairn will never be allied with him—never."

His voice was low but held an urgency that penetrated Gillian's inner turmoil.

"I love you more than my life, Gillian. There's naught I can say for tonight save that I was a fool . . . a drunken fool filled with his own accomplishments." His mouth touched a bruise on her shoulder.

"I'm sorry, Jamie. It was my fault as well . . . I shouldn't have spoken as I did. My anger caused me to say terrible things to you. I never meant to go so far!" Gillian stared tearfully at the angry welts on his chest, seeing them for the first time. "Oh, sweet Virgin, what madness made me do that to you?" When she touched them, he winced with pain. "Those gashes must be attended to now. I've some salve in the small leather coffer by the bed." She tried to rise but he held her back.

" 'Twill be a reminder to me that my northern rose has thorns," he said wryly. "Nay, love, it can wait till morning." He stared searchingly into the large haunted eyes until she felt her heart move within her and her mouth lifted fiercely to his. He held her tightly, fearing to let her go. Never had they been so totally separate as in their anger toward each other, and never had they come together with such furious, insane passion. They sat together quietly, their souls merging in the mystic bond which flowed between them. Gillian felt his lips on her temple, and was suddenly gripped by a dreadful sense of foreboding, as if this night had somehow placed them on a dangerous path neither had contemplated treading.

"Jamie . . ." Her voice was hesitant and trembling. "Tonight . . . never has it been like this before . . ." She felt his arms tighten about her. "There will be another child," she whispered. " 'Tis there . . . it's happened, I know it!"

"Aye, lovely, somehow 'tis something I know too," he replied quietly.

She searched his face, seeing that he was not humoring her. He put his hand on her body gently, his eyes strangely opaque in the firelight. Her foreboding returned.

"I'm afraid! Something dreadful will happen . . . I feel it! Jamie, I don't want to bear a child conceived in anger."

Gillian clung to him and he tried to calm her, uneasy over her premonition. For the moment there was but one solution.

"I'm taking you home, lovedy . . . 'tis time we both see our children again . . . and Glairn, sweetheart—home!"

The sudden call of a nightbird came through the open window and they heard the wind soughing through the trees surrounding the manor. In time the marks from Gillian's nails would disappear and the ugly bruises fade from her body, but the memory of that bitter, passionate night would stay with them to shadow many nights to come.

Cousin Thomas of Lancaster was in utter disgrace, and the barons were in a fury, while the realm lay stunned beneath another catastrophic defeat at the hands of Robert Bruce. The king, surrounded by his courtiers and his advisor, Hugh Despenser, and Despenser's son Hugh the younger, at his side, listened with great relish to the tales of Lancaster's inept generalship which had given the Scots the chance for a sweeping drive into England. The abbeys and monasteries were particularly easy game, lying for the most part open and undefended—ripe with the riches of centuries. They fell with little difficulty into the invader's hands. England's folk once more faced famine and disease as the aftermath of defeat. Unrest grew in all parts of the land, erupting in open rebellion which, while quickly suppressed by force, smoldered and refused to die. Self-proclaimed uncrowned king of England, Thomas of Lancaster soon learned that ambition and ability were not necessarily inseparable.

Aymer de Valence, already heartsick at the events brought about by the greed, ambition, and stupidity of the barons who constituted the faction opposing the crown, at last began to speak out openly for moderation. As James

Kilburn had predicted to Roger de Mortimer, the great lords of the realm began to flock one by one to Pembroke's banner. John de Warenne and his brother-in-law, Arundel, formed the nucleus of those Lords Ordainers more kindly disposed toward Edward. Returning from Ireland, Roger, with his uncle of Chirk and several of the other Marcher barons, decided to support Pembroke's proposal of a middle party. Reluctant as always to ally himself with any faction, Kilburn wanted to believe in the sanity of Pembroke's actions. He had seen too much of Lancaster's bungling—how the land was laid waste through the blind, black hatred between countries unable to come to terms with each other.

When he received word that the earl of Pembroke was requesting all the barons and earls of equal mind to gather at Leicester in April of 1318 for a series of meetings to lay the foundations for the formation of a middle party whose main role it would be to bring the king and his cousin of Lancaster together once more on amicable terms, Kilburn was still not sure that Pembroke's plan would work.

He hesitated in part to leave Glairn, since the Scots had begun their spring raiding earlier than usual. In order to keep the enemies on their own side of the border, he joined young Henry de Percy and several other border lords at Alnwick Castle and, with their combined forces, staged several raids beyond the border into Scotland. Making lightning forays for the most part, they learned to be as elusive as their adversaries. While many of the lords gave their men full rein to pillage and loot in the already ravaged countryside and to rape and brutalize the terrified women who fled from burning crofts into the woods, Kilburn kept strict discipline among his own forces. They rode westward, leaving a trail of devastation and burned-out crofts and villages behind them, finally sweeping over Douglas lands. With savage bitterness, Kilburn came to the holdings once held by his grandfather and rightfully his own through inheritance but taken from him by his cousin, James, the Black Douglas. Surprising himself, he drew back, sickened by the sight of what should have been his put to the torch. Astride his black destrier at the edge of the forest overlooking the rolling, cleared meadowlands, Kilburn watched the flames lick at the pale green, delicate young spears of grain just beginning to come to life in the black tilled earth of the fields. He dismounted and, drawing off a gauntlet, dug his hand into the dark soil, feeling the moist richness of the spring earth flow between his fingers. The acrid smoke of the burning fields reached him, and he was filled with a helpless anger at the senseless futility of their actions.

This was his land—the land his grandfather and his Douglas ancestors before him had possessed. His hand remained as if rooted in the soil as he knelt wishing desperately for an end to the destructive warring. He was an Englishman, an earl of the realm, and yet the half of him that was Scottish he refused to deny.

He withdrew his men following the raid, telling Lord de Percy that he had urgent business in the south. It was then he decided to commit himself to Pembroke and his middle party. Perhaps in the clever and shrewd thinking of that lord he would find an answer to his own needs. But more troubled him than the political situation of the border country. He felt uneasy about leaving Gillian behind. Although she had bidden him good speed and a safe journey with a gentle smile and insisted that he put all concern for her from his mind, he could not, thoughts of her intruding constantly.

True to her premonition, she was pregnant, and while she never complained, almost from the first she tired easily and sometimes drew within herself where none could reach her. Master Brassard was worried and not a little angry, for he had already shown deep disapproval over the short span of time between the births of Hugh and Jennifer. When he confirmed Gillian's state, he spoke sharply and plainly to both of them, telling them without his usual careful courtesy that this child should never even have been conceived. Bearing children yearly, the French physician firmly, believed was the reason so many mothers died in childbirth.

That night, at their camp in a small meadow by the roadside, Kilburn saw to it that his knights were settled down in their tents and the guards posted to keep watch before he finally stretched out on his cot. He drained a cup of wine and watched the glow from the burning braziers turn the chain mail of his hauberk into gold as it hung on the sturdy canvas wall of the large red and gold pavilion.

Dear merciful Saviour, how he had dreaded leaving Gillian, he thought, his mind returning to the last evening at home. He had spent hours in his small study with his constable, Simon Jardine, and his steward, Master Blount, into whose hands he entrusted the keeping of Glairn. When Master Brassard requested a word with him, he agreed, although he had groaned inwardly, for he was tired and wanted only to spend the remaining hours with Gillian. Declining the goblet of wine offered him, the Frenchman leaned toward the earl, his long, sallow face serious and troubled. They spoke in general terms of the health of the household and of the Kilburn children. Then, to the earl's surprise, the older man began to speak of his first encounter with Gillian at Windsor Castle, when she had been Lady de Broze and a favorite of the queen. Barely out of girlhood, Gillian had carried her lord's child without benefit of any physician's counseling, ashamed to reveal the bruises and other abuses inflicted upon her by her husband. In icy tones, James Kilburn ordered the physician to stop talking about those days, for his hatred for the Gascon still could flare fresh and hot within him.

"Nay, my lord, you misunderstand me," the Frenchman said quietly. "When the queen asked that I tend to her lady-in-waiting, Lady Gillian was dying . . . the child already dead within her. I will not horrify you with medical descriptions, but luckily, she survived my ministrations, and to my own surprise, was still able to bear children. However, the dreadful manner of the loss of her child did leave its scars, much of them in her mind and her soul. Too little is known of the effects of physical ordeals on the mind, but I believe many of the wounds dealt her during the days of her unfortunate marriage have never truly healed, although she has tried to forget them. While she wishes to give you children, Lady Gillian also has a tendency to fight the simple process of birth, making it doubly perilous. Mistress Non has told me that young Alain's

166

birth was a difficult one when it should not have been, and I need not remind you how close both she and the little maid Margaret came to death during those dreadful hours in York. Only your strength and love saved her then." The physician shrugged his shoulders and frowned unhappily. "Hugh's birth was normal in every way, but your lady was not ready to bear another child so soon after him."

"Master Brassard, you've told me this before. You lectured me at great length over Jennifer's birth . . . I'm not a stupid man, nor an insensitive one, and I do listen and understand your meaning. But there are things about me you have no knowledge of, nor will you have." Kilburn was annoyed and not a little discomfited, for this was women's talk, not men's, and he resented the Frenchman's continuous cautioning.

"Do you wish to lose your wife, Lord Kilburn? Yes, my lord, I'll be that honest and direct with you, for 'tis that simple. She is not strong this time, and also seems most unhappy over carrying this child."

The physician saw a strange expression cross the earl's face and linger in the long hazel eyes. He hesitated, debating with himself, but finally drew a vial from the leather pouch at his waist. Holding it between thumb and index finger, he showed it to Kilburn.

"Do you know what this is, my lord? Agnes found it quite by accident hidden beneath the countess's linen. 'Tis an infusion of hemlock!"

"But that's poison!" Kilburn whispered, shocked by the physician's words. Gillian had no reason to seek death!

"True, but only in certain quantities and forms. This fortunately would have only made her ill." Master Brassard returned the vial to his pouch. "I confronted your lady with it and she confessed to me that she had indeed taken it from my pharmacy in a moment of utter desperation, hoping to possibly cause a miscarriage."

"Nay, good physician, I'll never believe that!"

"Ask her yourself," the elderly man said in an even tone. "You'll find that she doesn't want this child."

Sweet Jesu, what price will we pay for our wild, baseless rage, Kilburn asked himself silently, burying his head in his hands. He certainly could not tell Master Brassard the truth for Gillian's unhappiness and obvious desperation, but he saw now that she still clung to her foreboding about this child. Realizing how his words had upset the earl, the Frenchman rose and reached for the stick he used to aid him in his walking. He set his red physician's cap upon his graying hair and it made a bright splash of color in the dimly lit chamber.

"Your lady will bear her babe, my lord. She's too far now to rid herself of it. But I must warn you that this may be her last child!"

The news had been very difficult to accept, and yet, Kilburn admitted to himself that the relationship had not truly been the same between them since that night in Hurley. Kilburn faced her with Master Brassard's revelations later when they lay together in the large bed, the velvet curtains enclosing them in their private world. Turning to him, she put her arms about him and he felt her tears against his cheek.

"Jamie, I'd not have done it, I swear to you! No matter what I fear, 'tis still our child. But I'm so afraid . . . if only I knew why I have this terrible dread of what is yet to be."

Feeling the child move within her, James caressed her with loving hands, reassuring her again that he loved her above aught else in life and that this child, too, was an affirmation of their love. She fell asleep in his arms, fitting herself to him as she always did, her head buried in his shoulder, while Jamie lay awake, her loose hair a silken pillow for his cheek, knowing that he would be leaving her in the morning and suddenly as convinced by her forebodings as she was.

The bells of St. Paul's Cathedral rang out joyously as the churchyard began to fill with barons from all over the realm. Entering through the gate from Bowyer Row, they walked through the churchyard toward Paul's Cross, a wooden cross used as a gathering place for malcontents, a pulpit for royal proclamations, papal bulls, and the settlement of grievances. The barons and knights in full regalia, each with a surcoat ablaze with his own family arms, made an impressive and colorful sight. The streets leading to the great cathedral were packed with folk clamoring to catch a glimpse of the powerful lords who ruled England. Some passed through the gates amidst loud cheers and friendly banter from the London citizenry, and others were greeted by a dark, sullen silence as they dismounted. The people of London were exercising that special freedom of expression denied many others in England less fortunate.

After weeks of discussions in Leicester relating to the middle party and its increasing number of adherents, Pembroke had managed to have Lancaster invited to attend the next Parliament. This was no easy accomplishment, for first Pembroke needed to persuade the king and his councillors to agree. The earl, with his talent for diplomacy, then persuaded Lancaster and his adherents to enter into a treaty at Leake, in Nottinghamshire, which once more strengthened the power of the Lords Ordainers, brought into being when Piers Gaveston had caused such chaos among the realm's baronacy.

In order to seal the truce, the earl of Pembroke, along with the earls of Hereford, Surrey, and Arundel, had arranged a love day, to be held, as was the tradition, in the churchyard of St. Paul's Cathedral in London. Kilburn, by now deeply involved in the political machinations behind Pembroke's newly formed party, had arrived in the company of the earl's staunchest adherents. He stood near the cross with Edmund Fitzalan, watching with great interest the arrival of a young lord of perhaps eighteen years. He was tall, handsome, and with that special fairness which most Plantagenets shared.

"'Tis Thomas Brotherton, of Norfolk, James, the eldest of the two sons of our first Edward's old age." Arundel's eyes twinkled. "He's not only the king's half-brother, but our queen's own cousin—as is our good cousin Lancaster. Their mothers were sisters!" He laughed, knowing of no other way to lessen the confusion, and added with a hint of malice in his pleasant voice, "What an incestuous lot we are!"

Kilburn stole another look at the exceedingly fair young man, for the earl of Norfolk was rarely seen. The youthful queen dowager had kept both her sons by her side, living quietly in the country away from the attention of Edward's court. When she died the previous year, still grieving, some said, for her royal husband, even her stepson had wept over her passing, for Marguerite, sister to the dead King Philip of France, had been greatly loved.

A fanfare of trumpets caused all eyes to turn in another direction as the barons of Chirk and Wigmore arrived. A coldness settled within James as he looked at the arrogant dark head towering over the crowd.

"God's blood—here come the de Mortimers! They cause as much stir as the king's entrance!" Edmund exclaimed. "I hear Roger did not cover himself with glory this time in Ireland and was sent home in disgrace. He has openly vowed to devote himself to making life as uncomfortable for the younger Despenser as possible, since they covet the same holdings in Wales. And of course, his uncle Roger of Chirk always agrees with his nephew! They're a damned clannish family!"

Eyes blank, Kilburn turned toward Edmund and over his shoulder saw Aymer de Valence approach. His hauberk covered by a long ceremonial surcoat of blue and white striped linen, he looked taller and thinner than ever. His great sword hung from a wide, richly and ornately tooled leather belt tightly buckled about his narrow waist.

"I've just had word that the king is making his way along Chepesyde with great panoply and that Lancaster proceeds along Flete Street, surrounded by his advisers and men-at-arms. The townfolk are treating this entire matter as some public holiday—shops closed, apprentices allowed to roam about. The ferrymen on the Thames are charging double their usual fares to bring visitors over from Southwark and Lambeth. 'Tis sheer madness. Would that this day were at an end."

"Aye, we all agree to that, Aymer, but let's pray that the peace will be a lasting one."

Kilburn looked at the pale, gaunt face with its prominent hawk's nose and the silver-streaked black hair. How long had it been since he had seen Pembroke smile, he wondered. Looking beyond the two men, James's eyes suddenly met those of Roger de Mortimer. He nodded in polite greeting and de Mortimer said something to his uncle which made the older man laugh as he stared at Kilburn. He's trying to provoke me, Kilburn realized and turned back toward Arundel, ignoring de Mortimer's sudden scowl.

The royal banner came into view, and while Edward dismounted outside the churchyard, there were shouts and hooting from the onlookers for both the king and Lancaster. Edward was clad, as were all the barons, in battle dress—hauberk, leg armor, long ceremonial surcoat bearing his own Plantagenet arms—and the sword at his side was held about his waist with a belt studded with gems. The sun shone on his uncovered head, turning the wheat-colored hair into gold. He had lately begun to wear a beard, and it successfully masked the weakness in his handsome face from those who did not know him well. Tall, with the body of an athlete, he presented an impressive figure. For once, the Despensers had wisely decided to stay in the background, so when the king faced his self-avowed mortal enemy, all eyes were focused on the two men. Thomas of Lancaster, nephew to the first Edward, was slightly shorter than his royal cousin and not so fair, but the Plantagenet resemblance was strong between them. Clasping each other's gauntleted hands, they leaned forward and gave each other the kiss of peace while a great roar of approval rose from the assemblage.

While the bells still rang out joyously, the doors to the cathedral opened wide, and the bishops of Wells, Norwich, Chichester, and Winchester led the way, bearing a large gold cross studded with precious jewels and tall lighted candles, as the king, the earl of Lancaster, followed closely by Thomas Brotherton of Norfolk, and all those who had attended the love day, entered the cathedral to offer their prayers for a lasting peace among the factions now firmly united through the earl of Pembroke's middle party.

Seated between Edmund Fitzalan and his brother-in-law, John de Warenne, James Kilburn listened to the intonations of the mass while the golden censers swung vigorously to perfume the summer air. For once the barons and earls were united, although less than happy faces could be seen throughout the crowded nave. It was an auspicious day, but as the mass wore on and the candles flickered and flared, illuminating the carved figures of saints and heads and bodies of cherubim supporting the old pilasters, James began to feel increasingly uneasy. The same sense of foreboding he had felt when he parted from Gillian returned and an odd sensation of pain swept over him. He heard her voice call out to him and grew pale as sweat began to pour down his face.

"James, what's wrong? Are you ill?" He heard Arundel's concerned voice from a distance, for his spirit was torn with pain.

He shook his head, murmuring to his friend, " 'Tis naught but the incense. 'Twas always troublesome to me."

Excusing himself, he managed to slip out of the cathedral without drawing too much attention. Standing on the side porch of the cathedral, taking deep gulps of air, he knew that he had to return to Glairn immediately. As she had done before, Gillian was calling to him, desperate and in great pain, spanning the distance between them. Answering her in his mind, he hammered his fists against the cold, uncaring stones of the church, filled with a frantic, terrifying need to reach her, and knowing that no matter how quickly he rode, he would arrive too late to be of help to her.

The drawn-back bed hangings slowly began to come into focus, the deep folds of the heavy velvet casting strange shadows on the draped ceiling. Gillian moved her head carefully and saw three golden shafts of sunlight stream through the window divided by its fluted stone columns. For a moment her weariness pressed down upon her, dulling her mind.

"My lady, see the bonnie lassie ye've gi'en the Laird . . ."

Gillian turned her gaze toward Non's cheerful voice and saw that the old woman's face was wreathed in smiles. Memory flooded through her and she closed her eyes.

"I don't want to see her . . . take her away!"

"My lady!" Non was shocked and stared disbelievingly at the drained white face framed by smooth dark hair which now lay in two neat plaits over the coverlet.

"Oh, Non—please let me be . . ." Gillian whispered and tears began to trickle from the corners of her closed eyes.

Never had she been so wracked by pain, hour after relentless hour, while she felt the strength slowly ebb from her straining body as she held back the screams which rose in her throat. They had placed her on the birthing couch, braziers alive with red coals placed all about her. Sponging her naked, sweat-drenched body with cool water faintly smelling of vinegar, Non soothed her with meaningless crooning until Master Brassard pushed the old woman aside with barely concealed impatience. Gillian looked at him with pain-glazed eyes.

"Gillian, scream if it will help—don't hold it back, it only makes you tense and the pains stronger. Breathe deeply . . . that's right . . ." Her hands reached out for him as another spasm shook her, and he held them tightly until a gasp escaped her and her grip weakened. His lined face was more serious than she had ever seen it before.

"Master . . . please, I can't take it any longer . . . the pain!" Tears streamed down her face. "I want to die—please let me die!"

"Nay, my child, we will not allow that," he replied sternly as Agnes came toward the couch behind her father and poured more water into the basin. When she tried to bathe Gillian's face, she was pushed away by the laboring, panting woman. Non and Eilys, sitting by the hearth folding cloths, watched the physician bend over Gillian again.

"Is there nothing you can do to ease her pain, Father? There seems to be no end to her labor . . ."

"I don't like it," the physician muttered to himself as he rummaged through the large wooden coffer containing his medicines. "Not once has she called for Lord Kilburn—she's taking the pain to herself. I warned them . . . I warned them both, but she needs must supply her lord with children, and he gladly obliges." He was worried and angry at his own seeming helplessness and did not notice Agnes's scandalized expression. "If this continues,

I must take the child from her. If only the earl were here . . . I must have his consent."

Reaching into the coffer, he removed a small flask of a yellowish liquid. Mixing a small measure of it with a quarter cup of wine which Non brought to him, they forced Gillian to drink it.

" 'Tis the water distilled from gillyflowers, my child, and mixed with a pinch of powdered mandrake root. 'Twill ease your pain for a while." Master Brassard smoothed the strands of wet hair from her forehead and laid her down again on the narrow, hard couch. Lying there, feeling a strange numbness flood through her at last, Gillian watched the elderly Frenchman as from a distance. He looked like an old crow in his black robes, she thought, and it seemed to her that he spread his robes like wings and began to fly about the ceiling. A beam of pale sunlight suddenly fell across her distended body and she saw with little interest that another day had dawned. How long had it been since the pain began? Why couldn't she remember? She moved her head restlessly . . . she felt so wet . . . Lifting a hand to touch herself, she pulled away the damp, tangled hair snaking over her naked, swollen breasts. Naked, Gillian realized dimly—she was lying before all their eyes with naught to cover her nakedness. Did it truly matter what they thought of her shamelessness? For a moment she had forgotten why she was stretched out on the uncomfortable couch while Non, Eilys, and Agnes hovered over her and Master Brassard stood at the foot, waiting. Waiting for what?

Then a knife suddenly thrust itself once more through her vitals, and another followed close behind the first. Sweet heavenly Mother, deliver me from this pain, she prayed, memory breaking into her drugged mind. A scream escaped her as searing, unbearable agony flooded her being, blocking out all other thoughts. She felt Master Brassard's hands press against her as her screams echoed through the overheated chamber. Agnes and Eilys held her, encouraging her, and she fought them as a tremendous wave of rage shook her. Rage at herself, rage at the child who was causing her all this agony, and rage at the fate which had placed her on this couch of flaming pain.

"Jamie!" she shrieked, tearing wildly at the two women, straining to rid herself of her painful burden. "Oh God, Jamie . . . please help me! Jamie . . . where are you?" she called, wanting his arms about her, to feel his strength bolster hers. Another scream rose, bursting from her as Agnes, following her father's instructions, held her tightly. Eilys wept for her as Gillian's fingers closed over her arm with a grip of iron. "Jamie . . ."

"Gillian . . , my love!" she heard her name called softly from a great distance—Jamie's voice. "Gillian, I know . . . we're one, my darling . . . 'twill be all right. I'm with you . . ." and she felt mailed fists batter at the pain, pushing it from her.

The babe's wail drifted through the chamber, but Gillian was oblivious to it. She had finally called out for Jamie and he had answered her. Placing her gently on the great bed, Master Brassard observed his lady's sleeping face, at peace, with a slight smile curved on the sensuous mouth, and wondered again at the force that could span leagues to link the earl and his lady.

"Shall we call her Mathilde, after your mother?" Kilburn asked, sitting in his old chair by the hearth, watching as the infant's tiny hands pressed against Gillian's full breast, the small dark head cradled in her arm. "Somehow 'tis fitting, for of all our children, she resembles you the most."

Gillian, seated opposite him on the settle, did not answer him, her attention fixed on her daughter pulling painfully and greedily at her breast. It was strange, she thought, that the babe had been given unsuccessfully to a succession of wet nurses, unhappy and wailing endlessly with unsatisfied hunger until Master Brassard, fearing for its life, had put it in its mother's arms. Instinctively seeking for its source of nourishment, the tiny infant suckled eagerly, content finally to lie peacefully against Gillian's breast while she waited for the love to stir within her that she had felt so overwhelmingly for Alain and Margaret. The same love had welled within her for both Hugh and Jennifer when they were placed in her arms as she still lay on the birthing couch. Her one regret had

175

been the custom, which she had finally resigned herself to, that high-ranking ladies did not nurse their children, giving them the freedom to travel about the countryside with their lords.

But she felt nothing at all toward this new child. Nay, that was not quite true, she told herself, looking up suddenly and catching an expression of total, rapturous love on Jamie's face as he contemplated his daughter. She felt a stab of jealousy—surprised again by the unexpected reaction to his obvious adoration of the infant.

She could not know that when the babe was placed in his arms and he saw the dark hair and small features so like Gillian's, his heart had swelled with a love that was different from the love he held for his other children. He brushed his lips lightly against a round cheek soft as silk and her eyes opened, large and blue. Something stirred deep within him as he looked into those eyes—Gillian's eyes. He was bewitched.

He rose from his chair and seated himself beside Gillian. She was still looking at the babe, a strangely unreadable expression on her face. Upon his return two days before, Master Brassard had told him of the difficulties Gillian had suffered and that there indeed would be no more children. Oddly enough, she had taken the news calmly, almost indifferently, but then he also admitted to the earl that she seemed to take very little interest in the new child. Gazing at her with troubled eyes, Jamie found her still drawn and too pale, but now, nearly a month after the birth, she was beginning to once more return to her duties as chatelaine of Glairn.

"Lovedy—did you hear me?" he asked her, putting a finger beneath her chin to lift her face to his. Her dark blue eyes rested on him, not truly seeing him. Her mind was still on her children, and then she smiled, the gentle, sweet features full of love for him. "Shall we call her Mathilde?"

As he repeated his question, he leaned over and picked up a small hand which still rested against Gillian's breast, holding it in his own, marveling at the perfection of the five tiny fingers.

Gillian frowned. Mathilde had been her mother's

name . . . the mother she had loved so much and had lost too young—whose death had also brought Jamie into her life.

"If it gives you pleasure to call her so, Jamie, I'll not argue the choice."

He laughed. " 'Tis not an order, my lady, merely a suggestion, for she does favor your family more than mine." He cupped her chin and kissed her mouth, soft and pliant against his, drawing back with a start as the door opened suddenly and Non bustled into the chamber.

"God's blood, Mistress, can't you ever knock?" Kilburn asked irritably.

"I'd nae thought ye'd be here, Laird, with all ye must do after sae lang an absence!" Non retorted, unfazed by his displeasure. "I've come for the wee nameless lassie . . ."

Disapproval stamped on her wrinkled face, she took the child from Gillian, wrapping it in a large shawl. Kilburn laughed at her temerity.

"Nameless no longer, Non! She's to be called Mathilde!"

He lifted his daughter from the nurse's arms for a moment, taking a last look at this, to him, very special babe, for it was as if he had recaptured the child Gillian. "My Maddie, my heart's love," he murmured, and Gillian's eyes filled with guilty tears as jealousy coursed through her again.

" 'Tis a fine name." Non remarked. Retrieving the child from her father, she disappeared through the door leading to the robing chamber where a small nursery had temporarily been installed. James turned toward Gillian and saw her tears with surprise.

"Lovedy, you're exhausted . . . 'tis time you were in bed."

He picked her up and carried her to the large bed, helping her remove her chamber robe before drawing the coverlet over her. The servants had long been dismissed by Kilburn, and other than Non's interruption, they had spent a quiet evening together. She lay propped up on large, soft pillows, watching as he loosened the ties of the bed hangings so that the curtains were only partially drawn.

As he stripped off his garments, Gillian realized how little he had changed from when he had first brought her to Glairn. For her it had been a night when Jamie's love totally erased the shame and degradation of the loss of her virginity at the hands of a man to whom she never should have been given. Standing near the hearth's warmth, long-muscled and slim-hipped, he was still hard and lean, not coarsening as so many men did when they neared their fortieth year. She felt a pang as he turned toward her, the white scar of the spear-thrust he suffered at Bannockburn marring the pale skin. There were scars from wounds received in other battles, but this one was a reminder of not only all that he had lost, but what they had gained as well. Her love for him was as deep and overwhelming as when he had first kindled it so many years ago. Yet, something had changed, come between them, and her sense of joyous peace at his return was marred.

His gaze turned toward Gillian, as if divining her thoughts, and she said almost shyly, " 'Tis strange to find ourselves totally alone."

"Aye, I've been away far too long, and there's much to be seen to in the next few days. I decided that tonight would be completely ours—without benefit of Hal, Agnes, or any of the other servants." James's face was somber, the firelight accentuating the hollows beneath his high cheekbones and the straight, narrow nose. His chestnut hair gleamed brightly as he slipped into bed, breathing a sigh of relief as he stretched his long frame on the crisp, freshly laundered sheets. "Unfortunately, I must also see to my other holdings. Master Blount suggested that I should leave in two weeks."

"Two weeks! Oh, Jamie, you've just returned to me!" Gillian wailed softly, moving into his arms. "Take me with you," she whispered, feeling his body awaken as she moved against him.

"Lovedy," he chided her gently, "you forget Maddie . . . she needs you now more than I!"

She pulled away from him, pushing his caressing hand petulantly from her breast. It ached from the babe's hungry assaults. Already his new daughter was first in his

178

mind, she thought spitefully. Amazed at her reaction and sudden withdrawal, he rose and lit the small oil lamp beside the bed. She was turned from him, the smooth, slender line of her back somehow indicating her hurt disapproval at his words.

He knelt on the bed and quietly turned her around. She lay on her back, staring up at him mutely, the large eyes haunted—seeing something in his face he could not fathom.

"What is it, Gillian? Why this child? She's beautiful and perfect in every way . . . as are all our children! Sweetheart, she is our last child. Don't let anything happen to her because of our selfish need and desire for each other."

Her eyes closed and she held her hands over her ears, trying to shut out his words. He took her hands and held them at her sides as he leaned over her, speaking quietly.

"I was in the cathedral in London . . . St. Paul's . . . when your voice called out to me . . . I felt pain as I had never thought possible!"

"You heard me?" Gillian gazed at him then, seeing the long hazel eyes filled with love . . . love for her alone.

"Aye, lovedy, I did. I always do—and it near drove me mad with fear, for I was so far away. I couldn't help you as I had in York. If I ever lost you, 'twould be the end of my life!" He kissed the soft, sensuous mouth, salty from the tears streaming down her face. "Would that I could have been here!" he murmured.

"But you were." And she twined her arms tightly about his neck, answering his kisses with her own. This time she let him draw her into his arms and, lying quietly together, their bodies pressed close, the dread and foreboding which had stalked her for so many months receded.

Perhaps all will be well after all, she prayed as she listened to Jamie's deep, even breathing. Secure again in his love, she buried her face in his shoulder and joined him in sleep.

PART THREE
1319

Chapter 6

1319
York

The hammering fists against the door brought Jehan out of a restless sleep. Sitting up on the narrow pallet, she did not know for a moment where she was. Her head ached from the thick, dank air and she held the wrinkled folds of her gown from her body with a grimace of distaste. Brushing strands of hair away from a face still flushed from sleep, she peered through the gloomy darkness, and in the dim, flickering light from the dying embers of the hearth could barely make out the small form of Peter de Gilles curled up on another pallet nearby. The queen's young page was sound asleep, his blond head resting on one hand while the other clutched his soft velvet cap against his blue tunic with the gold fleur-de-lis embroidered on it.

Christ's wounds, Jehan remembered peevishly, she was in the antechamber of the queen's apartments, becoming aware of her unkempt state. On duty during the night in case the queen desired anything, she had stretched out on the pallet for just a few minutes, or so it seemed to her. Damn that little bitch Alisa de Peverell who was supposed to be sharing the duty with Jehan—she had disappeared again. Filled with resentment, she glared at the queen's closed door. As if anything would interrupt the sleep of that feline creature after she had lapped her last bowl of cream for the night. Jehan scowled at the thought of having to be at the beck and call of a bored, self-indulgent woman whose sole purpose in life seemed to be to make others feel as miserable as she was. Never one hour's peace did she allow her ladies—seeming to single out the poor, widowed Lady de Maudley. Where else could she go—where indeed! Jehan's face took on a sly look, and she stretched her stiff limbs.

"Lady de Maudley," a voice called loudly, "unbar the door . . . 'tis most urgent!" The knocking began again, shaking her from her reverie. Damnation! 'Twas not yet dawn and the queen was never to be disturbed. Annoyance at the loud intrusion rose within Jehan.

"Do you hear me, my lady? Unbar this door at once!" the voice stridently demanded.

Awake at last, Jehan leaned over to shake the sleeping boy. "Peter!" she hissed in a low voice. "Wake up, little one . . . 'tis the queen's steward. He sounds most persistent to gain entry."

The child woke, rubbing his eyes, still caught in his dreams.

Jehan ran to the door, throwing back the heavy bolt.

"My lord, take care you do not wake Her Majesty," she said as imperiously as she could, but the gray-haired man entered without replying to her warning, pushing her aside impatiently. He was accompanied by several guards with flaming torches held in gauntleted hands. Her green eyes widened when she saw that they were all dressed for battle. The chamber was flooded with light, and, white with alarm, she shrank instinctively from the steward's fierce face. His voice shook.

"Rouse the queen this instant," he demanded, ordering some of the guards to strip the chamber of its tapestries. "Prepare her for flight. We've just received word that James Douglas is almost at the gates of York and the whole city is in danger of falling into the hands of the Scots! We must move quickly."

"Sweet heavenly Virgin," Jehan whispered between lips suddenly dry as her throat. The Scots here? How was that possible? Everyone knew that the English army had most of the Scottish forces besieged at Berwick. Even the king was there. Where had the Scots come from? Peter began to cry and she turned swiftly toward him, cuffing him sharply. Now was not the time for tears. She told him angrily to gather together the royal gold plate which stood on the dark wooden table against one stone wall. As she moved toward the inner door, it opened and Isabella stood on the threshold, staring into the crowded antechamber.

"Your Grace . . ."

"I know what has happened. I was awake and heard your voices. I'm not deaf!" The queen caught a glint of sardonic humor in Jehan's eyes and stifled a sudden desire to slap her lady-in-waiting's sly face. This was just the sort of situation Lady de Maudley would enjoy— particularly at her sovereign's discomfiture.

A brocaded robe held loosely about her, the queen swept barefooted into the small chamber. Stunned by her unexpected appearance, the guards stared at her with un- feigned admiration, momentarily forgetting the urgency of their mission. Pale golden hair flowing down her back, her well-shaped head held high and blue eyes sparkling coldly, Isabella controlled every man in the chamber with her regal, untouchable beauty.

"My children?" she asked, thrusting a velvet-covered coffer heavy with jewelry into Jehan's hands.

"Already on their way to the postern gate, Your Grace," the steward told her, wishing she had taken time to properly fasten her robe, for with each movement awareness of her slender, lovely limbs grew in the men surrounding her. God's blood, but she was an exquisite creature! Every time he saw her, he was caught by the perfection of her features. Angrily he thrust his thoughts from him, and was relieved to see that several of the queen's ladies had arrived to help her dress.

"My lord, will you have these coffers of the queen's plate taken to our destination!" Jehan ordered, still hold- ing Isabella's jewel case. "Leave your guards here and I will see that Her Grace joins the others as soon as possible."

Her voice quivered with excitement and her blood began to race. She felt alive for the first time in months, and her eyes sparkled in anticipation. Half of her almost wished that the Scots would capture them! Then she might catch a glimpse of the Black Douglas himself. Jehan had heard much of that handsome lord and was filled with curiosity. Increasing sounds of tumult brought her attention back to the urgency of the moment. Pushing the tantalizing thought of James Douglas from her, she ran into the bedchamber to find the queen's coffers opened wide to receive robes, gowns, cloaks, and other garments which several of the ladies, terror-stricken and weeping loudly, were throwing into them with total disregard of order. Jehan could smell the fear emanating from the women. Turning to the closest one at hand, she slapped Alisa de Peverell to stop her rising hysteria.

"You damn wanton—had you been here instead of in your lover's bed, you could have been of some help." She slapped her again. "And don't deny it—I know who it is, and if you don't stop this ridiculous weeping, I'll tell the queen." The young girl gaped at her, wiping her tear-streaked face with the sleeve of her robe.

"Jehan . . . the small crown with the sapphires—'tis missing," Isabella called, busily fastening the clasp of her cloak. Her ladies were giving her a headache, and she was relieved to see how self-possessed Jehan had remained ever since they had heard the news.

" 'Tis in the jewel coffer, Your Grace," Jehan replied, beginning to push the weeping women out of the chamber as a dull roar came to them through the narrow windows. Her eyes met those of the queen's. "Please, Your Grace, you must hurry—the children are waiting!"

"I will carry the jewels, Jehan. You bring the coffer there," and Isabella pointed toward a small ivory casket sitting on the rumpled bed. " 'Twas my father's gift to me. I'd not want to leave it behind." One of the few things Edward had left to her, she thought bitterly as they made their way rapidly through the winding corridors of York Castle, down twisting stone stairs feebly lit by small torches. The farther they descended, the damper the air became, the walls glistening with moisture, and then they found themselves being led through a narrow, low-ceilinged tunnel which sloped slightly upward. Drawing her cloak tightly about her, Isabella suppressed a shudder.

Their footsteps echoed eerily as the queen, attended by Jehan and two guards, quickened her pace. Far ahead of them they could make out flickering torches lighting the way for another fleeing group. Behind them most of her ladies followed with the last of the guards and her personal men-at-arms.

'Twas Edward's fault, she reasoned. Had he not insisted that she wait for him in York, she might be safe at Westminster. Why had he developed this sudden desire to have her close to him, Isabella wondered as she hurried through the dismal, stifling tunnel with only the guards' torches to show them what lay directly ahead of them. After all, she told herself, Edward sat before Berwick surrounded by most of his barons. What need had he of her when young Hugh Despenser was at his side. The spiteful thought came to her unbidden as a rush of cool night air hit her clammy skin. The torches were snuffed as they emerged without warning from the tunnel, and one of her equerries escorted her down a winding path between high bushes whose prickly branches tore at her clothes. There was a glint of water as a lantern flared suddenly, revealing masts etched sharply against the darkness. Isabella saw with an easing of her inner tension that they had reached the banks of the river Ouse.

The landing was crowded with members of her household in every state of dress. Some wept with fear while others quietly helped stow coffers and boxes aboard one of the vessels as quickly as possible in the little light allowed them.

"Your Majesty," a voice whispered hoarsely, and she watched as a tall, dark-haired man fell to one knee before her. "There are two ships in readiness to take you to safety." His chain of office with its seal attached glittered in the lantern light. "Young Prince Edward and the two other royal children are already aboard the first one."

"Master Fleming, we are most grateful for your help," Isabella said quickly, acknowledging the city's lord mayor for his assistance. He rose, prepared to speak further, but she was gone, eager now to join her children. Walter Cherrell, the master of the guard, saluted her and watched as the last of the men came aboard. When the lines were cast off, the small ship began to pull silently away from the shore, followed closely by the second.

Isabella stood near the prow, refusing to look back as Captain Cherrell explained that they would follow the Ouse to where it emptied into the Humber. They would either sail south on the Trent until they reached Nottingham, or travel overland as quickly as they could.

"Nay!" the queen protested hotly. "Not Nottingham Castle! I loathe the place." She shivered, feeling desperately cold at the mention of the gloomy castle.

The grizzled old soldier shook his head and stood firm, his face fierce from an old battle scar that snaked across one cheek.

"My apologies to Your Grace, but my orders are to see you safe, and there's no fortress stronger in these parts than Nottingham." His tone allowed for no further protests. She turned angrily from him and shivered again.

"Majesty, you look weary." Jehan was beside her now while Peter, white-faced and snuffling, brought her a velvet pillow and a stool. "Sit down and rest if you will not go below." Jehan still held the ivory casket. "The two princes are sleeping in a tiny cabin with their tutors, and the Princess Eleanor is in Lady Markham's care."

Eleanor! The queen thought of her little daughter with sadness, silently taking the casket from Jehan. If only she had been another son, Isabella might be done with having to endure Edward's indifferent invasion of her body. Was that why he wanted her near? Another son, healthy and strong, would secure the throne. How she had prayed that the child she carried would be another boy! But it had been pretty, golden-haired Eleanor, named after Edward's mother.

Isabella's hands tightened on the ivory casket. Her father had bestowed a dowry befitting a princess of France when she had married Edward a lifetime ago. Would she ever forget how her maid's heart had trembled at the sight of the handsome, blond young giant who was England's king when he had come to Boulogne for the marriage ceremony. This was her future lord and she would be his queen. Innocent desire for him had been an ache deep within her and she wished vainly that her age would allow him to come to her bed. But her father's physicians had forbidden it, and she was left to her dreams of romantic love while Edward pursued his own reality. Her almond-shaped eyes hardened as they stared blindly at the dark waters of the river moving the ships downstream, and her mouth twisted, remembering her slow, heart-breaking disillusionment. Day by day she had discovered with a mounting sense of disenchanted futility what manner of creature her lord was. He showered his beloved Piers Gaveston with her father's jewels, and the Gascon strutted before her, condescending and arrogant in his dark handsomeness, secure in Edward's love, knowing she was no rival. Bastard, she whispered, hating him still. When the barons slew him, her heart had sung with a fearful joy. Edward turned to her at last and she held him in her arms while he wept for his dead childhood friend. By then she was heavy with her first child. Admittedly, Edward had done well in his duty to provide the kingdom with an heir . . . and so had she, Isabella reminded herself, for had she not borne the pain of giving birth to her beautiful son. How full of pride the king had been, holding his firstborn in his arms. Now things would change, she had told herself, and indeed for a while her lord had been hers. But it was too late. She did not love him—how could she after all the humiliations—and discovered that she did not care.

Her fingers roamed over the carvings covering the casket. Inside, resting on blue velvet embroidered with the golden lilies of France, was her Book of Hours, her name illuminated with great beauty on the first page. Her father had presented the book to her the night before her marriage together with a golden crucifix set with sapphires and a small ring. The book and the crucifix she had kept, but she gave the ring to the only friend she had made in this alien land. She had sent it to Gillian de Broze, requesting naught but friendship in return.

Her blue eyes rested on Jehan, perched uncomfortably on a coil of rope near her, her hair still uncombed and tumbling wildly about her. What tangled lives we lead, Isabella mused, thinking suddenly of Jehan and the doomed Arnaut de Broze. She sighed, fighting the sudden

189

weariness that engulfed her. She would never quite trust Jehan. There was much about her the queen could not fathom, yet she had welcomed her back to court gladly after Lord de Maudley's death, hoping to find her a wiser and more prudent woman. Isabella smiled thinly at the thought. Jehan had cut a swathe through all the courtiers with her green-eyed, red-lipped sensuality. Every man seemed to be her prey. But why, the queen wondered, for it was whispered that for all the liberties she permitted, no man reached her bed. It was all too complicated for the queen's fatigued mind, she decided, resting her head against the rail.

There was a pale yellow glow in the eastern sky and the stars were glimmering ever paler as night began to recede. She closed her eyes and an image of a man came to her. She had glimpsed him but once, but thought of him often, his dark, glittering eyes staring at her boldly from a wildly handsome face, drawing the heart from her breast. It had been the recognition of two kindred souls . . . and yet, not one word had passed between them. Aymer de Valence had told her that the stranger was the baron of Wigmore. The following morning he was gone, sent from Tynemouth by Lord de Valence, who had observed the glance shared with the queen. How often had she whispered his name within her heart. Roger . . . Roger de Mortimer. And the queen slept, the cold unhappiness temporarily erased from her beautiful face.

The large coffer stood open, its deep blue velvet lining enhancing the luster of the ropes of pearls and gold chains, some fashioned of carved links and others elaborately set with precious stones, which spilled over onto the dressing table. Pendants, brooches, and rings glittered and gleamed with gems whose hearts were splintered by the light of the candles set in ornate holders about the chamber, already darkening in the late afternoon.

Isabella's face stared back at her from the mirror and she scowled, dissatisfied with her reflection. The pale hair was drawn back smoothly from her white forehead, its heavy plaits entwined with lustrous pearls. Her slender shoulders seemed bare, for the under-robe she wore was fashioned of silk so fine and thin as to be almost transparent. She shivered in the castle's perpetual damp chill that no number of lit hearths or braziers could banish.

"Nay—I hate it! 'Twill not do . . . 'tis too plain," she shrieked and, with an impatient gesture, tore a proffered fine gold chain from Jehan's hand, throwing it petulantly to the floor.

"Your Grace, 'tis a beautiful chain and will truly complement the neckline of the blue brocade," Jehan protested wearily. The queen was fraying her nerves and she fought a rising irritation as she bent down to retrieve the chain. With very little hope of agreement from Isabella, she suggested a rope of pearls, controlling a strong desire to scream. The queen's temper worsened each day they remained in this accursed place.

For a few moments Isabella hid her face in her hands. Sweet Jesu, how bored she was with sitting in Nottingham Castle day in and day out with naught to do but listen to the ridiculous gossiping of her ladies. The musicians displeased her, sounding raucous and out of tune, while the food served in the Great Hall was tasteless. Even her children, in their infrequent visits to her, annoyed her with their nonsensical prattle. She loved them—they were hers, yet she always felt relieved to see them disappear through the door, hearing their happy laughter echo faintly through the hallway. God's blood, why would no one tell her what was happening! Despite her vehement protests to the castle's constable, Lord Robert de Heland, he would tell her naught. While she lodged one formal protest after another, he listened politely, his handsome, regular features stony and expressionless. When she had exhausted herself, he went back to his own duties as if she and her court did not exist. Ever since their arrival the castle had been secured against the outside world. Only her eldest son was permitted to stride the battlements, accompanied by the constable and Captain Cherrell, vainly looking for attacking Scots. Poor Ned was doomed to disappointment, for none had been sighted, but at least he could pass the time with men he would someday rule, and who seemed to find pleasure in his lively company. His brother John, at three, was still too young to be a companion to him, preferring his toys to Ned's company.

With a burst of rage Isabella swept her dressing table clear of all but the heavy jewel coffer, sending everything else crashing to the floor.

"By the heavenly Virgin, I've had enough of this silence," Isabella said furiously as her ladies stared at her in sudden fright. The lovely face was pale and composed but her blue eyes glittered angrily as she ordered her page to seek out Robert de Heland. "If I'm to stay a prisoner in this accursed place, I will know what is happening and our good constable will certainly be forced to tell me, if I must threaten to have him sent to the Tower!" Although the idea was delightfully appealing to her, she doubted that the situation truly warranted that extreme an action.

As young Peter de Gilles left on his errand, the queen rose and allowed her ladies to finish dressing her. The blue brocaded tunic Jehan had chosen for her fitted her slender figure well, lying a trifle snugly over her softly rounded bosom. Its sleeves were tight to the elbow and flared out in wide fur-trimmed cuffs falling gracefully to the floor. Her silken under-robe of contrasting color shone through the slitted panels of the full skirt, and a beautifully woven girdle of gold mesh enhanced her small waist.

"The robe suits Your Grace remarkably well," Jehan exclaimed as she placed several ropes of pearls about the slender white neck.

"Remarkably enough to find out a man's secrets as well as you do, my lady?"

The question shafted Jehan as neatly as the blade of a dagger and so swiftly that she reddened in confusion. Isabella had the satisfaction of seeing her lady-in-waiting caught without words. She laughed and placed a delicate hand on Jehan's arm.

"Pray do not feign innocence, my lady. Did you think I should not find it odd that while you play the seductress with all my courtiers and equerries, we are probably the only two women in this castle who sleep alone!"

"Your Grace! Have I offended you?" Jehan looked at the queen with new eyes. Had she so underestimated the young Frenchwoman's perception? Isabella laughed again, white teeth gleaming between soft, moist lips.

"But nay, my sweet Jehan. Your ability to charm all men is well known. 'Tis just that I wish to know your secret."

Jehan's heart skipped a beat in sudden apprehension. Did the queen suspect what she was about . . . 'twas not possible, for she had taken great care not to become involved with any one man too deeply. She began to protest, but Isabella turned sharply when the door burst open with a great crash. Young Peter ran into the chamber out of breath and in a state of great excitement.

"Your Grace . . . my lord de Heland requests an audience with you in the small hall near the east tower as soon as possible. He has another lord with him, newly arrived in the castle! He is very tall and fearsome of face!"

Lord de Heland asked that she come to him? Isabella was astounded at his affrontery and her cheeks flamed in indignation. No one noticed, for the child was babbling on, falling over his words, round gray eyes shining, intoxicated with all he had seen.

"You should have seen all the archers marching over the drawbridge—I've never seen so many . . . mostly small men with oddly shaped bows—not as we know them . . . and mounted knights in armor—and pikemen!"

Welsh archers! Could it be possible?

"Peterkin—the archers . . . what badge do they wear?" Jehan asked.

"I did not notice, my lady, but they are in the outer bailey now, making camp."

Isabella glanced curiously at Jehan, the insult to her royal dignity forgotten. Again she found the red-headed young woman baffling. As if archers were of any importance. Unless there was a particular lord . . . ? Her eyes narrowed thoughtfully. Why had she not noticed before now that Lady de Maudley lacked the look of a grieving widow, nor one starved for a man's passion despite her rumored abstinence. She shrugged her suspicions aside. The whole idea was absurd. Jehan was as she had ever been. That was all there was to it. Every man was her natural prey! And, of course—she came from the Marches

—only barons from the Marches used Welsh archers. Perhaps a kinsman had arrived.

"I will wear the gold crown with the sapphires," the queen told her companion, closing her mind to her speculations, unaware of how close to the truth she had come. She never saw the trembling of Jehan's hands as she placed the crown on the pale brow.

"Word of the attack on York reached me while I was still in Shrewsbury. I thought it best that I come here first rather than proceed directly north to Berwick in case you needed reinforcement of the garrison."

"We've been fortunate so far that no Scot has gotten farther than the vicinity of York, or so the last message received told us. I've a large force here—enough to withstand a prolonged attack, but I must admit you still were a welcome sight, my lord."

Robert de Heland, slim, fair-haired, and in his midthirties, handed his guest a goblet of wine before pouring himself one. It was the first time he had met the tall, dark Marcher baron, but he had heard many tales of his arrogance and savagery. There had also been rumors of disgraceful conduct in Ireland which had caused his hasty return to England. Still clad in hauberk and leg armor, the baron's face was smudged from the road's dust mingled with sweat, and there were lines of weariness about his dark eyes. His leather gauntlets banded with metal, dented and scratched from much use, lay on the table beside the wine flagon, and de Heland had no doubts that the great sword hanging from the wide belt at Roger de Mortimer's waist had often drawn blood. The Marcher lord strode restlessly about the constable's study, stopping finally to stand by the windows and stare out with great interest at the town of Nottingham huddled far below the castle.

"This is indeed a well-placed fortress!" de Mortimer exclaimed with admiration, his eyes sweeping the horizon. Mountain born, he had always been fascinated by heights, and it was obvious that this was a castle from which a man could rule all that his eyes encompassed. " 'Twas right that the queen sought safety here." Isabella here! Would she remember him, he wondered, and his mind moved on to the hope that Jehan would not betray herself. Lord de Heland swore loudly as he came to stand beside his guest.

"Aye, the queen resides here, but not without continuing and violent protest, my lord. She fought the idea of coming here and complains constantly that she finds our hospitality greatly lacking," the constable said dryly. He disliked the youthful queen and avoided seeing her as much as possible. His grim expression softened as his thoughts turned to Isabella's lady-in-waiting. The Lady Jehan, on the other hand, was another matter, and he sighed as he remembered how her eyes had gazed guilessly into his for a heart-stopping moment before her sensual mouth opened beneath his assault. Was it just last night that he had trapped her on the small twisting stairs leading to the west tower? She had smelled of roses as his lips caressed the soft skin of her neck while she whispered to him. What had she asked him? De Heland tried to remember, but the warmth of her silk-covered breast under his hand and of her mouth reaching for his again had made his senses reel—and then she was gone, trailing soft laughter and broken promises behind her, leaving only a gossamer scarf redolent with her perfume in his hands. He had been obsessed with her from the moment her strangely slanted eyes had stared with green fire at him during one of the queen's endless tirades. His own wife's sweet face paled to nothingness in his memory, although he prided himself on his faithfulness to her during the many long separations they had had to endure in their life together.

Roger waited for his host to continue and saw that the man had been caught in some private dream. He smiled to himself, for he had observed that look many times before. Jehan was doing his bidding exceedingly well.

"My lord . . ." he called sharply and the other's blue eyes focused once more on the tall figure of the baron. "My lord, should we not present ourselves to the queen? I wish to see to the disposition of my men."

Roger placed his emptied goblet on the table. Sapphire blue eyes and pale blond hair—would the queen have changed greatly since Tynemouth? Roger found himself filled with the excitement of that moment in the hunt when his quarry had been flushed and was running to escape him.

"My dear Lord de Mortimer, how can we thank you for your protective presence here. Our gratitude cannot be measured."

The words were spoken in a soft, musical voice as Queen Isabella extended her hand to the weary knight kneeling before her, his green and yellow surcoat soiled from the hours of traveling the high roads and his unruly dark hair gray with dust from the day's march. She waited for him to raise his head, and when he did, the impact of those bold black eyes on hers was the same as so many years before. Her almond-shaped eyes widened in instinctive fear as his mouth brushed her fingers lightly. Her heart began to race as his gaze returned to her face again, but his words were commonplace, assuring her of his loyalty and pledging his life and those of his men to her safety. She bade him sit before her, offering him wine and cakes. The constable, seated beside de Mortimer, was aware only of Jehan as she stood by the queen. Her eyes had not left de Mortimer from the moment of his entrance into the hall, and a warm flush crept over the white skin as her sovereign welcomed the baron to her court, presenting some of her ladies to him.

"Of course, you are already acquainted with Lady de Maudley, my lord." She observed Roger's face closely as he raised Jehan from her curtsy and Isabella found it difficult to breathe.

"Her late husband was one of my most trusted lieutenants, Your Grace, and I still mourn his death." De Mortimer's expression was unreadable as he looked at Jehan with veiled eyes. She acknowledged his words with a soft sigh.

"As do I, my lord." Had she imagined a slight pressure of his fingers before he released her hand.

"How do you fare, my lady? Are you content at court?"

" 'Tis an unmeet question to ask before me, my lord, but I can answer for her. She fares most well and would

196

be more content were I not so difficult a mistress." Isabella laughed, unable to wrench her gaze from de Mortimer's. He was older yes, but otherwise he was exactly as she remembered him.

"Your Grace . . ." Jehan murmured, resenting the queen's interference. She felt the constable's attention resting upon her and darted him a dazzling smile, hoping Roger would notice. Last night she had come close to losing her head for the first time since coming to court, for Lord de Heland was a very comely man as well as a persistent one, and she found his kisses far from unpleasant. The queen seemed very pleased with herself, basking in the glow of Roger's flattering charm, Jehan thought with a spurt of spiteful jealousy, immediately forgetting the constable's existance.

Servants offered the two men refreshment while Isabella helped herself to a sugar plum, the favorite comfit she was never without.

Her teeth should rot and turn black, Jehan wished maliciously, waving a servant away with barely concealed irritation.

"How long do you plan to stay with us, my lord?" the queen asked as she watched him lift a golden goblet from the tray. She was struck by his grace and gentility, which seemed oddly in contrast to the fearsome warrior his appearance implied. She felt a wave of dizziness overcome her suddenly and rested her head against the back of the carved chair beneath the royal blue and gold canopy. What is happening to me? she wondered, as de Mortimer's magnetism reached out to her. Taking deep breaths, she began to feel better, and without looking directly at him, she heard him reply.

"Until I know that the countryside is safe for Your Majesty to travel south. Lord de Heland and I have decided that my men will sweep the entire area about Nottingham just to make sure." His eyes sought hers again, but she evaded his gaze. Frightened by the unfamiliar intensity of her awakening emotions, she had an overwhelming desire to escape from the danger which seemed to be concentrated in the man seated before her.

"We will make sure that your stay is most comfortable, my lord de Mortimer," Isabella assured him, amazed that she could manage so calm a tone while she gazed with fascination at his mouth. How would those hard, sensual lips feel on her own? The thought came to her unbidden and she shrank from it, thrusting from her the odd, disturbing fantasies which seemed to suddenly becloud her mind. Jehan watched her closely, fascinated by Isabella's reaction to Roger's presence, for never had she seen the queen struggle so to maintain her usual frigid, regal composure.

For a short time the two men sat in Isabella's presence, engaging her in desultory conversation and she slowly relaxed, for the baron showed only the deepest respect toward her. The moment of danger had passed for her and her cool common sense ruled supreme once more. Dismissing them at last with gracious courtesy, she excused herself from joining them in the Great Hall for the evening meal, reasoning that there would be greater informality and ease were she not to appear. The constable was unable to conceal his relief at her decision, while his companion remained silently indifferent to her words. Jehan followed them as they took their leave, an unspoken question in her eyes as she bade Roger good day. Bowing over her hand, he gave no sign of further communication, and she was left staring at the dark, seamed wood of the door as it closed behind him.

Bitch, Jehan thought angrily as she stood in the dimly lit hallway outside the queen's apartments. For hours Isabella had inspected her gowns, tunics of gold tissues, velvets and embroidered silks, selecting those which she would wear for the formal audience she would grant Roger de Mortimer and his knights the next day. For two days she had drunk in the fawning flattery he bestowed on her in their brief encounters while her lady-in-waiting had stood watching in helpless, angry frustration. Not once had Roger glanced her way in aught but polite courtesy. Tears of anguished disappointment trembled on her eyelashes as she leaned against the damp stone wall. Bastard! She longed to scream out at him, deeply hurt that he chose to ignore her so completely. He was courting the queen, although she had managed to avoid any commitment. Isabella was no fool—what game was she playing now, Jehan wondered, for rarely had the blue eyes sparkled so brightly and the dimpled smile been more prominently displayed.

"My lady Jehan." The whispered words seemed to float out of nowhere and she stiffened at their lilting, familiar sound.

"Who is it? Where are you?" she called in a low voice, peering into the gloom. Set into the opposite wall was a small entry to a tower stairs leading to the upper battlements. The torch above the stone archway had been snuffed out, leaving shrouded darkness.

" 'Tis Emrys, my lady, with a message from the Arglwydd." The small figure of the harper stepped out into the hall's dim light. Jehan drew closer, hope stirring within her.

"Does Lord de Mortimer wish to see me?" she asked, her voice trembling with expectation. She could not see the pity in the Welshman's eyes as he repeated his master's words, contempt for himself biting ever deeper into his embittered soul.

"My master bids you retain your distance, for no one must suspect your involvement with him. His plans forbid it and he is much disturbed by your too close observance of him. If you have a message for him, I will deliver it. Your presence in the queen's court is of too great a value to be placed in peril by any romantic foolishness."

"Romantic foolishness? Nay, I'll not believe he said that," she retorted, stung by Emrys's words.

"I speak as he spoke, my lady. Now is not the time to place passion before politics, and you are therefore ordered to be careful in even how you look at him."

"Enough, harper, no more need be said." Jehan whispered and fled as one in pain down the long, cold hall, Emrys's words echoing in her head, until she reached the safety of her own tiny chamber. She was under no illusion as to the reasons for Lord de Heland's allowing her the luxury and privacy of a bedchamber of her own, since all the other queen's ladies dwelt four and six together in similar chambers. But the constable's desire and vain hopes of fulfillment were the last subject which occupied her. Though Jehan felt like weeping, her anger refused her the indulgence of such emotions and she was relieved that Berthe was not waiting for her.

Sweet Jesù, how can he do this to me? she asked herself. She had been possessed by the desire to be alone with him since his arrival and now he had denied himself to her. 'Tis the queen, she decided grimly. He has set his ambitious will on her. For what purpose, she wondered, honestly puzzled, for Isabella had little power to wield, being ignored by most of the influential barons save her own cousin, Lancaster, and Lord de Valence, who was a true and kind friend.

How ripe she would be for Roger's kind of conquest! Jehan thought of Isabella's contemplation of herself when she believed herself unobserved late the night before, standing naked before the long, polished metal mirror. Her hands had caressed every part of a body still young and undeniably beautiful, although it was almost completely ignored by Edward. No doubt imagining another's touch, Jehan had thought meanly as she quietly closed the door on the scene.

Anger and disappointment surging through her, Jehan lay on the narrow bed, her mind alive with a thousand thoughts. Roger had tricked her into spying for him, knowing that she could deny him nothing, using her for his own purposes. She had known it too, and had not cared. Roger! Her small body curled into itself as she fought the hot throbbing desire growing within her to feel the naked weight of him, his hands caressing her until she was mindless with the passionate love she held for him. She moaned and beat her clenched hands against her body.

Nay, Jehan muttered, giving in to her tears. She'll not have him.

A thought struck her suddenly in the midst of her self-indulgent misery. It would be so simple to reach Roger —and once she was alone with him, all would be well. After all, he was a man. Arglwydd indeed! Jehan laughed in the darkness as a plan began to take form in her mind.

For days the countryside had been scoured thoroughly, villages emptied of their inhabitants and searched, bushes beaten and trees scaled, but the soldiers had failed to find one Scot. Today Roger de Mortimer had ridden out himself to supervise the undertaking and it was late by the time the drawbridge was lowered to readmit the weary baron and his men into the safe confines of the castle. All was deathly still within—even the constable had long since retired—and most of the castle folk lay deep in slumber as Roger seated himself in a high-backed chair and allowed his body servant to draw the dusty boots from his tired feet. Soiled surcoat, hauberk and tunic were quietly removed, and he sighed with relief as he washed the last of the day's dirt from his naked body with hot water brought by servants awakened rudely by Emrys. The harper was already busily polishing his lord's shield and seeing to his other equippage. Looking through the open door of the antechamber into his master's room he watched as a retainer sleepily poured wine from a small cask into the large gold flagon set on an ornate tray resting on a large carved wooden chest. He hissed in warning when several drops fell on the tray and the servant gave him a grateful look as he wiped them away with the cloth tucked into his belt. Roger paid little attention to the activity about him while he allowed himself the luxury of sitting at ease by the hearth's warmth for a short while before slipping into the bed which beckoned invitingly. The coverlet was drawn back from crisp sheets and the bolster and plump pillows waited for him within the darkness of partially drawn curtains.

Dismissing his servants, he ordered Emrys to shut the small outer door and closed his eyes, surrendering himself to his thoughts.

He was wasting time here, he decided morosely, for he had been unable to make any progress in breaking through the barrier Isabella had built between them. As long as he played the role of loyal baron, she sparkled and glittered enticingly, but attempts toward anything hinting at a personal relationship turned her cold and distant. Yet she was drawn strongly to him—every instinct told him so. Last night she had kept young Edward beside her. The blond child with his clear skin and intelligent blue eyes had been full of questions regarding Ireland and Wales. It was amazing how knowledgeable the seven-year-old prince was about his father's realm . . . and how totally innocent of the buffer role he played between his mother and the man she refused to see alone. Then there was Jehan, who was desperately trying to reach him. He couldn't risk it, for the tilted green eyes and sensual mouth still stirred him when he dared look at her.

He sighed and stretched, feeling tired muscles move beneath his fire-warmed skin. Why could she not tell Emrys what she had learned from the obviously love-besotted de Heland. Women! he thought irritably. 'Twould be best to leave for Berwick as soon as possible. But to leave without seeing Jehan at all—Roger hesitated . . . He would be a fool to chance seeing her, and yet he could not rid himself of the need for her. She alone could satisfy the devilish passionate hunger which seemed to burn endlessly within him!

A touch, deft and light, on his temples brought his mind back from the floating, peaceful darkness it had sought and could not find. Opening his eyes, he saw a pale, heart-shaped face contemplating him with concern. Jehan! Blood of Christ, how had she gotten past his men and guards in the antechamber. He saw that a heavy dark cloak enveloped her from hooded head to invisible toe. What mischief was she up to now?

"Are you totally mad?" he asked guiltily. It was as if she had felt his thoughts. Why had she not heeded his warning?

"You look so weary," she murmured, a finger tracing the taut lines about his eyes and cheekbones. Touching him again filled her with indescribable joy. He pushed her hand aside and rose from the chair. His back to her, he placed both hands on the warm stone mantel, eyes searching the flames. He was furious with her.

"I told you we could not meet . . . 'tis too dangerous here. The castle is crawling with members of the queen's court and the king's men."

She laughed deep in her throat, slanted eyes drink-
in the sight of the familiar features, black silken hair
which fell nearly to his shoulders and lean-muscled body
she had ached for since leaving him in London. She stood
behind him, pressing herself against his back.

"There's much about this castle I must tell you!" she
whispered.

"Emrys was instructed to give me your messages. He
warned you not to contact me—not here! The danger . . ."
he repeated.

Jehan's arms encircled him, her hands slipping inside
his linen chainse to caress lightly his warm smooth skin.

"A danger for you?" she asked, eyes closed, the
loosely woven cloth cool against her cheek. " 'Tis your
lady de Maudley who risks treason each time she sends
you her secret messages."

She felt him turn and place hard hands on her shoulders, holding her away from him. The white lids slowly
opened and her eyes watched the scowl fade from his
tense face.

"Besides," she added, studying his face closely, "I
fear the queen would be much displeased to know that we
shared more than just the loyalty of my dead lord."

Her heart sank as she saw a flush spread over the
handsome features. So I was right, she thought. Isabella
has captured his fancy as well. Jehan pushed the hood
from her head and let the shimmering red mass of her
hair tumble down her back, catching the fire's glow.

"You are mad!" he repeated softly, catching a glimpse
of her soft body beneath the cloak.

"Nay, Roger, not mad. But I must speak with you of
all I've learned these past weeks."

She unfastened the cloak and it fell about her feet.
Her body taunted him, for he knew all too well what sensual pleasures it offered.

"You come to tell me important secrets clad as you
are?" he asked her, sarcastic humor heavy in his low-
pitched voice. "How could I possibly concentrate on your
words when you stand before me as you do!"

With a suddenness that caught her off guard, Roger

swept Jehan high into his arms, whirling her about so that her hair streamed wildly about her.

"To the devil with it all," he said, laughing. Jehan clutched his shoulders tightly, arching her body as she felt his lips brush against her breasts through the thin silken shift. "God's blood, 'tis good to have you in my arms again." His mouth reached up and captured hers as he slowly lowered her body until it rested fully against his.

"Roger, I must tell you . . ." she gasped, evading his kisses for a moment.

"Later," he said thickly, giving in to the hunger she had awakened in him.

"Tell me honestly how you managed to evade my guards and Emrys in the outer chamber," Roger demanded as his fingers slid lightly over the velvet flesh of her body. Jehan lay against him, her eyes still dazed with passion. She felt his lips against her throat.

"I sent a flagon of wine to your guards with the compliments of Queen Isabella and a special one for Emrys," she murmured and her fingers touched him lightly, gliding expertly down his long-muscled body.

"And?" he prompted her, although he knew what her reply would be.

"And it happened to also contain a sleeping draught . . . compliments of Lady de Maudley."

Roger laughed, rolling onto his back as he lifted her easily in his arms so that her hair covered them like a curtain. He buried his face between her soft breasts as she lay full length upon him. Her skin was warm and pliant to his touch and smelled of sun-drenched roses.

"I should have suspected that you would attempt this sort of thing." He tumbled her abruptly back to the pillows and sat up. "My clever little dove . . ." The low, musical voice sounded amused. Rising from the bed, he strode to the chest where the flagon of wine waited.

"Let's hope this wine has not been drugged," he said, bringing back a filled goblet for each of them. The goblets were the handsome gem-encrusted gold ones she had always coveted, Jehan saw with a twinge of envy. She sipped the wine, feeling its warmth spread through her.

"Now what is this important news you risked all to tell me?" Roger asked, unable to resist touching the smooth skin of her bare shoulder. She began to tell him of their escape from York Castle and how they had gone through the tunnel leading to the river. Roger's dark eyes bored into hers, his hand still on her shoulder.

"And do you remember where the entrance is?"

Jehan nodded. "I'll never forget it . . . although there is a postern gate, the tunnel is secret, known only to a few."

"And what have you discovered about Nottingham Castle?" he asked casually, setting down his emptied goblet on the candle stand beside the bed. The flickering, sputtering candle turned his naked body into a study of golden light and dark shadow, accentuating the unsuspected strength beneath his slimness.

Jehan sat cross-legged before him, her eyes wide with excitement.

"There are many secret passages within the castle and several tunnels running beneath its walls whose entrances are a goodly distance away and well concealed."

"And where are these secret passages, and where do the tunnels lead?" Roger asked quietly, leaning toward her tensely.

"I know not. Lord de Heland would not tell me all he knows. There's not been enough time to find out."

"So it was the castle's handsome constable who told you of its secrets!" Suddenly Roger's voice was black with jealous anger. "What did you do to get this much information from him?"

Startled at the violence of his reaction, Jehan protested. "Naught that I've not done with all the others—a few meaningless kisses and caresses . . . promises not kept—questions asked and answers given. I was most careful . . ."

"Liar! The man is beside himself with desire for you." His hands gripped her arms. "Whore! I should have known you could not keep yourself from another's bed."

Jehan went white at his accusations. She had not expected praise for her discovery, for it was not in his nature to give her any. But it had been an accomplishment, for the constable was no fool and she had used nearly every wile she possessed to pry the secrets from him without involving herself too deeply.

"I warned you, you damn slut, that I owned you till I was done with you. You were to give yourself to no one else—no one!" Roger was working himself into a towering rage, dropping the baiting, half-amused manner he usually used toward her.

His hand lashed out, striking her face a stinging blow. Her head snapped back with the force of a second blow and the pain brought tears to her eyes. Her cheek was on fire where he struck her.

"How dare you speak to me so vilely! Need you remind me that I'm naught to you but a possession that you bought—a possession to be either ignored or kicked about," she spat out at him, her own anger rising.

Still holding the goblet tightly in a hand whose knuckles had turned white, she suddenly threw its contents over him, at the same time twisting her body sideways to evade another blow. The goblet fell with a heavy thud onto the floor. Wiping the wine from his livid face, he saw her eyes blazing with hurt fury and in that instant all thoughts of Isabella vanished from his mind. This outraged being was the Jehan he had deceived, betrayed, and wounded beyond measure time and time again by his selfishness and ambitious pride, but he had no true hold on her save their mutual need. Never could his wife drive him into a frenzy as Jehan was capable of doing. When he believed she had given herself to de Heland, it was more than he could bear, refusing to admit the reason behind his own violent reaction. He reached out for her, tangling his fingers in her long hair to pull her flailing body back. She fought him with all the strength she had, but he slammed her down hard, pinning her to the bed with one knee.

"You ungrateful bastard," she screeched at him, unable to move beneath his weight. "I've done your bidding, but I swear to you I've lain with no man but you since Ralph's death." She sank her teeth into his hand as he tried to stop her words. "You judge everyone by your own foul, amoral instincts. Whoreson! No woman is safe from your lustful appetites—yet you dare accuse me of the same . . . Do you also believe such behavior from your lady when you leave her to herself for so long a time? I hear she is most comely! I'm sure there are many men who would gladly share her bed."

Jehan burst into tears as he caught hold of her with hard, ungentle hands. His face was wild with rage, the dark eyes glowing with a murderous light.

"Never mention my wife to me . . . she has naught to do with you . . . naught!"

His wine-drenched black hair fell about the high cheekbones in sodden disorder and his mouth drew back in a furious snarl as Jehan fought his hands, bruising her as he forced her down against the pillows.

"Oh my God, Roger, 'tis true—you are indeed the Devil's spawn! Nothing touches your heart—sometimes I believe that you lack one at all," she sobbed. Her plan had worked too well, she realized, a feeling of panic coursing through her that she had pushed him too far this time. Desperate in her fear of losing him to the queen, she had unleashed a jealousy in him she had not known existed. But it was not love—how could it be when that emotion was totally alien to him, she thought bitterly, looking into his face, black with intemperate fury.

Then she found her arms wound tightly about his neck, her mouth feverish against his, feeling the anger pouring from his trembling body.

As he took her roughly and cruelly, she screamed out her love for him—the love forbidden her, denied by him, and finally confirmed by his towering jealous rage. Before the darkness of his savagery engulfed her, the words flashed triumphantly into a mind already blurred by agonized passion—"I've won! Sweet heaven, I've won!"

Chapter 7

1319
Berwick

"We are accomplishing naught by sitting idly before these walls waiting for the city to fall!"

Pembroke's deep, quiet voice broke the uncomfortable silence of the pavilion as he sat back in his chair and looked around the table. The remains of the evening repast had been cleared away, but the mood had not lightened. At a signal from his lord, Geoffrey brought out the maps for the customary evening's discourse. The earl was becoming increasingly aware that their enforced idleness was beginning to wear on the nerves of them all. In the encampments before Berwick's walls, barons and knights gathered, restless and dissatisfied with the stalemated campaign. He had seen Lord Badlesmere and Henry Plantagenet, Lancaster's brother and heir, ride toward that earl's tent, accompanied by others who were partisan to him. No doubt both Despensers were spending the evening in the royal pavilion filling the king's head with praise for his mustering of all the lords of the realm for this glorious campaign.

And what glory had it brought them? Thwarted by Robert Bruce's possession of as many ingenious siege-machines as they had themselves, the besiegers were as imprisoned outside the city walls as those within. While his secretary unrolled the detailed map charting the known defenses of Berwick, Pembroke's dark eyes rested on the dour face of the earl of Surrey. John de Warenne was the grandson of his father's sister, kin to both himself and Edward—yet Pembroke sensed a lack of commitment about him that made the older man wary. The sullen gray eyes never could quite meet another man's gaze squarely. While John cared little about the feelings of others, he was himself extremely sensitive to the slightest hint of impugnity against his own name. And Heaven only knows that there is good reason for it, Pembroke thought grimly, for it was no secret that he had sired several illegitimate children, barely providing for them and their well-born mothers while totally rejecting his own lady. She had refused to agree to an annulment of their marriage, successfully petitioning both king and church to deny his request. It must have been a relief for him to escape from his domestic troubles into the stagnant atmosphere of Berwick. De Warenne, feeling Pembroke's gaze, drew a hand nervously through dark blond hair which needed a trimming.

"Robert Bruce is also getting nowhere with most of his fighting force trapped within the city," he muttered, holding his empty wine goblet to be filled by a servant. His brother-in-law, Edmund Fitzalan, looked at him in disgust.

"John, the only task which seems to suit you these days is to empty wine casks." Arundel felt restless, hating each endless day and the even longer nights. He rose, casting a long, wavering shadow against the wall, and pulled aside the flap at the tent's entrance. The two guards outside looked at him curiously, but did not relax their stance as he glanced at the star-studded sky, filling his lungs with air heavy with the rank odors of unwashed bodies, horses' offal, and human waste mingling with the acrid smoke of cooking fires and torches flaring outside the countless tents and pavilions surrounding Pembroke's own camp. "Feel the air, my lords . . . already there is autumn's coolness in it! Damned folly!" The night air flowed through the tent, causing the suspended oil lamps and the heavy candles on the table to flicker wildly in the drafts. The camp's stench pervaded the tent and Geoffrey coughed, gagging with disgust.

"Close that entry, Edmund, and stop playing the eternal fool," de Warenne snapped peevishly. "There's no need to prove to us that 'tis September, nor where we are."

Arundel shrugged his broad, velvet-covered shoulders in apparent indifference, but the blue eyes, usually filled with good humor, darkened in sudden anger.

"Sit down, Edmund, and let us listen to what has been proposed by the king for the morrow, if anything."

James Kilburn's quiet words turned all eyes toward him. Arundel laughed mirthlessly as he threw his muscular body into the chair beside de Warenne. Sitting across the table from Pembroke, Kilburn had contributed little to the evening's conversation, his eyes thoughtful as he listened to the others' complaints. As the servant leaned over to replenish his goblet, he placed a hand over it, shaking his head. There had been enough drinking tonight. Arundel was right about de Warenne, although the more Surrey drank, the more morose he became. Sour-natured and humorless—that was what Edmund had called him once, thanking Heaven that his lady did not share her brother's unpleasant nature. Kilburn smiled thinly. He shared Pembroke's distrust of de Warenne. He would change sides to suit his own interest as freely as he changed his linen.

"James, you're most silent tonight and have a troubled look." Pembroke gazed at the younger man with concern, for he sensed in him a tension different from the others.

"Don't you find it strange that Robert Bruce has made no great effort to break this deadlock?" Kilburn said slowly as the other barons stared at him. The finely chiseled features were taut and white, mirroring the mounting fear within him. Geoffrey, standing by his lord's chair, realized that Pembroke too was equally concerned but had voiced none of his misgivings aloud. The Glairn hawk glittered on Kilburn's slender hand as he pointed a long finger toward the forgotten map. "Where are the rest of Bruce's men? 'Tis not possible they are all within Berwick. Look at the chart. I can't speak for you, but I admit I am puzzled and worried."

"Are you thinking of your kinsman, James?" The question was asked quietly, but Pembroke leaned forward eagerly, studying Kilburn's serious face. He was right, of course, but there was little they could do. A sudden horrifying thought struck him, and he bade Geoffrey bring another map from the rolls secured in a heavy coffer banded with iron. As the map was hastily unrolled, it revealed the entire border area. Berwick, in the extreme northeast corner, was marked in blue and the placement of the English forces in red. Obviously many sections along the border had been left poorly defended. James glanced at the area where his own holding lay, but forced his mind to concentrate on the matter he had broached.

"James Douglas is a clever, tricky man and extremely mobile. You can see that since our forces are all concentrated in this area, here, we've left practically no rear guard or defenses. If I were the king, the mystery of Lord Douglas's whereabouts would worry me exceedingly."

"I can understand your concern, my lord Kilburn, but you must admit no one thought it would take Berwick so long to fall," de Warenne said thickly, but Aymer de Valence shook his head.

"Nay, James is right. It has bothered me as well, although 'tis taken till now to make me realize where the danger truly lies." He raised his eyes from the map as the muted sounds of shouting filtered through the pavilion's walls, breaking the chilling spell Kilburn's words had cast over the other two barons. As the entry flap was drawn back to allow Thomas Fitzhugh to enter, they could see dark figures silhouetted against hand-held torches brightly flaring in the night air.

"My lords," Tom called in great excitement, "messengers have just arrived bearing news of a disastrous battle against the Scots. 'Tis spreading through all the camps that the Black Douglas tried to capture the queen, but she and her court escaped and are now safe in Nottingham! All the lords are summoned at once to the king's encampment."

Pembroke's eyes locked with those of Kilburn as they

all rose, alarmed by the news. Hastily leaving the earl's tent, they joined the throng of men hurrying to the encampment where banners with their three golden leopards on a red field snapped and sparkled in the torchlight. A path was made for the earl of Pembroke through the mass of knights gathered before the royal pavilion, and he entered without being announced, followed closely by the other three barons. The pavilion, though large, was crowded to overflowing with lords eager to hear the news. King Edward, flanked by the Despensers, father and son, was seated in an ornate gilt chair, his handsome features pale above the curling yellow beard. Thomas of Lancaster, with his brother Henry beside him, stood nearby. Catching sight of Pembroke's tall, thin figure, the king summoned him to come closer.

Taking a deep breath, Edward said solemnly, "My lords, we have just received word that a large force of Scots, led by Lord James Douglas, has attempted to take York in the hope of seizing our most gracious queen."

"How did you fathom their plans, James?" Pembroke murmured through the angry shouting in response to the king's words.

"Because I know my cousin," Kilburn replied. "And I'll wager that he found an English traitor to show him the way," he added grimly, falling silent as Edward held up a hand. In as few sentences as possible, the elder Despenser, as spokesman for the king, told the assembled barons of the army which had been hastily gathered together by Archbishop Melton of York in defense of the city. Composed of townspeople, farmers, priests, and monks, they had tried bravely to stop the invaders, but in the savage battle on the banks of the Swale near Myton, the Scots proved too strong and too well led for the inexperienced defenders and they were soon scattered or slain—many drowning in the river attempting to escape the savagery of the attackers. The archbishop had fortunately escaped with his life, but the Lord Mayor of York had not been so lucky. He was felled by an enemy spear.

And where were the Scots now, one of the barons asked Lord Despenser. He reddened, glancing quickly at Thomas of Lancaster.

"The report was that they were heading toward Pontefract."

"Pontefract!" Lancaster shouted, starting forward. "God's blood, I must withdraw my forces immediately. If those murdering pack of thieves take my castle . . ." He was ashen, his eyes wild with shock. Other barons, too, with holdings in the north joined in the protest. The king sat without moving, watching the milling crowd of barons who were rallying about Lancaster. A sense of helplessness pervaded his being.

"My lords," Pembroke's deep voice rose above the enraged, frightened shouting. "My good lords, contain yourselves and don't panic. 'Tis true that the Scots have managed to bypass us, but give some thought to the fact that they must now return whence they came."

The earl, in a long tunic of burgundy velvet, stood in the center of the pavilion while Edward, forgotten in the general turmoil, remained immobile on his thronelike chair and looked at him with envy. Had it not always been Lord de Valence who offered the calmest, sagest advice? The king raised a finger to his lips, worrying a hangnail with his teeth. No one ever asked his advice—nor would they listen if he offered any. The king was told what to do. The old nagging question returned to him—of what was he king? Not England surely—the barons had seen to that. He felt a comforting hand on his shoulder and looked up to see Hugh Despenser's smiling eyes.

" 'Twill work out quite well, Your Grace. Have no fear. Notice how they all listen to Pembroke . . . they'll not desert you," the younger Despenser spoke softly into the king's ear. "You see who's with him, don't you, Sire? Arundel, Surrey, and of course the earl of Glairn. They'll do his bidding and the others will follow." Audley, D'Amory, and several more belonging to Pembroke's Middle Party were also nearby, Despenser perceived, but declined to mention it to Edward.

"Not Glairn, Hugh. He was ever a man to go his own way." Of that Edward could be sure. The remembrance of their confrontation in York rose before his eyes, when he had publicly humiliated the border lord before the entire court gathered for the New Year's celebration.

That proud, stiff-necked baron had refused to be chastened, turning the royal insult into an indictment of the king's bad manners. Pembroke had been with him then, too. He knew they were steadfast and staunch friends. Would that he too could be so sure of those surrounding him. He pressed the hand still resting on his shoulder warmly. At least this was an ally whose counsel could be trusted. His dark eyes focused on his cousin Thomas—detestable man, he thought—coveting always what had never belonged to him. The crown which lay on Edward's brow seemed to press heavily into his flesh. The list of grudges to be settled with Lancaster was long, including the murder of his beloved Brother Perrot, and someday that lord would be made to answer them. Oh, that would be a glorious day, Edward mused, divorcing himself from the noisy wrangling surrounding him.

"Your words are always heavy with wisdom, Lord de Valence—what would you say if it were your holdings in peril?" Lancaster spat out, his hand instinctively reaching for the sword which he was not carrying.

"Thomas, think . . . Douglas must bring his men back through England. Rally your forces and meet him before he escapes back into Scotland."

Pembroke looked around him at the worried and alarmed faces of the northern barons. It was no use . . . the situation had changed from a political one to a personal one, and no blame could be placed upon a man whose family was in jeopardy.

The matter was not settled quickly, however, and while several barons hastily withdrew the next morning, it was two days before Lancaster formally advised Edward that he would ride south with his own force to see what could be salvaged.

" 'Tis exactly what Robert Bruce intended with this maneuver," Pembroke told the king irritably. "We're totally divided on this matter, and he knew it would happen."

"So even our great statesman couldn't stop Thomas from running home," Edward said spitefully, cracking a walnut with the handle of his dagger. He had invited his kinsman to supper and enjoyed baiting him, basking in the hearty laughter of his supporters at Pembroke's expense.

"No one has ever succeeded in stopping Thomas from doing what he wanted, Your Grace—including you." The words were sharp and their meaning not lost on the king. Pembroke was tired and suddenly out of patience with Edward's childishness.

"My lord Pembroke, you forget yourself!" The gray-haired Lord Despenser admonished him.

"Nay, I forget naught, Hugh . . . and neither do you. You and your son have remained at your king's side throughout this shameful episode. You are one of his most trusted advisers and your son is his closest friend. There was a time you would have spoken as I do." Pembroke did not flinch from the anger which flared in the other's eyes. "It does not please me to see so many barons pull their forces out to return home. I'll always consider it a grave error in judgment, but I cannot in good conscience condemn them."

"Conscience, dear cousin, was ever your strong point." Edward lifted the gold circlet from his head, holding it up for all to see. "This, my dear lords, is my conscience and I can tell you it weighs heavily on my soul. Yet no one seems to care. My father despised me. His crown was worn proudly, although it was drenched with blood most of the years he reigned, and you all admired him for it. I am aware that it was passed on to me with great reluctance, yet I must remind you all—it did become mine and I wear it still!" Taking umbrage at the lords' habit of speaking as if he did not exist, the king was shaken by a fit of stubborn rage. "You," he shouted suddenly at Pembroke, "you speak of abandoning Berwick to halt James Douglas before he can reach the border. Well, my fine, noble lord, I will not lift the siege. And we shall all remain here until the city is ours once more."

Edward replaced his crown and his dark eyes flashed with the anger that overrode his fear.

"I'll not meet Lord Douglas in the field . . . I'll not. Thomas can be damned to hell for deserting . . . and all of the others. And if Robert Bruce wants to treat with us, then you, my dear cousin Pembroke, may have the glorious pleasure of debating the issues with him, since you do that sort of thing so well." No one dared speak or look up as the king rose, brushing crumbs from his elaborately brocaded tunic. He struck an extraordinarily handsome figure.

If only the man within were as noble as the man without, Pembroke thought, rising with the other lords and bowing as Edward strode past him without another glance. His eyes caught the look of malicious glee on young Hugh Despenser's handsome dark face as he hurried after his king. You misbegotten, ambitious whoreson . . . don't rise too high lest your downfall prove too long a drop. The earl was furious. Speaking to the king was like speaking to air. He left the royal pavilion feeling humiliated by Edward's attitude.

Very well, my callow, cowardly liege lord, he said to himself. If you refuse to meet the enemy face to face, Berwick will have to be forfeited, and we'll expedite the process in spite of you! and he sent Geoffrey to summon Kilburn to his tent.

The riders could hear the tocsin still ringing stridently from village church to village church as they galloped ever closer to Glairn. Kilburn's heart sank as he saw plumes of crimson flames rise from struck villages and ruined crofts. The air reeked with spilled blood and death, and smoke hung dark and acrid over the burned villages. For two days they had cut their way through isolated bands of marauding clansmen, drunk with victory and not a little of the wine from the monasteries whose wealth they had plundered. Laden down with stolen silver and gold plate, goblets and religious objects, the Scots were unable to move as quickly northward as their general would have wished, although reports were that the main force had already reached the border.

Ever since Kilburn and his men had left Berwick, they had seen increasing signs of the havoc and destruction the invaders had wreaked on the English countryside. The roads were thronged with those who had lost all but their lives and now sought sanctuary wherever they could. Newcastle was filled to overflowing and many of the monasteries and abbeys which were left standing had closed their doors because there was no more room.

When Pembroke had advised Kilburn to withdraw his men and see to his holdings, the younger man had already made that decision. Arundel impulsively offered to accompany him, and when the Glairn hawk fluttered bravely at the head of Kilburn's troop of knights and men-at-arms heading out southwest from Berwick, the Fitzalan leopard rode beside it.

"'Tis difficult to comprehend seeing this sort of devastation here," Arundel said, covering his nose with a corner of his mantle, for the stench of burning flesh was nauseating.

"I grant you that it's hard to accept, but 'tis no worse than what our own soldiers and border raiders have done to the Scottish countryside," Kilburn replied grimly, his eyes fixed on the horizon. The towers of the castle should soon be coming into view, although it still lay some distance away. They were both riding with the visors of their helms open in order to breathe the thick air with more ease.

"There's more burning up ahead," Arundel cried, pointing toward an increasingly black cloud of smoke rising above the almost mocking brightness of the fall foliage. A sharp current of wind shredded the dark curtain for a moment and the top of a crenellated tower could be seen before being hidden once more.

"Edmund—God's blood, 'tis Glairn!" Kilburn exclaimed, terror crawling up the back of his neck and coiling itself insidiously into his mind. "Tom—see that the ranks are closed—force-march the men. Lord Arundel will stay close behind you to guard your rear." He turned toward Edmund, who nodded in agreement. "The mounted men-at-arms and knights will proceed with me . . . I feel we're not expected."

"Aye, my lord." Tom pulled on his destrier's reins, preparing to ride back to the pike men, his eyes glittering with anticipation as he closed the visor of his helm and swung his shield into position.

Kilburn held his black stallion back with difficulty,

for the animal sensed the coming battle with excitement. The lance sat loosely in its guard, and the shield bearing the golden hawk on its red field rested against his mailed arm as the earl slipped his left hand through the leather straps. His sword too lay easy in its scabbard, waiting to be drawn as he slammed his visor down, the crimson plume of his helm waving in false gaiety with his every movement.

"Till later then," Arundel called as the large destrier sprang forward, galloping down the winding road toward Glairn. It seemed an eternity before the earl and his men emerged from the trees, surprising a large force of Scottish soldiers attempting to storm the castle. They had attacked the outer gateway and scaled the lower walls, but the capturing of the causeway did not bring the victory they had expected. The heavy drawbridge was raised, securing the castle itself from a direct attack, and Kilburn knew that behind it the massive doors and portcullis were also closed. Arrows showered down upon the attackers from the battlements. Small figures could be seen moving along the walkways high above the castle's thick walls. Several bodies floated in the placid waters of the moat while scaling ladders dangled uselessly against the roughly cut stones near the west tower. A siege catapult was set up on the meadow where in happier times village revels and feasts had been held, and a fiery ball rose through the air with a loud whirring sound before Kilburn's horrified gaze and disappeared beyond the inner battlements of the castle. A large cloud of smoke rose suddenly skyward from where the missile had struck.

A murderous rage took hold of him, and with a wild keening scream, he bore down on the nearest Scot, breaking his lance with the force of his thrust, leaving behind a pierced, lifeless body whose two hands grasped the shaft as if to pluck it out. His sword was in his hand before he was aware of it, the afternoon sunlight running down its sharp edge as he swung it to either side with devastating effect, cutting a path through the men swarming about him. Distracted by the sudden attack from their rear, the Scots found themselves fighting for their lives against formidable savagery.

His eyes green with wild rage and his mouth pressed into a grim line behind his visor, Kilburn was not consciously aware when his sword slashed at a hand foolishly clutching at his stirrup, and with a howl of pain, his attacker slumped to the ground. He noticed that the Scottish invaders were poorly armored, with mantles of roughly woven wool or animal skins and the small round shields he remembered from Bannockburn. On foot and armed mainly with claymores and spears, nothing seemed to frighten them as they attacked Glairn's men with wild howling shrieks. A horn sounded through the din of battle and several Scottish knights rode down the causeway leading to the castle. Sword clanged against sword as they were engaged by Kilburn and his knights. The earth shook as horsemen clashed, and the frightened screams of wounded and dying animals mingled with those of the battling men. A stinging blow to his shoulder unseated the earl as his own sword whistled through the air to come down heavily on the neck of his unknown attacker. Blood poured from the body as it slid sideways from its horse, the dead knight's gauntleted hand still clutching his sword. The proud shield bounced after the body and came to rest a few feet away. The sounds of battle surrounded Kilburn as he found himself standing on the ground. His sword gleamed redly as he grasped it tightly in his right hand while his other held his shield protectively before him. A loud shouting from the forest told him that Thomas Fitzhugh had arrived with the rest of Glairn's armed force. His mailed feet slid on earth made slippery from spilled blood, and it was difficult not to stumble over the fallen bodies littering the ground. Hal brought the black destrier to him, and as he swung himself up into the high-cantled saddle, he ordered the catapult destroyed. His shoulder ached badly, but he paid it no heed as he looked about him slowly, realizing that the battle was all but over.

"My lord Arundel is in pursuit of the Scots who fled northward through the woods," Thomas Fitzhugh reported to him, and Kilburn carefully sheathed his sword, seeing his gauntlets wet with blood and slime. He was drenched with the sweat which streamed down his face and body.

He lifted the helm from his head and took several deep breaths to quiet the pounding of his heart.

"How many men did we lose?" Kilburn asked, seeing the smoldering ruins of Glairn's own village with slightly blurred vision and growing nausea.

"One killed and three wounded, my lord. One knight with a broken leg—'tis Robert Brampton. I've not yet had the report on the men-at-arms, but I think that the losses were heavier for the Scots."

Kilburn closed his eyes for a moment. Pray to God all were safe within Glairn—Gillian! His heart called out to her, but there was no answer. Tom's voice was sharp as his lord swayed suddenly, clutching at his horse's mane, the pain in his shoulder shafting through him hotly.

"My lord, are you well?" The young knight's voice was anxious, for the earl's face was drained of all color. Shaking his head, Kilburn managed to force a smile.

"Aye, Tom, I'm fine."

"We've taken three knights prisoner, and there are more than a dozen men-at-arms still alive."

"Kill them," Kilburn said coldly. "We take no prisoners." They had tried to destroy his life's blood. Had he not warned James Douglas of this very thing the last time they had met. "Either execute them now or give them to the village folk."

"Not the knights, surely, Lord Kilburn—one is a nephew of the earl of Moray!"

What did it matter who one of the prisoners was, the battle-weary man thought, watching the drawbridge slowly lower with a great thunderous creaking of chains to span the moat. He was the enemy and had tried to sack Glairn—and yet, he could be of value in exchanging English knights the Scots held prisoner. Turning his gaze from the castle, he shrugged and looked indifferently at the three prisoners standing defiantly in the midst of his own knights.

"Bring Moray's nephew along, Tom, and we'll send him to Newcastle. The other knights' heads can be displayed above the gate as a warning to any future bands of Scots who may venture near that they'll get no quarter from Glairn."

The black destrier's hooves clattered hollowly on the wooden planking as he began to cross the drawbridge. The massive doors slowly swung inward, and as he rode through the narrow passageway between the two raised portcullises into the inner bailey, he saw where fires had been extinguished and battered pieces of armor and discarded weapons still littered the ground. Sir Simon, in full battle dress, his face grimy with soot and sweat, waited in the yard before the central keep, surrounded by some of the knights and older apprentices, all bearing the marks of battle. Falling heavily on one knee before his lord, the old man thanked him for having saved them all. He looked drawn and weary as he told Kilburn they had been under siege for two days but withstood the attacks well. Glairn Castle was a fortification nearly impregnable to any attempt to capture it.

Sir Simon hastened to assure him that the children and the womenfolk were safe, having stayed together with those members of the household who could not take part in the defense of the castle. They were still in the sanctuary of the chapel in the care of Father Godfrey and Master de Blount. He added that young Master Alain had been greatly disappointed when armor and sword had been denied him.

"The countess?" Kilburn's throat was dry as he followed the constable's gaze to the walkway above the gate. A figure was running down the worn stairs, and he dismounted hurriedly, forgetting his pain as he slipped the helm from his damp hair and held out his arms. Hysterical laughter rumbled deep within him as he watched Gillian, clad in the hauberk he had worn as a boy, with a short sword clutched in one hand, hurry awkwardly toward him. A disheveled dark braid tumbling down her back, she might have been some warrior maiden from the ancient chronicles. Her smudged face glowed at the sight of him, and her sword clattered to the ground as Kilburn clasped her tightly in his arms. She wept with joy at his safe return, her tears salty on his mouth. Slowly they made their way up the few steps to the entrance hall of the keep.

"Jamie . . . we watched the battle! I was so afraid!"

Her fingers touched his face, love pouring from her and surrounding him with its soothing balm.

"Lady Gillian refused to stay safely with the others, my lord, so I insisted she be armed."

" 'Tis fine, Simon—I thank you for your concern."

One arm about Gillian's slender shoulders, he turned toward the wide stairs when the floor suddenly tilted crazily and everything spun wildly about him. He sank down slowly, his legs unable to support him, pulling Gillian with him. His last conscious sight before darkness claimed him was Gillian's frightened face bending over him. She called for help, pillowing his head in her lap. Sir Simon quickly tore off Jamie's surcoat and unfastened his hauberk. A red stain was slowly spreading over the unconscious man's left shoulder, and blood trickled down his arm. His face was deathly pale as his head lolled limply against Gillian's body. She smoothed the damp tousled hair from his forehead. He felt dreadfully cold.

"Sir Simon, he's not dead . . . ?" she sobbed, fear clawing at her with icy talons as she cradled Jamie in her arms.

"Nay, my lady, he's just fainted from loss of blood. A lance pierced the hauberk and grazed his shoulder. Master Brassard will see to him. Calm yourself—'tis not as bad as it looks. Once the blood is staunched and the wound salved and bandaged, he'll be fine. Especially when he's had a cup or two of heated wine. Remember his return from Bannockburn? Now there was a dire wound . . ." Sir Simon's voice was calm and matter-of-fact.

"Gillian . . . lovedy!" The words were whispered against her lips as she kissed him, her tears drenching them both.

"Maddie . . . she's safe, lovedy? My Maddie?"

"Aye, Jamie—they're all safe," Gillian replied, her heart twisting within her. "All of them," she repeated, jealous anger at his concern banishing her fear for him. Damn that child, she thought—what was it that made him love her so? When he had been carefully carried up the stairs to their bedchamber, Gillian remained sitting on the stone floor of the entry beneath the tattered banners of past battles, her joyous welcome made bitter by Jamie's question.

"Mama, why do you sit here—everyone is staring at you." The young voice trembled with apprehension as Alain knelt beside her, his child's fingers clutching her arm. "Hal told me Papa was hurt . . ."

Gillian looked with tear-blurred eyes at her son's concerned face. Drawing him to her, she buried her face for a moment into the small, thin body and felt his hand shyly touch her hair.

" 'Tis naught, sweetheart," she murmured, drying her eyes with the back of one grimy hand. "Come with me, sweeting, and we'll find out how your father is. Master Brassard will have seen to him by now."

Alain held his mother's arm protectively as they slowly walked up the stairs together. Looking down at the shining mop of chestnut hair and the long hazel eyes so like his father's she thought wistfully that Jamie might love his youngest daughter above all else, but this child, so rapturously conceived in a burned-out croft on the edge of a Scottish meadow eight years ago was the true culmination of their love. And, would Alain not have thought it unmeet and undignified, she would have clasped him to her and kissed him.

Sir Simon was proved right, and by the time Arundel arrived, Kilburn was installed in a large chair close to the warm hearth of the solar, comfortably leaning against soft cushions. A fur-trimmed woolen tunic concealed the white bandage Master Brassard had bound over his wounded shoulder and the pain was diminished to a dull throb by an infusion of bitter herbs he had been given to drink.

The children, sternly cautioned not to tire their father with their exuberance, were brought to see him. Fearful of their mother's displeasure, Margaret and Hugh regarded James solemnly, not venturing to approach him until he smiled and held out his hand. Jennifer, two years old and overcome by shyness, hid behind Agnes's skirt, her large hazel eyes watching wistfully as Mathilde was deposited in her father's lap, to be kissed and caressed as she nestled against the soft cloth of his tunic. Alain,

224

having already seen his father, sat with an attitude of superiority in the windowseat.

With rising irritation, Gillian watched James's naked expression as he held Maddie to him, his love for her so transparent that she felt hot jealousy pulse through her. No matter how often she told herself that it was not right that she should feel jealous of their own child, she could only remember the rage which had coursed through her at the moment of Maddie's birth. With grim satisfaction, Gillian listened to the child's howls of protest as she lifted her from her father's lap, handing her firmly to Agnes.

"Stop your wailing, Maddie, for 'twill not give you what you want," Gillian snapped. Turning to Agnes, she said, "I think Lord Kilburn should rest now. Seeing the children has allayed his fear that all was not well with them." She studiously avoided looking at Maddie, whose sobs had not diminished. Although she was still naught but a babe, a few months more than a year, young Mathilde already knew that few could deny her anything and used the knowledge to full advantage. Gillian was the only one unmoved by the quivering rosebud mouth and the enormous dark blue eyes abrim with tears. She listened with a sense of relief to the fading sounds of her daughter's weeping as the children were taken back to the nursery.

"You too, young Master Alain," she said to her eldest son, finding him still sitting by the window.

"Lovedy, you're too harsh with them," James chided, but he motioned to his son to obey his mother.

" 'Tis just that I want you to myself for a little while . . . I've not seen you all these months, Jamie," Gillian replied, her eyes drinking in the sight of him.

Servants brought flagons of wine, hot spiced ale, and a platter of sweet cakes into the spacious chamber, the glowing colors of the fine tapestries covering the stone walls and the comfortable, well-worn furniture enfolding them with a warmth unusual by the standards of the time. Gillian handed her husband a mazer of wine and their fingers touched. They looked at each other and smiled, their hearts at peace.

When Edmund Fitzalan strode into the cheerful solar,

he brought the coolness of autumn and a faint odor of wood smoke with him. A tall, broad-shouldered man with dusty brown hair and merry blue eyes, he was still clad in hauberk and surcoat, not having taken the time to change clothes before presenting himself to the castle. Gillian rose to meet him.

"My lady," Arundel said, bending over the soft white hand extended to him, "I would have wished a first meeting under happier circumstances."

Gillian lifted her dark-lashed blue eyes to his bluff, cheerful face and smiled gently. She had exchanged her armor for a more comfortable, simply cut robe. The deep red of the loosely woven cloth accentuated the pallor of her skin, and Arundel felt a tightening within himself at her loveliness.

"We will always be grateful for your help," she said. " 'Twas a terrible thing to have happen to the holding."

"Edmund! How did it go?" James asked, a trifle disturbed at his friend's entranced expression, although he understood all too well the impact Gillian had on other men.

"Very well . . . we were very successful in our hunt, and I've added to your collection above the gate." Arundel turned his attention reluctantly to Kilburn. "You seem none the worse for your wound—your constable told me what happened."

" 'Tis naught but a spear's graze . . . a few days stiffness and 'twill be forgotten." James shrugged off his injury and watched Edmund settle himself on the bench before the fire. A servant poured wine for him and he drank it thirstily.

"Excellent, James! 'Tis just the thing to clear the stench of burning flesh and bloody death from a man's mind."

Gillian shuddered at his words, but James sighed, resting his head against the back of the chair.

"Aye, the day's been a full one!" He closed his eyes. "But Glairn is safe."

"And since it is, I'd best tarry no longer. I plan to leave at first light, so I've set up a hasty encampment on your mired battlefield, James."

"So soon, my lord Fitzalan?" Gillian exclaimed. She found Arundel much to her liking, surprising herself, for she had held both Alain's betrothal to his daughter and Margaret's betrothal to Walter Deveron against him, naming him a meddler in her life.

"I fear so, Lady Kilburn. 'Tis meet I ride to Newcastle and find out what's happening to our siege." Edmund smiled at her and she smiled back, for his good humor was infectious.

"My Alianor will find a happy home here, I think," he remarked suddenly and was pleased to see a blush suffuse Gillian's pale cheeks. "I'd hoped to meet Glairn's young heir, but I'm afraid there's no time."

He rose and the chamber was filled with his explosive energy. Over both Gillian's and Edmund's protests, James insisted upon accompanying him downstairs.

"You'll not even sup with us, Edmund?" Kilburn asked, standing on the steps of the keep, his shoulder aching from his movements.

"Nay, James . . . 'tis best you not overtax yourself. Besides, with such as the Lady Gillian to wife, I'd not want a guest to keep me from her!" Fitzalan said, laughing. No wonder James had risked everything for her, he thought. Much had been said about the countess of Glairn, but few had seen her in the past years, for she remained in the north. "I'll send men for your prisoner before I leave," he called as he mounted the gray destrier, for he had promised his friend to deliver Moray's nephew to Newcastle. With a final wave of his gauntleted hand, he rode through the portcullised gate to the outer bailey, accompanied by his squire.

"My lord Kilburn."

James turned bemused eyes toward Simon Jardine, who stood before him at the foot of the steps to the keep, his face white and the eyes glazed with shock.

"My lord, I think you'd best come with me . . . I've some bad news to tell you."

Under Tom's supervision, Glairn's men-at-arms had scoured the perimeter of the castle both from within and without to ascertain the damage done by the attackers,

Simon told his lord as they walked slowly beneath the archway leading toward the kitchen wing and its vegetable and herb gardens. There seemed to have been relatively little harm done and few injuries. It was only now, as the torches flared and the candles gleamed golden in the evening dusk, that Graeme's body had been found a few yards beyond the postern gate. They had carried the body through the gate and stretched it out on the graveled path. Sword in hand, caparisoned for battle, Graeme lay with a look of deep contentment upon his dead face. Kilburn stared sadly at the man who had been his companion since childhood. A single sword blow had felled him, but sightless though he had been, he had drawn blood. Kilburn bent down and picked up his old friend's sword.

"The guards told me 'twas Graeme who gave the alarm for an attack on this gate, my lord," Sir Simon told him. "He was by the postern gate before any of the others could reach him." Looking anxiously at the grave man standing beside him, the constable added, "We can't understand how he was able to get this far alone . . . not in his paralyzed state."

"'Tis something we'll never know," Kilburn murmured. "Desperation or a strong will can oft lend unheard-of strength to a man."

Ordering a stronger guard at the gate, he followed Graeme's body into the keep, still holding the blood-stained sword.

Another door in my life shut, Kilburn thought sadly. Another light extinguished forever. And he shivered involuntarily. Touching the rough stones, he looked up at the walls of the keep towering above him. No matter, he told himself, Glairn survives, and was for the moment comforted.

"Jamie?" The whispered name floated softly through the empty chamber. Gillian looked between the drawn bed curtains, unable to penetrate the deep, unmoving darkness. There was no moon this night to fill the chamber's windows with silvered light. She received no answer and knew that he was gone. Lying back against the large soft pillows, her hand groped for the warm depression on the sheet where Jamie's body had rested.

How many hours earlier had she held him in her arms as he had wept for Graeme, his tears burning her skin? His need for her had been as comforter and receptacle for his devastating grief. So had he wept for the other friend of his childhood, Hugh Martleigh, when he heard of his death at Bannockburn. Now, of the accursed triangle, Jamie alone was left, Gillian thought, unable to feel any sorrow at the former squire's death. She had long ago known what made the other two cling to Jamie so jealously, but it had not mattered, for he refused to acknowledge the truth, recoiling from it angrily.

Rocking him gently as she would a child, Gillian understood that for the lonely, shy and sensitive boy, it had been a wonderful thing to have two close companions to grow up with, but it had led to a warped, dark friendship which had ruined Hugh's marriage and driven Graeme into the solitary wild world from which he could not be drawn.

"Jamie, he wanted to die!" Gillian murmured into the darkness. " 'Tis guilt which haunts you now—Graeme saved your life and you believe that it ultimately destroyed him. But he was destroyed long ago."

The words lay all about her, but she knew she would never say them to him. She guessed where he had gone in the depths of the battle-free night . . . to the chapel where Graeme's body lay on the catafalque he himself had ordered, there to face his grief alone, without her.

And Gillian wept . . . for Jamie's lonely childhood and oddly enough, for Hugh Martleigh whom she had grown to love in the short years she knew him. But never for Graeme, for she had feared him and was glad he was dead.

His shoulder throbbed painfully and for a moment James was overcome with dizziness. He gripped the edge of the bier, waiting for it to pass before allowing himself to stare into Graeme's dead face. Sleep had eluded him as forgotten memories of his childhood taunted him relentlessly. Perhaps here he might find the bridge between the days that had been and the present.

The chapel lay in darkness save for the flickering votive candles and the light from the tall waxen tapers standing near the bier.

Graeme's blunt features were at peace, the thick flaxen hair hiding the deep scar on his forehead. He looked so frail, so unlike the fierce, tireless Scot he had been. Only the small round shield with its strange marking and the long, heavy sword lying on his body, partially covered by the full mantle of animal skins, gave evidence of his once-powerful warrior's prowess.

How entwined their lives had been from those early days of childhood's equality to the time Graeme became James's squire, and his wild spirit was tamed. James swallowed painfully, his throat constricting as the memories of their standing back-to-back in battle flooded his mind. How invincible they had been together . . . until Bannockburn. Bannockburn! Would that that day be wiped out forever! And the grief that had walked silently beside him since Hugh Martleigh's death welled up, mingling with that of Graeme's loss.

Nay, he told himself sternly, I'll not bear the guilt for them. 'Tis past and the guilt was theirs, not mine! And yet he buried his face in his hands, unable to look at Graeme. A slight movement startled him, for he believed himself alone. Raising his head, he saw a figure huddled at the foot of the bier, barely visible in the shrouded gloom.

"Who's there?" he called softly.

" 'Tis I, Laird—tae be wi' my laddie for the last time." Non's words were broken and blurred with tears. She was on her knees, head bowed and covered by the woolen shawl which had always been a part of her. James could faintly smell the familiar odor of wood smoke and sheep which still clung to it.

"Come, old woman, sit here. 'Tis bad for your joints to kneel on the cold stones." He sat on the hard wooden bench and took one of her thin, gnarled hands in his own.

"Och, I hadna' noticed," Non said, drawing the shawl closer. "A' the thoughts a'whirlin' about in my head . . .

such a sonsie bairn my wee Graeme were." Her voice dropped sadly. "But doomed."

A flicker of light caught the shimmer of tears on the wrinkled cheeks. She seemed to have shrunken in those short hours since learning of her son's death. James sat silently beside her, holding her hand. Sunk in his own thoughts, he paid little heed when she began to speak softly, but her faltering words soon caught his attention.

" 'Twas a stranger's corse I washed today . . . I ne'er knew him!" Non's voice broke. "A' these years . . . he was my ain son—yet, he had a de'il in his blood—He knew, Jamie, he knew and 'twas my guilt! Ye were the auld Laird's grandson . . ."

James made a deep sound in his throat, gripped by a sudden aching pain. Kissing her cold forehead, he tried to draw her closer and said gently, "You're overwrought . . . try to rest a little. I'll stay with you."

But it was as if she did not hear him, her mind wandering back to the days when she had still belonged to the Douglas family. James listened to the whispered, meandering words, his face pale and intent. She spoke of things he had no knowledge of—of his grandfather's world—how many lifetimes past?

"He ne'er looked at me when he rode past, sae tall and clear-eyed wi' that burnin' look that turned my limbs to water. 'Tis he ye image, Jamie . . . like the Douglas laird ye are."

The old eyes glowed and the years seemed to drop from her. She was young again, and in love, leaping over the fire at Lammastide with the shepherd who had come over the brae with his ewes and lambs to capture her heart. One year and he was gone, leaving behind only the memory of their shared love and the babe born after his father's death. On and on the aged voice rambled, and James found his face wet with tears. Had he ever given Non any thought save that she belonged to him as everything in Glairn did, although his own father had removed her serf's collar years before. He cursed his blind indifference, seeing within the grieving old woman the vestiges of the vital human being who had felt passion and sorrow as much as he did himself. Her tear-drenched blue eyes gazed at him suddenly with blind love, and then they clouded with pain.

"I tried to luv him proper, and 'tis the guilt of it I carry," she said slowly. "Sae help me, Jamie . . . I luved ye mair than my ain laddie! 'Twas sinful, but 'tis nae shame I hae for luvin' ye." Non swayed, crooning softly. "Ye're the auld laird's grandson . . . a true Douglas, Jamie . . . ye e'er were a true Douglas!"

James picked up Non's limp hand and held it to his wet cheek, kissing it gently. He cradled her in his arms as she began to weep bitterly, the full impact of her loss sweeping over her.

"Graeme . . . och, my Graeme . . . forgi'e me . . ."

Graeme had known and not hated him for it! James looked without flinching at the squire's body, understanding him in death as he never had in life. Graeme had died as he wanted to, in battle, and for that he could not mourn his warrior's death. Their farewells had been said long ago, James realized, for a stranger had inhabited Graeme's crippled body during the last years. His spirit was now free to forever roam the dense forests and broad, windswept meadows he had loved, unshackled at last from the turbulent violence of his chained emotions and the blind, paralyzing darkness which had been his final world.

PART FOUR
1321

Chapter 8

1321
Salop

"You have lost your wits! Lost them entirely!"

De Mortimer spoke lightly, but Jehan caught the slight tinge of irritation beneath his apparent air of amusement. Not thirty minutes earlier he had stridden into the solar, causing the atmosphere to crackle with the force of his personality. Still weighted down by a hauberk and his surcoat spattered with the caked mud of spring roads, he handed his helm to Emrys. He never took his eyes from Jehan's defiant face as he impatiently unfastened his own cloak, letting Emrys catch it as he strode toward her.

"Nay, Roger, you're wrong. I've found myself."

It was difficult to remain aloof and indifferent in his presence, for no matter how she tried, Jehan felt small beside de Mortimer. He looked down at her heart-shaped face, her green eyes solemn, intent on her words to him.

" 'Twas a difficult decision to make . . . to leave all the pleasures and excitement of the world I've known and have the convent gates shut behind me forever, but 'tis better so. I've seen the peace of mind and tranquillity of spirit in the good sisters' faces. How I envied them their contentment!"

De Mortimer snorted in derision. "Rather say weariness and lack of spirit from too much labor and kneeling at prayers, my lady. They'll not put up with your tempers and willfulness once you've committed yourself to life within a nunnery!"

He refused to believe that her intentions were serious, Jehan realized. Without waiting for an explanation, he had insisted that the packed coffers standing in the courtyard ready to be loaded on the wagon be opened and emptied of their contents immediately. For more than a year she had heard naught from him—why could he not have waited one more day? She would have been gone, Jehan thought with annoyance. She took a deep breath.

"I've had much time to think in the months since I left the court—"

Jehan's words were cut short as Roger laughed darkly, without mirth.

"Nay, my dove, as ever, you never cease to delude yourself. 'Tis common knowledge—even in Ireland—that the queen cast you out because you allowed yourself to be discovered with a lover. I take it that de Heland was granted your bed as just reward for all he divulged to you, since the Lady Jehan has always had a way with men! 'Tis just fortunate that your spying was not brought to light."

The green eyes blazed in sudden anger. Treacherous whoreson! How dare Roger throw his own intrigues in her face like that, ignoring his own emotional involvement. He was unbelievable! Jehan struggled to control her rising temper, telling herself that despite his cruel words, he was not completely wrong, although Robert de Heland had never succeeded in his attempted seduction. She chided herself at her own unconscious refusal to admit that the queen had dismissed her in a fit of spiteful and jealous malice. Her eyes flew to his face, the true meaning of his remarks suddenly penetrating her rage. Veiling her astonishment, she could find no trace of mockery in his expression. So Isabella had not revealed the truth. What must the keeping of that secret have cost her, Jehan wondered, hoping venomously that it had caused the cold-blooded bitch to feel a measure of the pain she inflicted so easily upon others.

"You'll not shake me from my decision, Roger. You're released from caring to my needs. I would have thought you glad at the prospect of not having me to re-

236

mind you of a past mistake." Jehan's voice trembled and she turned away from de Mortimer's dark gaze, afraid of his nearness. She sat down on the padded seat of the recessed window. "As for me—I'll have a place to belong to without wondering where fortune's wind will blow me when you tire of me. I can pray and sit in the convent garden to meditate on the joy of serving God. 'Tis comforting to know that at the end of the day there will be food to eat and a peaceful slumber."

Roger's sword clanked against his armored leg guard as he strode restlessly about the small solar. It was incredible! The fantastic creature actually believed all she was saying. His expression was black as he threw his gauntlets to the floor. Had fortune truly turned on him, he wondered furiously. His stay in Ireland had been a disaster, and he had barely escaped from that accursed place with his life. Returning to England he found passionate anger and hatred against the usurping Despensers mounting to a near uncontrollable pitch among his fellow Marcher barons. When he reached Wigmore Castle, the news awaited him that the younger Despenser had seized one of his castles in South Wales, obviously with some sort of royal blessing. It had been taken with much violence, for the constable had refused to surrender without a fight. God's wounds, how he had raged at his impotence to act against that arrogant whoreson. And now this! In scathing tones he heaped abuse on the woman who had added fuel to his already considerable anger. His fingers itched to strike out at Jehan, to erase the unfamiliar look of pious humility from her face, which served only to increase the sensuality of the passionate features. But he hesitated, unsure suddenly how he should treat her. Venting his pent-up rage on her would serve no purpose but to harden her resolve to defy him.

Jehan contemplated Roger's outburst with apparent calm, keeping silent until he turned with a strangled oath and stormed from the solar, seemingly drained of words. Leaning her head against the cold stones, she rested her gaze on the hills surrounding the manor. The trees were already tinged with a soft green, mingling with the verdancy of the stands of pine. The second spring since she had taken up residence had come without her awareness of it. Isolated in her reluctant memories, Jehan was blind to the shaft of golden afternoon light which enfolded her in its glow.

Sweet Jesu, how she had bound him to her! Jehan's heart still raced, recalling how neither of them had been able to quench the insatiable hunger each had for the other. Until his departure for Berwick, Roger had come to her small chamber several times, having forbidden her entry to his own quarters. The last time they were together, she had been as one demented, fear clawing at her that this time he would disappear from her life, despite all that lay between them. Lips drawn back in his devil's laugh, he had held her against him.

" 'Tis not the end of the world, little dove," he had murmured. "Are you mine, Jehan?" Whispered words floated in the darkness as his mouth found hers again, drawing the very essence of life from her.

"Yes, my lord, I'm yours." Her answer was wild and she pressed herself to him with such urgency that she ached.

And no matter how I deny it, I'm still yours, Jehan breathed, unwanted tears seeping through closed lids. What would he have replied, had she dared to ask the same of him?

The door opened without warning and Jehan was distracted from her musings at the sudden activity surrounding her. Several servants, wearing the de Mortimer badge, had burst noisily into the solar, bringing more wood to replenish the fire. They gave no sign of having noticed her as they lit the large candles standing waxen yellow in their metal holders against the tapestry-covered walls. Now that the baron was in residence, they no longer feared his mistress's sharp tongue and flaming temper. Even the servants belonged to Roger and cared naught for her welfare, Jehan thought peevishly. Had he bidden them to tend a mendicant monk, they would have done so without question, for it was their master who commanded them. She shivered as the dusk-shrouded chamber emerged once more into light. Outside the hills loomed darkly against the dying sun. She brushed the tears from her cheeks with cold fingers. Peace—would it always be denied her? Jehan did not want to think of the weeks that followed Nottingham, but her mind would not obey, tormenting her with the kaleidoscope of days which blended into the nightmare still haunting her.

After the court's safe arrival at Westminster everything seemed well. England's panic over the Scottish invasion and the ensuing political news had consumed them totally for the first weeks. The queen was pleased to return to the sprawling palace, and the court settled down for a long stay. News reached them of the king's continuing siege of Berwick and the Black Douglas's safe retreat across the border for a triumphant reunion with his royal kinsman, Robert Bruce. The baron of Wigmore was never mentioned save in thankful phrases of loyalty displayed in time of danger. In any event, Roger had returned to Ireland and, for once, Jehan could breath more easily, knowing that although he was separated from her, he was also removed from the temptation of the queen's presence.

Did Isabella feel the same? Jehan had no way of knowing, for she could never fathom what truly went on in that delicate, well-shaped head. Even when the earl of Pembroke returned from Scotland at Yuletide, bringing with him the welcome tidings of a successfully negotiated two-year truce with Robert Bruce, Isabella's blue eyes remained cold and expressionless in her smiling face. The peace, however uneasy, also brought Edward and his courtiers to Westminster from York where he had gone after finally lifting his futile siege. Leaving Lord Badlesmere in charge of the army remaining in the north, he turned, in his usual way, to more preferred pleasures as the Twelfth Night festivities drew near.

Jehan moaned softly and buried her face in the arm resting against the windowsill, a familiar cold and angry futility consuming her. She had not been prepared for what happened that night in early January when she was suddenly summoned to the queen's presence long after everyone else had retired. She could still feel the fatigue which pressed continuously down upon her no matter how much she rested and the dizziness which swept over her without warning as she stood before Isabella's chamber, afraid to discover what lay behind the heavy wooden door. The humiliation of that interview was painful to remember. The queen sat as one etched in stone in the dimly lit chamber, heated beyond endurance by braziers placed near by. Alisa Peverell, a triumphant smile on her plain, sallow face, stood by the queen's side, fingering a beautiful chain set with small green stones, obviously newly acquired.

"You've been accused of spying on your queen, Lady de Maudley, and of consorting with the baron of Wigmore."

Isabella's voice shook with barely concealed outrage, although she remained perfectly still. The royal circlet glittered brightly in the flickering light as she leaned forward to gaze into Jehan's ashen face.

"Adulteress! Spy!" she hissed.

Jehan had stared at her in disbelief. Two thirds of the court was guilty of adultery. The chamber tilted crazily as she gagged in the oppressively thick air, but she took a deep breath, determined not to reveal her sudden panic.

"Your Majesty! What is there to spy about? And who would gain from anything I might hear? As for adultery— I am a widow!"

"Ask her what Lord de Mortimer had been doing when he was seen leaving her chamber before dawn the last night before his departure from Nottingham." Lady Alisa's voice trembled with malicious glee. "And her words with that same lord's harper outside Your Grace's chambers one night when she thought no one was about! She is spying for him—I heard her."

Jehan could not deny it, yet dared not admit it to a queen suddenly ablaze with jealous anger. White-faced and fighting a growing nausea, she remained silent as Isabella told her that she herself had observed her unfeigned interest in the handsome baron. She had not realized until then how deeply she loathed the Frenchwoman who used her power to cause others to suffer because of her own inadequacies. Wisely, Jehan had kept her eyes lowered, lest her hatred be revealed to the queen.

Unable to control her jealousy and not truly wanting to hear a confession of fulfilled passion with a man she herself coveted, a furious Isabella, in a carefully worded pronouncement delivered by one of her equerries, banished Jehan from court. The accusation of spying was not pursued and she had left Westminster Palace a few days later without seeing Isabella again.

When Jehan, feeling forsaken and clinging to her newfound key to peace, had seen the cavalcade ride through the gate earlier that day, a wild joy coursed through her at the realization that Roger had not forgotten her, but it had died in the face of her determination not to change her mind. She raised her eyes to the small tower set in the west corner of the fortified house to watch a barely visible yellow and green banner flutter from the crenellated top, and was startled by the unexpected blare of a trumpet shattering the stillness. Hearing the protesting squeal of the lowering drawbridge, she stepped up on the windowseat and peered into the courtyard, which was suddenly alive with flaming torches, yelping dogs, and retainers hurrying out to attend to the knights clattering through the large open gate. She could see Roger come forward to eagerly greet a black-visored knight on a large gray horse. His tall figure, bright in a deep scarlet tunic trimmed with gold embroidery, was dwarfed by his companion. It was Chirk, his uncle, for whom Roger had been named. What mischief were they up to, Jehan wondered, her own problems forgotten in her curiosity over the older man's arrival. She smiled in relief, for this was indeed a welcome intrusion. Perhaps she need not face any more of Roger's probing, for she had sworn to herself that he must never discover the true reason for her decision, for it would change nothing.

" 'Twas fortunate you found me, Uncle. I had thought to send you word where I was. How did you know to find me here?"

De Mortimer motioned to the tall, white-haired man to take the wide wooden chair before the fire. A servant hurried to place pillows behind the guest's back and another drew a small table near. A log fell in the hearth,

241

sending out a shower of sparks, and Roger turned toward the servants, speaking sharply to them. If they laid the fire carelessly because he had not been here, then it was time they were sent out into the forest to supply the manor with firewood. They blanched at his words, both running to tend to the offending log. He stood close by them, staring moodily into the restored neatness of the crackling hearth while his uncle observed him shrewdly. The baron of Chirk was a younger brother of Roger's father, and the family resemblance between them was very striking. Hard-bitten, cruel, and implacable in his hatred, this de Mortimer had gained his not inconsiderable power by every means available to him—a characteristic which was much admired by his ambitious nephew.

" 'Tis no secret that you've a mistress ensconced in your mother's favorite manor house." Replying to his nephew's question, the baron's words were dry and edged with sarcasm. The younger man darted a startled glance at Chirk and flushed, scowling darkly.

"My mother's possession no longer. It came to me with my father's lands and titles, as you damn well know. 'Tis mine to do with as I wish. My mother is well provided for elsewhere, and has no need for this manor. Lady Jehan is the widow of one of my staunchest lieutenants. He fell in Ireland against the Scots."

"How fortunate," Chirk murmured. Looking from under heavy white brows, his eyes sparkled maliciously. "Spare me your excuses, Roger. I know she's the daughter of Lord Gouland, whose lands neighbor yours in Clun. 'Twas a happy and not unsuspicious coincidence that she was made to wed one of your liegemen. However, I've no interest in the beds you share, save one. How Joan can calmly put up with your flagrant infidelities and still allow you near her is totally beyond my understanding. That she does is evident in how often you occupy her in childbearing. You use your wife as you use everything—to your own advantage." His harsh, wild face twisted in a smile. "I must admit that your red-haired leman is a toothsome fiery piece of female flesh. I'm not unfamiliar with her adventures at court. To keep you interested this long, she

242

must indeed be a wanton in bed! She fair made me itch to taste her wares myself."

He was delighted at his nephew's reaction, for Roger's black eyes burned with a cold fire as he turned toward his uncle with murderous fury.

"You're a fine one to sit in judgment on me, Uncle! I've heard that half the bastards in Powys resemble you."

Now was not the time to be teased about Jehan, for he was still disturbed by her earlier pronouncement. She had worsened matters by refusing to remain in the Great Hall with him after the evening meal, telling him she was retiring and that she did not wish to be disturbed at her devotions. When he ordered her to remain, her face had blanched in a burst of temper and she turned venomously to him in feline fury. Only the presence of his uncle had stopped him from following her as she swept from the hall. Chirk's well-placed shafts had hit their mark with stinging force.

"What lies between us concerns no one but ourselves, Uncle. Do not press me too hard, even in jest, or . . ."

"Easy, Roger. I'd no idea the wench meant so much to you." The old man had been startled by his nephew's reaction, but emotional entanglements were negligible in his philosophy. He dismissed Jehan's existence with a shrug, for there were more important things to discuss than Roger's amoral fancies. Drinking deeply from the heavy silver goblet a servant had already refilled, he stretched out his strong, muscular legs covered by a long, dark blue tunic banded with gray fur.

"I hear tell your creditors hounded you out of Ireland." The bantering tone was gone, and his words hung with icy disapproval in the chamber's stillness. "You've managed to play right into the hands of that whoreson Despenser and his whelp."

"The king's parchment charged me with incompetency, Uncle, and you know as well as I do that my competency was not the cause of my dismissal. My debts are no greater now than they ever were and I refuse to admit that I gave the Despensers reason to turn me out."

Dark fury seethed deep within Roger at the memory

of the formal words attacking the corruption of his administration. He had taken a measure of comfort from the way the flames licked hungrily at the offending parchment when he threw it into the fire. It took little imagination to fathom who had instigated that move against him. Particularly now in the light of the theft of his castle. The firelight cast Roger's shadow, tall and darkly menacing, against the far wall as he continued to stand before the hearth.

"Everywhere I turn, I hear of the power the two Despensers have attained over Edward. It angers me beyond reason."

"And for good cause. They've turned their attention to our holdings in Wales again. My position as Justiciar of Wales sits poorly with the elder Hugh. It lends credence to my laying claim to certain lands he covets. Since Gloucester's death at Bannockburn without leaving an heir, his three sisters have been pawns in a game of avaricious chess because of his Welsh holdings. That the Lady Eleanor is wife to his son is just the sort of lever Despenser needs."

"Was there ever a time Edward would not have given his nieces in marriage to a favorite, as he did to Gaveston?"

Chirk laughed lewdly.

"Why not? It would have made very little difference to our king which of Gloucester's sisters went to either lord. Those three royal nieces are ripe, rich plums for ambitious men to pluck through the king's favor. 'Tis interesting to watch how Lady Margaret's second husband is in league with his other brother-in-law, Roger d'Amory, against their common foe. D'Audley is no fool. I hear he's been in touch with Hereford."

The dark eyes flashed as Chirk continued his tirade against the Despensers, but Roger's attention strayed. Damn Jehan! Her words kept intruding as he tried to concentrate on his uncle's words. She was keeping something from him . . . he knew her well enough to have surmised that much, but what could it be? He sat down heavily opposite Chirk. Interrupting his uncle, he called loudly for Emrys. Music—yes, perhaps music would calm him.

Quietly the harper came from out of the dark corner he had inhabited and knelt before his master, eyes cast down and his small harp cradled with love in his arms. He felt de Mortimer's foot against his thigh, prodding him to rise.

"Must you always dress yourself as some lord's fool, Welshman?" Roger was irritated by the harper's motley attire, which was noticeably frayed and in need of repair. Emrys did not reply, waiting for his lord's wrath to break over him. He was inured to de Mortimer's abuse, and knew that it was not truly aimed against him, but was rather de Mortimer's anger at his own inability to resolve whatever disturbed or frustrated him. Seeing the closed, resigned look in the strange eyes, Roger's anger dissipated and he sighed.

"Play your harp, Emrys . . . 'tis time to sweeten our souls."

As the soft golden sounds of the gently plucked strings floated lightly about them, Chirk leaned forward urgently, ignoring the harper's presence and his music.

"We're the targets of a slanderous whispering campaign, Roger. We're being accused of corruption and treasonable ambition against the crown. What's worse is that Edward wishes to believe all of it."

"Splendid. Then we have just cause to defend our honor and reputation, Uncle."

Chirk nodded. "Agreed. But we'll need the aid of the other Marcher barons who stand to lose by the Despensers' unquenchable greed."

"I doubt you'll have any trouble finding others to join with us."

For the moment, all thoughts of Jehan were banished from Roger's mind, for here was movement at last toward the downfall of the Despensers.

Unable to contain his hatred of the royal favorites, Humphrey de Bohun, Earl of Hereford, had already attacked Despenser holdings with the help of several knights. Discussing Hereford's actions, both de Mortimers were convinced that Lords d'Amory and Audley would be eager to join with them, as was Lord John de Mowbray, for he stood to gain back much of Gower which had been lost to him by the younger Despenser's claims on behalf of his wife.

" 'Tis indeed a tangled web," Chirk commented, staring at the map of Wales spread out before them, the various holdings marked in different colors for the lords who owned them. Roger pointed to a large area near Clun.

"What about Arundel? Do you know where he stands?"

"Not with us, nephew. His son was recently wed to the younger Despenser's daughter. He'd not be inclined to view our grievances as we do. He's still the king's man."

"Fine—then the light-minded Edmund can look to his own holdings." Roger laughed suddenly and his eyes gleamed. "Now if we could get Pembroke on our side as well ..."

" 'Tis doubtful. He's not even been in England in recent months. When the term of the Scottish truce came to an end, Edward hoped to have him go north as leader of the royal delegation to meet with Robert Bruce in order to seek a permanent peace with Scotland, but he'd not returned and the king ordered the meeting to be postponed. I hear tell that he's now back and that he was with the king when Hereford was summoned to Gloucester to explain his warlike behavior. That meeting was to be held two weeks ago."

"I can tell you about that myself," Roger stated, leashed excitement in his voice. "I've just met with Hereford. He sought me out at Wigmore a few days ago. I've never seen him so angry. He's refused to answer the king's summons, and sent word that he would only come when the younger Hugh departed Edward's company."

"Which is indeed doubtful!" Chirk replied grimly and stared morosely at the map.

"Wait, Uncle, there's more. He also suggested that Despenser be put into Lancaster's custody until such time that everyone could be heard in a special session of Parliament."

The old man roared with mocking laughter, drowning out the harp's voice, and pushed aside the map.

"You've had me here all this time, and now you tell me of this—you devil's whelp! What else have you to say to curdle my blood and freeze the humors of my body with this continuing stupidity?"

"Only that the king stood fast in his refusal, claiming that Despenser had not been charged of any crime." Seeing his uncle's face redden in sudden rage, he drew a letter from his tunic and handed it to him. "Read what Edward now proposes. It seems he deems it possible to call Parliament together. Hereford has received the same summons to go to Oxford in May to discuss the matter."

"The king wants to meet with both you and de Bohun?" Chirk was incredulous. "Why did you wait till now to say aught of this to me?"

He looked at his nephew with new eyes. Why had he not seen the change in him before? The lean planes of the dark, ruthless face had hardened and the sensual mouth taken on a grimmer, more determined expression. Roger was more involved in the rebellious movement against Edward than he had imagined, and a new respect for the younger man took hold within his battle-scarred soul.

"Because I wanted to know where you stood and what you could tell me that I'd not heard." Roger took the letter and laid it on top of the map. "We're not going to Oxford." The words were short and matter-of-fact. "We've done with discussing and asking. 'Tis time to take what is ours and teach the others what happens when words are wasted on those too stupid to listen. Are you with us?"

The baron of Chirk raised his head and the firelight gleamed on his white hair as he smiled with satanic glee at his nephew.

"Need you ask? I'm with you, my boy—all the way. And may fortune attend us."

He rose to his full height and stretched while Roger rolled up the large map. Emrys was asleep, his body leaning against the warm hearthstones and his dark head bent over the muted harp.

"Nephew, 'tis time to find my bed and ponder all we've spoken of tonight. I suggest you do the same . . . at

247

least you've a soft body waiting for you." And with a final harsh laugh he was gone.

His last words woke Roger from the almost euphoric state he had been in as they made their plans, and reminded him of what he had momentarily forgotten.

"Emrys!" His voice hoarse with sudden impatience, Roger grasped the harper roughly by his collar, hauling him to his feet. "Bring Mistress Lowndes to me at once!"

"Mistress Lowndes?" Emrys murmured, still groggy with sleep. "But, Arglwydd . . . 'tis deep midnight . . . the manor sleeps!" the Welshman protested feebly.

"Don't argue with me," Roger spat out at him. "Bring her! Now!"

Too long had he held in the frustrated anger at Jehan which had plagued him all evening. Out of patience with all who stood in his way, Roger was determined to root out the true reasons for her behavior. If her tiring woman did not know, then he vowed that he would beat it out of Jehan's tender white skin himself.

Pulling aside the heavy bed curtain, de Mortimer held the small oil lamp close to Jehan's sleeping form. Its feeble light shone on a tangle of bedclothes and red hair spilling wildly over a pillow she held clutched in her arms. She seemed to sense another presence and moved restlessly, burrowing deeper into darkness. Placing the lamp on a nearby stand, de Mortimer sat down on the bed. Lifting back a long lock of hair, he looked somberly at Jehan's face, robbed by sleep of its mask of tempestuous willfulness. There was a vulnerability to her which oddly displeased him, for it was difficult to retain his anger against her. She was locked away from him in a world he could not enter.

"Jehan!" He called her name brusquely and shook her with an ungentle hand. At first the green eyes were darkly opaque and dulled with sleep, but when she realized that he was sitting beside her, she pulled the bedclothes closer, shielding her nakedness from him. Silently they stared at each other and then Jehan glanced away, unable to bear the look of angry shock on his face.

"You know." Her voice was flat, without expression.

"Yes, Jehan, I know." Impulsively he held out his hand to her, but she ignored it. "Why didn't you send word to me in Ireland?" He sounded resentful and baffled.

"Would it have made any difference?" she asked him, knowing before he replied what his answer would be.

"I don't know . . . I truly don't know."

Roger looked at the pale face gleaming like ivory from its frame of dark red hair. Her features were stubborn and unyielding. She shook her head.

"Sweet Jesu, what good would it have done, had you known. It doesn't matter anyway. Your presence wasn't needed . . . it would have changed naught." Her small chin lifted defiantly and the eyes flashed in sudden anger. "You were never to know—and only Berthe could have told you. Holy Virgin, I'll have her skin for this!"

"You'll leave Mistress Lowndes alone. I forced her to tell me, for I could not believe in the reasons you told me you were leaving me to enter a convent. 'Twas not like you." His words were sharp with annoyance.

"Roger . . ." Jehan leaned forward, her words urgent with finality. "What was between us is ended. I've put you out of my life and you must accept it."

His hand shot out suddenly and grasped the back of her head, tangling his fingers in the heavy hair. He pulled her toward him, making her look at him despite her struggle to escape his hands. She had refused to tell him the truth! He was furious with her and his rage lashed out at her.

" 'Tis not for you to make that decision, my lady. 'Tis for me to make. We've spoken of this before and I've not changed my mind. You accepted the terms of our relationship readily enough when you found yourself a widow with nowhere to turn. There's always been money for your needs and servants to attend you. When I gave you this manor house, you were well pleased with it. Now you dare to tell me that you regard it as a temporary gift! You ungrateful bitch—how often must I tell you that I believe your protestations of innocence when you tell me you've given yourself only to me." Roger's voice dropped to a seething, dangerous tone. "How well you followed my instructions—and yet you allowed yourself to be caught! How Isabella must have enjoyed bringing you low. You damn little fool, you could have ruined me! I had thought you more clever and too adept at dissembling."

"Stop it! By the holy rood, Roger, stop blaming me for everything that upsets your plans." Jehan's body shook with fury. "I was caught because you used me to further your own scheming ambitions. You're right—I was indeed a fool. A fool to agree to do what you asked of me. The reasons for my doing your bidding mean naught to you. I was caught because we were spied upon by Alisa Peverell. She was the one who told the queen. I've never been a favorite of Isabella's—I have no sympathy for her plight and she knows it. Why should I care that the king prefers the companionship of others and ignores her existence."

"Jehan, that's enough!" Roger wanted to hear no more of the queen, but the angry woman before him was beyond caring.

"I detest her as much as she detests me. She used her knowledge as a reason to rid herself of me. I'm glad I'm gone from her presence. I never should have returned to court. 'Twas a mistake from the first!"

"And the child, Jehan? Why did you keep it a secret from me? I had a right to be told." The words were torn from him, his pride allowing her no privacy.

"Nay, you did not! The child was mine, Roger, not yours—not like the son you took from me. I was not even sure until those last days at Windsor that I was with child. In all the years since I bore your son, I've not conceived ... 'Twas mine! You were never to know."

The slanted green eyes filled with bitter tears as she desperately tried to escape his grip. Somehow she would have hidden the child's existence from him . . . Sweet Virgin, how she had gloried in that knowledge. It had sustained her for the two days she traveled westward over the icy winter roads until her world had turned into a nightmare she did not want to remember. The ever-present resentment against Isabella lay like a twisted weight in the pit of her stomach until it was routed by the sudden pain ripping through her as she fought to remain in the saddle. Mistress Lowndes and the three armed guards she hired with almost the last of the coins Roger had given her had brought her, white-lipped and half conscious with pain, to the old convent of St. Ermagild, and there her dream had ended.

"At first I refused to believe that I had miscarried. I feared it a trick—a ruse . . . but then I knew." Jehan spoke wildly, unaware for the moment of Roger's presence. "I felt so . . . so empty! The abbess told me I was still young—that there would be other children." She laughed, her mouth twisting in pain. "Other children! Will you give me those other children as you give them to your lady? Not willingly, I vow, for my children would be bastards . . . burdensome bastards—a constant danger to their father and his ambitions! Where is the one growing up now who'll never know that I loved him once long ago?"

Stripping her soul bare, Jehan revealed herself as she had never done before. Roger held her shoulders tightly as she swayed, spent by the vehemence of her emotions. He was shaken by her words, resentful that she had accused him of placing his ambitions above all else. And she would have withheld his own child from him. How could she have even come to that thought! White with fury, he felt sick and disgusted with all that had happened. Never had he been so torn by conflicting emotions. Jehan! Desiring only to escape the one person she felt had caused all her pain. He could feel her trembling as his hands tightened their hold on her.

Misreading his silence for indifference, she screamed at him. "I'm glad I miscarried your damned seed! I'm done with you. I'm done with all of it. I only see you when you have need of me for one of your ambitious intrigues —'tis then that you remember the existence of Lady de Maudley." Slender fingers plucked frantically at the velvet-covered arms which were beginning to draw her closer. "For three weeks the sisters tended me—'twas the first time in my life that I knew what peace and contentment meant, and I envied them."

Shivering in the chill air, Jehan's eyes rested wearily on Roger's closed face. Had he heard anything, she wondered. There were no more weapons to use against him, and she realized the futility of her anger.

" 'Tis folly for you to enter a nunnery, Jehan. I'll not allow it!" Roger's voice was matter-of-fact. He had listened to her and now it was over.

"Oh, my dear lord—I know how little a part of your life I occupy. You're right—'tis all been said before and yet . . ." Sweet Jesu, she felt drained and made no effort to evade him as he finally held her to him.

"You lie to me and you lie to yourself. I never promised you more than I've given you. I've shared my dreams with you—you of all women truly know what drives me through my life." He buried his face for a moment in Jehan's soft hair, breathing in her familiar scent.

"You're not meant for the stark, bloodless life of the celibate," Roger said softly, caressing her satin smooth cheek. His finger traced the outline of her trembling mouth. "Never to know a man's passion again . . . Jehan, be honest and imagine a life like that." He took a deep breath and whispered quietly, "Besides, Lord help me, you're still a part of me . . . and the next months will be hard, for we rise against the Despensers. I need you to make me feel human."

Jehan leaned her forehead against his shoulder while his hands stroked the bare flesh beneath the bedclothes which had fallen from her shoulders. A feeling of relief flooded her as she realized the truth of his words. A convent would never be her destiny. Not so long as he claimed her for his own. She stifled a sob. So the barons were in revolt once more. Would he always be torn from her just when she had found him again.

Lifting her face to his, she murmured, "Why can I never win against your logic, Roger? Someday—someday 'twill end differently for us . . . but for now—yes, my good lord, yes, I'll stay."

Chapter 9

1321
Westminster

Eyes round with wonder, Alain Kilburn found the sights and sounds of the street leading to the huge gate set into the wall surrounding the city of London enchanting to behold. Never in all his nine years had he seen such a throng of people as on the road leading to the city. He had been full of excitement since leaving Glairn, for the prospect of being at his father's side for so long a time was beyond his wildest dreams.

Because of the continued savage uprising against the Despensers by the Marcher barons since early spring, the summons to a meeting of Parliament at Westminster, to be attended by all the magnates of the realm, had not been unexpected. James Kilburn thought it timely to introduce his heir to the intricacies of the world he was to inhabit. Despite Gillian's fears that Alain was still too young, James stood fast in his decision, allaying her misgivings somewhat by taking along her young page, Arthur d'Umfraville, as a companion for the child. They cheerfully bade her farewell, the two boys bursting with exuberant glee at the thought of being a part of the splendid cortege assembled in Glairn's outer courtyard at daybreak. Alain turned once as the party rode down the stone causeway leading to the king's road and caught a last glimpse of his mother's anxious face as she watched from the walkway above the huge gate. His brother's face had been dark with scowling envy as he stood by Gillian's side while his three sisters waved brightly colored scarves which fluttered wildly in the morning breeze.

It was late afternoon nearly ten days later when the weary party passed at last through the entrance of the earl of Pembroke's small palace on Flete Street near one of the main gates giving access into London City. The August sun shone warm upon them as they dismounted in the courtyard to find a delighted Geoffrey waiting to greet them. Alain allowed himself to be hugged, trying vainly to hold on to the dignity he felt he should maintain before the retainers swarming about them. But he was not allowed it, for even Pembroke, welcoming them warmly, could not resist embracing the handsome child.

"He looks more like you each time I see him, James!" Aymer de Valence remarked, ruffling Alain's bright hair affectionately.

Handing his cloak and gauntlets to a servant, Kilburn looked with loving pride at his son . . . the priceless gift that Gillian had given him. The two men smiled at each other as they listened to Alain's excited voice sharing his adventures with his uncle as a tired Arthur trailed silently after them to the quarters they would share.

When Kilburn was shown into the large walled garden set behind the stone building and surrounded on all sides by high walls, he found Pembroke sitting quietly on a bench beneath an old apple tree which spread its thick branches protectively over him. The sound of rustling leaves and the musical splashing of water from a small fountain successfully barred the intrusion of the outside world. As Kilburn sat down beside his host, he saw how drawn and tired Pembroke looked. Pale by nature, the older man appeared unusually ashen, and the tautly stretched skin emphasized his strong features. He seemed so isolated from the living world that Kilburn impulsively reached out a hand, clasping his friend's arm.

" 'Tis been a year since your lady's death and I can well understand that your grief has not yet passed, but has your new marriage not eased the pain somewhat? I've had no chance till now to wish you and your new countess well."

The earl's fine dark eyes turned away for a moment, for he did not trust himself to answer. The loss of his wife had been sudden and unexpected, and there were times he still could not believe she was dead. He held out a goblet to be refilled by the retainer standing near him, and ordered another filled to the brim with cooled white wine for Kilburn. When the servant withdrew, Pembroke sighed, allowing his grief to show.

"Beatrice meant much to me, James. I believed I knew how much, but 'twas only when she was gone that I thought of all the things I should have told her and never did."

" 'Tis that way with most of us," Kilburn said, fearing to say more.

"I come here whenever I can to escape from what awaits outside the walls," Pembroke murmured. "These times are dire and will worsen. Had I not been so long a time in France, perhaps I might have been able to stand between the Marcher lords and Edward. But this time I had myself to think of." He looked closely at Kilburn, whose hazel eyes were full of concern. "Do you think ill of me that I wed so soon again?"

"Nay, Aymer—'tis a necessary thing and no one condemns you for it."

"All know that I need an heir . . . but the girl is so young, James! It disturbs me still when I look at her— what kind of life can she hope to share with me? I'm fifty-one years old!" Pembroke sighed and shook his head, ashamed somehow to have revealed his misgivings to the younger man, hoping they would not be interpreted as weakness on his part.

" 'Twas rumored that Edward petitioned for papal dispensation on your behalf to allow the marriage." Moved by his friend's frank confession, Kilburn tried to ease the awkward moment. "Some say the contract was a political move in order to bind England and France still closer together."

"No, James, 'tis wrong. We needed the dispensation because our close kinship forbids marriage without it. The alliance is to fill my needs, not Edward's nor Charles's," the earl said quickly, gratefully aware of Kilburn's intuitive tact.

"Have you brought her back with you?" Kilburn was puzzled, for the palace seemed oddly still, missing the presence of a chatelaine and the usual chattering of her ladies.

"Marie is with me . . . we've been wed scarce one month, but she clings to the privacy of her own apartments. I permitted a distant relative—a widowed noblewoman who has been with her since birth, to accompany her to England. She will stay at least for now, until the child becomes more used to her new home. Save for my own visits to her, and an occasional one from Geoffrey, Marie has seen no one." Pembroke hesitated for a moment. "Lady de Marc is a formidable harridan whose sole purpose in life seems to be to protect Marie from the world. I fear she has been overly sheltered and I've had to take great care with her." His anguish was unmistakable. "James—I cannot put Beatrice from my mind . . ."

Kilburn was surprised to hear the uncertainty in his friend's voice. He had thought the earl too assured to have any doubts about his actions—and yet, he could understand the difficulties a sensitive man such as Aymer de Valence would face in a marriage with a young, untried maid while holding grief, still fresh, within his heart. Pembroke's voice broke into his thoughts.

"I'm relieved you've come down. At least we'll have another reasonable presence among our wild and passionate nobles who are screaming for Despenser blood."

The earl had closed the door to his personal life for the present, and his guest was only too glad to be able to turn his mind to what they would face in the next days.

"While I was in France, the younger Despenser appeared without warning, apparently fleeing from all the unpleasantness here. I came face to face with him suddenly in Paris, much to his own discomfiture. I must confess I did naught to hide my dislike or contempt for him before the French court." He laughed shortly. "He returned to England not long after. 'Tis a bad business, James, that these two continue to incur the wrath of all the other

256

barons. They've even managed to turn away those lords loyal to Edward." Pembroke leaned forward, speaking with an urgency commanding Kilburn's full attention. "De Warenne and Richmond have remained loyal, and only Arundel and I remain neutral among all the Marcher lords, although neither of us condemn them for their actions."

"It begins to look as if the Despensers are a greater danger than Piers Gaveston ever was."

Pembroke nodded agreement. "You're right, because they are no Gascon upstarts but peers of the realm. 'Tis another matter altogether."

"So the barons took matters into their own hands," Kilburn commented.

"With a vengeance, James. All their neighbors— Hereford, Audley, d'Amory—combined into a force which destroyed, burned, and laid waste much of the lands young Hugh holds through his wife. Our friend Roger de Mortimer, together with his uncle, led the invading army. Chirk claimed it all within his rights as Justice of Wales. One of my liegemen told me that the de Mortimer badge of a green tunic with its yellow right sleeve brought terror throughout the Marches."

Kilburn's face reflected his shocked uneasiness as he told Pembroke, "Lancaster met with Hereford and the other Marcher barons at Sherburn in June, while you were in France. He bade the northern barons also attend, but I refused to heed his invitation. I still want no part of this uprising. 'Twill solve nothing." His voice was grave. It was frightening to contemplate that all of England might erupt in full civil war because of the actions by the furious Marchers. "From what I've heard, Lancaster is now very much the leader of both the dissenting Marchers and most of the barons from the north."

Pembroke shrugged. "You should know your neighbors better than that. Even if they agreed to the continued assaults on Despenser holdings, I doubt that they would directly involve themselves." He smiled grimly, without satisfaction. "I was told that only Bartholomew de Badlesmere openly declared his adherence to the Marcher cause. Since he was steward of the king's household, Edward is furious at what he deems treasonable disloyalty to himself. 'Twas said that de Badlesmere was angry because he was replaced as Constable of Dover by young Kent, but I'm apt to think the fact that his daughter is wed to Wigmore's eldest son Edmund has more to do with it."

Emptying his goblet, Kilburn watched silently as a retainer deftly refilled it from a flagon covered with an icy film of dewy moisture.

"And it continues to worsen—the hatred and personal grudges grow ever greater on both sides."

"They're all demanding that Edward take some sort of action. Lancaster has now openly joined them and there have been so many attempts to placate them, everyone has lost count. Some of the barons are staying in Holborn and others in the New Temple because London's citizens have refused them entry into the city. Although Parliament has been in session since the middle of July, Edward turned deaf ears to their demands, branding them all traitors. A royal message was waiting when I arrived from France, ordering me to go directly to Westminster. Edward is truly frightened and desperate, for he cannot bear to face them alone. I finally convinced him that there is just one solution. Bring all the barons together at a meeting of Parliament." The dark eyes narrowed with worry. "It doesn't bode well for anyone, James. The barons are out of patience with Edward's continuing weakness. Even I agree that something must be done to stop the Despensers' influence over him. As a matter of fact, I've taken an oath to defend the barons' demands for their immediate exile. I had no choice if it will put an end to murder and destruction. But it will not change my adherence to the crown."

"And the de Mortimers, Aymer? Was their behavior truly as savage as you say?" The question was asked before Kilburn had time to think, for his mind shrank from mentioning Roger.

Pembroke set his goblet down on the bench and stretched, flexing muscles still supple from the strenuous life he led. He noticed that the shadows were lengthening. A light suddenly flickered behind a small mullioned window as a candle was lit to banish the darkness within.

"Were they not wealthy, powerful, and born of noble blood, they would be branded cutthroats and outlaws. For all their pretensions to courtly manners, they follow their own code of morality, one which I've yet to fathom."

The words which Pembroke spoke quietly were voiced with scarcely withheld loathing.

"I've surprised you with my frankness!"

He sounded amused by his companion's startled look. Yet, for an instant he had seen a strange expression in the clear hazel eyes. Kilburn did not reply, lifting his goblet to drink the remains of the wine.

"Come, my friend, let me introduce you to my lady. 'Tis time she comes out into the world she must soon occupy."

As Aymer de Valence rose in the gathering twilight, he wondered what lay between Kilburn and de Mortimer, for he had felt sheathed violent rage in the other man. He allowed his guest to precede him through the small arched doorway, watching the tall, slender figure of the border lord thoughtfully.

The morning of the barons' confrontation with the king dawned clear and bright. The sun sparkled on the Thames as the barons began to arrive, some by water barge from the vicinity of London or farther downstream, and others on horseback, surrounded by their retinues of knights, retainers, and servants.

Alain, astride the small, docile bay mare which had belonged to his mother, accompanied his father and the earl of Pembroke to the Hall of the sprawling palace of Westminster, which had been given over to the meeting. The golden hawk glowed on his surcoat, identical to his father's, and a small dagger sat snugly in its sheath at his waist. Beautifully made, it had been a gift from Isabella years earlier at the time of his sister Margaret's birth. Because of its value, he was only allowed to wear it for special occasions. He was nearly beside himself with pride. It was a new experience for him to be treated with the deference due Glairn's heir, and he gloried in it. Arthur rode near him, wearing the Glairn badge of the earl's page, his face mirroring the younger boy's excitement.

Alain stole a shy glance at Aymer de Valence, who was deep in conversation with his father. Although the strong dark face wore a forbidding expression, he did not fear him, for he knew the earl as a kindly man with a quiet, gentle voice whose dark eyes smiled warmly at him as he listened to the excited tales of the journey to London. The child had seen little of either his father or the earl since their arrival, but his uncle had kept him occupied with excursions through the city. He had also taken him to visit a pretty lady who smelled wonderful as she allowed him to kiss her hand, and had given him sweetmeats to eat. Uncle Geoffrey told him that she was Uncle Aymer's new wife, and that they must do everything possible to make her feel welcome in her new country, for she came from France, and everything seemed very strange to her. Alain had puzzled over it for some time, for he missed seeing Aunt Beatrice, but it seemed very unimportant beside all that he was seeing today. Geoffrey rode beside his nephew, intent on the great panoply displayed in the open ground before the palace.

"See there, Alain, that large banner with the gold leopards—'tis the king's own coat of arms!"

"As ours is the hawk?" Alain asked.

"Aye, and as the red martlets on a shield barred blue and white represent the de Valence arms!"

"Uncle Aymer's?" The child raised his shining eyes to the standard fluttering wildly in the morning breeze beside their own. There they were, the small red martlets marching along the border of the blue and white stripes. He followed his uncle's gesturing hand, for Geoffrey had spied another banner, drawing his nephew's attention to it.

"And coming toward us is the Fitzalan lion—do you know who it belongs to?"

The child shook his head, watching the standard approaching them, followed by a tall well-built man bearing the standing lion on his surcoat.

"'Tis that of the Fitzalan family, the earls of Arundel."

"Arundel!" Alain's face lit up in understanding as his uncle laughed shortly.

"Aye, my boy, your future father-in-law!"

The knowledge that he was betrothed to Alianor Fitzalan meant little to the young boy, for he had never seen her, and the marriage was so far in the future as to make it seem totally unreal. All the same, when the earl of Arundel drew abreast of Pembroke, Alain grew suddenly shy. He had never seen so grand a lord, attired in obviously costly garments and glittering gold chains. His knights, all similarly clad, clustered about him in an array of colors. Alain found that the earl made his father and Uncle Aymer look as drab as ravens, although they both were richly clad in silken tunics of deep, lustrous hues. Uncle Aymer greeted Lord Fitzalan civilly, and even smiled at something he said in a low voice. When Kilburn presented his son, Alain brought his small mare close to the black stallion before lifting his gaze to meet that of Arundel's. Laughing blue eyes met diffident hazel ones, and the earl's pleasant face broke out into a broad smile. He leaned over to slap Alain lightly on his back, liking what he saw.

"So this is my future son-in-law! James, I confess that in a few years my Alianor's heart will surely beat faster just seeing this handsome lad. Well, Master Kilburn, are you going to wear a white band like most of us?"

For the first time, Alain noticed the white silk bands many of the barons wore about their arms. He looked at his father, who returned his look with an enigmatic smile. The small brow furrowed for a moment. Neither his father nor Uncle Aymer wore a band, yet many of the others did.

"My lord," he answered softly in his clear, bell-like voice, "I would listen to what was said, and if I thought it right, I would join with you."

Arundel threw his head back, laughing in great delight while Kilburn gazed at his son with unexpected respect. The boy never failed to amaze him.

"By the holy rood, James—he's your son, 'tis not to be denied. He gave me an answer that could have come from your own lips. Sweet Jesù, I think my Alianor will be fortunate!"

With a promise to see them later, Arundel wheeled his mount about and disappeared in the general confusion of men and horses. The morning was on the wane, and

Alain could feel the air warming uncomfortably in the throng of people pressing into the open area before the entrance to the Great Hall. Trumpets blared and the sunlight gleamed on polished metal and lance tips of men-at-arms whose badges represented the greatest families of England. Banners fluttered in the hot August air as the courtyard erupted in excited shouts for the cavalcades making their way past crowds of onlookers scarce able to be held back by the king's guards. Although no baron this day wore armor, all shields and helms were carefully guarded by the squires who accompanied them. Young pages, in service to their masters, darted envious looks at the handsome boy astride the small mare who rode in company with the earls of Pembroke and Glairn. Alain was unaware of all save the dazzling display of which he too was a part. Arthur was close beside him as he dismounted before the wide entrance festooned with garlands of flowers, and followed his father into the Great Hall whose length was almost beyond measure. At one end, set upon a high dais, stood a large golden throne beneath a huge canopy bearing the leopards he had seen outside. Above his head, suspended from the high vaulted wooden ceiling, hung the banners of every baron present that day, and carved wooden chairs lined the sides of the hall. The Lords Ordainers' more elaborate chairs were placed on either side of the royal dais, facing each other. As befitted a lord of royal blood and proclaimed leader of the Ordainers, a chair only slightly less ornate than Edward's throne was placed a few yards down and to the right of the dais for Thomas Plantagenet, earl of Lancaster.

Alain's attention was suddenly diverted by a strange voice speaking almost into his ear. He turned to find a black-haired knight of tall stature and bold face standing beside his father. He was handsomely attired in a tunic of dark gold brocade and obviously was a great lord, for he was accompanied by many knights. His page, a boy of some twelve years, stood behind him holding his plumed helm. The green tunic with its yellow sleeve made the boy's auburn hair burn with a flamelike sheen and the odd-shaped eyes looked with sullen interest at the small boy whose tunic bore a golden hawk and who wore so costly a dagger at his waist. A mocking smile crossed the strange knight's recklessly handsome features as he addressed James Kilburn, although the smoldering black eyes seemed to impale Alain with their directness.

"So here is Glairn's heir! I must say I've never seen a son more like his father. Your lady has most certainly proven her fidelity to you with this one, James."

Alain grew cold as he saw his father's face pale and the slender hand hover near his sword. Recognizing the signs of his father's growing anger, the puzzled child felt a stab of fear, wondering why the stranger was also not aware of it. Something in the other man's manner made him recoil in dislike as he felt the tension mount between the two men.

"Roger, have the good grace to at least behave yourself before all your peers. You've no cause to speak so to Lord Kilburn." Because of James's silence, Pembroke took it upon himself to reproach the other lord whose eyes were now locked with Kilburn's furious ones.

"You think not, Aymer? When Arundel, not to mention a nonentity such as Bardestour, is preferred over Wigmore in the choice of alliances? I've a long memory." De Mortimer's voice took on a sneering tone.

"Bastard," Kilburn snarled softly, but stopped when Pembroke touched his arm in warning.

"That's enough!" The earl's voice was sharp. He heard James exhale his breath. "If your pride is such that you cannot accept the facts as they occurred, 'tis your private affair, my lord de Mortimer, but ours are different. We must settle what we've come to settle. After that, do what you will."

With his words hanging heavily between the two furious lords, Pembroke left them, making his way toward a small door which led into an inner chamber of the Hall where Edward waited for him. De Mortimer turned from Kilburn with a shrug of his elegant shoulders and, followed slowly and reluctantly by his young page, who had missed nothing of the exchange, crossed to the other side of the Hall where he took his seat. A few minutes later, amidst a great fanfare of trumpets, an ashen-faced king was ushered into the Hall, accompanied by Pembroke and

John, the earl of Richmond. Resplendent in a blue velvet robe embroidered with gold, the king had, on this day chosen to wear the ceremonial crown which glittered and sparkled in the light streaming through the long windows set high into the Hall's stone walls. From where he stood on the dais, the king could glimpse the large church his grandfather had begun to rebuild on foundations laid by Edward the Confessor. The sainted ruler's tomb was the focal point of the entire Abbey and drew thousands to kneel before it. But he had lived and died long ago.

It was quite a different Edward who now faced the wrath and disgust of the very barons who were the backbone of his kingdom. The symbols of his kingship, the royal mace and scepter, reposed on red velvet cushions held by pages dressed in royal livery. Looking into the sea of hostile faces turned toward him, a trembling, apprehensive Edward seated himself only when the younger Despenser came to stand defiantly beside him as a loud growl rumbled through the Hall. It grew even louder and more menacing as the elder Despenser took his seat.

Alarmed, Edward turned toward Pembroke, who sat with the Ordainers nearest to his left hand. When the earl shook his head in warning, he struggled to relax. How he hated them all! The king's hands clutched nervously at the arms of his gilt throne.

God's blood, Pembroke thought with a sinking heart, will he never learn to show strength before his barons!

The remaining lords hurried to their seats, heartened by the king's obviously fearful distaste to take part in the meeting. Kilburn, too, took his place beneath the banner bearing the golden Glairn hawk. Parliament's first session to break the deadlock between king and barons had begun.

Alain, with Geoffrey, Arthur, and Hal, watched the proceedings with great interest from the benches reserved for the various households, and were witnesses to what later became known as the Parliament of the White Bands. It proved to be a series of stormy sessions. Only on the subject of the Despensers was there general unanimity. When all the shouting and swearing died down, charges had successfully been brought against both the Despensers by a triumphant earl of Lancaster, and a decree issued ordering them into immediate exile while all the property gained through their scheming and treachery was to be forfeited. The barons had triumphed, for in addition to agreeing to their demands, a sulking Edward formally pardoned all those who had taken part in attacks upon the Despensers.

Parliament had lasted but a week, and the king made his final exit from the Great Hall, pale and beaten, rushing to the queen who was at Eltham. Once more pregnant and discomfited by the summer's heat, she considered her detested state fortunate only in that she did not have to suffer the king's indifferent but necessary visits to her bed. Since Isabella's flight from York, her cold, dutiful, and resigned acceptance of Edward's attentions had taken on an added dimension of loathesome disgust. Despite her feelings, she gave no outward sign of even dreaming of the existence of love and its total fulfillment.

Although Isabella had never expressed her political views openly, she despised the Despensers as violently as she had hated Piers Gaveston. When word reached her of the barons' victory, she knew that Edward would come to her, seeking consolation as he always did when things went awry for him, forcing a short-lived devotion on her which she found odious. The hatred that had festered within her soul for so many years had begun to ripen, and with her increasing emotional maturity, she wished only to be left alone to nurture it.

The road seemed to stretch endlessly over the increasingly wild countryside, and the riders were grateful to rest in a grove of trees near a small stream offering shelter from the hot sun. It was cool beneath the trees and Kilburn sank down on the grass, his back against a rough tree trunk. They had left Westminster a week past, but their pace was slow because of Alain. He could hear the boy's laughter as he helped the men water the horses in the stream. On the other side of the stream, serfs tilled a field lying open to the sun. They paid no attention to the knightly party, for they had learned long ago that it could be dangerous to see too much. The air scarcely moved in the midday heat and James could feel wetness trickling down his back beneath his hauberk. Hal approached with a basin filled with water, while Arthur handed him a towel. The water felt cool against his face as he washed off some of the sweat and grime.

"Alain is splashing about in the stream as happily as a fish. At least he doesn't seem to feel the heat," Geoffrey remarked, as he sat down beside Kilburn. He was returning to Glairn with them, there to wait for Pembroke, who was expected in Newcastle shortly with his new countess. It was one of Geoffrey's rare visits since Pembroke's kidnapping four years before. He was anxious to see Gillian again, for his attachment to her had never diminished in spite of their long separations. Kilburn glanced at him idly. At twenty-five he was no longer a boy, and should have left Pembroke's employ long ago for a position of greater importance. It had not been for want of offers that he remained with the earl, for he was much sought after. Kilburn thought that he did not look well. Each time they met, it seemed to him that Geoffrey became exceedingly more gaunt and pale. Pembroke, uneasy over his secretary's state, confided to Kilburn that Geoffrey had taken to spending hours on his knees in fervent prayer, seemingly still searching for a meaning to his life.

"I could lie here forever," Geoffrey murmured, stretching out beneath the tree. He could see the deep blue of the sky through the lacy tracery of the dark green leaves of the ash tree. The grass and earth gave off the strong, pungent aroma of late summer.

"One would never think that the political unrest of the past weeks existed, when one is in a glade such as this."

" 'Tis deceiving, Geoff, just as the barons' accord to the decree against the Despensers is deceiving. Do you actually believe that they'll remain in exile?"

"Why not? 'Tis what was decreed! They're already gone."

"Nonsense—exile never stopped Gaveston from returning. And mark you well—we'll have baron against baron the next time."

Kilburn sighed, wishing that his pessimism was not so strong within him. Sitting together at ease, they spoke in quiet tones of how sincerely Aymer de Valence still mourned the death of his countess, despite his remarriage.

"They were together many years, and shared much together. One cannot put such memories away—they must be given time to fade." How well he knew it from his own life, Kilburn thought. " 'Tis odd how much I missed Lady Beatrice's voice and quick step while we were at the palace," he admitted to Geoffrey.

"Aye, I still find it so . . . and now we must accustom ourselves to the new countess." Geoffrey grimaced and smiled an apology.

"Have you seen her often since she arrived in England?" Kilburn asked with curiosity. "Aymer tells me she prefers to remain hidden in her own chambers."

Geoffrey shook his dark head, and the gray eyes took on an odd expression.

"She seems a trifle strange and hides her true self. No one save the earl saw her prior to the marriage, and we were told that she spent much of her time in a convent since her father's death. She's of a most religious nature. But as countess of Pembroke she will have to change her ways, for my lord will not allow her continued reticence." He shredded a flower in his concentration and seemed not to notice that he had already mentioned her pious ways. "I join her at times at her devotions. At prayer she seems to come alive."

Then the two of you should get along quite well, Kilburn thought cynically, smiling to himself. Personally he had no opinions as to the merits of the countess Marie, save that she was pretty enough in an austere way and seemed overly shy and retiring. Pembroke had treated her with a gentle, almost paternal courtesy when he presented her to Kilburn. Seeing her small slender figure and immature face with wide blue eyes painful in their clear, innocent gaze, he had been shocked, for Marie de Valence could have not been more than fourteen or fifteen. He understood then why his friend had hesitated before consummating their union. Yet, Kilburn reminded himself, Gillian had also been barely fifteen when his desire for her had been aroused, but the sensuality of her nature had already been strong within her, lacking only her own awakening.

Watching Alain pursue a butterfly over a sunny bank of the stream, Kilburn ordered Arthur to tend to him before trouble befell him, for the child was like quicksilver at times. Spending so much time with his eldest son during the past weeks had been quite a revelation. He had feared the journey too strenuous for Alain, but the child had withstood it well. Wherever they went he had behaved himself with great charm and poise. Smiling at the thought of himself at his son's age, he remembered his own shy withdrawal from anything unknown. Not so Alain. Kilburn found a great deal of his uncle Robert in him. Arundel seemed quite enthralled with him, and had taken him for a barge ride on the Thames one morning, which had been a great success. Packed in among his belongings were gifts for everyone, including Non and the Fitzhugh twins. He had found a small pomander for his mother and for Margaret a length of silk ribbon the color of her eyes. Coveting a tin whistle for himself, he had bought it for his brother instead, and for his two younger sisters he had found prettily decorated balls. The gifts had been chosen by him from the booths and stalls set up in the small village of Chelsea near Westminster where Geoffrey had taken him one day when a fair had been held in honor of one of their local saints. He had quickly spent his small hoard of coins, to which his uncle had added a few pence.

How tall he is for his age! his father thought, as his son's eager face turned suddenly toward him. The bright chestnut hair gleamed in the sun, contrasting sharply with the short dark green tunic and hose he wore beneath a white surcoat identical to his father's. He had found an oddly shaped stone in the stream and was coming to show his father when their attention was drawn to a horseman riding rapidly toward them. As the rider saw the Glairn standard by the roadside, he veered and was quickly surrounded by Kilburn's men.

"Geoffrey, that rider bears the Glairn badge!"

Kilburn nudged his brother-in-law, who sat up quickly, looking with curiosity at the man striding toward the earl.

"My lord, thank God I've found you . . ."

The messenger sank down on one knee before Kilburn, who slowly rose, a cold feeling of apprehension gripping him. He recognized the young man as Sir Simon's squire, but had no time to wonder why his constable had parted with him, for he blurted out, "There's sickness at Glairn, my lord, and Sir Simon urges your immediate return."

"What kind of sickness, Will?" Kilburn's voice was urgent. "Don't make me guess! Is it plague?"

The young man shook his dark head.

"Nay, my lord. There was an accident—no one thought aught of it at first . . . the physician is trying his best, but feels you should come at once."

"The countess?" Kilburn feared the answer.

"My lady was well when I left. The lady Eilys and Mistress Non are tending to the older children, but Lady Gillian refuses to leave the nursery."

"The little one . . . ?"

"Aye, my lord, and the physician fears for her life!"

Everyone stood about in shocked silence. Kilburn turned and looked blindly at Geoffrey who was close beside him. He felt Geoffrey's hand on his shoulder. His mind refused to accept what he had heard. Surely not Mathilde . . . ! He looked at the young squire's wretched face.

"Rest yourself, Will, and have something to eat while we prepare to leave."

The earl stretched out his hand and helped the young man to his feet. Will smiled wanly at his lord, wishing vainly that it had fallen to someone else to bring him the news. Kilburn's mind was busily organizing its thoughts. He decided that he would ride immediately to Glairn with Hal and some of his men. Geoffrey would bring Alain at their normal pace, accompanied by the rest of the party. Arthur could remain with Alain as well, he decided.

Sweet heavenly Virgin, he prayed silently, don't let me be too late, and caught sight of Alain's anxious face as he hovered uncertainly among the knights. Summoning him to his side, he carefully explained what would be expected of him. Alain raised frightened eyes.

"Mama?" The name came out in a childish quaver and Kilburn realized how truly young he still was.

"Mama is well . . . 'tis Maddie who needs your prayers," he said and embraced the slight figure of his son. "We'll pray that she will recover," he added quietly. Bending over quickly, he kissed the soft chestnut hair and committed his son into Geoffrey's care.

They warned Kilburn of Gillian's stony, tearless grieving state when he entered the keep to find Sir Simon and Thomas Fitzhugh waiting for him, neither wanting to be the first to break the tragic news to him. With Hal and those knights and men-at-arms not left behind to accompany Alain to Glairn, he had ridden northward at full speed. Nearing Glairn, an unnatural stillness seemed to settle over the countryside. The fields they passed lay strangely idle and forgotten in the hot afternoon sun. Nothing stirred in the villages, and he noticed that all the doors were barred against the news he had yet to hear. Only the dreadful tolling of the church bell broke the silence, and the fear that he had successfully pushed away for a while once more laid its cold fingers upon him. The castle was filled with the same unearthly quiet which followed him into his study. There, Tom, with a weeping Eilys beside him, told Kilburn all that had happened in the past week. James listened quietly, wishing he could hold back the words which he knew would bring him anguish.

The weather had been so fine, Tom said in a flat voice, and the countryside so peaceful that Sir Simon had declared a holiday for the castle folk. The notion of a picnic had been greeted with great enthusiasm and they set out for the Dair in a festive mood. How the late morning sun had sparkled on its slow-moving waters! Tom turned to Eilys. Aye, she agreed, it had been a beautiful day. Only Lady Gillian did not join the picnickers. She had pleaded a slight indisposition, but willingly gave her permission for the children to accompany the others, provided that good care be taken of them. The food was laid out beneath the trees on the stream's banks while the children played vigorously on the green meadow, joined by several village children. They had come unexpectedly, and Sir Simon allowed them to stay, even giving them something to eat. It had been plain, wholesome food— roast fowl, meat pasties, cheese, bread . . . with wine and ale to wash it down while the children had milk, cooled in the waters of the Dair. Tom reminded Eilys that later there had been wild berries covered with clotted cream. How the children had loved that dish! Only a few small berries were left for the birds to finish.

The pages assigned to watch the children took care that none ventured too close to the riverbank. Small Hugh had already been fished out, having gone to seek some colored stones lying in the bottom of the river near its banks. Eilys saw Margaret and Master Brassard wander through the meadow, looking for herbs, her own twins following, for they adored the merry and warm-hearted little girl. She remembered seeing Jennifer and Mathilde sitting by Non and Agnes while they plaited wildflowers into circlets for the girls' heads. Jennifer, with her gentle nature, had been delighted to wear the one Non placed on the shining chestnut hair, but Mathilde, spoiled and willful, baulked, wanting other flowers than the ones Agnes had used for her circlet.

"Suddenly, before anyone knew of it, she was by the stream, leaning over toward some flowers growing nearly in the water. One of the pages ran to stop her, but she slipped, my lord . . . slipped into the water and for a moment completely disappeared. She came to the surface already in the grip of the page who had gone into the water after her. I remember that she laughed as Sir Simon lifted her out."

Stopping to wipe away her tears, she looked at her husband for reassurance.

"My lord, the little maid seemed fine—not even frightened. Non scolded her for having upset everyone, but you know Mathilde—she laughed at Non's words. The child's wet clothes were stripped from her at once and Non wrapped her in a rug after making sure she was rubbed dry. Of course, 'twas the end of the picnic, for we had all been so frightened."

Eilys looked fearfully at Kilburn, but he said nothing, his face unreadable. She took a deep breath and, in a voice which shook with emotion, continued to tell him how during the night the child woke screaming with pain and complaining of feeling hot. Alarmed, Non picked her up from her cot and found she was burning with fever. When Master Brassard was summoned to the nursery, he gave her a potion to calm her, for she would not stop screaming. By then the lady Gillian had also come, and, between them, they managed to get Maddie to sleep. Master Brassard voiced the fear that it was lung fever.

On and on went the tale as Eilys sat before him, clutching her husband's hand tightly between her own, tears streaming unheeded down her cheeks until Kilburn could hear no more. Craving to be alone with his thoughts, he sent them away with thanks, promising them further speech. He leaned back in his chair. His sweet, sunny Maddie . . . the small daughter who had brought such happiness to them all! He moaned . . . the pain which swept over him was one he had not felt in many years, but it was familiar to him. His mind sifted all that had been told him.

From the first sign of sickness, Gillian had remained with her child, allowing no one save Master Brassard to enter the nursery. When, at the last, Maddie had been out of her head with the fever, which would not break, she had lifted her from her cot, holding the child in her arms, rocking back and forth, her face wet with tears she did not even know were there. Eilys said that Gillian still refused to leave the nursery, seemingly unaware of all but her daughter's death. She had been there since the dead child was taken from her arms, mute and unmoving.

Maddie! The cry rose from his soul. So like her mother it was as if he had the child Gillian to love again. He remembered how the large dark blue eyes glowed in her oval face as he held her in his arms, the silken dark hair soft against his cheek. He could still feel her small arms twined about his neck and the sweet red mouth pressed for a moment against his when he had left for Westminster. Non had berated her for having lost a shoe, and looking down he saw five pink toes peep out from beneath her gown. Laughing with delight, she knew no

272

one could resist her charm. Maddie was too young to die . . . she was only three! He buried his face in his hands. What had she tasted of life?

Desperately in need of comfort, Kilburn went in search of Gillian.

The doll had lost an arm, Gillian noted idly, looking at the well-worn toy she held in her hands. No matter, she thought numbly—there was no one to love it or sing it to sleep anymore. The small chamber was silent in the blue dusk which crept through the narrow window. She had lost track of time, but somehow it mattered little. She could still feel the small body, burning with fever, in her arms, the dark blue eyes in the flushed face looking at her, not recognizing her. Now is the time to love her, a voice had whispered deep within her . . . your child is dying . . . the child you bore in such angry pain and that drew its life's sustenance from your breasts.

Nay, 'tis Jamie's Maddie, her heart screamed, not mine!

Maddie's arms had clung to her, and she pressed her cheek against the little maid's hot one, the surge of jealous resentment slowly ebbing. You're mad, she told herself. She's your own child.

"Aye, sweetheart, Mama's here," she crooned, trying to soothe her.

"Papa . . . where is Papa?" Maddie wailed weakly. "Papa . . . I want Papa . . ." Over and over Mathilde called for her father, while Gillian held her delirious child close. She tried to calm her with gentle caresses, brushing back with a trembling hand the tangled dark hair plastered wetly about the pale forehead. Bathing Maddie's hot face with cold water, she noticed that the cloth soon was as hot as the skin it touched. And then the piteous cries had slowly stopped and the labored breathing stilled. By the flickering light of the oil lamp, Gillian watched the large eyes dim and the white lids seal them from her forever, while a whisper as delicate as thistledown came to her . . .

The dull ache which had begun deep within her then had slowly spread throughout her being. Emptiness should not ache, she told herself, for she should feel nothing. The chamber door opened softly and she heard Jamie's voice call to her. Gillian closed her eyes. He had no place here, in Mathilde's nursery. He had not seen her die. She felt a hand stroke her head gently.

"Gillian . . . lovedy . . . I know how you feel!"

She looked blankly at him, not seeing the dust of the king's road on his travel-stained clothes, not the sorrow and shock etched on his weary face, grown suddenly old with pain. He could not know how she felt . . . no one could.

"You've come back." It was a statement of fact. "You've come back too late, Jamie. Maddie is dead . . . and you weren't here!"

Dead. The word echoed in her head without meaning.

"Aye, sweetheart—and 'tis something I'll never forgive myself for. I've spoken to Eilys and Tom."

"You weren't here . . ." Gillian said again without emotion.

"They told me about the picnic. It was an accident, Gillian—Maddie caught a chill and . . . and she was too little." His voice broke.

Gillian did not listen to him. Now she remembered. The other children were there. Everyone had been there —it was such a beautiful day! They had all been spared, and Maddie was gone. Only I was not there, Gillian told herself silently, a knife twisting in her soul.

Trying to make her aware of him, James put his hands on her shoulders, pressing his cheek against her bowed head.

" 'Twas the lung fever, Master Brassard said—he could do naught for her. Maddie couldn't fight it . . . Lovedy, he's distraught and sick over what has happened —everyone is!"

"Does it matter what it was?" Her voice was flat and without expression, but he saw how her hands clutched frantically at the doll.

"Gillian, look at me—please."

He knelt before her, grief tearing at him, but she turned her head, not daring to meet his eyes, fearing he would see the truth in her own. Wanting to comfort and be comforted, he found her turned inward, dismissing the fact of his existence. For the first time since he had known her, he could not reach her. Kissing her cold cheek, he rose and left her alone.

Glairn lay in stunned slumber beneath a night sky whose brilliance only intensified the blackness of sorrow within the castle. Mathilde Kilburn lay as if asleep on a bier in the Glairn chapel, the flickering candles heightening the waxen pallor of the beautiful little face covered by a white gossamer silk veil. The small dimpled hands held an old, intricately carved ivory cross, and a small gold band set with tiny pearls encircled the dark hair falling loosely over her shoulders. She lay surrounded by white roses from her mother's favorite bower, filling the chapel with their delicate scent. Father Godfrey knelt by the bier, not having left the child's side since she was brought to him. He would remain with her through the night, insensible to the pain-filled hours spent on his knees, knowing only that he must guide the little maid's soul to rest with his prayers.

Non, unable to reconcile herself to Maddie's loss, lay on her bed in the chamber she had occupied throughout her years at Glairn. She had taken the child's death badly; and fearing for the old woman's frail state of health, Master Brassard bade his daughter stay with her. Tears streaming down her withered face, she was beset by memories of all those she had loved and who had left her behind.

"Och, nae—'tis not true!" she said suddenly.

Hearing her voice, Agnes bent over her, dark eyes filled with concern. The young woman, whose own grief tore at her heart until she felt it would truly break, answered quietly, "Yes, Mistress—'tis true, and there's naught to change it."

"When my Graeme died—puir soul—sae sorrow I had, but mair a feelin' o' gladness, too, for at last my braw laddie didna hae to li'e chained to his dark world."

She struggled to rise, throwing back the blanket. Agnes wrapped Non's large woolen shawl about the old shoulders.

"The wee bairn . . . Agnes lassie—ne'er to see that

sonsie face . . . aye, didna the laird spoil her . . . daft for her, he was! And my lady, my puir lady—sittin' alone askin' why she could nae luv her ain lassie."

"Hush, Mistress, you mustn't speak like that. All say Lady Gillian's fair mad with grief."

A keening sound began deep inside Non, and Agnes, weeping openly, sat beside her as the old woman suddenly threw the shawl over her head, wailing her anguish in the tongue of her childhood. Together they each expressed their sorrow in their own way while Hal stood watching helplessly from the doorway.

Placing the maimed doll on the empty cot, Gillian left the nursery at last, wandering aimlessly through the winding, empty corridors of Glairn, Kilburn's large wolfhound trailing silently after her. Where was she going, she asked herself when she found herself standing for a moment at the entrance to a tower, looking blankly at the narrow stone stairs winding upward toward the battlements.

"I must see to my lord," she murmured, catching the attention of a solitary sentry standing guard near the tower entryway. "Aye, now 'tis my lord I needs must go to," she told him. The young guard gave her a curious look, for there was an unfamiliar brittle coldness emanating from her. And then she was gone, walking through the musicians' gallery above the silent and deserted Great Hall, the wolfhound a pale shadow. When she finally reached the door to the bedchamber, she hesitated. Jamie was there . . . Jamie who had loved Maddie above all else. She felt the dog brush past her as she entered.

"Jamie?" she called softly into the darkened chamber, lit only by the dying fire in the hearth. He stood forlornly by the open window, clad only in a short linen chainse and hose, the bright hair falling uncombed and lank about his taut white face. Jamie had never felt so alone, gazing at the star-filled sky, lustrous and sparkling in contrast to his own dark feelings. Gillian's voice brought him back from his musings. Her pale face gleamed in the dim firelight and he saw how reluctantly she moved toward him, clad in a wrinkled and stained white silk robe. She called his name again and blindly held out a hand to him. He took it, drawing her toward him. How cold she was, her body stiff and unbending. Wordlessly he buried his face in her hair, and the agony of his loss washed over her. She turned away from his pain, rejecting it, not allowing it to fill her own emptiness.

"How I loved her," Jamie whispered brokenly, tears burning his eyes. "Never was there a child happier than she, nor a child who gave more happiness to us all!"

Gillian listened to his low, heartbroken voice and wondered guiltily at her own lack of feeling.

Disengaging herself from his arms, she walked to the large carved chest where a silver tray holding a crystal flagon filled with claret and matching goblets stood on its flat surface. Pouring him a goblet of wine, Gillian said quietly, "We should try to sleep. 'Twill be a busy day for us. I assume that announcements have been sent. We must also order a special mass for Mathilde—perhaps in Newcastle later this month . . . or York—aye, York would be better."

Kilburn strode over to her, deeply shocked.

"Gillian, what's wrong with you? Have you no feelings? How can you discuss Maddie's funeral mass now? 'Tis—'tis indecent."

He looked down on a face frightening in its pallor, the large eyes dark and drained of tears, and he realized that her words had been spoken without thought. There was a wall about her suddenly which he could not penetrate.

"I need you, Gillian—please don't shut me out! Let me share your grief." he pleaded with her, taking her in his arms again. "Please." Her hand slowly caressed his bright hair, touching the pain-filled face lightly. Why didn't he understand, she thought, pity stirring within her.

"Sweet Jesu!" she whispered, and with a totally unexpected suddenness, she stiffened in his arms. Covering her face with both hands, she let out a heartbroken wail. Alarmed, James carried her to the bed where she lay against the pillows, fighting him when he tried to hold her, refusing his attempts to comfort her.

Gillian had remembered! Mathilde, the babe conceived and born in rage, bitterly resented by her jealous mother and spoiled by her doting father and an adoring household, had, in her dying breath, spoken one name. In the penetration of her numbness by her pity for Jamie, Gillian had heard again her child murmur, "Mama."

In the days following Mathilde's death, life began once more to stir at Glairn. Kilburn assured Master Brassard that he did not blame the physician for his inability to cure the lung fever which had claimed his daughter's life. Since she could not be returned to them, he ordered that the sooner everyone resumed their normal lives, the better it would be for all.

Despite his brave words, Kilburn found himself listening in vain for the happy laughter and light steps of the little maid who now reposed in the chapel. Bowing to Gillian's wish, Mathilde's small tomb had been placed beside that holding the body of Alison Kilburn, the earl's first wife, and of the son who had cost his mother her life so many years before.

James also missed Non's tart tongue and their habitual clashes, which nearly always ended with the nurse retiring in the face of his anger. The child's death had aged her beyond belief, and she had become as a child herself, tended by one of the younger serving maids, recognizing no one but Kilburn.

Striding along the castle's battlements, Kilburn felt the warmth of the sun on his face. Too long had he been out of its light during the past months. His holdings stretched out about him, all the varying greens of forest and field and rich brown earth and golden crops seeming to welcome his attention. Here and there a thin plume of smoke rose toward the bright blue sky, denoting the presence of a village, and he noticed that already fall was beginning to change some of the foliage to its bright colors. He leaned against the battlement's rough stones, looking northward toward Scotland.

Scotland! His mind returned suddenly to the ruined tower near his own lost Douglas lands where he and Gillian had first tasted their love for each other. He regretted the memory, for it brought to mind his greatest worry.

Frowning, he thought of Gillian, still surrounded by her inner wall. No one was permitted past the barrier she had erected—not even her children, who were beginning to avoid her icy presence. He was unable to hold back a groan as he thrust a hand nervously through his hair.

Robert and Elizabeth had journeyed from Kestwick to be with Gillian, staying two weeks while she smiled and spoke in a seemingly normal manner, although the frozen expression in the dark blue eyes never changed. How grateful they had all been at first that Geoffrey was there, for he had always been able to penetrate her guard. But he too finally could take the pain of her coldness no longer and left to join Pembroke at Newcastle.

"Damn life's pain! he shouted suddenly to the breeze which was freshening as he stood on the battlements, swept by frustrated anger that he could not understand Gillian's continued detachment and at his own grieving, uncomforted soul.

Gillian's face stared at her from the mirror, the eyes unnaturally dark against the ivory hue of her skin. Had the haunted look returned to her eyes after Maddie's death, she wondered, or was it her inability to communicate with Jamie. Perhaps if they were able to share their grief as he had begged . . . yet she did not deserve his comforting, nor could she bring herself to ease his anguished sorrow.

Her coffers were packed, waiting for morning to come so they could be stored in the wagons lined up in the courtyard below. Not only her coffers, but Jamie's as well, for he too would be leaving Glairn a few days after her.

The brush drawn through her long dark hair did not break her concentration as Agnes ministered to her lady, heavy at heart for her coming separation from Hal. The servants were building up the fire in the hearth, busily turning back the counterpane on the bed and loosening the ties of the hangings in preparation for the night. The countess remained oblivious to them, sitting before her silver-backed mirror, her thin hand playing nervously with the comb lying atop the dressing table.

When the royal messenger brought her the queen's

summons for her presence two months after Maddie's death, she had grasped the chance to escape from Glairn where the poignant reminders of her dead child surrounded her. She knew she was being selfish, but she could bear Jamie's nearness no longer, reminding her eternally of her own guilt, each silent day driving them farther apart. The sounds of her children's happy laughter were as hammer blows to her heart. How soon they had forgotten their sister! Gillian hardened herself against their love.

The queen's message was brief, saying only that she desired Gillian's most welcome presence. Her courier also brought news of a new royal daughter, born in the Tower of London where Isabella had taken up residence. It was obvious to all that she was lonely, for Edward, in a fit of spite against the barons who had deprived him of the Despensers, had forced his queen to dismiss all but those most loyal to the crown from her court. Gillian, with a new cynicism, felt it was malicious defiance on Isabella's part that she wished to have the countess of Glairn attend her. No matter the reasons, a royal summons to court could not be ignored.

When Gillian showed James the queen's message, he read it without expression. If he was surprised or angry at her almost eager acceptance of the order, he gave no sign of it, and raised no protest against her joining Isabella in London.

Now he too would leave Glairn, for two days after the arrival of the queen's messenger, one of Pembroke's knights appeared at the gate bearing disturbing news. England was wild with rumors that Cousin Thomas had tried to make a secret pact with Robert Bruce, accepting a large sum of gold from him, and that the earl of Hereford had openly pledged support to Lancaster. The earl of Pembroke requested the gathering of all adherents to his middle party, and so Kilburn began his preparations for his own departure.

The hour was late and the chamber quiet save for the thumping of the wolfhound's tail as it sat watching its master move about, drawing off his clothes. Uncertain as to what he should do, he stood briefly by one of the open windows, breathing in the freshness of night. Already the air held the sharpness of autumn.

Tonight was the last he would spend with Gillian for quite some time and he wondered if she would turn from him as she had since Maddie's death. He closed the window and walked toward the bed. The darkness stifled Jamie as he parted the bed hangings and slipped into bed, but he could sense her awareness of his presence. Lying beside her, he heard her even breathing.

"Gillian," he called softly.

"Aye, my lord." It was said so simply.

" 'Tis our last night, Gillian."

"Aye, my lord."

He reached out a hand and touched her shoulder. She did not move but he felt a quickening in her. Turning toward her in the darkness, he let his hand gently caress the soft curve of her cheek, and felt the pulse beat at the base of her throat as his fingers lightly slid downward, finally finding the silken pliancy of a breast, filling his hand with its taut-nippled fullness for a moment. She caught her breath at the touch her body craved for and steeled herself against it. He felt her tremble as his hand continued to stroke the familiar body.

"Jamie, please! Stop! I can't bear it . . ."

He froze at the anguish in her voice and felt hot tears as he cradled her face in his hands.

"Lovedy, talk to me," he said softly, his mouth touching hers lightly. Her breathing was labored, coming in short, quick pants, and her heart beat wildly. He tried once again to penetrate her coldness. "This silence is driving me mad . . . You lie beside me night after night— I feel your need, yet you turn from me. We can't go on like this!"

"We needn't—tomorrow I leave to join the queen and you ride with Pembroke. Perhaps 'tis best we part for a while," Gillian said through her tears, the numbness his hands had almost vanquished settling over her again.

"Who can refute your logic, my lady?" Jamie replied

coldly, moving away from her. It was useless. She refused to allow him entry to her soul. " 'Tis obvious that what lay between us has vanished, at least for now."

And they lay in the large bed next to one another in icy silence, staring blindly upward toward the velvet drapery neither could see. Gillian started in surprise when Jamie said softly, "If you ever have need of me, Gillian, call to me."

He thought she had not heard him, but her answer came as a whisper across the chasm they had both created.

"Aye, my lord."

PART FIVE
1321

Chapter 10

The Tower of London

"How do you intend to avenge this insult?" Isabella's voice shook as she stood before her royal husband, livid with fury. "Edward, I was fired upon!"

"Calm yourself, my lady. You're not alone in your rage, for I share it. I've been quite beside myself since the news was brought to me. Believe me, there was no thought that you would be denied access when I suggested that you break your journey at Leeds Castle."

The king's voice was low and bland, belying his words. Sitting at ease in his council chamber with only a few of his courtiers about him, he was a sharp contrast to the agitated woman who had swept into the room unannounced. His dark eyes rested dispassionately on his distraught wife. It was indeed a rare sight to see Isabella give a public display of such emotional outrage, but he reasoned that it was a welcome change from the usual attitude of indifference she showed to his court. She had not even bothered to change her clothes upon her arrival at the Tower. Her woolen surcoat was wrinkled and stained from the frenzied ride to London.

Isabella pushed back her pale hair, which had escaped from its confines beneath the narrow crown. Her blue eyes were icy with contempt as they looked down at him.

"You may share my rage, but I wager you'll do naught about it," she snapped angrily. Opening the tooled leather purse hanging from her girdle, she withdrew a white silk handkerchief and held it out to Edward. "Here, my lord, take it and see where the blood of young Peter de Gilles has stained it. I used it myself to staunch his wound after he was hit by an arrow. Had it not been for my men-at-arms, who encircled me, I too might have been wounded or even killed as two of my knights were."

How could this incident have happened! Isabella was still stunned by the climax of an otherwise uneventful journey. The pilgrimage to Canterbury had been pleasant enough, and for a few days she had even forgotten her animosity toward Edward. Under incredibly blue skies they had ridden along the high road, through the eternal throngs of pilgrims making their way to St. Thomas à Becket's shrine in the cathedral. To her surprise, Edward rode beside her, ignoring his subjects who knelt or stood with bowed heads as the royal cavalcade passed. It never failed to amaze her how unaware he always seemed of the folk who called him king. The talk between them had been about their children and of other journeys they had shared. Having Gillian with her again had also raised her spirits, although the sight of her friend's closed, frozen face had shocked her. Who would have dreamed that Lady Badlesmere, in the absence of her lord, would refuse the queen entry to her own castle, claiming that her lord had forbidden her to allow anyone admittance while he was away.

"I want that woman hanged from her own battlements," Isabella spat, remembering the insolence with which Lady Badlesmere had replied to her marshal's demand to open the gates of the castle to the queen. She felt hot tears sting her eyes. "She and her lord are both traitors . . . 'tis well known that they are sympathetic to your cousin's cause. Why else this deliberate insult against us?"

She swayed dizzily and an arm suddenly encircled the slender shoulders. Isabella leaned gratefully against Gillian, spent from the violent and frustrated fury which enveloped her.

"Your Majesty, I beg you . . ." The soft words caught Edward's attention. "Permit the queen to be seated, and

286

perhaps she could be given a cup of wine to soothe her."

The king reddened from the gentle reprimand and he caught the looks exchanged between his courtiers and Isabella's ladies. Without rising, he motioned servants to place a chair beside his. While her ladies helped her to sit down, another retainer poured wine into Edward's own goblet and offered it to the queen. She drank gratefully, feeling the wine's warmth course through her. Leaning her head against the chair's high carved back, Isabella held Gillian's hand, knowing full well that it would annoy her lord.

Edward stared at Gillian without expression. He had little liking for her husband and still remembered his countess from the early days at court, when she had been wife to one of his Gascon knights. A shadow crossed the handsome face as the memory of Piers Gaveston took image in his mind. He thrust it from him reluctantly, aware that everyone was watching him. It was a mystery why Isabella clung so tenaciously to her fondness for the pale, sad-faced young woman who scarce spoke and seemed to take no interest in any of her surroundings. The countess's continued air of cold detachment and avoidance of him was beginning to irritate Edward. It now seemed that she had the same ability as her lord husband to remind him of his social graces and make him look a fool before his courtiers. He shivered in the damp chill which pervaded the chamber and drew his velvet mantle closer, seeing with relief that Isabella's color was returning as she drank the last of the wine.

So she demands vengeance, he thought with grim satisfaction. It certainly was what she would get. He had much to settle with the barons who had taken his only true friends from him. What would they say if they knew that he was in constant touch with the exiled Despensers! After the pilgrimage to Canterbury was ended, he had even briefly visited the younger Hugh on the Isle of Thanet, that remote corner of Kent nearly forgotten by everyone save a few fisher folk and pirates. They had discussed the manner of Hugh's return . . . oh, but he was a clever man, was the younger Despenser! Edward smiled to himself. Perhaps they would be together sooner than anyone dreamed.

The threadbare, moldering tapestries moved constantly in the drafts filtering insidiously through the walls of the queen's bedchamber. In the flickering, wildly dancing light cast by huge candles set in rusting iron holders, the stones reflected the shiny film of moisture covering them. It was nearly as cold within the Tower's royal residence as without, and no matter how many braziers were lit, they did little to ward off the dampness rising from the river. Gillian looked wearily about the chamber and was struck again by the unbelievable conditions of the queen's apartments. The hearths did not draw properly and the chambers reeked of smoke and mildew.

Reaching up to unfasten the bed curtains, Gillian leaned on the thick rug of fur pelts over the other coverlets for additional warmth. Its luxurious softness only emphasized the scratched, worn bedposts and rotting folds of the shabby velvet curtains. Why did Isabella accept the conditions under which she lived in the Tower, she wondered anew and could find no answer, for it was totally out of character for the queen to fail to raise objections. Yet they had been here for nearly two months, secure from the turmoil which raged about the forbidding walls of the Tower.

Sweet Jesu, but the queen allowed her little rest. In a way Gillian welcomed Isabella's demands, for she had discovered that total exhaustion could blot out the memories which refused to die. She shook out the queen's discarded under-robe and tunic, giving them to a serving maid. How long would Isabella consent to her state of virtual captivity? Already she had shown her restlessness through acts of pettiness and stubborn willfulness—everyone had been victim to her short temper. Gillian sighed, recalling one of the interminable games of chess she had had to play with her. Perceiving that her opponent's strategy would checkmate her, the queen had swept the pieces from the board in spiteful rage.

They saw little of the king since he first ordered the siege of Leeds Castle. No one had believed him capable of such swift action, and despite the menace of a baronial army which had been raised to relieve Leeds and headed by the earl of Hereford together with the two de Mortimers, Edward remained calm. Gillian shuddered at the thought of Roger de Mortimer—he had come so close.

It was Isabella's page, Peter de Gilles, recovered from his wound, who excitedly brought them the news of the castle's surrender. Lady Badlesmere was taken prisoner and would be lodged in the Tower, Peter said, but her lord had eluded the king and found refuge with Hereford. Eyes shining, he spun a wondrous tale of the citizens of London gathering together their own army to accompany the king's knights and soldiery to Kent in order to avenge the queen's honor. Isabella and her ladies had listened with rapt attention as the names of the barons besieging Leeds Castle were mentioned—Pembroke, Norfolk, Richmond, Arundel, de Warenne. Pembroke had finally declared his support of Edward, and many of the others had followed his example. Many—but not Glairn. Fingers absently stroking the fur's softness, Gillian wondered where Jamie was, and felt an ache stab at the emptiness still within her.

"*Chère* Gillian," Isabella's voice broke through her musings. The queen, sitting at her small dressing table, turned from the mirror to look at her favorite lady-in-waiting. Her freshly brushed hair fell in a thick, shining blond braid down her back. "*Chère* Gillian, young Alisa has just told me that the Marcher barons have met with Cousin Thomas. I wonder what mischief he is fomenting now!" She laughed—a brittle, cold sound. " 'Twas rumored that London was harboring enemies of the crown, but our cousin Pembroke has proven them false. My city is still loyal . . . for 'tis my city still, as it ever was." Isabella sighed, seeking reassurance and receiving naught but respectful silence. She frowned petulantly. "How I wish that my lord Hereford and the de Mortimers could have taken London and relieved the Tower instead of withdrawing as they did. Sweet Jesu, I languish here."

"Your Grace, you jest!" Gillian went white at the thought of possibly seeing Roger again.

For a moment Isabella's blue eyes sparkled at some

private memory, but she said, "Of course I jest. I'm aware as you are that the barons from the Welsh Marches bode the crown ill. But I weary of rumors and whispers. 'Twas the same in Nottingham after our escape from York." Her voice grew cold. "Alisa knows what can happen when one is shut away from the outside world."

Alisa de Peverell's pinched, sallow face reddened and her hand strayed to the pretty gold chain she always wore about her neck. Isabella laughed icily, the sound shattering the sudden silence which had fallen around her.

"She proved her loyalty to me . . . more than that de Maudley slut did."

De Maudley slut? Gillian stared uncomprehendingly at the queen.

"Jehan de Maudley, Your Grace? But she's dead these many years!" Gillian whispered, frozen with shock.

"Dead? Jehan?" Isabella gazed at herself in the small mirror. "Why do you say dead . . . 'tis true she tried to kill herself once, but my physicians saved her—unfortunately. Mother of God, how I detest her!" She chattered on, delighting in her vengeance. "I cast her out—I never want to see that sly face again. 'Twas good riddance, for she's a wanton bitch and I'll brook no disloyalty from my court." With a slender forefinger she rubbed a bit of perfumed unguent into an imagined blemish on her throat, thrusting the unpleasant thoughts of Jehan from her mind.

So Jehan had survived . . . it would take time to accept the reality of it, but Gillian felt an unexpected sense of relief. Jehan was alive—another victory in quenching the fading memory of Arnaut de Broze.

The queen's outraged shriek mingled with Alisa's painful scream as her head snapped back from the force of Isabella's slap. A silver dish with comfits clattered loudly to the floor, the sweets scattering all about.

"You stupid bitch," Isabella shouted. "I want the sugar plums—not these sickening confections." Her temper unleashed, she slapped the screaming girl again, heaping insults on her bowed head. Grasping a jeweled hand mirror from the table, the furious woman hurled it to the floor while her ladies shrank from her in sudden fear.

"I see you've not changed your habits or sweet, gentle nature, my lady!"

The derisive sneer in Edward's voice penetrated Isabella's rage and she raised startled eyes to her husband, whose tall, imposing figure filled the chamber with its royal presence. Alisa scuttled away, hiding her flaming, stinging face from sight. She took refuge behind the other ladies, but Isabella had already forgotten her existence. Gillian, still standing by the bed, could feel the unbridled animosity between Isabella and Edward as it flowed and pulsed from one to the other. How they loathe each other, she thought, somehow finding room to pity them both.

"What do you want, my lord?" Isabella asked, shuddering at the remote possibility that he had come to bed her. "I'm weary and long for my rest." She turned her back on him, wishing him gone. Without replying to her, Edward ordered her ladies to retire, and the door closed softly behind Gillian, the last to leave. Oh sweet Virgin, 'tis what he wants for a certainty, she told herself with a sinking heart. No hint of her revulsion showed on her face, and she steeled herself for what she considered her royal duty.

Edward's dark eyes were blank as he wordlessly watched his wife unfasten her fur-lined robe and let it fall about her feet. Her naked body glowed in the dim light and the sudden cold made the nipples harden on breasts still firm and beautiful. But her husband viewed her with little interest, annoyed at the insistence of his councillors to make his necessary visits to the queen. Although her beauty had increased through the years, it made him want her less, for it seemed to mock him. Because of her presence, his Brother Perrot had been taken from him . . . a poor neglected queen she had declared herself to the realm—spiteful bitch. And yet, when he finally held her in his arms and felt the fullness of her soft body against his own, desire came. But he knew that she would give herself to his unloving, caressing hands and passionless, seeking body as she always did—with stoic silence.

Shivering, Isabella slipped between the curtains and

lay on the bed motionless, waiting for Edward to come to her. And the mute, painful ritual began, repeating itself as it had throughout the years of their marriage, dutiful and indifferent, until Edward moved away from her inert body, both relieved that it was over.

Unaroused and unfulfilled, Isabella lay beside her husband, willing herself to sleep, but it was denied her. There was a tiny fiery ache deep within her which gnawed at her body whenever Edward came to her. She was filled with a vague sense of dissatisfaction as a tear slipped down her cheek. She wondered, as she had over and over, what it was that had driven Gillian to James Kilburn and Jehan into the arms of de Mortimer. A strange warmth pulsed through her at the thought of the Marcher baron. The ache quickened, sending tongues of flame licking at her vitals. She moaned softly, her body on fire. Put him from your mind, Isabella—'tis naught but the dreams of an untried maid, she told herself sternly. Not six months ago you gave birth to Joanna in this very chamber—remember your children. They are your duty and your future. Drawing the covers over herself, Isabella felt a pleasant drowsiness surround her.

She was nearly asleep when Edward said, "I'm leaving London tomorrow to see what is happening in the west. There's much unrest which must be quelled. Particularly since I ordered Roger d'Amory and Hugh d'Audley to return the lands they stole from the Despensers."

Isabella stiffened with foreboding. Holy Virgin—what idiocy was he embarking upon now.

"You will join me in Cirencester for Christmas," Edward told her, hard put to keep his smug satisfaction from her, for it all was going exactly as Hugh had predicted. Cousin Thomas and his friends would hang themselves through their eagerness to oppose him, the younger Despenser had said. When Hereford and the others came to assist Badlesmere, he had sent Pembroke and the archbishop of London to Kingston-on-Thames to treat with them. It seemed a lost cause until word to withdraw was received by Hereford from Lancaster. With a feeling of frustration, Edward wondered whether Thomas had suspected a trap. Of all those he saw as his enemies, Lancaster drew his strongest hatred, and when his chance for vengeance came, he would be ready for it. That he had promised himself at Piers Gaveston's grave at King's Langley.

He settled himself more comfortably against the large soft pillows and stretched out his long body beneath the covers.

"We may also be joined by both Despensers soon!" Edward ignored Isabella's sharp intake of breath at his words. "They petitioned the Council to set aside the sentence—'twas illegal, you know. I've always believed it so, and now the archbishop of Canterbury and the other members have agreed and will annul the order of exile."

You are a great fool, Isabella screamed at him silently. By the holy rood, this will lead to more trouble, she thought, and found herself saying, "Lancaster will never accept their return—never."

"He's not been asked his opinion. If he doesn't, I'm prepared to force him to," Edward snapped peevishly. She was talking to him as to a child. "I've ordered Chirk to join me in Cirencester. He's failed to apprise me of conditions in Wales for many months and 'tis time he fulfilled his function as Justiciar. Lord de Valence will also spend Christmas with us. I've asked him to bring his new countess along. She can give you news of your brother's court."

There was no reply from Isabella and he smiled in the darkness at his cleverness in resolving matters so well. He was well aware of the charges and countercharges which had begun to thicken and pollute the air of his realm. Soon, Hugh, we'll be together, and 'twill be your good counsel I can heed again, he thought sleepily. All that need be done was to push his barons a bit further . . . just a bit and he would have them all on his side. He was every whit as good a king as his father had been. Why would no one admit it?

The king slept peacefully in the wide bed, warm and comfortable beneath the fur rug. Isabella's sleep was fitful, for the image of a wildly handsome face with burning black eyes which usually dominated her dreams was obscured by the clouds of civil war which were gathering blackly on the wide horizon of her mind.

Cirencester

"Return to Glairn, Jillie—'tis where you belong! This court life is not for you."

Geoffrey's gray eyes were full of concern as he looked at his sister's closed white face. Gazing wistfully out of the small window, Gillian watched the wind fling sleet and snow against the small glass panes frosted over from the cold. She shivered and wished she had brought a cloak. The heavy woolen undergown and velvet tunic lavishly trimmed with thick fur could not keep the winter's chill from settling into her bones. Cirencester seemed to be at the end of a world growing increasingly unfamiliar to her, and it was beyond her comprehension that the king had been so adamant to have Isabella and her court in attendance. Even the royal children were here to celebrate Christmastide with their parents. Gillian sighed, thinking how their clear happy laughter seemed out of place among the grim-faced men, mail-clad and fully armed, who continued to ride in day after day and who spoke of naught save war. There was little time for feasting or celebration, for each day the town took on a greater semblance to an armed camp as Edward and his barons busily prepared to launch their campaign against the Marcher barons and their ally to the north, Lancaster. She turned toward her brother and shook her head. She did not want to think of what he insisted on telling her.

"I can't return, Geoff, not yet. Don't ask it of me nor my reasons, for I will not speak of them." The large eyes darkened with pain and Geoffrey saw how her hands pressed against her body as if to contain its anguish. "Naught has changed for me since we last spoke."

"But to be here at Yuletide and have your children alone in Glairn without you or Jamie—'tis hardly fair to them," he protested, but Gillian's expression did not change. "Heaven alone knows when your lord can return home. At least go to him—he's not so distant. We face a dire time and each moment is a precious one."

She put her hands over her ears to shut out his words, knowing the truth of them. But she wanted no more of his pleading and his constant probing into her soul. When the earl of Pembroke had arrived in Cirencester with his young countess, Gillian felt relieved to see that Jamie was not with him, for she had dreaded having to face him. Her joy at seeing Geoffrey quickly fled when he pressed a letter from her husband into her hand. Breaking the Glairn seal with shaking fingers, she had fearfully read the brief message wishing her well. The stilted formal words were obviously written in haste and revealed naught of his own state or his feelings. Gillian had stared at the unfamiliar cramped writing, trying to find Jamie somewhere within the letter, but he eluded her. Only the knowledge that his own hands had held the small piece of parchment gave her an odd sense of comfort. Geoffrey told her rather coldly that Jamie had ridden to one of Pembroke's holdings nearby with some of the earl's men to see to the strengthening of the castle's fortifications, allowing Pembroke to meet with Edward. Robert, who had joined his brother-in-law, had gone with him to Goodrich. Jamie was deliberately avoiding her, Gillian realized then, and sank even deeper into the despair which continued to grip her.

"My lord fears Marcher attacks on his holdings since he's cast his support to Edward," Geoffrey said quietly to Gillian, whose eyes were once more fixed on the window. She seemed unaware of his presence and he felt irritated by her perpetual avoidance of discussing what he felt must be said. After several unsuccessful attempts to speak with her alone, he had been able to find a measure of privacy for them in a small alcove at one end of the solar. Although the warmth of the large hearth did not reach them, a brazier standing nearby allowed them some comfort. The manor house occupied by the immediate members of the court was old and drafty, but everything had been done to make it as habitable as possible for its royal occupants.

Geoffrey leaned forward, trying to catch her attention. "The earl is greatly worried over the king's coming campaign, for he believes it will accomplish naught but to widen the breach between Edward and those barons opposed to what he stands for. From reports he has received, 'tis a certainty that not only Hereford, but Roger de Mortimer and his uncle will take to the field to prevent him from entering the Marches."

"Have you never learned that 'tis unchivalrous to fill a lady's ear with talk of politics and war, Master Geoffrey? One speaks of gentler things." Pembroke's deep voice interrupted his secretary as he held out a steaming goblet of mulled wine to Gillian. "You neglect your sister's health," he chided gently. "Here, my lady, drink this. It should ward off winter's chill."

A servant had followed him and silently offered goblets to both men. Pembroke settled himself comfortably down beside Gillian's too slender form on the pillow-strewn bench beneath the window. Lifting his goblet, he said, "Wassail, my dear countess, and to you too, you young rogue." Pembroke's dark eyes smiled at Geoffrey as he told Gillian, "Your brother slipped away from me while we were going over some very dull papers dealing with our usual lack of finances. Somehow I knew that I would find him with the only one he truly cares for . . . and I can't fault him."

The earl lifted Gillian's hand to his lips for a moment and was surprised to feel it tremble. So she still grieves, he thought, noticing the shadowed eyes and soft, vulnerable mouth which seemed to have forgotten how to smile. And not only for her dead child, he told himself as he urged her to drink the wine while it was still warm.

"Since I leave tomorrow, there's much still to discuss with Edward and the others, but I thought to permit myself a short visit to the solar." Pembroke drank the wine, watching the silent young woman beside him. She toyed with her goblet, looking unseeing into its depths. " 'Tis the first chance I've had to talk to you since my arrival, Gillian. I wish you as good a Yule as is possible for you."

"I thank you, my lord." Gillian spoke with difficulty, almost as if her voice had not been used for a long time. The earl's presence always filled her with shyness, although she knew he was genuinely fond of her. "May I congratulate you on your marriage—the lady Marie is a most charming young girl."

She would say anything to prevent the man seated beside her, in his kindness and desire to comfort, from speaking to her of that which she shrank from hearing. Neither noticed that Geoffrey had gone, glad to leave Gillian to Pembroke's gentle probing. Perhaps he could penetrate the wall she had built about herself, allowing no one to see beyond its boundaries.

"Thank you, Gillian." Pembroke pressed her hand. " 'Tis the first time since our marriage that she's ventured forth to court, save when I presented her to Edward. Our ways seem strange to her, I fear, and I would have wished a less warlike atmosphere for her, but Edward insisted I bring her."

He sighed and gazed at the group of ladies seated about the hearth, searching for the small, thin figure of his countess. She was listening to Isabella, who was chattering with great animation to her young cousin and brother-in-law, the earl of Kent. Sensing his gaze, Marie's attention left the queen. As her eyes met Pembroke's, a tremulous smile transformed her face, making it glow softly with mute affection.

"She's very lovely, my lord. Have patience with her shyness and reticence. I remember only too well how I felt in my early days at court. I was no older, but certainly less happy in my marriage." It was obvious to all but her lord that Marie de Valence was most assuredly content in her wedded state.

"Had I more time to spend with her, attendance at court would be less of a trial for her, but I fear that I'll not see her for many a month." His hand absently fingered the gold chain about his neck. He frowned, a rare anger rising in him. "Sweet Jesu, I'm weary of all the warring and yet there's naught I can do to stop it. I'm indentured physically to Edward and bound by honor to him. The burden of it weighs heavily upon me. He's determined to wreak havoc on us all and I've no power anymore to stop him."

It was a startling revelation for Pembroke to make and for a moment Gillian was taken aback by his candor.

She was further startled when he said bitterly, "I should have remained a widower and left that innocent child a maid."

"Nay, my lord, you're wrong about your lady," Gillian protested. "She truly cares for you and that knowledge should give you comfort. Geoffrey has told me of your misgivings of the coming campaign, but have no doubts that the countess will be well cared for. She has brought a breath of home to the queen, and for that, Isabella will make her a friend. Know that I, too, will be a friend to her." At last a smile hovered on Gillian's face as she leaned toward Pembroke and murmured, "Although a less formidable guardian than Lady de Marc would make things easier. I vow that even the queen trembles when she approaches."

At Gillian's comment, Pembroke broke out in unaccustomed laughter at the image she had evoked, for Lady de Marc was indeed a forbidding personage who had had finally to be put into her place—not a light task even for so clever a diplomat as the earl.

"My dear, 'tis good to talk to you, even though I spoke of things best left unsaid, and for which I scolded Geoffrey. But I've always found you the most perceptive of women, and so I've told James more than once." He saw the shadows return to her face. "Nay, Gillian, I'll not speak of him, nor of what you want to forget. I like you too well to deliberately cause you pain." His voice was low and gentle, reassuring her that she had naught to fear from him. Staying by her side, Pembroke called for more wine and coaxed her to eat sweetmeats from a small silver dish he held in his own hand while he spoke of unimportant things.

Gillian clutched the iron stirrup of Geoffrey's mount with cold hands as the animal moved restlessly, fighting the firm hand holding it in check. The manor yard seemed suddenly too small to contain all of the earl's men busily preparing to leave amidst the din of shouting retainers and the hysterical barking of the dogs. A sharp wind blew through the open gates, heralding more snow. Although it was already past daybreak, the leaden clouds forbade the sun to filter through, obscuring the light and lending an unholy darkness to the scene. Torches flared briefly and were quenched by the wind, which seemed to be everywhere. Gillian's cloak billowed about her and her feet slipped on the ice-covered stones of the paved courtyard. Geoffrey caught hold of her arm, steadying her.

"Geoff—take care that naught befalls you."

He could scarcely hear her, surrounded as they were by the tumult of leave-taking and the shrieking wind. Pembroke was already seated on a powerful destrier, the visor of his helm closed so no one could see his face. His standard bearer waited by the gate for his lord's signal, the blue and white striped banner with its border of red martlets snapping in the wild gusts. Gillian felt her brother's hand on her uncovered hair and then he cupped her chin, forcing her to look at him. His gray eyes glittered angrily as he bent down toward her. She had refused to answer Jamie's letter, telling him there was naught for her to say. Ignoring the bleak, lost look of her, despite her seemingly indifferent attitude, he chose to see only stubborn self-indulgence.

"Because I love you, I've tried to understand, but I can take no more of your childish refusal to speak of what troubles you. That's why I must leave the truth with you. I can only hope that it will haunt you as relentlessly as it haunts me." She tried to escape him, but his grip was too strong and his furious voice lashed out remorselessly. "You are destroying Jamie with your silence. You, more than any of us, know what manner of man he is. He will seek death rather than live without you! My lord fears for him, though he says nothing—Robert scarce knew him again—and all because you turn from him without telling him why. You both lost Maddie, yet you neither comfort nor let yourself be comforted. She's dead, Gillian—she won't return."

She struggled for breath, feeling as though she were drowning in his words, but her brother was impervious to the pain he inflicted upon her in his desperation.

"God's blood, Gillian—don't you know that naught

matters to Jamie but you." And then his own fear was wrenched from him. " 'Twill be your fault alone if he does not survive what we will face in the coming months, no matter who strikes the blow."

Gillian stared at him in horror, his words burning themselves into her soul, and she staggered back as he released her. For a moment longer, Geoffrey gazed down at her.

"Think well on it, sister."

Putting spur to his horse, he was gone, galloping through the gate after the earl. Gillian stood motionless in the sea of men riding past her, aware of aught but her brother's cruel, deliberate tone and the glacial hardness in his eyes.

Sweet Jesu, 'tis not possible! Her lord was strong and full of life. Jamie! Gillian was left alone with her guilt and her loss. It was too late now for a letter or even a message —everyone was gone. Her arms flailed out, groping futilely for support.

"Jamie!" The name was torn from her, thrown into the air by the wild wind and hurled over the manor walls into the white vastness beyond. She never felt the gentle hand which grasped her own as the emptiness within her suddenly erupted in a scalding flood of tears penetrating to the innermost depths of her being. Lost in the wilderness of her emotions, she allowed Lady Marie, her pale face twisted with anxiety, to lead her into the warmth and security of the manor house.

Chapter 11

1322
Salop

Snow filled the sky, drifting down softly, the thick
white flakes covering the stone and wooden fortifications
of the old house and obscuring the hills rising above the
small tower.

"Damnation! 'Tis beginning to snow again!"

Robert Harron turned from the narrow window overlooking the courtyard in disgust and looked at the tall,
haggard man clad in battledress standing by the hearth.
With a feeling of irritation, he realized that James had not
even heard him, so intent was he on his own thoughts. It
had taken them four days of hard riding from Ludlow to
Shrewsbury in search of Roger de Mortimer before learning of his whereabouts from a liegeman near Wigmore.
Carrying a white flag as a sign of their peaceful intent, and
accompanied by a small force, they had been permitted
access to the small manor house half hidden among gaunt
trees standing silent watch over the unfamiliar land. It was
strange not to feel the comforting weight of the long sword
at his side, but their arms had been taken from them before they were allowed within the fortified house.

Holding hands red with cold toward the fire's warmth,
James Kilburn's handsome face was somber, his eyes
turned inward. Saddle-sore, his muscles aching from the
long ride through freezing, wind-driven snow, he was

weary to the bone. He had dreaded the meeting with Roger ever since leaving the security of Goodrich Castle. Were it not for Pembroke's urgent desire to at least make an attempt to reason with the Marcher baron, he would never have agreed to come. It was a futile journey at best. Unclasping his fur-lined cloak, drenched from the melting snow still clinging to its folds, he threw it impatiently on the settle beside his helm and gauntlets. His wrinkled red surcoat was still damp and he longed to divest himself of his hauberk and armor, for they weighed heavily upon him. An involuntary shudder ran over him and he frowned. There was an unnatural stillness to the house which made him uneasy.

"I was told two knights under a white flag had demanded admittance to see me, but never would I have thought one of them to be the earl of Glairn!" The sneering derisive voice jarred James's already frayed nerves and the austere mouth tightened grimly. He raised his head slowly and contemplated his host with hostile eyes.

" 'Twas not of my own choosing, my lord de Mortimer," James said coldly. "I but bring an urgent message from the earl of Pembroke."

Still standing by the window, Robert nervously observed the two men facing each other, neither one giving ground. He knew that James would refuse to continue his mission if the baron of Wigmore adopted his usual sarcastic manner. His brother-in-law was in a dire state, and despite all efforts by those about him to lighten his spirit, he was retreating ever deeper into himself. He was like a tightly coiled spring, ready to snap. Pembroke should never have chosen him for this, the younger man thought, for de Mortimer was too volatile for Jamie to deal with in his present condition.

"Pembroke sent a fellow earl as messenger to a mere baron? By the holy Virgin, his opinion of me must have risen enormously since we last met." Roger's dark eyes mocked his visitor. James continued to stand before him, his lean, hollow-cheeked face expressionless. "James, you look dreadful! I can't flatter myself that it was fear of facing me again that has caused such a change in you."

Roger himself looked splendid—sleek and self-satisfied. The prospect of war excites and pleases him, Robert realized, seeing the dangerous glitter in the baron's eyes as he watched James warily. Serving men entered silently, carrying a large steaming bowl of mulled wine with great sops of bread floating in it and gold mazers bearing the de Mortimer crest. While his servants offered the two men the filled mazers, he seated himself before the fire.

"I forget my duties as host!" Roger said smoothly. Lifting a filled mazer, he saluted them. " 'Tis a time to say Wassail to you both, my lord Glairn and young Lord Kestwick. May this be a good year for us all." He drank deeply, feeling the hot wine stir his blood.

James Kilburn set his mazer on the mantel without having touched the wine.

"I've not come to drink with you, nor wish you a good year," he said stiffly. " 'Tis not for the pleasanter side of life I've traveled these many leagues to find you. The king and his army are in Worcester . . ."

Roger laughed. "Is he indeed! It has not escaped our notice, James. You may be sure that he'll not be allowed to cross the Severn, for we hold the other bank securely. Should he try, you may tell him that he has a great surprise in store."

" 'Tis a civil war, Roger . . . and very different from the one when we were all banded together against Edward because of his unholy attachment for Piers Gaveston. This war will be fought on your lands—and you'll not win."

With an impatient gesture, Roger cast the dregs of his wine into the fire, and great yellow flames leaped up hungrily to consume them.

"I'll not discuss my lands nor the reasons for our actions with you. You'd close your ears to any truth save what your good friend Aymer de Valence tells you or what happens in the north." He was suddenly filled with anger at the slender man still standing before him. "There's more to this realm than what encompasses your world. The forces that have been set in motion cannot be halted by you or your precious Pembroke. Do you think me too arrogant to care where we fight? This land has been bathed in blood before. I've been burned out countless times and have pillaged in return. I hold to what's mine as truly as you do, my lord. My hatred may be greater than yours, but 'tis deeper rooted, for my enemies are my peers as well. I doubt that your rigid morality can comprehend the lengths to which I will go to avenge myself."

Why does he persist in his refusal to understand what I'm trying to tell him, James thought, controlling his rising irritation against de Mortimer.

"The Despensers are to be recalled, Roger, and will probably join Edward in the field. You are out-numbered —you, your uncle, Hereford, and the others. If you fight, how many lives will be needlessly forfeited for an ambitious dream that has no possibility of success." As he spoke, James drew a folded paper from the sleeve of his hauberk and offered it to the Marcher baron. Roger made no move to take it from him, his black eyes smoldering as he remembered how he had once offered to share his dreams of power with Kilburn, and had been refused because of the other's overwhelming love for a woman. That too would always stand between them.

Kilburn looked down at what Pembroke had entrusted him with. Should the king or his barons hear of it before Pembroke had time to set his plan in motion, there would be hell to pay. If only de Mortimer could see the justice of their position.

"If you are willing to listen to reason and withdraw from this treasonable act of rebellion, Lord Pembroke believes that he can promise complete amnesty for you, as well as for your uncle."

"And how does he intend to achieve all this?" Roger asked, adding sarcastically, "I have no doubt that with his well-known diplomacy and tact, he will even find good cause for us to welcome the Despensers back and allow them free access to what they covet and we possess."

"Roger, at least think about it. Pembroke's not alone in his desire to avoid war. Norfolk, Kent, de Warenne, and even Arundel believe a confrontation can be avoided. If you agree to his proposal, they will request a safe conduct for you so that you may meet with them."

"A safe conduct?" De Mortimer rose from his chair, his voice shaking with fury. "A safe conduct so that I can

abase myself before those who seek my downfall? Never
. . . there's but one place I will meet my enemies—in com-
bat with a good sword and lance."

He strode restlessly about the room, his rage lashing
out wildly at his former friend and at Robert, whose
strong resemblance to his sister Gillian kept intruding upon
his concentration on the matter before him. Damn that
haunting bitch! He silently cursed Gillian for the uneasy
guilt which rose within him. He wanted no part of any
of them.

The two men said nothing, watching de Mortimer
struggle with his angry pride. Somewhere within that handsome head must lurk some common sense, James hoped,
for he had faced crises before and landed on his feet. He
glanced down at the proposed safe conduct Pembroke had
prepared for Roger.

"Roger," James's voice was sharp, cutting through
the other's rage. "Don't act in haste. And for sweet heav-
en's sake, don't allow your animosity toward me to affect
your decision. I warned Aymer I was not the man to place
this plea before you, but he contended that my presence
would convince you of the gravity with which he views
this entire matter."

Black eyes blazed out of the passionate face as de
Mortimer stopped before Kilburn.

"Do you know what you are asking of me?" His
words were edged in bitterness. "Can you comprehend the
extent of the Despensers' greed in wresting our holdings
from us?"

"Lands stolen from the Welsh princes who held it
long before the first Norman ever set foot in England,
Roger. Who is to judge our right?"

"Stop moralizing, James. 'Tis one of your more tiresome traits and has ever affected your judgment," de
Mortimer snapped. "You have a way of irritating me to
the point of detestation!"

"Aye, such as choosing other lords' offspring to wed
my children." The words were out before Kilburn could
control himself. He was instantly contrite, for the matter
which had brought him to Roger was too important to drag
personal pettiness into it.

"You bastard! 'Tis a miracle you ventured so far from your lady's bed . . . should I feel honored?" De Mortimer's lips drew back in a knowing sneer. "She's indeed worth your enslavement, for her talents make one's senses reel." It was a challenge flung down between them. Kilburn went white, his mind struggling against the rage which was seething within him.

"Nay, Jamie!" Robert put a restraining hand on his arm. "Now is not the time for personal hatreds." It had been a detestable thing to say, but de Mortimer was not known for either finesse or finer feelings. He felt Kilburn's muscles begin to relax as the anger drained from him. "My lord," Robert turned toward Roger, whose face mirrored James's aroused hatred, "we did not come here in animosity or anger, but to beg you to reconsider your position. It is hoped that you will accept the safe conduct for the purposes Lord Kilburn has mentioned."

De Mortimer shook his head and said slowly, " 'Tis not only the Marcher barons who are in this. The rebellion is far more widespread."

"If your friends are counting on Lancaster's assistance, best forget it. He was ever a lord to sit and wait while others fought and died." James laughed shortly. "Best look to yourselves if you refuse to treat with Pembroke."

As he laid the safe conduct on a small table, he noticed a small square of yellow silk lying in the padded chair standing nearby. A needle, threaded with green silk, was still attached to a partially embroidered rose. So that's why he's here, James thought wryly. He had heard tales of the Marcher baron's mysterious unseen mistress, for whom it was said he held so deep a passion. Reaching for his still damp cloak, he flung it impatiently over his shoulders.

"Think well on it, Roger, for the king is anxious for victory—and what whim he toys with today is oft forgotten tomorrow. He will reach Shrewsbury with or without crossing the Severn." Picking up his helm and gauntlets, James added, "Pembroke is presently in Newport and will await word from you."

There was no more to say. He had fulfilled the mission entrusted to him by Pembroke and now all that remained was a strong desire to put Roger de Mortimer behind him. Even the winter storm was preferable to the hate-filled atmosphere of the manor.

De Mortimer stood by the hearth, his face averted, and he found himself unable to bid his visitors farewell. Their mailed feet made a jarring sound as they strode from the chamber into the hall, and a short while later Roger heard the gates protest as they opened to allow Kilburn and his party to depart into the snow-filled afternoon. Still he remained by the hearth, his mind seething with all that had been said. A safe conduct! The humiliation of it! He struck his fist against the hard stone mantel in frustrated anger.

"You should have offered them shelter for the night, my lord. The weather is foul."

Jehan had slipped up silently and stood behind him. Leaning her head against his back, she heard the wild thudding of his heart. He was trembling.

"They'll find hospitality enough at Glasmore Abbey. 'Tis not far and they must have passed it on their way here," Roger said thickly. He did not turn and she sensed the anger still within him. Jehan ran a hand softly over his velvet-clad shoulder, caressing the long black hair which hung over the collar of his tunic.

"Roger, you are being offered amnesty . . . don't throw your freedom away because of personal grudges."

"You were listening!" He turned then, grasping her arms with ungentle hands. "Your opinion is of no consequence. What knowledge do you hold of my way of life?" His face was stormy and his voice harsh, but Jehan had no fear of him, for she saw how Kilburn's visit had shaken him. She had heard the words flung at Kilburn concerning Gillian and wondered again why she seemed to stand between them.

Stifling the familiar surge of jealousy she felt at even the thought of Gillian, Jehan said quietly, "The only knowledge I have is what you reveal of yourself when we are together, and that you seem to seek death even in the midst of life. 'Tis something I've never been able to understand." He stared at her, and she knew that perhaps for the first time since she shared his life, he was heeding her words. "I listened because I had to know what they wanted of you. Their offer was brought in all sincerity and I believe that it was without Edward's knowledge. Pembroke seeks peace above all else. With the Despensers returning, his influence over Edward will diminish—but not yet. Use his power, Roger. At least meet with him; listen to him without your usual rancor and impatience. And above all else, don't trust Thomas of Lancaster. He is a viper."

Roger looked down at her earnest, pleading face with surprise, realizing that her concern was totally for him. She seemed to have no thought for herself, although she well knew that her future depended on his decision. It was a different Jehan from the one he had found in Dublin Castle, he thought in wonder. His hand gently cupped her face and he traced the outline of the compelling mouth with his thumb. What was there about her that kept him so ensnared?

"Little dove—if it were only as simple as you utter it. There is much I must discuss with my uncle." He sighed, reluctant to tell her. "This morning a messenger brought disastrous news of raids into Clun by Welshmen supporting the king. I fear we've lost more than we gained when we burned out the Despensers."

She blanched, her heart beating painfully. Clun! Where her father's holdings were. She was suddenly filled with cold fear, for Roger's moroseness was unnatural. She was familiar with his moods and knew that from the depths of his despair he would soar into a state of unmanageable, savage hatred which allowed no logic to shake it from its target. Jehan pressed herself urgently against him as she searched his face.

"Please . . . I beg you, Roger. You have no chance of victory. Your life is more precious than vindicating your hatreds! If you have no thought for yourself, think of your children—think of Edmund, who will lose everything if you forfeit your life. Who will be the next baron of Wigmore then? And your other sons . . . what of your daughters—linked to the greatest houses of England? What would happen to them?"

He smiled at her, his sardonic humor for once not in evidence.

"The only one you've not mentioned is my wife . . . Nay, Jehan, don't look away. Joan is my wife and has borne me our children, each one of which I hold dear. And she would miss me, as would my mother—but I think none would mourn me as you would this moment."

"Roger, don't talk of death—please." Her eyes glistened with tears. " 'Tis not too late to save yourself. Pembroke is an honorable man. His word is true."

" 'Tis not Pembroke I distrust, but that pewling abomination we call king!" He freed himself from Jehan's embrace, silencing her protestations with a kiss.

"Enough of this," Roger declared firmly. "There's much to be seen to, for I meet with Chirk tomorrow." He picked up the paper Kilburn had left behind. " 'Tis best I take this with me as proof of Lord Pembroke's good intentions."

"Roger—please shackle your passions," Jehan begged, frightened by the demonic exhilaration which suddenly possessed him.

"My uncle will agree that there is only one road we can choose. We will take to the field and face that damn coward with all our strength at our backs. Our victory will be glorious and those who named me traitor will beg for mercy." He laughed then, a short, harsh sound which belied the almost feverish brightness of his eyes.

"Roger . . ." His name was spoken pleadingly, but he brushed Jehan aside. All else had paled at the prospect of battle and it was as if she no longer existed for him. In that moment of decision he had unknowingly severed the emotional bond between them, although it would take a long time before she faced the truth of it.

Burton-on-Trent

"Is it finished?" Pembroke's deep voice was rough with fatigue as he turned toward the knight who had just been ushered into his pavilion. Mud-spattered, his surcoat rent in a dozen places and stained with blood, Edmund Fitzalan nodded solemnly. For three days the armies had battled each other for the bridge spanning the Trent, with neither side victorious.

" 'Twas fortunate that a way was found to ford the river at Walton. I shall never fathom their ignorance of the bridge crossing—how else could we have outflanked them?"

Pembroke, having successfully routed the enemy at Walton, had deemed it possible to order his army's encampment on the newly won side of the river. Sitting in his tent, he had gratefully accepted the news that the rebel army was showing signs of disorderly withdrawal.

"From the size of the camp, I would think the main body of our soldiery survived." Arundel accepted the cup of wine offered by one of Pembroke's retainers, but remained standing in spite of the earl's invitation to rest. "I must find James. I've not seen him since we engaged several of Lancaster's knights near the bridge. I've never known him so heedless of his own safety as in the past days. 'Twas as if he were avenging some personal grudge, giving quarter to none who fell beneath his sword. 'Tis worrisome."

A brooding look came over Pembroke's weary face and he leaned forward in his wooden camp chair.

"There are many things which worry me, Edmund. Matters are worsening day by day. I know the king is jubilant over his victories, but he never gives thought to the price to not only those who support him, but all the rebel barons who believe that Lancaster is right."

"I know what haunts you, my lord. I too cannot erase it from my mind, for Edward's betrayal of the de Mortimers was a betrayal of our honor." Arundel unclasped his cloak, throwing it over a coffer. Although he had intended remaining only a few minutes, he realized that he wished to cleanse his soul of the de Mortimers' fate as much as Pembroke. While they had never truly discussed that day, it continued to fester with ever-mounting anger. With his wine cup replenished, he sat down beside his host and stared gloomily into the glowing heart of a brazier. The metal oil lamp suspended from its portable stand shed a fitful light over the two men, accentuating the shared exhaustion and unease of spirit stamped on their taut features.

"Had I foreseen it, I would never have offered them the safe conduct," Pembroke said bitterly, hitting the chair's arm with a clenched fist. "We both know all too well that Edward had finally agreed to a pardon, should they surrender."

"But why did they hold so fast to the belief that Lancaster would come to their aid? It only delayed their decision and now they're imprisoned in the Tower because of it."

Shrugging his shoulders, Pembroke frowned. There was no answer to Arundel's question. He had hoped that with the surrender of the two de Mortimers, the other Marcher barons would have followed suit. Even Hereford had sent word that, with the promise of amnesty, he would also surrender.

"They finally did what they had to do—their men were deserting, Lancaster had betrayed them . . . 'twas what I would have done. They truly had no other choice, but by then it was too late."

"I shall never forget Roger's face when he ceded his sword to the king. For him that moment must have been a horrendous humiliation."

"Who could have known what Edward intended? He has never sought our counsel save when his crown or his precious skin has been in peril."

"But, Aymer—to arrest them on the strength of a dubious petition by common folk accusing them of high-handed cruelty and then ordering them to be chained without allowing them to refute the charges—'tis totally unacceptable to me!" Roger in chains! Arundel recalled his feeling of shock as he watched the shackling of both men before all those present. Roger had struggled wildly in the grasp of his guards, insisting that he had been promised amnesty while the king blandly denied ever having agreed to it. He would never forget the blazing hatred in de Mortimer's face as he cursed them all. Chirk had stood frozen, the fierce mountain hawk seemingly drained of all strength, but the younger de Mortimer refused to surrender meekly. He had shouted down Pembroke's protests to Edward, drowning them with his wild promises of revenge, singling out those he considered party to his betrayal. Had Pem-

311

broke too shuddered when Roger's burning black gaze rested on him as he spewed out all the demonic malevolence in his nature. A cold fear had clawed at him for a breadth of a heartbeat.

"Edward relished that moment, for he had condemned them in his own mind long before they surrendered. How filled with his own power he was at that moment." Just thinking of it made Pembroke ill with angry frustration which consumed him in the face of his own humiliation at the hands of the king. He felt a choking grip on his throat for a moment as he fought the sudden breathlessness which had come with rage.

"Don't blame yourself, Aymer. You acted in good faith. That the king chose to betray his promises cannot reflect on your honor. And remember that you are not alone . . . there were others as betrayed."

"Well said, Edmund—how many of us secretly rejoiced at Hereford's escape north!" The tightness eased and he took a deep breath, grateful for the air which seemed to burn his lungs.

Kilburn had come in, tracking muddy earth from outside and bringing with him the chill moistness of early evening. His cloak glistened wetly from the fine rain which had begun to fall an hour earlier. Arundel leaped up with a shout. Slapping Kilburn on the back, his pleasant features reflected his relief.

"Thank the heavenly Virgin you're safe. I had lost sight of you."

" 'Twas easy enough to do, considering the battle allowed for very little thought." Kilburn smiled wryly, softening the grim austerity of a face alarmingly thin. "Lancaster, Hereford, and Clifford have fled, leaving Tutbury Castle to the king. 'Tis said that Roger d'Amory has been captured, but is so sorely wounded that he will not survive."

"Perhaps 'tis just as well, for there would be small chance of clemency at the hands of either Despenser." Arundel spat out the words, for one thing all the barons shared was disgusted rancor at the favorites' return to Edward's side.

"Come, James, rest for a while. I feel you bring us

news." Pembroke saw his hesitancy and assured him that his battle-stained state would offend neither barons nor chair. Kilburn unbuckled his sword gratefully, handing it to a retainer along with his cloak and helm. He ran a hand nervously through hair which clung damply to his head, falling in unruly strands over his forehead.

There was silence in the tent, as Kilburn closed his eyes for a few moments, trying to calm the wild clamoring of his blood. His entire life in the months since his child's death and Gillian's turning from him had become a nightmare. The endless hours in the saddle, riding through numbing cold, driving snow, and being buffeted by bone-chilling winds only intensified the soul-searing loneliness which tore at him when he was allowed a few hours of dry warmth and quiet shelter—that temporary, battle-free tranquillity which all save he sought so desperately. He tried constantly to find the reasons for their estrangement, sensing that the answer must be so obvious and simple that he was blind to it. He needed the assurance of Gillian's love as surely as he needed food to continue to exist. Only together were they complete—though parted by half the realm, the mystical bond between them kept them whole. But that too was severed, and as the months passed without a sign from Gillian, his soul had withered. Only once, while at Goodrich Castle that past December, he had thought he heard Gillian's voice calling him, but it was naught but the winter wind hurling itself wildly at the weathered stones of the old fortress. The unreasonable desire to be done with life continued to grow ever stronger within him.

"James." The voice was impatient, and a strong hand grasped his arm. "Is it known where Lancaster and the others have gone?" Arundel cut abruptly into Kilburn's thoughts, returning him to the urgent present. Though neither Pembroke nor Arundel remarked upon it, both had seen the expression of total hopelessness which suffused Kilburn's finely drawn features.

"Aye—I do. 'Tis believed they're heading for Ponte-fract. The king has ordered de Warenne and Kent to follow them." From his surcoat Kilburn drew out a rolled parchment with the royal seal affixed to it. "One of Edward's messengers found me as I was riding into camp. I leave for Carlisle immediately to join Sir Andrew Harclay in an effort to cut off Lancaster, should he try to escape north." He faltered for a moment. "The Scots have crossed the border again. In all the turmoil it has generally been forgotten that the truce between our realms ended at the start of the new year."

"Sweet Jesu, no. Have we not troubles enough?" Arundel protested, disturbed by the news. Kilburn shrugged, his face unreadable.

"After I have joined Lord Harclay and done what I need do, I will return to Glairn. With the Scots abroad once more I am needed in the north. My brother-in-law will travel a distance with me and then take his men to Kestwick." He grew cold at the thought of Glairn lying in the path of the invaders.

"So we can expect some of our other barons from the north to leave us as well," Pembroke said with resignation. They all knew it would be so. Kilburn was reluctant to speak of yet another matter even more grave.

"There's talk that Lancaster has been seeking an alliance with Robert Bruce, offering to join with him against the crown."

Pembroke nodded. He too had heard the rumors but could scarce believe them.

"If it be true, then Cousin Thomas is indeed a traitor and should be treated accordingly." Pembroke's voice was rough with indignation. "The man's a fool—he could have ruled Edward, had he had the wits for it."

Trumpets suddenly blared through the encampment and the three men exchanged glances.

" 'Tis probably John and young Kent calling their men to arms," Arundel remarked, rising with difficulty. He grimaced with pain and touched his left shoulder gingerly. "I fear that I was not spared—'tis naught but a bruise, but no less painful for not being serious."

"Come, Edmund, I'll see you to your tent and then prepare for my departure." Kilburn bade Pembroke farewell, clasping the older man's hand warmly before following Arundel into the raw, wet air of early March. They stood together for a few minutes before Edmund's pavilion, watching faceless knights, helms closed, shields held in readiness, stream past, followed by mounted men-at-arms bristling with pikes, spears, and battle-axes. The steadily falling rain seemed to have little effect on their mobility, for they rode out of the encampment at a goodly pace. John de Warenne, preceded by his standard bearer and herald, passed by without stopping, only taking time to morosely salute both men before disappearing into the mass of humanity moving northward toward Pontefract.

Drawing on his gauntlets, Kilburn said, "So must I too ride northward—pray God that all goes well." He pulled the hood of his cloak farther over his head, cursing the weather.

"James, swear to me that in the days ahead, you'll do naught to jeopardize your life in a foolhardy manner."

Kilburn looked at Arundel in amazement, for the worried urgency in his voice came as a shock. Had he been so transparent in his thoughts, he wondered.

Arundel's blue eyes glistened suddenly and he clasped Kilburn's shoulder, blurting out gruffly, "Know that your friends care what becomes of you, James. No problem was e'er so great as to be solved by a show of foolish reck-lessness nor the deliberate seeking of death." He could say no more and moved toward his tent. Kilburn stared after him, startled by his words.

"Edmund," he called out, and Arundel turned back for a moment. "I'll think on it. 'Tis all I can promise."

The narrow wooden bridge spanning the murmuring waters of the Ure slowly emerged out of the darkness as the first streaks of light began to appear in the cold eastern sky. James Kilburn, mounted and caparisoned for battle, kept a firm hand on the reins, for the black stallion was eager to escape his restraints.

"It appears your mount smells the coming battle, my lord."

The speaker, of middle age and with penetrating dark eyes, rode over to stand beside Kilburn, gripping the handhold of his shield tightly with a gauntleted hand. There was a calm assurance about him that belied the tension gradually spreading through the mounted men surrounding him.

"Aye, Lord Harclay, as do I!" Kilburn said gravely, his eyes sweeping the length of the bridge and the road beyond for any sign of movement.

" 'Twas a blessing that you chose to cross the river by the ford last night or you would have been struck down," Lord Harclay murmured softly.

Kilburn agreed, and following his own thoughts, said, "How I was able to avoid a confrontation with Lancaster and Hereford is a miracle, for I fear we would have been vastly outnumbered."

Lord Harclay laughed grimly. When his sentries had brought Glairn's herald in, so sure were they that he was from Lancaster they had almost slain the terrified man. Had he himself not recognized the red and gold banner of Glairn, there might yet have been a skirmish. Instead, with a sense of relief, Lord Harclay found his modest army swelled by Glairn's knights and men-at-arms.

"How have you positioned your men? Will you allow Lancaster to advance on the bridge?"

"When I reached Ripon and heard that the rebels were riding toward Boroughbridge, I realized that if I proceeded here with all haste, I could prepare a lovely welcome for those misbegotten traitors. If you will look to either side of the bridge—there, along the stone wall—my archers have orders to fire at any one who tries to cross. The rest of my men—and yours, my lord—are spread across the end of the bridge and on the north bank by the ford. Our enemy will have no easy task to find a crossing."

As the day slowly brightened, the small army became increasingly restless, knowing that with each minute, Lancaster, his loyal barons, and what was left of their army drew nearer. James had ridden north with no knowledge that Lancaster had left Pontefract for Dunstanburgh in Northumberland, or that he was traveling a lateral road with them toward Boroughbridge.

He stood in his stirrups to stretch his legs, and raised the visor of his helm. The fresh air felt good against his hot face. There seemed to be less bite in the slight breeze. Perhaps we'll have an early spring, he thought idly.

"Does anyone know how far distant they are?" Robert asked, dismounting. "I'm fair stiff from the saddle and this mindless inactivity."

" 'Twill be worth the wait, I'm sure," James replied to the younger man. "Sir Andrew is a capable man and well aware of what he does."

Both men looked up sharply as a warning arrow suddenly whistled through the air over their heads. Within minutes riders began to pour over the wooden bridge from the far shore, only to be greeted by an unexpected barrage of arrows. Horses plunged into the river in an attempt to ford it, and the air rang with the shouts of fighting men and screaming, excited animals. James, seeing the mounted attack on the ford, rode swiftly along the riverbank. Swinging his great sword to either side, he guided his horse through the melee, parrying attacks with raised shield. By the holy rood, he would take the day, he swore to himself. His blood sang a wild warrior's song in his ears, blotting out the noise of the battle. He felt his sword pierce flesh, slicing to the bone, pressing in deeply. Drawn out, it gleamed red in the sunlight. He gave no heed nor care to who had received his blade. A sudden blow to his back unhorsed him, but he swiftly regained his feet, angry at himself for not having seen the other rider advance on him. A whirring sound made him instinctively raise his shield and the mace bounced off its hard surface. Nay, he'd not allow such an attack to go unavenged. Growling deep within his throat, James turned and engaged a knight with Lancaster's badge on his surcoat. The mace again swung toward him and again he lifted his shield, meanwhile forcing the knight to defend himself against the ferocity of his attack. They were ankle deep in water, but neither noticed. He cast the shield aside, grasping the hilt of his sword with both hands. Screaming its song of death, the sword struck home. The mortally wounded knight fell heavily into the water, his blood a red eddy swiftly absorbed by the river's current. Kilburn swayed as he lifted his sword again, bringing it broadside against a helm. The sweat pouring down his face, he felt as if he were being stifled within a metal vise. With an impatient gesture, he pulled off his helm, throwing it heedlessly away. Bareheaded, the sun brightening his ruffled hair, he laughed wildly, seeing his gauntlets wet with blood.

Another knight bore down on him, lance lowered and aimed at his heart. Crouching low, he waited until the knight was almost upon him. Reaching up unexpectedly to grasp the shaft of the lance, he pulled the man from his mount. James realized dimly that he had lost his sword, but it did not matter, for its lethal music still echoed through him. His flesh ached suddenly to feel the coldness of metal burn through his own body. Naught mattered in that moment but death—his own death! "Slay me," James shouted, standing in the water, covered with the blood of the men he had slain, defying those about him. "Slay me now," he screamed, waiting for the sharp thrust of a lance or sword to deliver him into blessed oblivion as the battle surged about him. Down he went, a rough hand forcing his face into the water, a knee in the small of his back momentarily paralyzing him. He couldn't breathe . . . bright lights exploded in the blackness of his mind. He had asked for death, but not like this! His hand fumbled desperately for the dagger at his side. Finding it, he lashed out blindly at the weight pressing against him. He felt his dagger plunge into its target, meeting little resistance. The terrifying pressure eased and he found himself free to struggle to his feet. Water spilled from his nose and mouth as his vision cleared. James saw his unknown assailant stand before him, and he lunged at him without thought, his eyes blazing with green fire. Mindless with fury, his fingers found the man's throat . . . felt a snap . . .

"Jamie . . ." Hands were pulling at him. "Jamie . . . in all mercy, stop! You've broken the poor creature's neck twice over."

James lifted glazed eyes at Robert, who held his arms in a strong grip.

"Let go, Jamie," Robert ordered in a desperate voice, for the man in his grasp was like a wild beast, aware only of some inner force. James shook his head dazedly, Robert's voice penetrating his rage. Where in sweet heaven was he? His hands loosened their hold on the throat of an ordinary man-at-arms. Blood oozed through his leather hauberk from a dozen knife wounds, while terror-filled eyes stared sightlessly into his own.

"Robert . . ." The name was spoken hoarsely and James retched with sudden nausea. He crawled slowly up the muddy bank, seeing with surprise that the battle was over. What had come over him? Had he in truth broken the man's neck? He felt drained and dreadfully tired as he lay gasping on the ground, drenched and covered with mud.

"For a man who wanted to be slain—aye, even asked to be slain—you proved yourself a liar. God's blood, Jamie—what came over you? You were like a man possessed." Robert's dark blue eyes looked at Kilburn anxiously from a face robbed of its natural color. He helped the earl into a sitting position, noting that the labored breathing seemed to be easing.

James found that tears were streaming down his cheeks—tears which somehow alleviated the pain stored within himself for so long. Possessed? Aye, he probably had been possessed by the wish to die, to escape from life, but it was a desire contrary to his own nature. Asking for death, he had brought it to others and survived. Slowly he got to his feet and saw his blood-covered sword lying nearby.

Retrieving it, he said thickly, groping for the words, "Whatever possessed me these past months is gone, Robbie . . . 'tis a strange thing that in the midst of death, I found life." He smiled, and Robert saw the fine hazel eyes glow with an inner peace. With a lightening of spirit, he followed the earl to where Lord Harclay stood. The battle was over.

Hereford was dead, killed by a Welsh pikeman while leading an attack on the bridge by foot. Kilburn had looked down on the body, feeling a surge of pity for the hapless man who had wagered all and lost. What had it gained any of them?

Thomas of Lancaster, deserted by the survivors of his army, surrendered the following morning and was taken by Sir Andrew Harclay to York, along with several other lords, including a gravely wounded Lord Clifford.

While Robert, at Kilburn's insistence, rode north, he himself was to ride with all speed to Pontefract where the king and his assembled barons waited. The body of Hereford had yielded the damning proof of Lancaster's complicity in seeking an alliance with the Scots, and the earl of Glairn offered to deliver it safely into the hands of Edward, for such evidence could not be entrusted to a messenger.

The battle had been short but fierce, and James found that, harrowing though it had been, he could contemplate his experience calmly and dispassionately. What had happened at the ford had happened to a man beset by hopelessness and whose world had darkened all about him. How he had emerged from that frightening, lonely world, he did not truly know. Perhaps the very blood lust which possessed him with such ferocity had in some strange way purged his soul, bringing him back to the sanity of his known world. He could think of Gillian without flinching, loving her still, but without pain or bewilderment. Having faced his own demons, he could wait until she had faced hers.

Pontefract Castle stood massive and ominously silent in the gathering darkness. Pennants flying from the eight towers gave mute testimony of the peers assembled for Thomas of Lancaster's trial. Little movement could be discerned save for the guards patrolling the battlements and standing watch by the huge gate whose doors still stood wide. It seemed as if, with a sense of guilt, the castle were offering access to any who might request it. The invitation was a futile one, however, for the road leading through the town and climbing up toward St. Thomas's Hill was empty. It had not been so several hours earlier when the earl was brought out of the castle astride a small gray pony, his mien white and expressionless, the blue eyes turned inward. The crowd, gathering in ever growing numbers throughout the morning, had surged forward hurling mud and dung at him and cruelly reviling him until they were beaten back by the king's guards.

Sitting on the narrow bed in his pavilion, James Kilburn grew cold at the memory of Thomas Plantagenet, standing by the waiting block with the hooded headsman beside him, loudly beseeching God's mercy in heaven, for was he not forsaken on earth. The earl's trial had been swift, attended by the king, the elder Despenser, and the earls of Pembroke, Arundel, Surrey, Richmond, Atholl, and Angus. Even Edward's half-brother, young Edmund of Kent, had sat among Lancaster's judges. The letter found on Hereford's body was the final piece of incriminating evidence of treason against him—no baron could condone Lancaster's open invitation to Robert Bruce to enter England with his soldiers, nor the aid offered toward achieving a peace treaty which could only be construed as advantageous to the Scots.

The sentence of death was inevitable, and the earl of Lancaster, forced to face northward toward Scotland, had been beheaded before the jeering crowd. Feeling depressed and sickened by the spectacle, Kilburn rode slowly back to the large encampment surrounding the castle, declining invitations from both Pembroke and Arundel to join them in the Great Hall for the evening's repast. All these years Lancaster had been the stumbling block in Edward's reign, hated by barons who also bore no love for the king. And now he was dead. How the king must rejoice at the knowledge that no longer would he have to endure Cousin Thomas's studied insolence and open disobedience. James had no desire to sit among his fellow barons and gloat over the dead man's downfall. Once alone, he realized that to allow himself to sift through old memories and think on what would probably happen now that Thomas Plantagenet was dead held little interest. His mind shied away from the past and the future, taking refuge only in the present.

He was lightheaded with fatigue, causing Hal to inquire anxiously if he should call a physician to attend him. James smiled at his squire's concern, assuring him that all he needed was sleep. He had had little rest since leaving Boroughbridge, for Lancaster's trial had quickly followed his capture. After forcing down a few mouthfuls of soup, thick with gobbets of meat, carrots, turnips, and laced with beaten eggs, and a slice of bread spread generously with butter and honey, he stripped to a long chainse and stretched out gratefully on his bed. A servant brought him a cup of wine, but he waved it away, the weariness he had held back until now washing over him. Dimly he heard Hal move quietly about the large tent, seeing to his hauberk and long sword, and was already asleep when the candles were extinguished. The young squire left a small oil lamp burning near the entrance and moved a glowing brazier closer to his sleeping lord before slipping silently from the pavilion.

An urgent whispering drew Kilburn from deep sleep, and he fought against his waking consciousness.

"My lord Kilburn . . . my lord . . . please forgive me."

James opened his eyes and saw a pale face take shape beyond the brazier, eerily illuminated by its dim light. Though a hood was drawn over his head, the man's green eyes glittered in the brazier's glow.

"Emrys?" The earl's voice was filled with amazement. What did de Mortimer's harper want of him at this time of night in an encampment at Pontefract? How had he gotten past the guards?

"My lord, forgive this intrusion, but I could not do otherwise—the Arglwydd ordered that I tend his lady. She's near mad with fear and grief." The small Welshman was stumbling over his words in his anxiety to speak with Kilburn. James could scarce understand him, for he continuously lapsed into his own tongue.

"Slowly, Emrys . . . you mean Lady de Mortimer is with you?" James was perplexed. What could Joan de Mortimer want of him? "Why has she come in secret? Surely she could present herself without shame before us."

"Nay, my lord," Emrys wailed softly. " 'Tis not his lady wife I've brought . . . 'tis she who's been his all these years. Please, I beseech your patience in seeing her—she craves speech with you. There's no peace for her until you have listened to her. But if the Arglwydd knew she came to you, he would be furious." Emrys shivered at the truth of his words. De Mortimer would never forgive her interference, even though her thoughts were only for his safety.

Sweet Jesu, Kilburn swore silently to himself. De Mortimer's mistress! With an impatient gesture, he agreed and Emrys scuttled out, the lamp moving on its chain in the sudden draft. James rose stiffly and lit a candle. He did not relish meeting the unknown lady in darkness. He wondered how long he had slept, for nothing stirred outside. Shivering, he held his hands toward the brazier's warmth, idly noticing that its glow was still bright and hot. He stretched, longing to return to his bed. Looking curiously at the heavily cloaked figure Emrys ushered into the tent, he decided to make short shrift of his unwelcome visitors. The woman knelt before him, whispering her thanks in a voice oddly familiar to him.

"My lady, I can do naught for you unless I know what it is you want from me." James's voice was cold, cutting through the tearful murmuring. Intent upon offering her some coins before sending her away, he was unprepared for the sudden sight of Jehan's red hair and the feverish brightness of her slanted eyes peering at his from an ashen face as she pulled the cloak's hood back. He recoiled in stunned amazement and felt his heart lurch. Jehan de Maudley alive! And Roger's mysterious mistress he had hidden so well from all eyes. His mouth was dry, and for a moment he could not speak.

In the silence which grew between them, Jehan stared at Kilburn, surprised that the man standing before her had changed so little in the ten years since she had seen him. He had neither softened nor coarsened. The taut, lean look, the burning gaze, and austere mouth were the same. Her heart sank, remembering their last meeting. This man would not help her. She had been mad to even think of coming to him . . . and yet, he was the only one—there was no one else she could trust. Listening to him speak with Roger at the manor, she had sensed the honor and sincerity of his words, though he had made no attempt to mask his dislike of Roger.

Raising her eyes to his closed face, she said, "Lord Kilburn . . . I beseech your help—speak with the king on Roger's behalf. You have access to him."

"For what reason?" Kilburn had recovered quickly from the shock of seeing a woman seemingly returned from the grave. He bent down and lifted Jehan to her feet. "You need not kneel—here, sit down and tell me why you have come."

Sitting in the heavy camp chair, Jehan unfastened her cloak and looked down at the shabby wrinkled gown which she had worn since fleeing the manor hours before it was seized by the king's men. She had ridden over the countryside with Emrys ever since, searching for the earl of Glairn. And now that she had found him, she feared it would be a futile plea. For the first time, a sense of hopelessness rose within her.

" 'Tis Roger, my lord earl—the king has ordered his execution. Both he and his uncle are to be executed within the next few weeks." Tears began to stream down her face. "He was betrayed. The king wreaks vengeance upon him, for he has always detested Roger."

James nodded. "Aye, we all were stunned by the king's action—and ordering the de Mortimers' death caused many of the rebel barons to turn to Lancaster."

" 'Tis true Roger defied the king . . . and if there was to be punishment, so be it, but he surrendered willingly with the understanding that he would be granted amnesty. 'Tis unjust of the king to have condemned him to death." Jehan's voice broke, the thought of losing Roger forever too horrendous to contemplate. He was in the Tower, chained and helpless, each day moving closer to death. "I'm powerless to do aught for him—but he must not die! Please, my lord—he cannot die, he cannot!" Her hands reached out blindly, clutching James's sleeve. He loosened her fingers with barely concealed distaste.

"I really don't know what I can do, Lady de Maudley. I have no influence over the king—on the contrary. He holds little love for me. Have you thought to ask the queen?"

"Nay!" The word was spat out. "Isabella hates me." Jehan shuddered, hysteria creeping into her voice as the weeping increased. "I love him, my lord. My father has disowned me because of it. Since my husband was killed in Ireland, Roger has . . . has protected me. I've naught but him."

"What of his wife? Has she not tried to change Edward's mind?"

Jehan raised eyes glazed with tears to him. Her mouth twisted bitterly.

"Emrys told me that Lady de Mortimer petitioned the king as soon as she heard of her lord's fate. He refused to even accept the petition." She beat a fist on the arm of the chair. "But what do I care about Roger's wife! She at least has his children to comfort her. What have I, save my memories of him."

With a feeling of annoyance, James saw that Emrys had disappeared. Damnation—how was he to handle Jehan? His instincts told him to send her away. Yet he hesitated, for he knew she had done what her own passions had told her. The poor wanton bitch seemed to have a penchant for doomed lovers. Pressing a cup of wine into her hands, Kilburn urged her to drink it. He wondered when she had eaten last, taking note of how thirstily she drank. What could he do to help her? Perhaps Aymer de Valence could help. If he were to speak with Edward—convince him the de Mortimers' deaths were unnecessary now that Lancaster was dead and peace could be restored to the Marches. It was a possibility—remote, yet possible. Pembroke still had some influence over Edward, even though the Despensers held sway over him. Leaning toward Jehan's forlorn figure, he began to tell her of his plan.

" 'Tis all I ask, Lord Kilburn," Jehan whispered with gratitude. She gathered her cloak about her. "I'll trouble you no longer, my lord. I'll find Emrys and we'll be on our way."

"Nay, Lady de Maudley. Stay and rest. You didn't want attention brought upon you. 'Tis best then that I call him."

Throwing a cloak over his shoulders, James left the pavilion, relieved to escape Jehan's uncomfortable presence. The night air was cold and a slight wind was rising as he searched for the elusive Welshman without success. A sentry, warming himself beside a small fire, looked at the tall cloaked figure with curiosity, wondering what the earl was doing abroad at so late an hour. Emrys was nowhere to be found. Damn him, James thought irritably, angry at being played with by the likes of de Mortimer's harper.

Although he had been gone for just a short while, he

found Jehan asleep, lying on the bed he had himself occupied earlier. James looked down at the pale, exhausted face and shook his head. Best let her sleep, for Emrys would come for her soon enough. Drawing a coverlet over her, he threw several fur pelts on to the carpeted ground and lay down, wrapped in his cloak. The brazier by the bed shed warmth enough for both of them, and he felt himself slowly relax. As he drifted into sleep, he found himself smiling wryly at the ironic twists fate dealt his life. Jehan de Maudley—alive all these years. My poor Gillian, he thought drowsily. What fears you might have been spared, had you but known.

And Gillian followed him into his dream—the large eyes filled with love illuminating her beautiful, haunting face. So had she looked when he had first claimed her . . . she was in his arms and her soft mouth was opening beneath his. A burning ache rose in him as he felt her body against his own, soft, pliant, smelling of rose petals. He drew back, puzzled. Nay, something was wrong! He struggled to escape his dream. Jehan! He saw her bending over him, her unbound hair falling softly about him. Tears glistened on her cheeks as the sensual mouth found his, kissing him until she felt him respond. He felt her hands caress him and pulled away from her. The physical need for Gillian, which had come to him in his dream, ebbed in the waking presence of the woman who was so shamelessly offering herself to him. He found himself trembling.

"What are you trying to prove this time, my lady? How different I am from Roger? As you did when you shared the bed of Lord de Broze?" James felt a fool.

"How else can I repay you for your promise to save Roger's life! Nay, my lord," She held a finger to his lips, stilling his protest. "Even if the attempt fails, you will have tried. I'm grateful to you beyond words." The words were spoken softly, and she saw him hesitate. "My lord Kilburn, my body is all I have left to give. I'm yours to take."

Her tongue ran lightly over her lower lip, betraying her. She had watched him as he slept and knew she wanted him now as much as she had in Tynemouth when she had attempted to discover his vulnerability as a weapon for Arnaut de Broze and lost her head. It had naught to do with what she felt for Roger. Nay, after all those years, Lord Kilburn still fascinated her. James saw the truth of it in her eyes. Rising to his knees, he leaned over Jehan, gently smoothing the long strands of hair back from her face. He shook his head, the hazel eyes dark now with pity, the only tender emotion he would allow himself.

"Nay, Jehan, it can never be. There's too much that is impossible to forget." Her sensuality and the blatant sexuality of the body she had offered to him beckoned strongly, but a familiar coldness was settling in his soul. His voice was hard-edged and devoid of warmth. "As long as I live, I shall hate the memory of Arnaut de Broze with a consuming passion. I can never forgive him his perversions, his cruelty and, aye, I'll admit it freely—for being allowed to take Gillian's virginity from her. And he was your lover, Jehan, as Roger was your lover. Roger holds as little liking for me as I do for him, although for different reasons. I will not take you, Jehan. My hatreds are too strong within me against those to whom you've given yourself." He sighed, his voice softening. "I cannot take you, but be assured that it changes naught. I've given you my promise, and I will keep it. Now prepare yourself to leave. I have a feeling that Emrys is waiting for you."

Alone, Jehan rose slowly to her feet, aware of only one thing. He had rejected her again! And for what ridiculous high-minded reasons. As if her love for Roger had aught to do with it. Closing the buttons of her disheveled gown, she found herself flushing hotly. He had made her seem a lustful, shameless wanton. There was no passion in him—there never had been. And yet—her hands stopped braiding her hair as she remembered how his mouth had sought hers and the fiery pressure of his body hard against her own. He had been still snared in his dreams . . . and then he turned from her. Cold-blooded bastard! Roger would never believe that Kilburn had refused her. Oh sweet Jesù, why had Roger not listened. If only he had believed Pembroke sooner.

Roger! Jehan choked back a sob. He must not die . . . please, dear Lord in heaven, spare his life, she prayed, and pushed all thoughts of James Kilburn from her mind.

When the earl returned with Emrys, who had been

waiting quietly behind the pavilion, Jehan was sitting, pale but composed, in the large camp chair. James had told the harper of his promise to Jehan and there was little else to be said. Pressing a small bag of coins into Emrys's hand, he asked where they would go.

"I'll take my lady into Wales, my lord. She'll be safe with my people, and they'll tend her well until the Arglwydd returns." Emrys's green gaze rested on Kilburn's tense face. He was a good man who knew little peace. The Welshman felt regret that Lady Jehan had placed the burden of his master's fate upon his shoulders, but she had had little choice.

"Come, my lady, we must return to the horses before it becomes light and they are discovered." They had a long journey ahead of them before they would reach the mountain fastness of Wales. Powys ap Rhys and his wife, Lady Olwen, would welcome them, he was sure of it. A sudden thought struck him. The boy! He looked sharply at Jehan's unsuspecting face, and smiled to himself. Well, 'twas a risk that would have to be taken. The Arglwydd had entrusted Lady Jehan into his keeping and he would see her safe.

James watched them disappear into the mist that had risen, shrouding the earth as dawn began to push back the darkness of night. Roger de Mortimer and Jehan de Maudley. He laughed softly, for the combination seemed absurd. She was no match for the Marcher baron. It occurred to him that he had not asked her about the rumors of her death, but then, did the knowing of it really matter? Listening to the sounds of the awakening encampment, he decided that he would speak to Pembroke today . . . before they said their farewells. He would set out for Glairn as soon as possible, for there was no further need for him to stay at Pontefract. Perhaps Gillian would be waiting for him, he hoped wistfully, remembering his dream. She had seemed so near! He smiled, giving himself up to thoughts of Gillian. All that remained of Jehan was a faint, lingering scent of rose petals.

Chapter 12

1323
Tower of London

The narrow walkway connecting the central keep to the building which housed the royal apartments was short, scarce fifty steps, but long enough to allow Gillian to breathe in the crisp, cold air which was so sadly lacking in the cramped confines of the queen's apartments. Leaning against the crenellated walls, Gillian looked up at the sky, noticing with pleasure how one by one the stars were beginning to shimmer in the deepening darkness. Idly running a finger over the rough surface of the stone, she thought of all that had happened since the uprising ended at Boroughbridge.

The mounting fear which Geoffrey's words had instilled in her remained with her all through the long, anxious weeks of fighting. Each day had come heartbreaking reports of yet more dead and captured. To most of the people at court it mattered little whether they were royalist or rebel, for so snarled were family ties that loyalties meant naught. So many lives had been forfeited . . . Hereford and d'Amory killed in battle, Clifford and Mowbray hanged in York while Lord Badlesmere was executed in Canterbury—and then the final shock of Lancaster's beheading! When the earl of Pembroke returned to York from Pontefract, she forced herself to go to him, seeking news of her lord. At times she had been convinced of his death, for so distant had they grown, she could no longer feel his presence. Her overwhelming joy was unfeigned when Pembroke told her that Jamie was safe and had returned north. She sent a letter to him, and his only reply had been a terse note sent through Geoffrey. Yet, it was enough to awaken memories of him so sharp and real that she ached with her yearning. Slowly and painfully she began to come to life. Emotions which had lain dormant stirred within her, filling the cold emptiness of her soul.

Retracing her steps, Gillian looked uneasily toward the unlit entrance to the keep, finding the brooding darkness sinister. The Tower at best was seldom cheerful, but at least it offered safety. She had often wondered whose advice Edward had taken when, flushed with success, he had ordered that a campaign be mounted against Scotland. Gillian still trembled at the thought of Robert Bruce, with James Douglas as his able lieutenant, withdrawing his men from their paralyzing invasion of the northwest counties and driving the king's forces from his own scorched and war-stricken land. Edward, fleeing south, had brought the Scots in full pursuit deep into Yorkshire once more. Panic-stricken, the court joined other folk clogging the roads leading to the safety of the counties far removed from the turmoil. Arriving at Windsor, she received word that Glairn's household as well as Robert's family were at Hurley. With Isabella's permission, given only on her oath to return in three days' time, she had ridden the short distance to the d'Umfraville manor.

Gillian sighed, and drew her cloak more closely about her, for the late winter air carried with it the river's damp. Windsor had depressed her, as she knew it would, and it had given her pleasure to once more have her children about her, banishing the ghost of that other child which would always haunt her stays in that huge, unhappy castle.

Her sister-in-law had regaled her with long tales of the terrible weeks during the summer when the Scots had swarmed over the border, bringing terror and destruction. Never had they so feared for their lives, Elizabeth confessed in a voice tight with emotion as she relived the days and nights of suspenseful waiting.

"The tocsins rang without stopping and no holding

was spared. We never knew where they would strike next. Neither Robert nor your lord took part in the king's campaign—the peril was too great for us. They dared not leave." Elizabeth leaned toward Gillian, her face pale and shadowed. " 'Twas then that Robert decided to send us south. James wanted the children to go to a manor he has just been awarded in Suffolk, but finally agreed to allow them to join us here. With winter approaching, the raiding will begin to lessen and then we can return home and hope that somehow peace will be achieved before all is lost. 'Tis hard to believe that Northumberland is like a great deserted battlefield unless you've seen it for yourself."

"And Jamie?" Gillian hesitated. "How does he fare?"

"Oh sister, how can you ask!" Elizabeth exclaimed. "He seems well enough and makes a pretense of being content, but he never smiles and keeps to himself too much. Robert says that he speaks to no one of that which seems to lie heaviest upon him, but he no longer despairs of life. Still, my dear, I believe that he needs you above all else to make him truly whole."

"Not yet—I have no right to go to him," Gillian had whispered, tears streaming down her cheeks. Unwilling to say more, she turned away, but Elizabeth did not press her. She found little sleep at Hurley, for her mind was filled with memories of Jamie. Sweet Jesu—how she wished she could explain all that was in her heart to him . . . perhaps it was not too late! If only he would listen to her. Lying alone in the bed which had been their battlefield that rage-filled night five years before, she recalled the words they had flung at each other while every fiber of her body remembered the shameless ecstasy which had brought Maddie into their lives and ended with her death.

Returning to court, Gillian was restless and homesick, finding her duties an intrusion to her private thoughts. Her love for Jamie glowed ever brighter, and what she believed had been destroyed by her guilt-ridden grief still lived. Each day Jamie's image grew stronger and clearer until she felt a mere stretching out of her hands would bring him to her.

Summoning up her courage, she had gone to Isabella, requesting to be released from her duties. The queen, gazing in her self-absorbed misery at the young woman whose eyes pleaded for her understanding, had begged her to remain until the household was settled in the Tower. 'Twas all she could afford till spring, she confessed with surprising candor, but Gillian had caught a glitter in the cold blue eyes which belied her words.

"*Chère* Gillian—you're all I have left of my early days—only with you can I speak of when I was still a maid but already a queen. Please, 'twould but be for just a few more weeks. Perhaps the king will be kind and order the countess of Pembroke to attend me in your place." And Gillian agreed.

She shivered suddenly as the wind shifted without warning and knifed sharply through her, bringing her mind back to the present. Startled, she saw that she had been standing on the walkway longer than she had realized. The sky was completely dark, and torches flared brightly on either side of the arched entryway. A sentry brought word to her that the queen wished her presence.

"My lady . . ." The voice was low, with a musical timbre which jolted her memory unpleasantly. "Good evening to you—'tis a rare event to see anyone else in this godforsaken place."

A quiet laugh drifted toward her, and in the flickering light of the torch she made out the figure of a man sharing the walkway with her, a guard beside him. Where had he come from? A political prisoner surely, Gillian thought, peering at him curiously, for his speech was that of the high-born. Dimly she could see that he was tall and that his bearing was proud. He was shackled—a sudden movement brought the discordant sound of chains. It was getting colder, and the stranger's next words were lost in the rising wind. The sentry called again, so urgently this time that she stiffened in annoyance. Damn the queen, Gillian thought irritably, and without replying to the shadowy figure, hurried past him into the shelter of the keep.

"Was it cold on the battlement this evening?"

The words were spoken casually as Isabella sat frowning in apparent concentration at Gillian's black knight. She had not uttered a sound nor made a move for quite some time, and Gillian was surprised at her sudden question.

"Aye, Your Grace—the wind is from the river. But there's a beautiful clear sky. 'Tis always pleasant to take some air. Perhaps it could be arranged for you—'twould help you sleep."

"Oh, but I would surely catch a chill!" The queen laughed and pushed the chessboard away. "Nay, I'd best remain within these gloomy walls until my garden blooms again." She bit into a sugar plum with relish.

They sat by the small hearth, away from two others of Isabella's ladies who sat whispering and giggling together near the doorway. Peter de Gilles, still the queen's page, perched in the tiny crevice by a window barely larger than a slit, idly fingering a dulcimer. Lowering her voice, Gillian told Isabella about her strange encounter on the battlement. The queen began to smile, and her eyes sparkled.

"You wonder at his identity, my lady? How naive you are—you dream too much of your lord and pay scant heed to what happens all about you. 'Tis obvious that you spoke with the baron of Wigmore—he's here in the Tower."

Gillian stared at her in dismay. Of course he had sounded familiar to her. How could she have forgotten that Roger de Mortimer was a prisoner here? While they were lodged in the royal palace, the keep had seemed another world. Her eyes narrowed thoughtfully as Isabella chattered on with increasing animation—although she had not seen him, she knew that he had been imprisoned with his uncle since last year. 'Twas said that the old man was quite weak and ill from being kept in confinement, but now and again restrictions were eased and the younger man was permitted a few minutes of exercise twice a week. There were times he was also brought down to one of the larger chambers for questioning by the constable or the king's justices."

"But I thought he'd been sentenced to death!" Gillian whispered, uncertain as to what she should think.

"They both were. Then for some reason my royal

husband changed his mind and ordered that they be imprisoned for life."

Gillian shuddered at the image of Roger confined in chains to a cell for his untold span of years. Nay, 'twas not his destiny, of that she was sure, and the queen seemed to be of similar mind, judging from her expression. Though Isabella claimed no knowledge of Roger, Gillian did not believe her. There was something working in her cold, clever mind, but whatever it was, she had no intention of sharing it with even her most trusted companion.

The suspicions which were aroused in Gillian allowed her little sleep that night. She was grateful that her position permitted her the luxury of privacy in even a chamber barely larger than a closet. She could lie on her narrow bed alone with her thoughts, without having to listen to the idle chatter of the queen's other ladies.

Isabella—she was to be pitied actually, for since Lancaster's death she had been made to feel the full brunt of her enemies' ascendancy to power. Her court had been trimmed to the barest number of ladies, courtiers, and retainers tending her needs. The Despensers, with obviously malicious pleasure and a smug display of their control over the royal treasury, had proclaimed the necessity of reducing the queen's alleged extravagances and finally shorn her of all the loyal folk who had come with her from France. Even her old nurse, Claude, who had been with Isabella since she was a tiny maid, was sent from court, aflood with tears while her mistress watched her departure in icy misery. The remaining household, all English, were hard put to suffer Isabella's petulant complaints and fits of ill temper, which Gillian knew to be but shields to hide her wounded pride.

While the members of her court were dismayed at once more occupying the dank, moldering chambers of the royal palace, Isabella had seemed oblivious to the outrageously deplorable conditions until Edward came to visit her briefly before returning north. He had been truly shocked to find his youngest daughter asleep in her cradle sheltered beneath an old tapestry stretched over her to protect her from the rain which found its way through the leaking roof. The king, in a rare display of royal rage, had dismissed the constable, John de Crombwelle, in total disgrace. It was only when a new constable was appointed and ordered to begin immediate repairs that the queen began to complain of the impossibility of living in the royal palace. The constable, fearful of both Edward's wrath and Isabella's temper, suggested that her household be transferred to the old royal apartments in the White Tower.

Gillian sat up in bed, her eyes widening in growing understanding as she recalled Isabella's extravagantly reluctant acceptance. Finally settled, she expressed her delight in the apartments once occupied by her husband's grandfather, although they were only slightly better than those she had left. Why had no one realized the duplicity of her actions? But then, Gillian too had given no thought to it herself, even though she had never conquered her distrust of the queen. Isabella was interested in Roger de Mortimer! But to what purpose? In the spring the court would move to Eltham, and Roger, left behind in the Tower, could be of no use to her. It was never easy to fathom the queen's thoughts, and Gillian could find no ready answers to the questions she asked herself. It seemed to her that she lay for hours in the shrouded darkness of her curtained bed before falling into an uneasy sleep. She awoke a few hours later with a sense of foreboding that somehow fate had begun to weave a new pattern into the tapestry of their lives.

"Why does the queen refuse to see me?"

Roger de Mortimer's voice shook with anger. Twice before he had asked for an interview with the queen and been refused. It had come as a surprise that without any warning he had been brought into the small council chamber, accompanied by two guards. Instead of the queen, however, he was unexpectedly faced with the countess of Glairn. Besides being acutely aware of his shamefully disheveled and shabby appearance, Roger's dark eyes flashed with the angry resentment which consumed him each time a movement brought attention to his manacled state.

Seated in a high-backed chair with Peter in attendance, Gillian felt an uncomfortable warmth steal through her under Roger's angry scrutiny. He had stared at her in astonishment before greeting her with mocking courtesy. Gillian, almost fearing to meet his gaze, had been filled with rancor at Isabella's refusal to meet with him. Claiming that it would show disloyalty to the king, the queen ordered her trusted friend to discover why the imprisoned baron of Wigmore demanded an audience, despite Gillian's suggestion that she have her chamberlain deal with him. Isabella had grown suddenly furtive and refused to listen.

"What is it you wish of the queen?" Gillian tried to keep her voice calm in an atmosphere charged with Roger's vital personality. He laughed shortly.

"What I wish of her?" His skin, stretched tightly over a face grown alarmingly thin, was the color of parchment. He held out wrists rubbed raw from their shackles. "My appearance should be proof enough. 'Tis not for myself alone that I ask, but for my uncle, who has neither youth nor a strong body. Our imprisonment is political, not criminal, yet we've been subjected to the most abominable treatment imaginable."

Leaning toward her in his urgency, he was pulled back roughly by his guards. Taking a deep breath, he struggled to control the rage which their touch had unleashed. He had lost none of his untamed wildness in the long months of his imprisonment—rather it was intensified by the gaunt pallor of his features.

"Our cell is so damp in winter, the walls run with water which gathers on the floor in pools. Even after the stones dry, the straw remains unchanged, reeking and crawling from the vermin which breed in its filth. In the summer's heat there's scarce air to breathe. My uncle will die if he remains as he is. Though the words choke me, I am forced to petition the queen to intercede with the king for clemency on our behalf."

Gillian shielded her eyes from his blazing anger. He was indeed in a dire state and obviously concerned for his uncle. Though she held no liking for him, and shrank from his nearness, her heart was touched. His plight was obvious, and she could not help but feel that it was largely caused by Edward's spite. Motioning him to a chair near her, she ordered some food and wine be brought him, despite the guards' protests. She chose to ignore their existence. After all, was she not on the queen's errand.

"My lord de Mortimer . . . I give you my promise that I will tell the queen all that you have laid before me. 'Tis all I can do, for I myself have no power to alter the conditions of your confinement."

Sitting silent and still, Gillian watched Roger wolf down the cold meat pie which was set before him. She felt faint at the thought of the year he had already spent in the Tower and the untold number of years still ahead of him. She closed her eyes, thanking the Virgin that there was but a short time left before she could be gone from this accursed place.

Roger drained his cup, looking at Gillian over its rim. By the rood, she was still a beautiful woman, but her face reflected a haunting sadness he did not remember. He felt his blood stir within him. It had been too long since he had had, or even seen, a woman. Damnation, she would drive him mad. The black demon eyes swept over Gillian boldly, seeming to strip her bare of the soft velvet robe whose simple lines did little to conceal the warm, rich curves of her body.

As a servant refilled his cup, Roger said baldly, " 'Tis a wonder to me that James allows you so far from his bed. Or have you found better sport?"

"You go too far, my lord! I've given you no cause to speak to me in so crude a fashion," Gillian retorted hotly, her face crimson. "If you crave the truth, 'tis the death of our youngest child which brought about our separation." Hurt and shamed by his words, she told him what she had not told anyone before. " 'Tis my own guilt which drove me away from him."

Roger was silent as she flung her pain at him.

"Gillian . . . I didn't know. When I saw James last year, there was no mention of your child's death nor your estrangement." Nay, he thought, only the hatred which lies between us.

"Why should he have said aught to you of it. What are you to him, Lord de Mortimer, save a baron who cares

337

for naught but his own destiny and uses his friends in its pursuit."

"My destiny seems to end here," Roger said ruefully, his tone softening. "I apologize for my words. As you can see, my world is lately confined to four walls. I forget that others suffer misfortunes as well."

Looking down at her hands, Gillian found them clenched tightly together. Sweet Jesu, why had she told him? Her mind searched for some way to turn his attention from herself.

"I saw your eldest sons at Windsor. They are being held in custody together. They seemed quite well and not too discontented." At least she could tell him that much. Though handsomely dark in the manner of his father, at seventeen, the elder son had an intelligent sensitivity lacking in Roger. She had liked Edmund de Mortimer very much.

"Though I can imagine Edmund not minding his confinement too greatly, Roger is very like me and must chafe at being held hostage—for that is what they are, no matter what it is called." While he was eager for news, his voice was bitter. God help them! Even should they be released, there was naught left for them to return to.

"They share a household with Hereford's two sons, and all are under the care of Henry de London. I saw them but briefly."

Gillian dared not tell him of Edmund's frustrated anger at the Despensers for seizing the choicest holdings of his father's confiscated properties.

The next time that Roger was brought into the council chamber, the queen was waiting for him with Gillian beside her. Seeing her stand regal and coldly distant, wary of his presence, he fell heavily to one knee and bowed his head. He dared not look at her—not yet.

"My lord de Mortimer, 'tis not necessary." Isabella's clear voice filled the small chamber. "The countess of Glairn told me of your conversation with her. I was deeply shocked and saddened to hear of your dire straits."

"Your Grace, I can only assume that it was through your kind intervention that we have been moved into a less abysmal cell. And as for the removal of our shackles . . . my uncle and I thank you most humbly."

All his words were respectfully correct; yet Gillian thought she detected the slightest hint of self-satisfaction in the low-pitched voice. Looking at Isabella, she saw a smile illuminate her lovely face. Her hand hovered caressingly for a moment over the tangled dark hair of the man kneeling before her until she remembered that she was not alone. Gillian knew how vehemently the queen had fought with the constable to improve the conditions of both the de Mortimers' imprisonment. Where could they possibly go, Isabella had asked Stephen de Seagrave, stilling his protests. Within a keep as strongly fortified as the Tower, there was no possible chance of escape. She could see no purpose in so mean a treatment toward prisoners kept in the Tower because they had been betrayed by their trust in the king's word. He had agreed, for there were many men who believed the king had acted unfairly in the de Mortimers' capture. Wisely, de Seagrave was determined to keep his actions secret from the king's justices.

Roger rose to his feet and gazed fully at the queen in so intense a fashion that she was the first to lower her eyes. In sudden confusion, she turned to Gillian, chiding her for not offering Lord de Mortimer wine and the sugared fruit and sweetmeats she had ordered brought for him. Despite Gillian's guarded warning, Isabella dismissed de Mortimer's guards from her presence, instinctively knowing she had naught to fear from Roger so long as Gillian and her page remained with her. Peter's young face was a study of outraged disbelief as Isabella continued to treat Lord de Mortimer more as an honored guest than the prisoner he was. Throughout their interview, no further mention was made of the ailing baron of Chirk and it might have been as though neither Gillian nor Peter existed. When at last Roger was turned over to his guards and the queen retired to her apartments, smiling and chattering gaily with Alisa de Peverell, who waited for her in the bedchamber, Gillian cautioned the boy not to speak too freely of what he had witnessed. Hearing apprehension sharpen Lady Kilburn's gentle voice, the young page paled at the image she painted of Isabella's angry vengeance over betraying a trust.

It was but the first of three such meetings, and Gillian observed the queen and Roger with growing resentment at the deceit they were visiting upon her, each using her to reach the other. In Roger's presence, Isabella glowed, the porcelain skin taking on a rosy tinge. Her almond-shaped eyes glittered feverishly as she contemplated the visage of the man she had not forgotten since their last meeting at Nottingham Castle. She was awakening, and Gillian saw the other Isabella slowly emerge—the hidden Isabella she had only caught glimpses of through the years and who had frightened her.

Winter gave way at last to spring, and though Edward and his army remained in the north, England was heartened by the news that the earl of Pembroke had concluded a temporary truce with Robert Bruce. Hopes rode high that the peace which settled over the northern counties would be a lasting one.

Gillian found herself caught up in the excitement of preparations for her return to Glairn and kept Agnes Jardine busy airing out forgotten pieces of clothing, wrinkled and smelling of mildew from lying in the closed coffers for months on end. Shoes, girdles, chains, scarves, and all the countless items lent out to the ladies of Isabella's court were reclaimed and packed into the large iron-bound boxes standing outside Gillian's small chamber. Agnes herself was ablaze with joy, for soon she, too, would be reunited with a husband she had not seen since leaving Glairn.

In the midst of her activities, Gillian was disturbed by news of a secret meeting Isabella had had late one night with Roger de Mortimer. Peter de Gilles had observed the prisoner, accompanied by a young officer of the Tower, slip quietly into the queen's private chambers, but told no one save the countess. In spite of her mounting uneasiness, Gillian was relieved that she had not been drawn into joining Isabella's willful scheming. Whatever it was that the queen seemed to be plotting with an increasingly confident Roger, she feared it boded ill for them all. Trembling at the possibility that Roger had indeed divined the true facets of Isabella's character, Gillian prayed that it was just one more of her fancies which had no substance.

At last Gillian's coffers and trunks stood ready. A messenger was already en route to Glairn bearing news of her coming, and all that remained of her time at court were the few hours until dawn.

She spent most of her last evening playing chess with Isabella. The queen dreaded her departure, although she had said little to dissuade her from leaving. Thinking herself no longer a part of the royal court, Gillian retired early, only to be awakened from her slumber in order to keep the restless, sleepless queen company. Clad in a loose robe with flowing sleeves and her hair falling in two thick plaits over her shoulders, Isabella looked pale, drawn, and absurdly immature. Though the faithful Alisa and another lady were on duty to tend to her needs, the young woman preferred the serene company of the friend she was losing once more.

"*Chère* Gillian, can you not change your mind and remain with me? We may journey to Newcastle later in the spring, and 'tis but a short distance to Glairn. Surely your lord can wait that long for you."

"Nay, Your Grace, you know that I must go. 'Tis been far too long a time that I've been separated from my children, and I hold you to your promise to release me." Gillian smiled in understanding at Isabella's sad face. "Besides, Mary de Valence will be joining you at Eltham; and you can share with her your memories of France and the court. She knows your brother. You'll forget me and 'tis better so. You know quite well that your sovereign lord holds little liking for any Kilburn."

But Isabella assured her morosely that it would not be the same. She looked at Gillian across the exquisitely carved ivory and ebony chess set which her father-in-law had brought from the Holy Land and wondered when they would meet again. They both paid little attention to the game, Gillian longing only to return to her waiting bed and fearing to probe too deeply into Isabella's thoughts. She was always to remember Isabella's quiet words, spoken to her in sudden trust, knowing that they would never be repeated.

"My good and gentle Mortimer will someday be gone from this accursed place and I will join him, for we are meant to be together. All these years have I waited for him and soon my waiting will be at an end."

Appalled by her confidence, Gillian could not reply, nor did the queen expect an answer. The words still echoed in her mind when she returned to her chamber, causing her to stand by the hearth staring sightlessly into its glowing heart. In spite of her careful warnings to beware of Roger, Isabella had refused to listen and was obviously determined to follow her own counsel. Forget the queen, she told herself—you're going home. The long, frozen months of her self-imposed exile had come to an end and while there was still Jamie to face, she prayed he would welcome her return. Slipping the small buttons of her robe from their velvet loops, she smiled, already imagining Jamie's arms holding her close. And yet . . . her large blue eyes darkened as the nagging, doubting fear returned to overshadow her happiness. There had been no answer to her last letter and Jamie's silence mocked her. Perhaps he had not forgiven her for turning from him. He would not listen to her—she well knew how implacable his will could be. With trembling fingers, Gillian brushed errant strands of hair from her forehead and felt her skin grow cold with mounting dread. It was a risk she had to face—even if she discovered that Jamie no longer wanted her. Oh sweet Jesù—nay! And her fears began to tear at her again, the persistent doubts eroding her reason.

Had it not been for a slight movement behind her, she might have given way to her emotions. As it was, she stiffened with alarm as Roger de Mortimer's low voice spoke from the darkness of the partially curtained bed. She would never know how he had managed to evade his jailers, for he refused to tell her, saying only, " 'Tis your last night at court, my lady. What would you think of me, had I not come to say farewell." His voice was silken smooth, and Gillian's blood froze.

Turning to face him, she prayed that her voice would

not betray her, saying coldly, "Why should it matter to you what I think, my lord?"

Roger rose from the bed with pantherlike grace. The shadowed hollows beneath his cheekbones gave his face an eerie, ghostly look. Despite her aversion to him, Gillian was not immune to his considerable magnetism, and she found herself unable to move as he walked toward her. He reached out a hand and slowly tilted her head toward him.

"When last we said farewell, we were most rudely interrupted and I never had a chance to properly thank you for caring for me so tenderly." He smiled—a terrible, frightening smile. His hand slid to her throat where a pulse beat wildly, and moved down . . . by the Virgin, her skin was like velvet! His fingers lingered caressingly on the gentle slope of her breast.

"My lord . . . Roger—'tis madness to have come here," Gillian whispered, her gaze locked to his. She was turned to stone, unable to move away from him. He nodded and the smile faded, replaced by a burning hunger which heightened her fear.

"I made myself a promise that night at Glairn . . ." It was as if he spoke to himself. Painfully aware of his hands, every instinct screamed to her to try to escape him, but Gillian made no attempt to resist him. She felt his lips brush against her cheek and kiss the corner of her mouth. Turning her face away, she tried to plead with him, her voice barely recognizable. As he drew her closer, the heat of his body reached out, and at last, panic freed her from her paralysis.

"Nay . . . please, Roger—I beg of you . . . for sweet mercy's sake, let me go . . . don't—please don't!"

But he only laughed at her futile struggles, holding her fast. Before he stifled her cries with his mouth, Gillian saw his face, wild, blinded with desire, with all reason fled, and she knew that there was no escape from him.

The King's road lay open to his view, running straight and clear past tilled fields and meadows. Early morning mist rose steaming from the damp earth and somewhere in the distance, Kilburn heard bells singing sweetly. He

343

could not discern whether the sound came from a village church or small, hidden monastery, but it somehow heightened the urgency within him. His herald rode ahead, the earl's banner with its gold hawk flaring in the freshening breeze, eyes alert for any movement on the road before him. His men were uneasy, wary of the brooding, forbidding expression on their lord's grim face.

Kilburn was worried. Ever since Gillian's voice had roused him from sleep two nights earlier, he had known that something was terribly wrong. She needed him . . . he was sure of it, for her cry had been one of deep anguish. With his men, he had left Nottingham Castle in the morning and ridden south, traveling as quickly as he could toward London, for the queen was there. No one had asked the reason for his haste, nor had he offered any explanations.

With each league bringing them closer to London, Kilburn was beset with ever-mounting dread. Why had Gillian called out to him? He could still feel the fear which had knifed through him at the sound of her voice.

Lovedy, I'm coming to you, he whispered, putting anxious spur to his horse.

Two hours of unrelenting, forced riding brought them in sight of the hospice of Haverbury Abbey, and he had almost decided to call a short halt when Hal said, "My lord, the small group of travelers coming toward us . . . 'tis the Glairn banner!"

Gillian? Aye, there she was, astride the small gray mare he had given her when she left Glairn. His heart leaped at the sight of the familiar figure sitting so straight and slim, her hooded cloak falling back to reveal a tunic of dark green wool. Gillian! He cursed himself for a fool that he had allowed so long a separation between them. The breach could have been healed earlier were they not so stiff-necked with pride.

As they drew closer, Hal called out excitedly as he caught sight of his wife riding a brown jennet. Servants, maids, and baggage men brought up the rear, and Kilburn noticed with a start that Isabella had sent along four of her personal guards. Their blue surcoats bearing the golden fleur-lis of France made a bright splash of color against a countryside just awakening to spring.

God's blood, what had happened to her! Kilburn was stunned at the change in Gillian. The chalk-white face framed by the hood of the traveling cloak sprang out at him, amazement its only expression. She looked ill, her eyes enormous and glittering with unshed tears. She halted, waiting for him to approach, silent and watchful. Kilburn felt suddenly cold with a nameless fear, and his joy at their reunion died within him. They faced each other for the first time in nearly two years and could find no words. Impulsively he reached over to grasp her gauntleted hand and it lay lifeless within his.

"Gillian . . ." His voice sounded strange to him, stiff and cold.

"My lord," Gillian said in a low voice, never taking her eyes from his face. Seeing the familiar beloved features again, the knot of pain within her tightened.

"I see the messenger found you."

Kilburn looked puzzled. "Nay, I know of no messenger! 'Tis not why I came . . ." He said no more, for it was not necessary. She realized that he had heard her cry out for him, that he had come to find her, but she prayed he would not sense all else which had befallen her. Gillian watched him dismount, drinking in the sight of his beloved face, the spare litheness of his movements and the familiar red and gold surcoat which flashed out from beneath his gray woolen mantle. Then his hands circled her waist, lifting her down. For a moment she leaned against him, feeling the known, hard length of his body next to her own, and she yearned to touch him. She turned away toward a greening bank beside a flowering hedge.

"I've been to Nottingham." Kilburn walked beside her, trying to find something to say to her. Her large eyes contemplated him, pain clouding her gaze. How could she have turned her back on his grief, she wondered, truly understanding for the first time what she had done to him. Jamie, her heart cried mutely, how I love you! And the silence lengthened between them.

Wordlessly he helped her to mount once more and they began their journey northward. It was a nightmare.

Kilburn could not decide which was worse, the bright sunlit hours of day as they rode silently side by side along the same road they had ridden over years earlier, the young maid in love with the romantic, distant earl who refused to return her feelings and was finally forbidden her, or the nights when Gillian lay frozen and unmoving beside him while he stifled an overwhelming desire to draw her into his arms and with his love try to ease her pain.

She was a stranger, even to herself, suffering Agnes to help her dress in the mornings in the cramped confines of the small tent and draw her travel-stained outer clothing from her aching body at night, while she waited with a rapidly beating heart for Jamie to come to her. She fought his nearness, hoping desperately that he would make one tender gesture toward her and wishing that she could find the words to tell him. Her panic mounted as the walls of York became visible in the verdant dusk of a mild spring evening. Riding through the open gates of the Micklebar, the party wended its way through the narrow streets. They crossed the white stone bridge over the Ouse and rode past timbered houses crowded close together, the small streets emptying themselves of the townfolk as the bells began to toll the closing of the gates. The massive shape of the Minster was outlined against the yellow-white evening sky as they skirted the square, entering the wool merchant's familiar street.

Gillian swayed in the saddle as everything swam hazily before her eyes. She was cold with a fear she could no longer battle against. Jesù, sweet heavenly babe, she prayed, please help me! What am I to do? I can't tell him. She looked at his stern face, the long hazel eyes thoughtful and serious, the austere mouth unsmiling . . . why had she not noticed the slight silvering of the chestnut hair which lay softly curling behind his ears. I'll lose him, she thought. And if I lose him, I don't want to live. In that moment, her children did not matter to her, her home, Robert, Elizabeth, Geoffrey—naught mattered to her save Jamie. She had been such a fool.

Gillian made a mewling sound, unable to control herself any longer as the pain washed over her in endless waves. She never felt Kilburn's hands lift her down and carry her through Lionel Porcher's gate, past the wool sheds into the large house. Uncle Lionel's welcoming smile turned to concern as he watched his nephew carry Gillian up the stairs to the chamber which always stood in readiness for them. His heart stopped for a moment as he caught a glimpse of her white, sick face. As Agnes made to follow him, the earl turned, saying curtly, "Nay, Mistress, I'll tend to my lady myself."

The merchant took her arm, gently leading her to his his study.

"Come, Mistress Jardine, let's wait here for your husband."

And listened quietly as Agnes told him the little she knew of Gillian's terrified flight from the Tower.

A fire crackled in the hearth, warming the chill air, and tendrils of steam rose from the metal ewer placed on the hearthstones. An oil lamp suspended from the black-raftered ceiling cast wavering shadows against the white-washed walls as Kilburn moved quietly about the chamber. Gillian lay unmoving on the velvet-curtained bed where he had placed her. Bending over, he saw her eyes open slowly and a look of pure, naked joy spread over the white face as she recognized him.

"Jamie . . ." His name was whispered softly, liquid with love. "I was so wrong! I didn't know."

"Nay, my love . . . say no more. Everything will be all right."

Gillian blindly stretched out a hand to him and he caught it in his, pressing his lips against the blue-veined wrist where a pulse beat wildly at his touch. She pulled away, the dark blue eyes reflecting her awareness of the shameful knowledge which still possessed her.

"Jamie . . . you can't love me, you can't . . ."

She fought him weakly as he undid the fastenings of her tunic and removed her outer garments, but when she felt his fingers at the ties of her shift, she struggled to escape him, trying vainly to prevent him from revealing her nakedness. As he drew the shift from her, she whimpered and covered her face with her hands, afraid to look at him.

347

"Please don't. You must not see! Oh, God, please . . . I can't tell anyone. 'Twas wrong . . . wrong!" Her voice fell to a murmur in the face of his silence.

Kilburn was appalled and cold with shock. The tender white body was covered with bruises which were already beginning to fade. He needed no words of explanation to know what had happened, but he wondered at the pain she had endured on their journey northward. Rage rose within him, rage at his own blindness to the depths of her agony and rage against the filthy whoreson who had done this to her.

An image flashed through his mind, of bold black eyes and mocking laughter. He rose and walked to the hearth to pour hot water into a large basin. Placing it carefully on a carved wood stand drawn near the bed, he began to gently wash Gillian's bruised body with a soft cloth. The suspicion which was growing in his mind seemed impossible. Roger de Mortimer was a prisioner in the Tower, imprisoned in a cell far from the royal apartments. How could he find access to any of the queen's ladies? It made no sense. Besides, there were other men in the Tower—members of Isabella's retinue, knights, hundreds of retainers, guards, other prisoners . . . Then why did Roger keep coming into his mind? He looked at Gillian. Her eyes were closed but tears slowly trickled down her cheeks.

Nay, he told himself, I'll not ask her anything yet . . . there's still too much unspoken that lies between us.

He dried her body carefully and from a small jar he found in one of her coffers, applied an unguent to the worst of her bruises as gently as he could. When he was finished, he drew the covers about her shoulders.

"Gillian." His voice was low and husky. She opened her eyes, afraid of his words. He shook his head. "Don't speak, lovedy, 'tis rest you need."

He reached for her hand and her fingers clung to his as he kissed her gently, feeling the soft mouth tremble under his own.

"I don't deserve you." she whispered. His long hazel eyes smiled quietly at her. She felt his hand lightly stroke her hair.

" 'Tis you alone I love," she heard him say as she slipped into the dark serenity of sleep.

"She's told me naught! Scarcely one word has she spoken in all these days."

The words were uttered with a desperation Kilburn could not suppress as he shared a cup of his uncle's specially mulled wine with him. For nearly a week the earl had stayed close to Gillian while she lay upstairs in the small bedchamber, mute and still, avoiding his gaze until he felt he could bear her silence no longer. Although Agnes had told him all she knew, only Gillian held the key to what had actually happened, and he burned to know the truth. Long legs stretched out before him, Kilburn sat at ease in the merchant's comfortable study where he had so often sought the old man's wise and thoughtful advice. The ancient aumbry, dark wood glowing richly in the firelight, still stood against one wall, its shelves holding the finest pieces of silver plate and crystal, flagons, goblets, and mazers that Master Porcher's grandfather had brought with him from London. He noticed idly that the merchant had recently acquired a handsome carpet which covered the center of the well-scrubbed wooden floor, bringing an added warmth to the chamber.

"Don't press her too closely, James. Gillian will talk to you when she is able to," the merchant warned, disturbed by Kilburn's frame of mind. "I confess that I was appalled by her state when you brought her here, but Mistress Agnes tells me she's much improved. She's obviously suffered a great shock. You must give her time, lad."

Master Porcher looked with concern at his nephew's miserable face, and hoped that the truth would not be too much for him. He could not know that for Kilburn it seemed a miracle that Gillian had finally returned to him. There had been times in the lonely months without her that he believed she was lost to him forever. Replying to his uncle's question of his plans, Kilburn vowed that he would not leave until all was as it had been between them.

"I love her too much to lose her again," he said softly, adding that he felt Glairn held too many unhappy memories

349

for her to return there in her present weakened condition.

"Aye, James," Uncle Lionel remarked seriously, his square face with its dark, blunt features frowning in his concentration. "I understand how you feel. Something made her turn from you after Maddie's death—nay, nephew," he said anxiously, setting down the steaming silver cup and leaning toward Kilburn, whose eyes had filled with sudden pain. " 'Tis true . . . don't close your mind to it. Whatever it was, it made her desperate enough to run from you and her children. You've gotten her back now. Just let her feel your love . . . 'tis what she needs most from you."

"She knows. Oh dear God, Uncle, why does my love seem to bring her naught but grief?" Kilburn cried suddenly. He rose, moving restlessly about the low-ceilinged chamber, his mind full of unanswered questions.

"That's nonsense, James. You've shared great happiness together, and will again, I'm certain of it. What's lacking now is your patience. What brought her to this present state was not of your doing."

His hand trembling slightly, the earl refilled his cup and stared blindly into its ruby depths. He thought of the meal they had shared earlier, Gillian propped up on large soft pillows, picking with disinterest at the tasty custard and rich steaming broth placed before her. As he spoke of ordinary, everyday matters, he had fought the desire to take her into his arms, wanting to feel her close to him again. But she remained withdrawn, the large haunted eyes only rarely lifting to his.

"I've often wondered that if my grandfather had allowed my mother to speak of her love for your grandfather, she might not have retreated into her private world," Master Porcher said thoughtfully, breaking into Kilburn's brooding. The earl's hazel eyes rested on his uncle, seeing with a pang how white the dark hair had become. The once ample form had shrunken, and while his clothes were still made of the finest cloth, they were now fashioned for a much smaller man. " 'Tis a state I'd not want for your lady, James. My birth must have turned my grandfather's entire life into a nightmare, yet he survived it. But it destroyed my mother, and even your father's acceptance of me as his brother made no difference to her, for she had escaped into the safety of her dreams. Don't let it happen to Gillian."

He sighed and stood up, looking at Kilburn's tall, spare figure clad in a short tunic of dark blue wool, falling to just below his knees. The finely tooled leather belt was dyed a deep amber as were his soft boots with their cuffs fashionably scalloped. The slender hand resting against the mantel bore the Glairn ring, its fierce hawk glinting brightly in the firelight. But for all his simple elegance, he exuded a despair which touched the merchant's heart.

De Mortimer . . . why did Wigmore constantly intrude into his thoughts, Kilburn wondered, seeing once more the bruises on Gillian's body and remembering how she had looked after Roger's secret departure from Glairn seven years before. He thrust the memory from him, telling himself that his suspicions were foolish. He shivered as with a chill, and turned around to find that his uncle had left him.

Gillian, his heart cried out, my love, let me share your pain, please.

Sinking into the merchant's empty chair, he buried his face in his hands.

The silken folds of her chamber robe fell softly over a body no longer aching and sore, and Gillian felt an odd sensual pleasure at the touch of the smooth cloth against her bare skin. Looking into the small mirror placed on the table near the window, she saw the face of a stranger gaze back at her, pale and shadowed. With shaking fingers, she touched her cheeks, feeling the bones beneath the taut skin. She ran a hand apprehensively over her throat, down to her breasts, covered now by silk, but then . . . Gillian closed her eyes, trying vainly to empty her mind of the wild images which continued to haunt her.

As awareness had slowly returned to her, lying safe within the confines of the quiet chamber, she had felt Jamie's loving strength surround her. But she kept herself locked away from him, evading his anxious gaze. She knew what he was waiting to hear, but she could not speak of it—not yet. During the day, she watched the spring sun stream through the small window, casting patterns of light against the white plastered walls and dark wooden beams of the low ceiling. Sounds of the busy street beyond Master Porcher's gates filtered dimly through her consciousness and she listened to the voices of the merchant's workers, the low rumbling tones of the men an accompaniment to that of the clear young laughter of his apprentices from the courtyard below.

The nights were the worst, filled with unspeakable horrors, and she fought her dreams to awaken finally, trembling with the remnants of her fear. Turning in the lonely bed, which seemed to mock her with its emptiness, she would see Jamie's dark form stretched out on a pallet before the hearth and be comforted by his nearness.

Tonight a restlessness filled her, a yearning to be done with the dark, frightening silence she had watched grow ever deeper. Gillian knew then that she wanted above all else to return to Jamie, to hold his love and never let it go again. She rose from the table as the door quietly opened, greeting an astonished Jamie with a shy smile. He stood by the doorway, his pulses pounding as she walked toward him, her movements free of pain, the soft dark hair falling in a long, thick plait down her back. He cupped her face between his hands, the silken skin cool to his touch, and looked into eyes which shattered him with their bruised love. He brushed his lips lightly over hers, tasting again the sweetness of that sensuous mouth. His kiss deepened as he felt her mouth open beneath his, clinging with tremulous hunger until she pulled away, shaken by the emotions his nearness had awakened. Her body rested against his for a moment, and a familiar loving warmth filled his heart.

"Lovedy," he murmured, stroking the fine hair, his fingers tangling themselves in the heavy braid. He drew her toward the wide settle, his eyes capturing hers again until he looked away finally, trying to find the words in the leaping flames of the hearth. Gillian sat beside him quietly, waiting for what she knew was to come.

"Whatever happened . . . whoever it was—I promise it will make no difference between us!"

" 'Twas Roger de Mortimer!" she said simply. "You

fear to ask . . . 'twas Roger. That last night before I was to leave the Tower . . . he was waiting for me. All these years I thought myself safe from him! And he was there . . . I don't know how he was able to—bribed a jailer perhaps . . ." She laughed and it sounded like a sob. "He was there—in the shadows, waiting . . ."

"Gillian, don't . . ." It was a plea, for a fearful dread suddenly coursed through him. His words were a surprise, for Gillian had expected questions, accusations, even anger from him. When she dared to look at him, she saw the truth in his eyes.

"Aye, Jamie, I must, but I don't deserve your forgiveness or understanding." She pulled away and stood before him, tall, slim, and white-faced. She knew that he had to be told, that no doubts could remain—it was a desperate gamble, but one she must take, although it would take all of her courage.

"Roger came to me . . ." she began quietly. "I didn't try to escape him . . . I let him touch me . . ."

Her voice faltered as she slowly sank down before him, allowing the memory of that dreadful night to pour through her again. She remembered Roger's dark eyes gleaming in the firelight as he pulled her to the bed and began to caress her . . . Her fingers covered her eyes, hiding against the remembrance of his hands, ungentle and bruising, and his hungry mouth consuming her, drawing her life from her.

"The worst part of it was that I found I wanted him!" Tears began to stream unheeded down her cheeks as the words poured from her. Kilburn sat in frozen silence, scarce believing what she said. "Night after night I dreamed of you . . . longing for you so much I could hardly bear it."

She looked at him suddenly, seeing his shock and unable to stop herself.

"I was filled with remorse that I'd turned from you. Jamie, 'twas wrong of me . . . I know that now, but I felt so guilty over Maddie's death. You see, I never loved her."

Kilburn made a strangled sound, the pain her words

evoked rising in him mixed with pity for the woman crouched before him.

"But you didn't cause her death. I can't believe you didn't love her . . ."

"Oh, God, 'twas not her fault she was conceived in rage. Yet each time I looked at her, she reminded me of that night in Hurley when all we could do was wound each other. And she was the last! After her there could be no more babes to hold in my arms." She lowered her gaze. "I saw your face when you looked at her—I was jealous . . . jealous of your love for her. And I hated her for taking you from me!"

He did not know how to answer her, for he had never even suspected her feelings toward Maddie. You didn't understand, he thought sadly. Oh, lovedy—the needless agony you inflicted upon yourself.

"I wanted to come home," Gillian sobbed brokenly. "The children . . . Glairn . . . but most of all, I wanted you. 'Twas all I could think of. And it grew worse after I spoke to Elizabeth at Hurley. I should have answered your letter in Cirencester, but my guilt wouldn't permit it. When I finally did send you messages, your replies were so cold . . . I feared I'd lost you! I began to believe you didn't want me anymore. Not in all the time I was at court, did you come . . . But my need for you was greater than my fear—I had to see you . . . to explain. When the queen released me from court, I counted the days until I would see you again. How was I to know about . . . about . . ." Her voice faltered and stopped as her body began to shake.

"Gillian, did Roger take you against your will?"

She did not reply. Bending over, Kilburn lifted her up and made her look at him. He had to know. "Tell me!" he demanded.

She shook her head, the bruised, hurt eyes refusing to meet his. He felt cold.

Taking a deep breath, she whispered guiltily, "I did fight him finally, Jamie, but he was too strong. And then he was over me . . . his body against mine and . . . and . . . Oh, my God, Jamie, I wanted him!" She cried out the words, hysteria claiming her at last. "I knew in my heart that you didn't want me anymore . . . how could you after

354

hurting you as I did—turning from you without any words. I should have comforted you and instead I ran away. You couldn't want me . . . Oh, Jamie—I was so afraid . . . and then Roger was there. When he first touched me, I pleaded with him, but he refused to listen . . . and suddenly it didn't matter . . ."

Her mind had screamed out to a rescuer too distant to come to her aid until she was flooded with naught but a growing awareness of de Mortimer's unrelenting, driving strength and hardness. When the hammering on the door and the treble of Isabella's youngest page penetrated her consciousness, she found herself clinging to Roger as if she were drowning, her senses on fire and her body answering his with starved passion. Shaken by her reaction to a man she loathed, she shrank from him, calling out weakly to the boy, afraid he would enter the chamber and witness her shame. She was spared that humiliation, for he only replied that the queen craved her attendance once more, since she still could not sleep. For a moment she felt Roger's body tense, but when the page did not enter, he relaxed, lying quietly beside her on the narrow bed. His hands still touched her, gentle now where before they had been cruel, painfully bruising the delicate flesh beneath his seeking fingers, probing the secrets of a body she could no longer defend.

She had turned her head so that he could not see her tears, but he forced her to look at him. His eyes were puzzled as he stared down into her white, dazed face. Gillian could not know the unfamiliar feeling of remorse she stirred in him, and had she been less terrified, she might have better understood his words.

"What have I done to you? I did not understand . . ." Roger bent over her, his voice gentle. "I've always believed that chastity of body in a woman was a myth. I saw your loyalty and passion for James Kilburn as a web woven about him, binding him to you so tightly that he sacrificed taking his rightful place among the ranking barons of this land. James could have been a part of my world, Gillian. I offered it to him. Yet your husband has always spurned it, and for that I despise him. I know now that I was mistaken about him, for his feelings for you have naught to do with his other beliefs. I should have seen that when last I saw him. My ambitions still exist . . . I'll not remain here forever, and England's not yet done with Roger de Mortimer!" His voice grew hard and his grip on Gillian tightened, causing her to cry out in pain. Roger's moment of tenderness had fled. "I used his love for you to taunt him . . . and where there once was friendship between us, there now lies naught but hatred."

He raised the coverlet to cover her nakedness and she thrust aside his hands, trying vainly to evade him.

"I realize now that I've greatly misjudged and wronged you, my lady—you should never have been hurt."

"Hurt?" Gillian suddenly found herself able to face him with a contempt born of her shame. "You rue your deed by saying I should not have been hurt! You have no idea of what you've done to me . . . 'Tis not only your body but that fearful blackness within you which violates every decency it touches. I must face my husband with the truth . . . even if I don't, he will know." She surprised him with her vehemence. "And now I must go to the queen. How can I keep it from her?"

The words died in Gillian's throat as Roger's dark eyes burned into her own. His voice was cold and deliberate.

"Not a word of this ever to the queen! She is mine, and has naught to do with this. Do you understand?"

Gillian's tears wet the strong, lean hand clamped over her mouth as she gazed at him in terror. There it was again . . . the look of death and destruction she had seen at Glairn seven years before. Her eyes glazed over in sudden panic and closed, for she dared not contemplate the dark, doomed face any longer. And then she was free to rise from the bed. De Mortimer watched from the shadows as she donned her robe with trembling hands. She braided her hair and ran a wet cloth over her face, scarce knowing what she did. When she reached out for the door latch, he moved quickly and silently to stand behind her, holding her against him for a moment as a hand moved to circle her throat.

"Remember, my lady, not one word to Isabella . . ." The words were whispered into her ear and she almost screamed aloud at the menace in his voice and the pressure of his fingers.

For the rest of the night she sat in Isabella's apartment, even while the queen slept, afraid to return to her own chamber lest de Mortimer still be there. She waited for the dawn to break, her mind battling thoughts of Jamie as her abused and bruised body began to throb painfully while the burning ache within her slowly ebbed.

She remembered little of her departure from the Tower an hour later, knowing only that Agnes held the reins of her small mare and led her through the still empty, silent, winding streets of London. Dazed, she blindly followed the armed guards Isabella had insisted accompany her on the long journey northward, until all that was left her was the wild, savage pain which coursed through her, totally obliterating thought and feeling.

She had told Kilburn it did not matter. How wrong she had been!

"Jamie, please don't hate me. There's never been anyone but you—only you have mattered to me since I was a child. Naught's changed. You're still all that matters. I love you, Jamie, and I need you . . . Oh, sweet Virgin, I need you . . ."

Gillian wept wildly, desperate in her fear that she would lose him. She collapsed at his feet, unable to look at him, her body shaken by the terrified grief that welled up deep within her. Silently, Kilburn lifted her into his arms, holding her as he had held her the first time, cradling her as he had cradled the child Gillian, taking the searing pain of her shame and fear into himself, and sharing her guilt. Never would he forgive himself for having allowed this to happen to her, he told himself, for he had interfered with the king's original judgment against Roger de Mortimer.

"Please, Jamie, please forgive me . . ." Gillian sobbed, knowing that the truth had torn him apart. "Without you I am naught."

His arms tightened about her as he rocked her gently. Although he knew that she needed the comfort of his understanding, the words were difficult to find. The minutes passed as he fought the pain within himself.

"Try to forget what happened, my darling. 'Tis past and not to be spoken of again." His voice was muffled against her hair, and she did not see the tears in his eyes. "You are mine, Gillian . . . you always were and are still," he assured her.

At his quiet words, Gillian turned in his arms, pressing herself against him. Her tears mingled with his own then, and their lips met. From her shy but eager response, Jamie knew that she was returned to him. They clung together, shutting out all but the love they drew from each other.

Despite his brave words, his hatred against Roger intensified as time passed, not only for having inflicted such anguish upon a soul as tender and vulnerable as Gillian's, but for having turned her into the one weapon capable of shattering Kilburn's sense of balanced stability.

PART SIX
1323

Chapter 13

On the night of August 1, 1323, the Tower's entire garrison, as was their wont, celebrated the feast of St. Peter ad Vincula, consuming copious amounts of wine, while the royal kitchens provided course upon course of food generally reserved for the king's own table. Sir Stephen de Seagrave, as constable, presided over the festivities with a great show of ceremony. A worried aide had voiced concern over leaving the Tower's fortifications and dungeons guarded by only a handful of men, but de Seagrave laughed, replying that the Tower was secure enough, for all the gates were barred, the portcullises in the entry towers lowered, and what prisoners there were, safely locked behind the heavy wooden doors of their cells. Besides, how often was it that they were honored with as gracious a gift as wine from the royal cellars. Watching several of his men sink into a drunken stupor, the constable observed dryly that such quality was unfortunately wasted upon most of the garrison. In all the raucous merriment, the absence of a young sub-lieutenant went totally unnoticed.

Gerald de Alspaye at that moment was standing precariously balanced on the roof of the royal kitchens, nervously peering into the dark, cavernous mouth of the large chimney.

"My lord, I'm over here!" he whispered as a head and shoulders slowly rose from the opening.

"God's blood, but the soot in that damned chimney near stifled me."

Roger de Mortimer pulled himself free and swung silently onto the slanted roof. He took a deep breath and, smiling grimly, looked back at the massive shape of the White Tower, glowing faintly in the fitful light of a moon partially obscured by scudding clouds. Their plan so far was working remarkably well. Despite their fears, it had been surprisingly simple for de Alspaye to cut through the wall of his cell. The mortar was old and the stones easily loosened, so that it had taken only a short time before he was able to crawl through the hole. Without encountering guards, he had followed the stocky figure of his accomplice through a nearby passage leading into the large rooms of the kitchens. What a sight that had been, Roger thought with glee . . . Oh, Isabella, I've much to thank you for if the rest of our plan goes as well. His mind briefly touched the memory of the queen's face, her eyes sparkling with anticipation when he first told her of his plan. How willing she had been to become a party to his escape. Not only had she passed on messages to his friends and supporters outside the Tower walls, but she had even beguiled the unsuspecting de Alspaye into joining them.

Only with Isabella's help could they step over the inert forms of the cooks, helpers, apprentices, and serving men who lay about in sodden slumber. A cup, fallen on its side, had spilled its drugged contents over a marzipan confection, turning its fanciful innocence into a scarlet obscenity.

And now, standing on the edge of the roof, he broke the unnatural silence by allowing himself a quiet laugh. Were he a superstitious man, he would have crossed himself, but he was concerned neither about the absence of guards nor the lack of torches or lanterns.

Carefully they inched their way along the roof's edge toward the square, crenellated shape of the Garden Tower. A torch flared suddenly from below and drunken voices were raised in song as two guards emerged from a small door directly beneath them. The two men froze, melting into the darkness and protected by the stone ledge running the entire length of the royal palace. There too he had been fortunate, Roger told himself, for had it not been for the queen's influence, he would never have been transferred from the White Tower to a cell in the royal palace. His one regret was that his uncle had been too ill to take part, lying white and bone-thin on his pallet, barely able to swallow the thin gruel he was brought once a day. The wild face took on an expression of implacable loathing. That was another thing Edward would answer to someday. So he had vowed to himself each day as he watched the old man weaken and fade.

The light moved in the direction of Cole Harbor Gate, wavering in the same manner as the guard holding it. There was no doubt in either man's mind that those two would soon join the others in a drugged sleep. "This way . . ." de Alspaye's voice was sharp with urgency. Roger's hands gripped the rough stones, feeling them bite coldly into his flesh as he vaulted to the parapet of the Garden Tower. Crossing to the other side, he quickly clambered down a rope ladder the younger man had brought with him. His feet touched the ground and he ran toward the outer wall. De Alspaye had already twice thrown a long rope with a grappling hook at one end over the top of the wall when, with his third try, he felt the rope grow taut and hold fast.

A sudden feeling of distrust swept over Roger—it had all been too easy, a voice whispered inside his head. Was de Alspaye intending to betray him to waiting guards once the outer wall was reached? He fought against the blind fear which threatened to engulf him. Don't play the panicked fool. The young officer need not have involved himself with you at all . . . but he pulled the rope from de Alspaye's hand.

"I'll go first," he snarled in a low voice. Startled by his vehemence, the younger man stood mutely watching as de Mortimer grasped the rope in both hands. With agonizing slowness, Roger worked his way upward, hand over hand, stopping now and again to brace his feet against the wall. His breath rasped in his ears—were there alert guards on duty, they would of a certainty hear him. Silence!

Nothing moved in the nearby Wakefield Tower. His arms felt as if they would break from bearing his weight, but he tried not to dwell on the possibility of falling. Look up, he told himself sternly, look up, you're almost there. His hands touched stone, clung, and gripped hard. A sharp edge cut into his palm and wetness spread over his hand. Damnation! Roger swore silently, enduring the pain which shot through his arm as he pulled himself up and over the top of the wall. His breath came in great sobbing gulps as he lay on the narrow walkway, fighting a mounting nausea. His face was wet with the sweat which had broken out from his exertions. He could feel it trickle uncomfortably down his body while the beating of his heart gradually slowed.

Gerald de Alspaye joined him, leaning against the wall as he too fought to catch his breath. A dim light flickered from an overturned lantern.

"My lord, look over there—in the corner. 'Tis two guards, both asleep." Laughter bubbled inside of him; the drugged wine had certainly done its work well.

"Now we must hope that the guards at the postern gate have also been taken care of." Roger murmured. He felt the muscles of his legs quiver as he rose slowly to his feet. Anger coursed through him and he cursed under his breath, damning his imprisonment. His body had never failed him before. The palm of his hand tingled, but he thrust the pain from his mind. There was no time for weakness. Roger wiped his face free of sweat and began to draw the rope over the wall. In a few minutes, both men had clambered down to the outer ward and lowered themselves silently into the black, dirty water of the moat. The moon suddenly emerged, bathing them in its brightness as they swam across to the low wall of the wharf. Nothing stirred. Huge and menacing, St. Thomas's Tower straddled the moat like some mythological monster as the two men crouched in its shadow. They could hear the gentle lapping of the river against the stones of the wharf edge. The dank odor of rotting garbage, wedged in the iron grillwork of the watergate, assailed their nostrils. A slight breeze made them shiver in their wet clothes, despite the mildness of the summer night.

Roger's eyes strained to penetrate the darkness. A light flickered from the river and then was gone. There it was again, closer this time. A soft thudding of oars against metal locks reached his ears. Gerald de Alspaye clutched his arm.

"They will wait by the postern gate . . . 'tis over here," and he ran down the short steps leading to the river. The iron gate, set with the king's cipher, was unlocked and made no sound as it was swung open. Roger stepped over the body of a guard, snoring drunkenly. Dimly he could make out the shape of the small boat with a shuttered lantern hanging from its prow as it rode lightly on the water. One of the boatmen clung to the large metal ring embedded in the wall by the bottom step.

"My lord de Mortimer?" The whispered words were faint. Roger stepped into the boat, guided by eager hands to a seat beside a hooded figure. His companion crouched at the bottom of the boat, near the oarsmen, watching the river.

"You're safe now, my lord."

"Master Bakerel?" Roger asked, scarce believing his eyes as the long, pale face sprang into view for a moment, illuminated by a briefly unshuttered lantern.

"My lord Bishop Orleton has sent me to see you safely on your way." Although unassuming and self-effacing in the presence of his master's peers, this least and mainly ignored of the Bishop of Hereford's scribes was the most valued and resourceful of his agents. It had seemed natural to entrust him with the mission. Darkness shrouding them once more, the scribe spoke to Roger in tones of quiet deliberation as the boat drew slowly away from the king's stairs, heading for the far side of the Thames. The tide had turned, flowing toward the estuary, and they moved quickly and effortlessly downriver, putting distance between themselves and the Tower, which still lay steeped in silence, its guardians not yet aware of what had occurred within its high, impregnable walls.

When the mist which hovered over the coastal waters of Hampshire began to shred and wisp itself into nothingness in the milk-white light of early dawn, the dark bulk of a large merchant ship became visible, its tall masts pointing heavenward. Few on board suspected that the tall man wrapped in a long dark cloak, who had been quietly brought alongside the ship in the captain's boat shortly before dawn, was anything but a wealthy merchant whose passage had been paid for in gold. As the anchor was raised with a loud creaking and squealing of its iron chain, the vessel began to move away from shore, sails filling with the freshening wind which would aid their journey across the channel.

Roger stood by the rail, looking back at the receding coast. His face was drawn, the features shadowed by the hood which hid him from prying eyes. He knew that he had much to be thankful for and many to be grateful to. The bishop had seen to it that a band of his liegemen were waiting for him when he and de Alspaye were put ashore in Surrey. Adam Orleton had also provided him with merchant's clothes and a small leather bag heavy with coins, which was pressed into his hand by Master Bakerel as he was wished godspeed, with instructions to ride for the coast where the ship waited. The liegemen had ridden with him through the day and most of the night and had accompanied him to the coast.

"Where are we bound now, my lord?" Gerald, his military bearing all but submerged in the sober garments of a scribe, stood beside de Mortimer, his eyes wistful as England drew ever more distant.

"I understand that the ship is heading for a port in Normandy, Gerald. Once there, we can again regain our own identities. Then we go to Paris—to join others like ourselves who have taken refuge with the French king."

Gerald sighed. The queen had paid him well enough for his part in the escape, but he had given little thought to what the future would bring to his own life. For now he was bound to de Mortimer.

"And what will we do in Paris, my lord?"

An innocent question—too innocent to bring out the devil's laughter and the fire which poured from the dark eyes as Roger threw back his hood and felt the salt spray on his face. His mouth twisted as he smote the rail with a clenched fist.

"We wait, my friend. And when our waiting is done, we will return to England."

His face hardened as bitter, violent hatred rose within him. Oh yes, he would return, but under very different circumstances and on his own terms.

Pen-yr-bryn, Wales

He's free! Thank the heavenly Virgin," Jehan's voice rang out joyously, her relief echoing through the high-ceilinged hall. "Roger is at the French court and is safe!"

Her face glowed with unconcealed happiness as she looked at the letter held in hands whose trembling she could not control. She ran from Emrys to Lord Powys, uncertain with whom she should share the news, her small figure casting a wavering shadow against the rough-hewn wall devoid of tapestries. Several dogs, lazily basking in the warmth of the huge stone hearth which dominated one end of the long hall, totally ignored her existence. Not so Lord Powys, who watched her intently as he sat sprawled out in his wide, pelt-strewn chair. One hand absently fondled the head of an enormous mastiff which lay at his feet. A heavy leather collar about the dog's massive neck was attached to a chain confining its movements. As Jehan drew near, the animal growled in warning, baring its teeth. She stared at it and laughed, for once too distracted to take offense at the dog's animosity toward her.

Jehan wore a large shawl of soft fur, fastened to one shoulder of her heavy woolen tunic with a large, ornately worked silver clasp. Silhouetted against the fire, her loosened hair spilling wildly about her, she appeared as some pagan spirit to the two men who stared at her silently.

"I must begin to pack my things," she said excitedly, turning toward Emrys, who had not moved from his place by the hearth since she eagerly pulled the letter from his grasp. He averted his gaze, for her shining face was too painful for him to behold. "We will start for France as soon as I can ready myself for the journey." A thought struck her. "I shall have to take Mistress Lowndes with me." By some miracle, Emrys had located the tiring woman in Shrewsbury some months after their own arrival at Pen-yr-bryn, bringing her to her mistress. For Jehan it was the first ray of light in a life turned unbelievably bleak.

"By the gods, 'tis a foolish woman you are!" Sir Powys growled, discomfited by her obvious desire to escape. He was a huge bear of a man with a mane of tangled brown hair falling to his shoulders. Above an untrimmed beard, deep-set eyes glittered in a face astonishingly lacking in the coarseness his appearance would indicate. "No journey can be made safely in weather such as this. The snows are still with us—there'll be time enough to speak of leaving when spring comes. 'Tis right I am—what do you say, Emrys?"

"But my lord has summoned me." Jehan did not wait for the harper's reply. She could think of naught but that Roger was safe and she would soon be with him once more. Enduring her exile with ill-grace, only the belief that she would be reunited with Roger had kept her from going mad. To her, Wales was a hostile land with an alien tongue she could not comprehend. She found the primitive meanness of the small, isolated castle appalling to her luxury-dominated senses, and it had all served to drive her into abysmal, frightening loneliness.

"My lady!" The harper's low voice intruded into her happiness. "Lady Jehan—the message is not for you."

"Of course it is!—Lord de Mortimer asks that we join him at once." She pointed toward the fine black script on the much handled sheet. "Here, Emrys—you yourself told me so."

"The message came to me, my lady . . . it makes no mention of you at all." He tried to take the letter from her, but she drew back, holding it to her breast.

"Nay—'tis untrue . . . my lord would want me with him. I've waited since he was imprisoned." She would not believe it. "The letter has traveled many months—see how worn it is. Why would he write, if not to summon me?" Suspicion swamped the heart-shaped face. "You lie, Emrys. You lie for her! 'Tis Lady de Mortimer you serve—your true loyalties have always been with her. But she's at Skipton under house arrest—what good can she do her lord?" White-faced, her eyes moved beseechingly to Lord Powys, who stared into the fire, avoiding her gaze.

"He doesn't want you anymore, my lady! 'Tis quite obvious to all save you." The clear voice rang through the hall, spite clinging to every word. Stung to the quick, Jehan swung about sharply to face the boy sitting in a window recess several steps above the rush-covered floor. Thin and gangling, he seemed all awkward arms and legs, hovering in that half-world, neither child nor man—understanding both too little and too much of the frailties which surrounded him. "If you believe that after all these months your lord decided he needs you with him . . . You dream too much." His tone mocked her.

"Bleddyn . . ." Lord Powys grew angry at the boy's insolence, cautioning him to be still, but Bleddyn merely laughed. Sauntering down the steps, he ran a grimy hand carelessly through dark auburn hair already untidily ruffled. His green eyes sparkled with malice. The year he had served the baron of Wigmore as page had been a miserable time for him. He had detested the servility forced upon him. Suffering the animosity of the other boys in the de Mortimer household, he longed only for his lost freedom. Lord de Mortimer's arrest and imprisonment had meant a release from a state he had neither sought nor desired. Lady de Maudley, although a stranger, served to remind him of those hateful months. Bleddyn despised her because she so shamelessly loved the baron.

"Uncle, 'tis common talk that your liege lord takes his pleasure where he will . . . what need has he for a lady whose usefulness to him is at an end?"

"Pleasure?" Sir Powys's heavy voice was lifted to a roar. "What knowledge have you of a lord's pleasure—you're naught but a cub yet." His face grew red with the futile anger he felt toward the boy. "I've warned you ere now, Bleddyn, not to speak to Lady de Maudley as you do. She gave you no cause to say what you have." The sharp brown eyes caught a sudden look of arrogant resentment which crossed the wild, handsome young features. "We gave Lady de Maudley shelter and protection because the baron of Wigmore asked it of us—'tis true. But she

369

has also tended to your aunt Olwen with great care, and for that I'm grateful to her beyond measure."

" 'Tis not only Aunt Olwen she tends to, Uncle . . . I've heard——"

Bleddyn's head snapped back as Jehan delivered a stinging slap across his face. His cheek crimson, the boy stepped back as she blazed her scorn at him.

"You're naught but a filthy-minded, foul-mouthed young whelp who does no credit to his uncle . . . I can't fathom why Lord Powys countenances your continued insolence, nor why Lord de Mortimer bothered to keep you with him as page."

Her eyes brimmed over with angry tears as she turned away, leaving Bleddyn gaping with astonishment at her outburst. Jehan took several deep breaths, determined to pay no further heed to the boy. No matter how she tried, he seemed impervious to her overtures of friendship, showing her naught but resentment and dislike. She sank onto the narrow bench close to the hearth and Emrys knelt before her, holding the soft hand which she blindly reached out to him.

"My lord truly did not ask for me?" Jehan murmured. "Not once?"

Bending his head, the harper pressed his lips lightly to the hand still clasped in his, feeling the rushing, agitated pulse in the delicately boned wrist.

"He asks that I join him in Paris . . . and I'll not wait for the snows to melt."

Stunned by Emrys's words, Jehan sat quite still, her eyes closed, not wanting to see the pity on the men's faces. So Roger had not summoned her and she was trapped at Pen-yr-bryn. Of course he was a hunted man, she told herself, for the king had placed a price on his head after searching throughout the realm for him following his escape. Wales had been alive with rumors, causing Edward to believe Roger had sought refuge with his supporters, but he had been nowhere to be found. Now he was in Paris—at the royal court and probably existing on naught but what his wits could win for him. If he could barely support himself, how could he possibly afford the luxury of having her with him. Besides, 'twas possible he did not know she was with Emrys. It was a frail reason for his not asking for her, but Jehan clung desperately to the thought.

"Come, my lady, have some wine. 'Twill hearten you." Sir Powys motioned a servant to see to Jehan, but she shook her head. Even the sudden activity about her seemed far distant as servants went about their evening duties. The hall was suddenly illuminated by flaring torches, routing its dark shadows, but the light only served to enhance the chilling starkness of bare stone walls, which even the replenished fire in the hearth could not banish.

Lord Powys looked at Jehan thoughtfully over his large leather tankard of ale, wondering as he had many times before why his liege lord had singled him out, entrusting two souls into his keeping. Though the responsibility weighed heavily upon him, the trust had not been misplaced, for he would die to keep it. Both he and his lady loved Bleddyn as their own. He had never questioned the child's origins, nor had he truly cared until now. The boy had brought a joy and renewed life into the castle, causing the old walls to ring with happy childish laughter. But the sweet Virgin alone knew why Bleddyn had changed since being with the baron that year. He had returned full of wild bitterness, turned inward. As time passed, he grew ever more difficult to read. Lurking about the castle, silent and secretive, he would suddenly give vent to explosive fits of arrogant temper, which caused the servants to shun him. Only his aunt Olwen seemed to bring out the gentler side of his nature. Powys's dark eyes narrowed. As for the lady Jehan . . . now there was quite another problem! Bleddyn had come closer to the truth with his cruel words than he could know, the Welsh lord mused wryly, sweeping his gaze over Jehan's pale features. She could easily drive a man mad with her flaming red hair and those cat's eyes which seemed to look into one's soul. He fought the fantasies that had haunted him in recent weeks—imagining her soft, moist mouth opening beneath his, her arms twining about his neck. Inhaling the lingering fragrance of rose petals, Powys could almost feel the firm pliancy of breasts and thighs, merely glimpsed through her robes, pressed urgently against him as he drew her closer into his embrace . . .

"I'll not go! No one can make me!"

Bleddyn's enraged shrieks shattered Powys's dream and he raised himself angrily from the chair. The boy's face was white as he lifted a heavy flagon of wine and hurled it toward the fire. The hearth exploded in a shower of sparks as servants rushed to push back flaming logs.

"Have you lost all your wits?" Powys's heavy wrist bracelets made a jarring noise as he grasped Bleddyn by the shoulders. The mastiff, excited by his master's anger, barked and snarled, fighting the chain which held him in check. The servants stood frozen in an atmosphere charged with wild emotions. "What is all this shouting about?"

"I'll not go, Uncle! Wigmore wants me with him in Paris—Emrys just ordered me to get ready." The oddly slanted eyes were rebellious.

Powys turned to look at Emrys. The harper's face twisted in dismay. " 'Tis true . . . the Arglwydd has asked that I bring him with me."

"How dare you question Lord de Mortimer's command!" His dark eyes gleamed with annoyance as Powys spat out the words. "You have no choice but to go . . . there's naught to be done."

"But I must stay—Aunt Olwen . . ."

So that was it, Powys thought, his throat tightening. "Your aunt Olwen will be tended to, Bleddyn-bach." His voice softened. "You can't disobey your liege lord. 'Tis not permitted."

Bleddyn wrenched free of his uncle's hands and, young as he was, his passionate anger made the air crackle with its force.

"I will not go, Uncle! Lord de Mortimer is your liege lord, not mine. I hate him. I hate you all for being in his power. I'll never let him own me—never." He dashed tears from his eyes with boyish hands, angry even with himself for allowing them to have penetrated his defenses.

"I leave at first light tomorrow, young sir, and will expect you by my side." Emrys folded the letter and thrust it into the sleeve of his tunic.

For a moment Bleddyn stood before them, sullen stubbornness replacing his rage, and Jehan caught her

372

breath as she saw the resemblance to Roger for the first time. His head tilted back defiantly and with the fluidity of movement inherited from his father, he stalked from the hall, all righteous indignation.

"He'll come round," Jehan said softly, noting the shock on her host's face.

"Nay, my lady, I fear not. He's that stubborn, he is, and will not be found till Emrys is well gone from here." Powys shrugged. " 'Tis impossible to control him anymore . . ."

They sat in silence, pursuing their own thoughts, while Bleddyn rode furiously through the castle gate on his small gray horse, veering sharply away from the causeway to where a narrow twisting path skirted the edge of a deep ravine, leading to the mountain's crest and the dark valley forest beyond.

"I've almost forgotten the feeling of the sun's warmth . . . How long it's been since my eyes have seen the valley awaken to spring!" The soft, gently murmured words drifted lightly through the gathering darkness. "I remember when I rode beside my lord following the sounds of the hunting horns . . . my world was beautiful and complete then. Now I can but live my life through others." Lady Olwen's frail figure stirred in the deep, velvet-pillowed chair which threatened to engulf her. She smiled wistfully at the woman who gazed silently through the narrow window. Unmoving, she seemed oblivious to all but what seemed to hold her interest beyond the confines of the small chamber. "Your tales of the royal court and its intrigues banish the shadows which seem to draw ever closer. But the excitement of court life, and its glitter and ceremony, are quite overwhelming. 'Tis best suited to a nature such as yours, my lady. I know that for me, my quiet life here has given me all the happiness I've ever desired. You have been so kind . . ."

Jehan bit her lip to keep from screaming. Ever since Emrys's departure, her loneliness and sense of futility had driven her to endure the unrelieved tedium of spending her days in the company of a woman barely clinging to life. From where she stood she could see the melting snows on the mountain crags, glistening in the last rays of the sun, mocking her self-imposed imprisonment.

"It also pleases my lord to have you with us, for he misses the world outside more than he will ever admit. There was a time when his ambitions could have carried him far beyond these mountains." The weary voice faltered for a moment. "And he is much taken with you . . . it could not be otherwise!"

Sweet Jesù, why must I listen to this mawkish, tiresome nonsense, Jehan thought meanly, totally unaware of how her sensual vitality smote the other woman's heart. Turning away at last from the window, she shivered in the chamber's damp chill.

"It pleases me not at all, my lady. I did not think when Emrys brought me here that my stay would be so long. I care naught for your lord nor your household." Her tone was peevish. "And your nephew makes my living here totally intolerable."

"Ah yes, Bleddyn!" Lady Olwen's voice was sad. "My poor Bleddyn. There's too much feeling within him, and he sees far more deeply into the hearts of folk than his age should allow."

Servants began to light the large candles standing in their massive iron holders, and Lady Olwen's wasted features sprang startlingly to life. Tears shimmered in the mild blue eyes, and for a moment she could not speak as the familiar knot of pain tightened within her. Sitting down on the settle opposite Lady Olwen, Jehan chose to ignore her last words. Restless and beset by her own troubles, she did not want to think of Bleddyn, nor hear of his countless virtues. Her eyes were thoughtful as she stared wordlessly at the gaunt, white-faced woman. 'Twas said that Sir Powys's lady would not live till summer. What would happen to her then? She had no wish to remain at Pen-yr-bryn alone with a widowed lord who even now did not hide a growing interest in her. His wife had been ill for several years, and if castle gossip were to be believed, Sir Powys was a man of lusty appetites. Her gaze shifted toward the hearth. Fresh wood had been placed on the dying embers and she watched small flames begin to lick greedily at the bark-covered logs. Where could she go?

She had been able to bring what was left of Sir Ralph's gold with her when she was forced to flee the manor. A smile lurked in the corners of her mouth—James Kilburn had believed her when she said she had only her body with which to repay his favor. Perhaps she had even believed it herself, for he had always drawn her, but Sir Powys . . . a shudder swept through her at the thought of his heavy hands touching her. Yet—those closely hoarded coins would not keep her for long. Damn Roger! She cursed silently.

"Bleddyn fears you."

Jehan looked up sharply at the quiet words, her face mirroring her surprise.

"Afraid? Of me?" She laughed dryly—that young whelp had a tongue which flayed her each time they were together. "Of course—he senses that you are a part of a truth he fears to discover, and if he does, it will shatter the world he knows and believes in."

As Jehan's eyes narrowed with suspicion, Lady Olwen was convulsed with icy terror. What lay in her heart could no longer wait. As if to confirm her fear, she began to cough—a spasm terrible in its tearing, rasping sound. A fleck of blood crimsoned the corner of her mouth as she leaned back at last, spent from the effort it took even to draw a shallow breath. A young servant girl wiped the ashen face with a damp cloth.

"The truth?" Jehan's voice trembled with sudden apprehension. What could she mean?

With a slight movement of her hand, Lady Olwen dismissed the servants hovering about her. The two women sat for a few minutes quietly contemplating each other.

"I know who Bleddyn's father is . . ."

Startled by Lady Olwen's directness, Jehan stared at her with sudden interest, realizing that this woman was not the naive innocent she had thought her to be.

" 'Twas not difficult to fathom when Emrys brought the babe to us wrapped in velvet and fur. I'm sure my lord was told the truth, but he's ne'er said aught to me these thirteen years. A wet nurse came with the child—she's still here, and still a stranger, though wed to one of our own people." A sigh escaped Lady Olwen. "It has always saddened me to think that because our Bleddyn was put to her breast, her own child was lost to her. And yet she loves our boy and was ever good to him."

"Think of the babe's own mother, my lady, from whose breast he was torn!" The words were out before Jehan could stifle them.

"I do . . . and 'tis to her I speak." Lady Olwen fought for breath, fearing that what she believed had to be said would be misunderstood. "Bleddyn is your son . . . I've seen the knowledge of it in your eyes. And the boy senses it too. He doesn't understand, for he believes he is the son of my lord's eldest brother who was killed in a tournament. To us he is Bleddyn ap Rhys, our nephew. I'm the only mother he's ever known, and I love him as if he truly were mine."

There was no shock in Jehan's eyes as she continued to gaze at the woman opposite her. It had taken her very little time to realize who Bleddyn was, but to her surprise, she felt no maternal stirrings at the sight of him.

Lady Olwen's heart was pounding at a frightening rate and the pain began to spread outward as she drew upon the little strength left to her.

"Bleddyn's sire is a man to be feared. I know that you still love him, despite the hurt he has visited upon you—but if you don't forget him, he will destroy you." She saw Jehan's face drain of color, the green eyes begin to glitter with sudden anger, and was swept by a great sense of urgency. "Roger de Mortimer taints all those he touches with his arrogant, ambitious will, caring naught for the pain he inflicts nor the bodies he treads upon in his eagerness to attain his destiny. The very thought of him fills me with terror. Oh, Jehan," she cried, unable to hold back her fears, "my Bleddyn must be shielded from him, for there's too much of his father in him. It grows stronger day by day. Promise me, please, that he will never know who he truly is." Lady Olwen held out her hand blindly, and instinctively Jehan clasped it in hers, alarmed at its icy touch. "He must never be told the truth . . . I beg you to keep it from him."

Disturbed by the vehemence of Lady Olwen's outburst, Jehan tried to calm her, pressing her back against the pillows, but the sick woman would have none of it. Over and over, she begged Jehan's silence, weeping uncontrollably. In her agitation and pain-wracked anxiety, she did not see the smoldering resentment cross the other's face, replaced finally by a blank stony expression. Glancing down at the clawlike hand grasping hers, Jehan recoiled in distaste.

"What right have you to ask that of me?" she spat in cold, deliberate tones. "Every child should know who gave him life."

"Nay, my lady, not when he's the bastard of Roger de Mortimer. 'Tis a stigma he would bear all his life. I don't know why the baron wishes to have the boy with him, but 'tis unholy . . . He's your son too—try to love him a little . . . protect him . . ." She drew a shuddering breath, never taking her eyes from Jehan. Braided red hair glinting in the candlelight and her slender body stiff with angry indignation, the younger woman broke free from Lady Olwen's grip. Avoiding the beseeching look, Jehan turned away, refusing to utter the words Lady Olwen yearned to hear.

She was furious at her own blind stupidity. Why had she not guessed that the mysterious young page Roger's people had spoken of with such derision was her son. Berthe, repeating gossip told her by de Mortimer's body servant, had mentioned the favors shown a young Welsh page and the jealousy and hatred it had caused among all the others in service to the baron. Roger had never brought him to the manor, and since the subject was of little interest to her, she had soon thrust it from her mind. And now that she knew, did she truly care what happened to Bleddyn? The tall boy whose green eyes blazed with mocking dislike was not the babe she had borne or held in her arms. He was a stranger to her, while Roger . . . Oh, sweet Virgin, Roger was all that was left to her. Nearly three years she had existed without him, only the belief that he would someday return sustaining her. How difficult it was for her only she would ever know—but her waiting would soon end, for Jehan was convinced that Roger would send for her. What would Bleddyn matter then! Damn them all, she swore, her face set with cold, implacable rage.

"What have you done to my aunt?" The boy's frightened voice broke into Jehan's musings. She glared at him with annoyance, but he pushed past her, seeing only the parchmentlike pallor on Lady Olwen's tear-streaked face. The snowdrops he had found at the forest's edge and picked for her were scattered on the chamber's floor. Kneeling by her chair, he buried his face in her lap. With a trembling hand, Lady Olwen gently smoothed the tangled hair back from the wide forehead. He lifted his head, searching her face for reassurance, the slanted green eyes full of tears.

"I'm all right, Bleddyn-bach." She smiled at his anxious young face. "Naught's happened to me . . . Lady Jehan has been telling me wonderful stories of the queen . . ." and she held the boy close, kissing him as she calmed his fears. A cheek resting against Bleddyn's auburn hair, her eyes sought Jehan's, pleading. Jehan had seen Bleddyn's face suffused with love. So he would have loved me, she thought bitterly, had he not been taken from me. Reaching for Lady Olwen's hand, she murmured softly, "I promise."

Chapter 14

Riding beside Robert through the forested land about the manor house, Kilburn breathed deeply of the warm, moist odor of awakened earth. Between the branches of young-leaved trees, glimpses of the deep blue afternoon sky seemed to intensify the brilliance of the beauty all about them. Neither man spoke, relishing the eternal, unchanging tranquillity of the small pastoral holding which drew them so strongly each time they journeyed south. Kilburn realized with wonder that it already was a month past since they had joined the barons at Westminster for a meeting of Parliament. Since then, summer had spread itself almost unnoticed over a countryside suddenly alive with wildflowers and blossoming hedges, while fields and meadows lay greening in the soft, clear air. He felt far removed from the seemingly endless days of arguing and bickering which had ensued.

Though the meetings were called to discuss the increasingly troublesome unrest in Gascony and the worsening relations with France, he had been astonished at how many of his peers shared his concern over the Despensers. Since Lancaster's death, they had ridden the crest of the king's pleasure. The elder Despenser, created the earl of Winchester by a fawning Edward, had been chief spokesman for his king during the sessions, and few men dared to oppose his will. It was quite another matter outside the council chamber where both father and son were bitterly denounced. De Mortimer's outrageous escape from the Tower the year before was also still a major topic of conversation. There were barons who viewed it as a dangerous matter that Wigmore should once more be at liberty, allowing himself the luxury of creating mischief out of reach of English law. Arundel had laughed heartily, delighted by the foolhardy and desperate gesture, but Pembroke urged caution, reminding them that his acceptance at the French court could only have been allowed through the intercession of someone held in high regard by King Charles. Many minds flew to Isabella, but no one spoke her name.

Sensing his rider's distraction, Kilburn's large black stallion quickened his pace. A less firm hand on the rein would have allowed the animal to leap through the underbrush to gallop where the powerful legs would take it. An arrogant toss of the head set the bridle adornments to sing out his displeasure, drawing Kilburn from his silent musing. He laughed, knowing what his mount wanted. He patted the gleaming satin-smooth neck with a gauntleted hand.

"Aye, laddie, 'tis true that you've not had your run today . . ." and he gave spur to the huge destrier. Before a startled Robert knew what had happened, the earl's steed sprang eagerly forward, thundering down the narrow forest path. They emerged without warning into a sunlit meadow lying golden beneath the summer sky. Blowing heavily, the animal came to a shuddering halt, and his master waited for his brother-in-law to catch up with him. The younger man's blue eyes sparkled with merriment as he reined back sharply, for Kilburn's stallion was still restive.

"Jamie, whatever came over you to go charging through the trees like a fair loonie? I thought 'twas only my folly," and Robert laughed, remembering an earlier time.

The earl's bright hair was ruffled by the wind and his lean features had relaxed their grim expression.

" 'Tis possible to feel like a youth again at times, particularly when life seems especially dear." He laughed lightly, still exhilarated by the wild ride. Robert nodded his understanding.

"Aye, I can agree to that. 'Tis been a long time since I've had such a feeling of peace and safety. It seems a miracle that the border is still secure." He stood up in his stirrups, stretching his legs. The pleasant sound of a wood dove reached his ears and he sighed. "Do you think there'll be trouble with France over Aquitaine? Edward seems determined not to swear fealty to the French king this time."

"I have no doubt that Pembroke will manage to soothe the royal feelings of King Charles. It was to be expected that he would be sent to France. He's the best man to be chosen for this mission." Kilburn wiped his face with the sleeve of his tunic. The sun's rays seemed uncommonly warm, and the riders returned to the cooler shadows of the forest. "He had looked forward to spending a few idle days at Hertford Castle with us. 'Tis a pity, for he's had scant time for himself in the last year. Gillian is disappointed—she seems to have found a particular place in his heart. But I have no doubt that the countess will welcome her visit. I understand they find each other much to their liking."

"Will Alain be there, or did the earl take him along to France?"

Kilburn shook his head. "He's done well in the year that he's been in service with Aymer, but the earl felt he was too young for the rigors of such a journey. I was rather surprised that Gillian agreed to come with us, but we've not been parted since she returned to me. And seeing Alain again is all she talked of as we came down from Glairn. He's always been her favorite."

As he spoke, Kilburn glanced quickly at Robert, almost afraid of his reply, but the other only smiled and remained silent. There's always one who's special, isn't there, the younger man thought, seeing the earl's face cloud over for a moment. 'Tis not only Maddie's death which haunts him. No great wisdom was needed to see that whatever had happened between his sister and her lord prior to their reunion had changed them both. The brightness of the day seemed to have lessened as the sun disappeared without warning behind a cloud and they rode on without further speech. The house emerged warm and mellow out of the trees as they reached the road leading to the arched gate beyond the narrow moat.

"My lord," a voice called urgently and they turned to see a messenger approach them, the sound of his horse's hooves muffled by the soft earth of the pathway. He swayed in the high-cantled saddle, dusty and disheveled from his obviously long journey. They were astonished to see he wore the queen's livery, and Kilburn recognized him as a member of Isabella's household. Something in the flushed young face filled him with a sense of foreboding.

"I bring news, my lord. The earl of Pembroke . . ." The voice faltered. It was common knowledge that the earl of Glairn was a staunch ally, and the messenger quailed at his look.

"God's blood, young sir, what of the earl?"

"Dead, my lord! In France!" The words were blurted out and hung in the sudden stillness. Kilburn's face blanched, the air darkening about him. He had not heard properly.

"Dead? 'Tis not possible! I saw him just before he left."

The fleur-de-lis on the equerry's wrinkled surcoat gleamed dully in the late afternoon sun as he slipped a rolled parchment from the leather pouch suspended from his shoulder.

"Her grace, the queen, bade me deliver this into your hands."

He thrust the roll at Kilburn, who looked at it mutely, not moving. Robert took the parchment from the messenger, ordering him to the manor for a brief rest and some food, for it was obvious that there were others to be notified as well. For the young man it was a journey not yet ended. Robert broke the seal and unrolled the parchment, scanning it quickly, for the message was short.

"Jamie, 'tis terrible news! Shall I read you what it says?"

Kilburn nodded, not daring to speak. Sweet Jesù—

not Pembroke! Not the man who had been such a close and true friend over the years. He looked at Robert, trying to read the truth of Pembroke's death in his face, praying that it was all a ridiculous joke.

"A sudden fever, 'tis said! I can't believe that's all there was to it."

Kilburn sat by the hearth in their bedchamber, a goblet of wine clutched in his hand, forgotten. Gillian stood behind him, looking down at his bent head. She touched his shoulder gently, sharing his pain.

"My darling, I know. He was my friend too."

" 'Tis not only my loss I think of, lovedy. I think of all he still meant to do. I can't help but wonder at how relieved the Despensers must feel, now that the king's conscience is gone." His voice shook with bitterness. "The equerry said that when Edward received the news, he sent his own confessor to tell the countess. Had he only shown such solicitude when Aymer was still alive."

Gillian knelt before him, her large eyes filled with concern over the anguish tearing at his soul. Her face was ashen and drawn.

"Jamie, we should go to Lady Marie as soon as we can. It must be terrible for her . . . she loved him so deeply."

"Did she?" He had never truly known what the quiet young countess thought of her lord. She had always seemed such a child to him. But Gillian would have sensed the truth of it. He drew her into his arms, grateful that he could share the pain of this loss with her.

"Aye, I suppose she did, though the Virgin knows she had precious little time with him."

"It was enough for her to know that she loved him. He was a rare man."

Her arms tightened about him as he suddenly buried his head in her breasts, unable to keep his grief to himself any longer. All the years of their friendship crowded in about him, pressing him down with memories now too painful and poignant to bear.

Later, when she had persuaded him to come to bed, Gillian lay holding him in her arms. Though she too mourned an old friend's death, her mind turned back to other nights in what seemed to her now another life. So had she lain, comforting him when he had discovered Hugh's death, the childhood friend he had loved so well and lost at Bannockburn, and so she had tried to comfort him at Graeme's death. Then she remembered that there had been no one to comfort him in his grief over his dead child, and her own tears began to flow as the sense of her failure rose bitterly to haunt her.

Hertford Castle was shrouded in an unearthly stillness as Kilburn's party rode across the lowered drawbridge through the double gate lit by flaring torches which crackled and sparked in the rising wind. The castle steward, obviously still shaken by the news of his lord's death, was waiting silently for the earl and his lady as they entered the stone-flagged hallway of the central keep. Preceded by a young retainer lighting their way, he personally led them to the chamber which had been prepared for them. Gillian looked with concern at Kilburn as they ascended the steep winding stairs to the next floor, but his face was closed and unreadable, set into grim, forbidding lines. He had scarcely spoken on the journey from Hurley, and when he did, it was obvious that he had turned inward. It was a trait she never had accustomed herself to, for at those times he would shut her out, and she could not reach him.

The chamber was small and dark with only a tiny hearth set into the stone wall. A narrow window looked out onto the inner bailey and, peering through the aperture, she could see dimly the figure of a solitary guard walk the battlements opposite as he passed a lighted tower entrance. She turned from the window as Hal entered the chamber, bringing his lord's shield and helm, followed by servants carrying their baggage. With a sudden, burning ache, she noticed the blue and white striped badges on their livery. How often had she seen those arms fly from Glairn's battlements when Aymer de Valence had come to see them!

A small figure appeared suddenly in the open doorway, hesitating at the sight of the earl's still figure standing broodingly by the hearth.

"Sweetheart . . ." Gillian called softly, and her son's long hazel eyes turned toward his mother. Alain was very pale and she could see traces of tears on the fine, sensitive face. "We've come to take you home," she told him as he came into her embrace, his thin young arms circling her waist, his head burrowing tightly into her body. How tall he's grown, she thought, a sense of joy at seeing him sweeping over her in spite of her grief.

"Mama, they say that Uncle Aymer's dead!"

The words were muffled and she felt him tremble. Smoothing back the tumbled chestnut hair from the pale forehead with a loving hand, she said, "Aye, my darling, we know. 'Tis a dreadful thing, but one we must face together." She looked over his head to where Jamie still stood, and saw that his gaze was resting blindly on Alain.

"How is Lady Marie?"

As the countess's page, Alain would know how she fared. The boy shook his head, wiping his eyes with a bare hand.

"I don't know. I've not seen her since the news of Uncle Aymer arrived. Only Lady de Marc and the priest have been in attendance."

He glanced fearfully at his father, aware of the strangeness of his demeanor. He seemed to have taken no notice of him at all. Gillian drew away, kissing his child's cheek.

"Then I must go to her. Stay with your father and tell him all that's happened," she told him. The boy clung to his mother's hand, but she whispered encouragingly to him. As she opened the chamber door, Gillian saw James turn and hold out his arms. As he embraced his son, she knew with a sense of relief that he had returned to them.

The Abbey was ablaze from the light of thousands of candles, while the long windows illuminated the high soaring arches with suffused summer brightness. Since dawn, mourners had come to pray, slowly filling the long benches placed in the nave for them. The coffin containing Pembroke's body rested on a high catafalque before the high altar, covered with a heavy silk banner adorned with the arms of the de Valence family. His shield and the long sword which had served its master so well and now would forever rest in its scabbard was placed atop the bier.

Stunned by her husband's sudden death but still aware of his standing among the peers of the realm, the countess of Pembroke had requested the royal council to name the earl's burial place. To no one's surprise, they had chosen the Abbey at Westminster, for was he not kin to the royal family and cousin to the king? So Pembroke's body had been brought to the Abbey after a slow journey from London the day before. Clad in hauberks and surcoats emblazoned with their family arms, his kinsmen, John de Warenne, Thomas of Norfolk, and Edmund of Kent, as well as Edmund Fitzalan and James Kilburn, had kept vigil by the bier throughout the night while monks chanted the endless prayers commending the dead man's soul to heaven. And while the earls silently stood watch, the tall white candles at each corner of the catafalque flickered in golden loneliness.

Seated now in one of the chairs placed near the altar for the barons of the realm, Kilburn's eyes burned with fatigue. The past month had been a kaleidoscope of sounds and shapes which his dazed emotions refused to accept. His mind kept returning to the sight of Lady Marie's naked face, stripped finally of its contained, frozen grief, showing frustrated anger when she was forbidden to look for a last time on her dead lord's face, for his coffin was sealed in France. It had been a bitter moment for them all, for the reality of Pembroke's death had finally broken through the defenses they had all raised against the truth. He would never forget the moment when Geoffrey, unearthly pale and frighteningly gaunt, had knelt before Marie de Valence and released himself from his pledge to remain at his lord's side until they had once more returned home. Though having lived the longest with his knowledge, Geoffrey was still bewildered, railing against God and all the saints for having allowed the earl to die. He would not speak of Pembroke's death, evading any attempts to discuss the final days of his lord's life.

A sudden stir brought Kilburn's attention to the present and he found that Edmund Fitzalan had slipped into the red velvet-cushioned chair to his left. Acknowledging each other's presence with silent nods, they both looked intently at the procession making its way down the center aisle. The young countess, looking somehow too frail to bear her grief, was flanked by the earl of Surrey and the king's young half-brother, Edmund of Kent. He kept an uneasy eye on his cousin's widow, fearing no doubt that some hysteria would erupt. It was an unnecessary fear, for while distraught, she had not shed one tear over her lord's death. Alain had been chosen to carry the cushion holding the countess's illuminated breviary, and he carried himself straight and tall with the poise and presence befitting an earl's son.

"Young Alain looks indeed regal, James," Arundel murmured to him. "My small Alianor will certainly be smitten with him when they meet at Yuletide!"

"He's a good lad for sure," James replied, pleased at Edmund's observation. "I intend to take him back to Glairn and keep him with me for his training. This business has shaken him, for he regarded Aymer as a second father."

" 'Tis true . . . in some ways I think we all did. He was so strong and convinced of the rightness of his beliefs. How he despaired of me at times!" Arundel smothered a laugh, for his merry nature was difficult to quell. "Regard John . . . a solemn occasion suits his moroseness. I've never seen a man relish a funeral more than Surrey—he fair wallows in it." James stifled a smile at Edmund's apt description of his brother-in-law but sobered as Lady Marie lifted her head toward the catafalque, swaying suddenly as if the sight was too much for her. Kent patted her thin hand plucking nervously at the carved arm of her chair and she smiled wanly at him.

James caught sight of Gillian, seated behind the countess, a white-faced Geoffrey beside her. Sweet Jesu, the boy is naught but skin and bones, James realized with a shock, seeing the large gray eyes glow with an unnatural brightness beneath a tangle of unbrushed dark hair. He'll burn himself out if he's not careful, he thought and wondered what Geoffrey would do now that his master was gone. There was no way of knowing, since he was erratic and unpredictable, and Pembroke had been his only anchor.

"Your lady grows ever more beautiful, James! It always takes my breath away when I see her again. You're a fortunate man." Arundel's voice was full of admiration, for the sight of Gillian's lovely features and softly rounded figure was a pleasure he never tired of.

Aye, James agreed, he was indeed fortunate. Gillian was totally his again. Though it had taken time and patience to come to terms with the changes their long separation had wrought in both of them, their love was strong and had survived. De Mortimer was never mentioned between them, but he was there all the same, existing in the invisible scars Gillian would always carry, and in the knot of cold hatred which lay locked away in his own soul.

"The king," Edmund hissed and they rose with all the others as Edward, accompanied by a visibly shaken Isabella, entered, walking slowly toward the altar. The queen's hand rested lightly on her royal husband's arm while she stared fixedly at the bier before her. The two Despensers followed closely and, at their passing, the atmosphere grew hostile, but neither acknowledged the animosity directed at them.

Hypocrites! James thought, watching them take seats flanking the royal couple.

"Poor Isabella," Arundel murmured. "She's lost the only friend she's ever had at court."

They both watched her as she knelt beside the king, her head bent in prayer. There was a vulnerability to her pose which brought to James's mind the first time he had seen her twelve years earlier. Abandoned at Tynemouth Castle to the mercies of unfriendly barons by an Edward fully aware that she carried his child, she had been lost and frightened until Pembroke came to her aid, assuring her of his protection. Edmund was right—Aymer had proven to be a true friend, demanding nothing from her for that friendship.

James closed his eyes, blocking out the sight of those who had come to mourn and wishing again that it would prove a nightmare from which he would soon awaken. As if she fathomed his thoughts, Gillian sought out her lord from among the gathering of barons. In that instant, their souls touched and the lights seemed to dim, the low murmuring about them receding. Lovedy, 'tis unbearable . . . all of it, he cried mutely.

I am with you, my darling. You are not alone, and I share your pain. The answer came from her heart, and he felt a comforting warmth fill the aching emptiness within him.

Geoffrey was gone and no one had seen him leave. His meagre possessions were still in place in the tiny, monkish chamber he occupied in the Pembroke palace on Flete Street. Though he had attended the funeral feast in the Hall the day before, so remote and shut away had he been that even Gillian hesitated to approach him. The Hall, which hours earlier had echoed with the strident sound of voices, stood shorn of its guests. The remains of the feast still lay scattered on the floor, fought over by the unleashed dogs, neglected in the search for Geoffrey.

"He's nowhere to be found." James's voice was sharp with irritation as he looked at Gillian's worried face. He had found her in the earl's council chamber, sitting opposite Pembroke's empty chair.

"I fear for him, Jamie, for I feel he doesn't even know what he's doing." She wiped her eyes with a handkerchief and rose to stand by Kilburn. "I searched his room this morning and found this." She thrust a small blue velvet casket into her husband's hands. He opened the box, looking into it curiously. A chain lay coiled inside, exquisitely wrought of heavy gold, each link etched with the de Valence cipher.

"It belonged to Aymer—I've often seen him wear it," he exclaimed. "I wonder why it is in Geoffrey's possession?"

"Because I gave it to him." Lady Marie, standing in the doorway, had overheard him. Joining Gillian and Kilburn, she drew out the chain, and they stared at the gleaming links as she held it before them. "My lord has often said that of all which came into his possession upon his father's death, this chain holds the greatest value to him. It was presented to William de Valence by his brother, King Henry of England, when he was created earl of Pembroke. It is my lord's dearest wish that it one day be passed on to a child of his flesh." Her voice faltered. It

389

was still difficult to remember he was gone. "Since that will never be, I know that he would be pleased it be given into Master Harron's keeping, for the earl regarded him with as much love as he would have held for his own son."

Gillian's tear-filled eyes met Kilburn's and she turned away, unable to reply.

"No wonder he bolted!" James said quietly. It was an overwhelming gift and a gesture of extreme sacrifice and unusual understanding of the human spirit from one as young as the countess.

"He wept." The childish voice was strangely flat and expressionless. "I've not seen him since."

"I think I know where he's gone. There's but one place he would seek consolation," James told the two women. He felt pity for Geoffrey, but it was mixed with anger for having placed an added burden of worry not only on Gillian but the young countess, who could bear little more.

A short time later, surrounded by a press of people surging restlessly forward, Kilburn and his squire passed through the large open gate, entering the city of London without fanfare, their cloaks masking their identities. A young boy, burdened down by two wicker baskets filled with newly baked loaves of bread, directed them down a twisting, narrow lane reeking with the stench of rotting garbage and human excrement. At times little light passed between the tops of the houses lining both sides of the street, their upper stories jutting out so far that they almost met. The sun was a pleasant sight as they emerged into a small square dominated by an unassuming, obviously old church, its weathered gray stones covered with lichen. Dismounting at the side porch, they tethered their horses besides Geoffrey's. None of the folk tending their stalls set up in the square, nor those who had come to buy paid any attention either to the tall man with a dark cloak partially hiding a scarlet surcoat nor his auburn-haired squire standing beside his lord's black stallion. Leaving Hal to tend the horses, Kilburn entered the dark sanctuary of the church. There was a chill to the air, and the flickering candles at the small altar and before the figures of the Virgin and several saints were its only illumination save for a shaft of light which streamed through a narrow window set high in the wall. It fell on a crucifix, the like of which James had never seen. Carved from a single piece of wood, the agonized figure of Christ writhed eternally in pain while his lowered head seemed to move beneath a lifelike crown of thorns. Transfixed by the hypnotic effect of the cross caught in the beam of golden sunlight, James did not at first see the dim figure huddled in the corner of a bench. Wrapped in his cloak as if seeking warmth, Geoffrey sat white-faced and numb. He did not look up as the earl joined him.

"Are you all right, Geoffrey?" James asked, raking the wretched face with anxious eyes. Getting no reply, he began to speak quietly to the young man, never sure if he heard one word.

"Your actions have caused everyone great anxiety, and I confess that I can find little excuse for your running away. We have all suffered a loss through Aymer's death, and in a way, I suppose you have been closest to that loss. There's naught I can say to comfort you, I know, for whether real or imagined, your pain is your own. I can't feel it, although 'tis there, nor are you able to feel mine." He was putting it badly, disconcerted by Geoffrey's apparent unawareness of his presence. The younger man had not moved since James joined him. "To tell you now that in time it will pass and subside will bring you little peace. You're not alone in feeling as you do. Others have suffered and survived. 'Tis not your first loss and neither will it be your last."

"I've tried to pray, but I can't. I can't trust in a God who would allow my lord to be murdered." The words were whispered in an anguished wail. Geoffrey turned his face from Kilburn's shocked gaze.

"Murdered?"

"Aye, Jamie—they let him die, and I swear 'twas the hand of Roger de Mortimer which wrought the deed, though naught can be proved."

"You're talking daft, Geoff—'tis true Roger is in France, but he'd have no reason to want Pembroke dead." Kilburn felt cold. "Besides, Aymer died of a fever."

Geoffrey laughed harshly, his eyes dark with pain.

" 'Tis what's been claimed—he'd not been well for quite some time, so what better reason would there be than a chill which caused a fever. Nay, Jamie—I was with him when he died—'twas not natural!" His voice broke and he clutched Kilburn's arm, desperate now to share the knowledge he had kept to himself all these weeks. The words poured from him, spilling over each other in an unintelligible tangle. Kilburn looked about him helplessly and could almost believe that the head of the crucified Christ had lifted and the wooden eyes were contemplating them both.

"This is no place for what we must discuss," the earl muttered and insisted that Geoffrey join him in the sane brightness of day. They found a bench in the small yard behind the church, and for a few moments sat listening to the market's muted sounds. Kilburn watched a large bee hover over a small unfamiliar bush afire with red-petaled flowers. It all seemed so humdrum that Geoffrey's accusation seemed absurd.

"You called me daft, Jamie, yet have no knowledge of the truth." Breaking into the peaceful silence, Geoffrey's voice was suddenly calm as he faced his brother-in-law. "The journey was no different from any of the others we have made through the years I was with my lord. But this time, rather than traveling straight to Paris, the earl visited one of the countess's holdings near a town called Saint-Riquier where he decided to spend the night. It had been a long road, and he seemed exceptionally weary to me, but was in good spirits." The gray eyes were suddenly full of pain. "He ate little—some broth and I think a roasted fowl was placed before him . . . it matters naught how much he ate—but just as he was finished, the steward pressed a goblet of wine into his hand, insisting that it was the finest ever stocked by the manor. My lord laughed, and as he drank from the goblet, said he would be the judge of it. A few minutes later he rose from his chair without speaking and began to walk toward the door."

Geoffrey shook with the memory of those few minutes when his world had come crashing down about him. "They say it was a fever took my lord's life—what fever strikes a man down in the midst of his people, his face purple, choking and gasping for air? He was murdered! Poisoned—I swear it to you!" He could still feel Pembroke's hand on his arm groping desperately for support and then himself being pulled to his knees as the stricken man sank to the floor while his servants stood about too frightened to call for help. "He died there in my arms, unshriven—his eyes staring into mine. Oh sweet Jesù— had I not seen him die!" Geoffrey cried, his hands pressed to either side of his head, blind with grief. "I've had no life save with my lord all these years and wanted no other. He alone understood me and never called me fool. And now he's gone and I swear 'twas unnatural. He was murdered . . . poisoned! Yet you refuse to believe me—I can see it on your face. Aye, and you also wonder at the love I held for him . . ." His eyes glittered feverishly as he searched Kilburn's face. "I loved him, Jamie!" It was an admission wrung from the depths of his soul.

"I know, Geoff, I know." James saw how deeply etched the thin face was with the emotions Geoffrey had held to himself for so long. "I loved him too."

"All the years I spent with him . . . I was safe— protected from what I did not wish to know. I never questioned his decisions. There was no need, for he was the wisest of men."

"He was human, Geoffrey, and he had faults, but you loved him. You served him with your heart and supported him with your devotion when he despaired. No man could wish to have a better friend then you were to him, and as he was, in his way, to you. But don't misread that love, lad. There are all kinds of love." James paused, wondering how far he could go, for the younger man was truly an innocent, with no true knowledge of the complexities of human emotions. If only his father had allowed him to take holy orders, he might have been spared his agonies! The guilty thought came unbidden, and he felt instant remorse. "Let no one tell you that your love was wrong, but 'tis something you must put behind you, for you've your own life to lead now."

"My existence is an absurdity . . . I've no life save with the earl. I realized it when the countess gave my lord's chain to me . . . there's naught left for me." He was resigned to it.

"By the wounds of Christ, Geoffrey—stop wallowing in self-pity!"

The words lashed out harsh and cutting. The younger man recoiled in shock at the impatience in Kilburn's voice.

"You think you're the only one who mourns? The only one who feels pain? Why can't you see what a good thing it was that you were with Aymer when he died, for he did not die among strangers but in the arms of one who loved him. Death is always worse for those who are left behind than for those who die. 'Tis the living who must feel the pain of loss and bear the emptiness until finally all that's left are memories."

James's eyes burned with unshed tears as he revealed his own anguish. "Do you think I can ever forget my first wife? Or not remember the futile pain within me her death caused? I've lived with the guilt of Hugh Martleigh's sacrifice each day since Bannockburn, though his death was honorable. How often is it that the memory of my sweet Maddie's face returns to haunt me. Geoffrey, I loved them all and will never forget them, but life endures."

He stopped talking as Geoffrey put his head in his hands, unable to stem his frustration. James saw the lowered head with the dark hair growing childlike on the slender neck and ached with compassion at the young man's unworldly vulnerability.

"I'm sorry, Jamie. I've listened to all you've said, but just now it makes litttle sense to me. All I feel is a great hollow pain in the very center of myself. I've never felt such pain. And the only part of my lord left to me is a gold chain which should have belonged to his son."

"The son he'll never have, Geoff. Think of his Marie who he left behind—she's lost him, too, and in a way you can't fathom. You both loved him, and with her gift, she's reaching out a hand to you. Grasp it, for 'tis she who needs you now. You knew him best, and that which you knew is what you can give to her."

It was all he could say as he slowly reached out his hand and drew it over the young man's dark hair, brushing the damp strands back from the pale forehead as if he were a child. For the first time since he had found him, the wild, lost expression in Geoffrey's eyes began to fade and he drew a shuddering breath. Smiling wanly, he grasped his brother-in-law's hand between both of his.

"You have always understood . . . I should have known, for my lord told me often to turn to you should I ever have need of counsel. How wise he was," he murmured. "And yet—there's so much pain to bear!"

"There is always pain. Not always the same kind of pain, I admit, but the heart is never at peace . . . not really. Still, a measure of happiness will come again, in time. Allow it to come."

"There's so much I still don't understand."

"Don't try, Geoffrey, for it would drive you mad."

"I will tend to my lord's estates myself."

Marie de Valence spoke in a voice rigid with determination. Her words came as a surprise to them all, for she looked very childlike sitting in the earl's chair. Her small back stiff and thin hands clutching the arm rests, she had listened to James Kilburn voice his concern over her future welfare.

Her statement caused him to protest.

" 'Twill be an enormous task for you, countess. There are your lord's other heirs to consider."

"The consideration has been made, and we are in accord." Terse and to the point, Lady Marie made it clear that she did not require any assistance where none had been requested.

"Allay your concern, brother. My lady will not be alone in her battle to retain her lord's estates. I will remain with her for as long as she has need of me." Geoffrey stood suddenly beside the countess's chair. "I've already been in touch with the earl's nephew and his two nieces, and a meeting is planned as soon as possible to prove his will."

"He named me executor and I will do naught to shatter the faith he placed in me." Lady Marie's meaning was clear and James saw that she would find any further offer of advice an interference. It was no secret that she was already fending off vultures such as the Despensers from looting her dead lord's holdings and estates. "And I have no fear that I cannot overcome any obstacles as long as Master Harron remains by me."

James's gaze rested on Geoffrey's face and the gray eyes met his without flinching, clear and steady. The pain and bewilderment that had inhabited his soul was gone, vanquished by the eagerness with which Lady Marie accepted his decision to stay by her side. She had wept for the first time since learning of Pembroke's death, tears streaming down her face as she clung to him, drawing from him the strength she needed to endure the pain of loss still within her. They had sat together in Pembroke's study, with only the light of a single candle to illuminate their faces, a frightened girl too young to be deemed the widowed dowager countess of Pembroke, and the earl's brilliant secretary, whose handsome, ascetic face already mirrored an awakening devotion for his dead master's wife. Unheeded tears glistening on her white cheeks, Marie had listened to Geoffrey speak of Aymer de Valence, sharing with her the memories and images of the husband she had known too short a time. So they were bound together by their love for a man who would remain alive to them as long as they remembered him.

Although James had counseled Geoffrey that life should resume its normal course, he found it simpler for a few months following his return north to retreat with Gillian into a false state of tranquil serenity. The border remained quiet, the harvest was adequate, and naught occurred to unduly disturb their peaceful life. Alain began his training under the stern eye of Simon Jardine, who found the boy as difficult a student of the martial arts as his father had been before him. Despite the boy's apparent lack of interest, Sir Simon never slowed the pace of his instruction, tempering his teaching with good-humored patience.

At Yuletide, the earl of Arundel, accompanied by his lady and members of the household, brought his youngest daughter to Glairn for her formal betrothal to Alain Kilburn. Alianor Fitzalan, barely nine years old, proved to be a shy, quiet little maid with dark hair and large black eyes. While studiously ignored by her future husband, she was soon made one of their own by the other Kilburn children. It was a merry company who celebrated Twelfth Night in the Great Hall of Glairn, and the thick stone walls rang with the excited shouts of the children as Hal Jardine held aloft the golden bean found in his piece of the special cake stuffed with almonds, raisins, citrons, and other glazed fruit. Playing his dulcimer, he led the parade of children around the Great Hall, a paper crown perched crookedly atop his auburn curls as befitted the King of Revels. The musicians, seated in the high gallery opposite the dais, picked up the merry air Hal was playing, and soon all were marking time to its infectious beat.

"How quickly time passes," Gillian murmured wistfully. Reaching for Jamie's hand, she held it against her cheek in an affectionate gesture. Throughout the merriment, he had seemed oddly silent and distracted. Turning toward her, he smiled at her pensive face. He loved her more deeply than he had thought possible, and the realization brought his thoughts back from their early days together when naught had mattered to him save possessing her:

" 'Tis exactly what I've been thinking." He sighed. Soon they would have to part with Margaret, for her betrothal was to be held in the spring.

Sharing the thought, they watched their eldest daughter's laughing face as she coaxed Alianor to join her in a dance. Even Alain had thawed sufficiently to caper wildly with Tom and Eilys Fitzhugh's young daughter Blanche, while her twin brother Robert, in company with young Hugh, had shy Jennifer in tow.

"When Margaret leaves us, we'll still have the others," Gillian said in a vain attempt to reassure them both. "And she'll only stay with the Deveron family for a year." A feeling of depression gripped her—if only she could hold back the encroaching years. Their peaceful life made her uneasy, for just so was there an unearthly stillness before the breaking of a storm.

"Long faces at the revels are not allowed, my lady!" Arundel's blue eyes twinkled as his hand beat the table to the music's rhythm. " 'Tis a time for merriment, where all things are allowed." Turning toward her, he suddenly kissed a startled Gillian hard on the lips. "Take no offense, James—'tis what I've wanted to do since I first saw your lady. And you've leave to do the same to mine!" He roared with laughter as his wife leaned forward to frown at his high spirits. "I'm afraid there are times Alice displays her brother's lack of humor!" He sobered abruptly, crumbling the richly iced cake between his fingers. "Speaking of Surrey, I hear that John is to accompany Kent to Aquitaine with an armed force, should there be fighting."

"There's none among us who has the diplomatic skill or tact that Pembroke had," James replied.

"You're wrong! There's one, I warrant, who would do quite well." Edmund lowered his voice conspiratorially.

"My lord, you speak out of turn!" Lady Alice cautioned her husband sharply, her pale, rather plain face showing alarm. Fascinated by what was happening, Gillian looked from one to the other.

"Nonsense, Alice. I'm only repeating a remark my lord Bishop Orleton happened to make regarding the queen."

"The queen?" Gillian was startled. What had Isabella to do with all of this?

"Everyone is speaking of how the Despensers have reduced her to virtual prisoner status. 'Tis difficult to believe that her dower properties have been denied her, while she must make do with a pension whose sum is determined by Nephew Hugh. And now she must even suffer his wife as her constant companion." Arundel chuckled. "I know I shouldn't speak so of a family bound to us through marriage—but politics have naught to do with personal attachments—or so I've been telling myself. But I think both Hughs err in their treatment of Isabella. She is still the sister of King Charles of France. And Adam Orleton remarked that it would certainly be an obvious diplomatic advantage for Edward to utilize the queen in settling the problems of Gascony and Aquitaine in his stead."

"Besides ridding himself of a wife who refuses to keep silent any longer on the subject of her lord's favorites." Now that her husband had voiced his thoughts, Lady Alice added her own observations.

Isabella to visit the French court! Gillian suppressed a shudder and the gaiety about her receded as she heard Roger de Mortimer's words echo inside her head. The queen is mine! How cold his voice had been and cruel the pressure of his hand on her throat. Sweet Jesù, would she never be able to forget?

"Nay! She must not go!" The words were blurted out in sudden fear. Gillian rose blindly, her hands at her throat as if attempting to loosen an imaginary hold.

"Heavenly mother! The queen will go to France—and 'twill be a disaster for us all! We can't stop it!" Her eyes were wide, staring out at something she alone could see.

They gaped at her in stunned silence, shocked by her strange behavior and rare vehemence. James, alarmed by Gillian's almost trancelike state, held a goblet of wine to her lips, forcing her to drink. The pressure about her throat eased and she sank down into her chair, willing herself to return to the safety and warmth of the Great Hall. Slowly the color began to return to her face while the wild clamoring within her abated. For a brief moment Gillian met Jamie's eyes and she saw that he knew what had happened to her. She forced a smile, apologizing quietly for her outburst. Impulsively, Arundel kissed her hand, commenting loudly on the splendor of the feast. The guests returned to their food, drink, and private conversations, and gradually the hall began to come to life again. Edmund soon had Gillian laughing over the outrageously slanderous tales he was so fond of telling, while Jamie relaxed, relieved to see that the disturbing moments had passed. Yet the dark spectre of Roger de Mortimer had appeared to sit among them—silent and unwanted.

Chapter 15

1325
Paris

"I vow 'twas a welcome you'd not expected!"

Charles smiled at his sister, seated beside him beneath the blue and gold canopy of France. The long tables of the Great Hall were filled to overflowing with members of the court intermingled with those of Isabella's own household who had accompanied her on her visit of state. It was obvious that the king had spared naught to make this welcoming feast a lavish, memorable one, not only for his sister but for the English ambassadors who had preceded her and were so anxious to begin their negotiations. In the brightness of torches and candles set in golden holders, the bejeweled headdresses and gems worn by the guests glittered their brilliance against a dazzling background of silks, satins, and velvets. While the old palace resounded with happy laughter and gaiety, the bishops of Winchester and Norwich sat morosely contemplating the revels. With private amusement, Charles noted that despite their disapproving looks, they had managed to eat heartily while keeping their goblets well filled.

"Nay, brother—'tis not as if this were my first visit since leaving France, but I think it will be a very special one." Isabella's blue eyes sparkled as her gaze swept over the sea of faces before her, seeking but one.

Accompanied by the earl of Richmond and Henry

de Beaumont, she had ridden into Paris in the midst of a tumultuous welcome by its citizens eager to see the royal sister of France. They were greeted in turn by a radiantly beautiful Isabella. Her heart had beaten wildly as she listened to the excited shouts and cheers of the folk lining the path of the procession as it made its way down the Rue St. Antoine toward the bridge spanning the Seine. Even before the Ile de la Cité was in sight, the great bells of the cathedral of Notre Dame could be heard ringing out joyously. Banners and pennants, gay with bright colors, were everywhere, in doorways, fluttering from small windows set into whitewashed walls, atop stone gateways and the small private residences of wealthy merchants and petty lords, as well as the imposing palaces belonging to high-ranking nobles. The freshness of a spring day washed the scenes unfolding before Isabella with the pastel colors of pure happiness. She was home!

"No man who sees you can understand or sympathize with a husband who is so neglectful and indifferent as 'tis said Edward is of you." Charles spoke with quiet deliberation, his cold blue eyes searching Isabella's face. She smiled, sipping her wine silently.

"I've given up trying to fathom Edward. After all our years together, he's still a stranger."

"We've heard stories."

"I'm sure you have, brother, and most of them true, for the Edward who kneels before you to do homage for his French lands is not the man I call husband—but it somehow matters less, now that I'm home again." Isabella leaned over and touched her brother's hand. It was good to be with him. Younger than she by two years, he had been closest to her in age, and until her marriage, they had been inseparable. As children they had often been taken for twins, so alike in feature were they. And we still mirror each other, she thought proudly, finding Charles's fair handsomeness compelling. Clad totally in white and gold brocade, the king glittered in royal majesty while his sister proved a breathtaking contrast in a black velvet robe heavily embroidered with pearls and gold thread. Though her crown might not sparkle as brightly as the king's, Isabella knew that all men's eyes were drawn to the expanse of milk-white bosom exposed to view by the fashionable low cut of the fitted bodice. With a rare feeling of satisfaction, she smiled grimly to herself. Warning Edward that his penury would find little sympathy with the extravagant French court, she had seen to it that her wardrobe rivaled any court lady's in France! And for once, Edward had listened to her, turning deaf ears against the protests of Winchester and his detested son. She had even managed to escape her lord's niece, that frozen bitch wife of the younger Despenser. Her hand tightened about the stem of the wine goblet, its costly gems biting painfully into her tender skin.

"Your Grace . . ."

The two words, though simply spoken, took on an unexpected eloquence as Isabella heard the longed-for musical voice. She felt her cheeks grow hot as the quickened throb of her heart sent the blood rushing through her veins. She turned to find Roger de Mortimer kneeling before her, resplendent in a knee-length tunic of plum velvet trimmed with a band of gray fur, his sleek dark head bent over her hand. His lips brushed her trembling fingers, lingering perhaps a trifle too long. Afraid to look into his face, she murmured a greeting, scarce knowing what she said. His nearness was reaching out to her, as it always had. She laughed lightly, in an attempt to cover her confusion, and Charles, seeing her unusual agitation, came to her aid.

"Lord de Mortimer has been a most valuable asset to our court, for he is indeed a hawk among our doves."

Isabella's eyes widened at her brother's words, and she finally gazed down at the Marcher baron who still knelt before her on one knee. He was smiling and her heart lurched as she saw how little he had changed, save for a new hardness which sharpened his handsome features. His unquenchable arrogance was apparent in the set of his head and the expression in the bold black eyes.

"His Majesty refers to the hunt, Your Grace. For some unknown reason, I've always shared a rare bond with every hawk I've hunted with."

"'Tis true, Isa," Charles said. "The birds seem to know what he wishes before the prey is even sighted." He laughed. "Our people claim he's kin to the devil!"

"If I were, Sire, I could use my powers to attain that which I desire most." Roger's gaze rested on Isabella's face, his meaning transparent to the brother who loved her.

"I know better than to ask what that might be," Charles retorted in apparent good humor. "But now I will take my sister for a short stroll in her favorite garden."

"You should remain with your guests, brother," Isabella protested, not wanting the moment to end, but allowed him to escort her from the Hall. Roger rose slowly to his feet and watched them leave. He was acutely aware that the king had deliberately cut short the interview for reasons of his own—it did not matter, for the queen was here, within his reach.

Though the garden was small, surrounded on two sides by high walls, it was quiet and serene, with several trees, already gnarled with age, to offer shade in the summer.

"I'd forgotten how isolated this corner of the palace is," Isabella murmured as she seated herself on a marble bench beneath a tree beginning to show its first blossoms. The night air was deceptively mild and the sky filled with stars.

"I think there is much you have forgotten—and remember less." Charles's words were short. He had seen the look which passed between his sister and the Marcher baron and was angered by it. "I allowed Lord de Mortimer at my court because you requested it, Isa—and because he dared defy Edward. 'Tis no secret that I bear little liking for your husband."

Isabella tried vainly to see her brother's face in the light which fell from the long windows of the covered walk leading to the garden. "I know, and am grateful for your help."

"I need not remind you that a scandal of your making will meet with little sympathy. 'Tis to be hoped that you will not use the mission you were sent on to achieve some purpose of your own. I'll not countenance it." The king's voice was cold and his warning well understood by Isabella. How like their father he was, she thought. She would have to be wary of him, for he would weigh her words with his intellect rather than his heart.

"My dear Charles, you need not fear. In all the years of being Edward's queen, I've been watched and spied upon not only by his friends but his enemies as well, hoping that I would indeed commit some folly or indiscretion which could be used against me." Masking her true thoughts, she answered him with scorn. "We are very alike, Charles, not only in feature but in our natures. Like you, I know best how to hate, for 'tis the only emotion I've ever been allowed, and it has had much time and opportunity to grow into maturity." Isabella rose, resentment sweeping over her. How dare he presume to police her actions! "Tomorrow I will stand before you as Isabella, queen of England, but tonight I am still your sister, the Isa of our childhood—and she will not be judged!"

To her horror, she found herself weeping, the years which had separated them seeming to drop away. Charles drew her into his arms as she allowed all the hurt and misery of her life with Edward to spill out. He was no stranger to pain and unhappiness, for he had lived with betrayal and loss for most of his life, but what Isabella told him of the constant humiliation and intrigues of Edward's favorites filled him with sick loathing. Yet, he refused to acknowledge her plight in the life she led as England's queen, fearing she would look upon it as his consent for any revenge she might contemplate against Edward. "With all his faults, Isa, he still gave you children. 'Tis what you were brought to England for," he reminded her. Charles knew his sister well, and was amazed that her patience had lasted this long.

"I know—but with what reluctance he was driven to my bed." She shuddered. "My children are strong and beautiful—yet their father pays little heed to them, preferring the companionship of his courtiers and the barons who pander to his tastes."

A burst of laughter and the high clear voice of the young French queen drifted into the garden. Charles cursed softly under his breath as Isabella moved out of his arms guiltily.

"Damnation, Jeanne is probably coming to join us."

"Please, Charles, I don't want her to see me like this —I've ne'er told anyone. I would not want her burdened with the truth—'tis shameful," Isabella whispered, shrinking into the shadows in an attempt to hide her tear-stained face. "Leave me here . . . I'll be all right." She dried her eyes with a square of silk and watched her brother stride rapidly through the stone arch giving entry to the royal apartments, and disappear.

We are an accursed family, Isabella thought bitterly, for even the happy laugh of Charles's new queen as she greeted her husband could not lighten her mood. Poor Charles—if this girl did not give him a son, then who would inherit the crown of France, she wondered gloomily. Sitting quietly and alone in the secluded serenity of the garden, she felt suddenly as if time had been allowed to stand still.

"I want you, Isabella!"

The words were low but clear and her cheeks flamed beneath the veil covering her face. Kneeling at her devotions in the royal chapel, Isabella had not noticed the presence of anyone else save her old nurse with whom she had been joyously reunited on her arrival in Paris. Mistress Claude, respectful of her place, knelt some distance away from her former nursling. At the sound of de Mortimer's voice, the queen glanced nervously at the old woman, whose eyes were closed in prayer.

"She's quite deaf—or have you forgotten?" Roger sounded amused as he moved closer. He could see the confusion she was vainly trying to hide and resisted the temptation to touch her. The ivory and gold beads slid through her fingers, yet no pious words formed in her mind. How did he know Claude was deaf! Oh, but he was a clever, scheming creature—yet her awareness of him lived and breathed more strongly in her than she had thought possible and she knew it did not matter what he was.

The ecstatic welcome Paris had shown her and the obvious pleasure her brother seemed to find in her company had gone far to salve the pride battered for years by the debasing actions of Edward and his friends. During the weeks following her arrival, the court was caught up in the gaiety of the festivities Charles had planned in her honor. Were it not for the presence of the renegade baron of Wigmore, she would have entered into the excitement and merriment with a happy heart. Though she could feel his dark, passionate gaze follow her every movement, he made no further attempt to approach her. With ill-concealed impatience, she was forced to wait for another opportunity to speak with him. None of her women escaped her tantrums and fits of petty malice as her frustrated desire for him grew even stronger.

"You have lost your wits, my lord de Mortimer . . . If someone should see us . . ." she whispered coldly.

"They would but see two people praying, Isabella." He reached out his hand and covered hers. They felt cold.

" 'Tis difficult to have you so close and yet find you so aloof and distant."

"Aloof and distant?" Isabella raised her head, barely able to see him through her veil. "You jest—'tis you who have shown little interest."

Roger lifted the hand still clutching its beads and pressed his lips to a pulse beating wildly in her white-skinned wrist, betraying her agitation. Prying open her fingers, he took the rosary from her, slipping it into his tunic. His mouth, warmly caressing, kissed the palm of her hand. Isabella stifled a moan, for his touch was unbearable.

"Why do you do this, Roger?" Her voice shook as anger rose within her—anger aimed mainly at herself for having so low a threshold of resistance against him.

"I do it because I must touch you. If I don't, I'll go mad. To see you constantly—know that you are within reach and yet forbidden me . . . 'tis more than I can bear."

"Forbidden?" Her anger fled in the face of his words.

"Yes—forbidden by your brother. You forget that I can only stay here because of his goodwill. 'Twas obvious to me that he disapproves of my even speaking to you. But I could stay away no longer. There are no thoughts in my mind save of you." He caught the sound she made at his words and smiled to himself with satisfaction. A little more wooing and she would be totally ensnared. But he found that he was not quite as in command of himself as he pretended to be. She did distract him. He longed to penetrate the regal, untouchable facade behind which she took refuge. The very thought of leaving her defenseless against his assault on her senses excited him.

"You are indeed mad . . ." Isabella lifted the veil from her face. For the first time, she met his gaze—and knew she was lost. To her own bedazzled eyes, the muted light filtering through the long panels of stained glass bathed him in the colors of enchantment. She looked at his mouth, imagining it covering her own, and grew faint at the thought.

"Isabella!" Roger caught her arm as she swayed, eyes closed in an effort to shut out his face. Mistress Claude rose painfully to her feet, her attention caught by the stirring figures opposite her. The queen's face wore an oddly strained look, and the old woman, suddenly concerned, began to approach her, retreating hastily in the face of de Mortimer's imperious black look.

"There is a small door in the west tower—leading to a flight of stairs—'twill be unlocked." Isabella whispered, drawing away from him. She was pale but in control of herself again.

"When?"

The cool blue gaze slid to the old woman who stood within reach of her voice. Isabella knew that she would have to chance taking her into her confidence, for she could never be able to accomplish it alone.

"Tonight . . . Claude will be at the postern gate . . . Yes, 'tis the best way. Trust her. She'll bring you to me." Her heart was beginning to race again at the thought that they would soon be together. She had committed herself. "After the second watch—no one will be about."

Before Roger could reply, she had risen, her slender back straight and her head held high, the golden circlet on her brow shimmering in the shower of sunlight which streamed through the open door. The narrow staircase leading to the low-ceilinged chapel beneath was shrouded in darkness, for the palace servants had little time to worship save at mass. Without a backward glance, she swept out, the old woman hurrying after her.

Roger stared at the empty doorway with admiration —she had been so glacial that her acquiescence had come as a shock to him. God's blood, she was magnificent! He pulled his gauntlets from his belt as he stepped over the threshold, blinking in the sudden brightness. Tonight! At the thought, he allowed his suppressed hunger for her to flame within him, while a voice inside his head whispered, And now it begins—the adventure he had waited for his entire life.

Isabella's almond-shaped eyes looked almost shyly at him as he walked slowly toward her across the floor, his footsteps muffled by the Oriental carpet spread out over the cold stones. How long had she waited for this moment, she wondered as his hands drew her to him. The pale blond hair cascaded unbound down her back and his slender hand brushed back a silken tendril clinging to the soft cheek, lingering there for a moment. Isabella could not wrench her eyes from his, staring as if hypnotized. Holding her face with both hands, he lowered his dark head and lightly brushed her lips with his, feeling her tremble.

"Roger . . ." she murmured, but could say no more, for his lips took possession of hers, deepening as her mouth opened under his assault and she began to respond to the passion that she felt was rising within him.

She had drawn him from the first with the cold diamondlike quality of her beauty, brittle and unawakened. He sensed instinctively that once aroused, the kindled fire of her sensuality would burn with an icy, searing flame. His hands slid down her slim throat and slowly undid the narrow ribands of her robe. She felt the air chill her flesh as the silken cloth fell away. His gaze moved over her face and throat and she prayed he would not notice the pounding of her heart. Her mind froze and her body stiffened in sudden panic as his hands touched her naked breasts, caressing them gently as she tried to draw away.

"Nay, Roger . . ." It was an entreaty, a plea to save

her from her own emotions. Shaking as if with ague, she laughed brokenly.

"I feel like an untouched maid . . . I've borne four children and yet . . ."

He held her tightly, feeling her softness against his body, and buried his face in the silken mass of her hair.

" 'Tis because you are untouched, my love. You gave your body to your lord, but never yourself. That you will give to me."

He lifted her up in his arms and carried her to the bed while the firelight cast their fused shadows against a wall bare of any hangings save a heavy jeweled crucifix. Isabella lay waiting for him, aware of the cool smoothness of the sheets against her face and the plush richness of the brocaded coverlet where her feet rested against it. The golden tassels of the velvet bed curtains glittered in the room's flickering light and she noticed the deep red folds of the embroidered canopy over her head. Images whirled before her eyes in mad profusion . . . Edward's handsome face when he had lain with her the first time and had given her no love but only pain . . . Piers Gaveston's arrogantly amused eyes mocking her at the coronation, bedecked with the jewels she had brought to England as her dowry . . . her firstborn's wrinkled red face when, exhausted but filled with happiness, she had held him in her arms . . .

And then all thoughts were blotted out as de Mortimer came to her, dark eyes burning with the hunger he had felt first at Tynemouth, so long ago. The untamed, arrogant face, pale skin stretched taut over the high cheekbones, took on a predatory, hawklike look as his mouth regained its possession of her, his hands and tongue discovering the secrets of a body as beautiful as he had imagined it to be. She lay beneath him and found that this was no dutiful, bloodless Edward, but a passionate, violent man whose body demanded a response from her, which she gave him with joyous rapture. Isabella loved, and the wall she had built about herself suddenly crumbled. She gloried in the waves of unbelievable, golden emotion which poured over her, drowning her with their burning, ecstatic violence, and she clung to her lover, tearing his flesh as she discovered a world unknown.

He found her insatiable, passionate, and as demanding as he was himself. Entwined, they lay together in the royal bed, exhausted and still, his hand on her breast. Isabella slept in the serene knowledge that he was with her.

And Roger smiled in the darkness, an exultant smile, devoid of love or tenderness. This night he had won a great victory, and he knew that he held England in his arms.

It was early dawn when Roger left the queen's chamber, silently descending the twisting tower stairs behind a sleepy and disapproving Mistress Claude. Keys to the tower door and to the postern gate lay secure in the small purse attached to his belt. The night had been a revelation to him, and triumphant beyond his wildest dreams. Lying in his arms, her naked body pressed tightly against his, Isabella had recklessly revealed the deep-rooted and hopeless desire never to return to England, to leave Edward to his flatterers and the greedy corruption of the Despensers. Caressing her smooth satin skin with a gentle hand, he quietly dissuaded her from any rashness, reminding her that it was far more satisfying to seek vengeance than to face the frustration of unfulfilled hatred. He had felt her tears as she confessed almost girlishly that she had wanted him from the first time she had ever seen him, but that his unbridled arrogance and wildness had frightened her. Roger did not reply, wisely stifling the cruel sarcasm which would have destroyed what he had just gained. He merely kissed her until she trembled with her newly awakened passion, drawing him down to a body that seemed to have been created for his use.

Striding through the garden in the growing light, he knew that he could return to her as often as he wished, for she was caught by violent emotions she had not dreamed existed. Because of all the tales he had heard of her coldness, the uncontrollable tempers and cruelty she inflicted on those about her, he was amazed to find her astonishingly naive and innocent.

411

She had begged him to move into the palace, but he refused, telling her he could not accept her brother's hospitality beyond that which had already been given him. It was too soon to make her completely dependent upon him, and besides, he preferred the privacy of his own home to that of the rambling corridors and overpopulated chambers of the royal palace. He had rented a small dwelling just large enough to house himself, Emrys, and a cook who, for lodging and a few coins, prepared indifferent meals for them. The house stood unpretentiously in a quiet street between the Rue St. Antoine and the river, and was a place not to be shared by anyone save the harper, who understood his rapidly changing moods. Accepting them without question, Emrys knew the cause for his master's descent into the bitter dark rages which would often engulf him.

The early sun sparkled on the Seine as Roger crossed the already crowded bridge to the right bank. During the seemingly endless months of his exile, he had grown restless and dissatisfied with his life, finding Paris stifling to his mountain-bred nature. The only real physical activity he enjoyed was when the king invited him to the hunt, which was but seldom, or on the rare occasion when a tournament was held. Even then, he felt the humiliation of being patronized by folk too steeped in their own indulgences to know the rigors of his fugitive life.

Muffled in the anonymity of his dark mantle he briefly stood looking back at the walls of the royal palace and the spire of St. Louis's chapel soaring high above the circular towers. Within one of them lay his future—he had possessed the queen and heard her cry out his name in passion. Roger smiled grimly. Now that Isabella was his, he could begin to lay the plans for his return to England, for she was necessary to its success. Confident of his conquest, he doubted that she would need much persuasion.

When he returned, he would punish that damned young whelp who had refused to come to France with Emrys. Why did the boy oppose him so? There was also the matter of Jehan. Even now she intruded into his thoughts, and his face darkened. When Emrys admitted that he had taken her to Pen-yr-bryn, the realization that she had found her son filled him with rage. Shaking the harper until the small man's teeth clattered, he accused him of deliberate mischief. It seemed to him then that luck had totally deserted him. She had become a weight about his neck which he did not need—not with all the other things that beset him. Her joyous submission and the passionate release his body enjoyed when he made love to her faded into nothingness in the face of his troubles. His children were scattered throughout the countryside under Edward's custody, and he despaired of his wife who, while still confined to Skipton Castle, had had her allowance cut off by the king upon hearing of her lord's escape from the Tower. Though he was never emotionally held by her, she carried his name and had borne his children. For those reasons alone, his strange devotion to her never wavered. His estates confiscated, his possessions seized, he lived upon the largesse of his friends, a position unbearable to one such as he. Only his hate sustained him—that black, burning hatred he held so passionately for Edward and all those who supported him. He had been close to despair when Isabella arrived. But holding her in his arms, he realized that she would be the one to restore to him all that was now lost to him. And perhaps even more. Yes—with Isabella beside him, there was no one to stop him from grasping that which he had long ago decided belonged to him.

"A letter came from Edward this morning."

Her thin silk veil fluttering in the warm summer air, Isabella stole a glance at the man riding beside her along a well-worn path winding its way past huge old trees whose branches obscured the hot blue sky. De Mortimer, aware of her scrutiny, kept his face blank although his hands tightened their grip on his mount's reins. Damn her, he thought with irritation—she would dangle the news before him, enticing him with it until his nerves stretched near to breaking. Nay, my queen, he decided, you'll not have me beg aught of you—ever. He breathed deeply, the clean smell of earth and trees filling him with a sense of pleasure dampened only by the restlessness which haunted him still. Seeking to escape the fetid heat of Paris, Charles had moved his household to the Bois de Vincennes. While a steady stream of messengers traveled the road between the city and the rambling old hunting lodge built one hundred years earlier by their sainted great-grandfather, Louis IX, the royal family enjoyed the shadowy coolness of the trees and the sparkling waters of small streams fed by springs rising deep within the forest.

"He actually found time from his dalliance with the Despensers to write to you?" Roger's voice was heavy with sarcasm as he guided his horse close to hers, not wishing to be overheard by Emrys or the two young pages accompanying them. Isabella shook her head and laughed.

"Nay, *mon coeur*—not to me. To Charles. 'Tis his reply to the agreement we reached. Although I was sure that he would be pleased to hear that his French holdings will be returned to him intact, I've been dreading his answer. If he comes to swear fealty to Charles, it would mean an end to our meetings." Isabella's voice faltered over her last words. The thought that she would no longer be able to spend her nights lying in Roger's arms was painful, but she knew that as long as Edward was in France, Roger could not be seen at court. The danger would be too great for both of them. She doubted that she could keep her newly awakened emotions from Edward. With a hot rush of resentment, Isabella felt that she had played his game too long to risk betrayal now. Never in all her life had she dreamt that there was such fulfillment in the act of love as she experienced since the first rapturous night Roger had come to her.

With much dissembling, cajolery, and diplomatic tact, Isabella had managed to have Roger de Mortimer attached to her household as one of her knights, allowing him to accompany her to Vincennes. So far they had managed to keep their liaison secret, although Isabella sensed that Charles suspected that Wigmore had become her lover. She was also well aware of the frowning disapproval with which at least one of Edward's ecclesiastical ambassadors had greeted de Mortimer's acceptance within the royal circle, fearing they would be blamed for his behavior. There was little they could do, Isabella thought smugly, for Charles enjoyed nothing more than to remind them that they were beyond the reach of English law. And if they knew that she welcomed him to her bed . . !

In answer to her fears, Roger replied curtly, "Nonsense! There would always be a way."

Setting spur to his horse, he drove Isabella's startled mount before him, and they galloped wildly through the forest, losing themselves in the tangled wilderness where there were no paths to follow. Within minutes, their companions were out of sight as the trees closed in about them. When the horses at last came to a shuddering halt, Isabella turned a white face to her lover. She had lost her veil, and the full sleeves of her robe were rent where they had caught on the bushes and brambled undergrowth. Dismounting quickly, Roger lifted her down and held her in his arms. He could feel the excited thudding of her heart against his own.

"Did you wish me dead?" she whispered shakily, lifting her mouth to his. Although able to keep pace with him, fear had licked at her more than once as she clung to her mare's bridle, bending over the animal's neck to escape from being unhorsed by low-hanging branches.

"I wanted to show you how simple it is to be together," and his lips covered hers, tasting the cold fire which consumed her.

"We would have to live in the forest then," Isabella replied, smiling at the absurdity of their thoughts. She looked about her with pleasure, surrounded by the deep silence of the dark forest. A few beams of sun drifted through the heavily foliaged branches, dappling the moss-covered earth with golden light. She sank down at the foot of an old tree whose roots spread out on either side of her like cradling arms, and relished the rare solitude. Roger joined her, leaning his head against its thick, gnarled trunk.

"Perhaps that would be the answer to all our problems," he said cynically. Pushing back the heavy plait of pale gold hair, he kissed the soft skin behind her ear, letting his lips drift down the graceful curve of her neck.

" 'Tis not like you to be so romantic," Isabella murmured, her eyes closed. She gave herself up to the ripples of sensual delight which Roger's slyly caressing hands were awakening in her.

"Or you to be so shameless," he said mockingly, gently squeezing the soft roundness of her breast. A fiery ache gripped him as he touched her, but he fought against it, forcing his mind to focus on more important matters than his desire for her.

"When does Edward leave for France?" The question was asked so quietly that Isabella did not notice the duplicity of his behavior.

"He's not coming," She drew away from him, her fair hair in disarray, the lacings of her gown undone and her cheeks flushed. She was in love and could not hide it from him. "At least not yet. He claims that he's been ill and cannot travel . . ."

"Or that the Despensers fear to be parted from him. 'Tis difficult to understand a man who would agree to sacrifice a kingdom rather than risk a friendship."

"He's a fool!" Isabella said with contempt and shrugged, her tenderer feelings forgotten as she thought of her husband.

The almond-shaped eyes glittered with an icy brilliance and Roger could feel the violent, passionate hatred in her. He smoothed back errant strands of hair from her face, asking casually, "And what of young Edward? Couldn't he come in his father's place?"

"He's too young, Roger—he's not quite thirteen. Besides, he has no authority." Her eyes were wary of him suddenly, for she had seen that calculating look before.

"My love—authority can be given to him—say, as the duke of Aquitaine. What harm could there be if you were to suggest it to Edward? 'Twould be for the good of England."

For a moment she stared at him in stunned surprise.

"The Despensers would never agree to it! 'Tis an outrageously mad scheme, Roger!"

She looked down at the dark head as he leaned forward to press a kiss in the hollow between her breasts. His breath was warm against her skin. Her fingers slowly caressed the heavy tangle of hair at the nape of his neck, waiting for him to speak.

"You can but try, Isabella, if you truly want to end your bondage to Edward and all he stands for."

Lifting his head, Roger's black devil's gaze burned as he searched the queen's face, meeting an answering fire in her cold blue eyes. The enchanting mouth curved into a smile which transformed her visage. The demon which had lurked behind Isabella's innocent beauty for so long stirred, awakened at last by her lover's words—the words which unlocked her soul. She laughed, a deep, seductive, and tantalizing laugh, and her lips drew back over white, even teeth. Hypnotized by the transformation, Roger's heart leaped in recognition of a kindred spirit.

"Oh, *mon gentil* Mortimer," Isabella whispered, her hand resting lightly on the side of his face. "Your thoughts are my thoughts and your desires are my desires—and so shall my revenge be your revenge." Drawing his head down, she pressed her mouth against his, parting with a hunger no longer necessary to deny. "Together, *mon coeur* . . . together naught will stop us."

And while overhead the summer breeze moved rhythmically through the trees and birdsong drifted innocently about them, Roger de Mortimer and Isabella of England lay clasped together, forging the first link in a chain that only death would sunder.

As the days grew into weeks, Isabella's obsession with her lover became so obvious that all knew of it. After the arrival of the young prince, newly created duke of Aquitaine, all pretense was abandoned by both the queen and Wigmore in exultation over the success of their scheming. Young Edward, excited and bursting with pride over his title and the responsibility entrusted to him by his father, had impressed the jaded French court by his regal bearing and the fair, blue-eyed handsomeness inherited from both his parents. Queen Jeanne's younger ladies were enchanted by the boy's charmingly accented French and coaxed him also to speak his country's tongue. He complied amidst much hilarity by his audience at the barbaric sounds. Smiling broadly and stuffing himself with comfits, he accepted their gentle teasing with good grace, not caring what they thought of him.

The entire court watched him kneel before his uncle in the Bois de Vincennes, swearing fealty to France on behalf of his father for the duchy of Gascony and the county of Ponthieu. The old ritual, with all its pomp and ceremonial glitter, brought tears of pride to Isabella's eyes. Walter Stapledon, the bishop of Exeter, who had been entrusted with the young prince's welfare on the journey to France, stood by her side, watching her warily, for he had been charged by his king to seek out the truth. She listened to the boy's clear young voice recite the ancient words of homage which would retain peace between both realms, scarce believing that this self-possessed youth was the babe she had once held in her arms. Fearfully searching for any of his father's weaknesses, she was relieved to find her son totally devoid of Edward's shortcomings. To de Mortimer's jaundiced eye, it seemed that the young boy showed an uncommonly keen grasp of his purpose in life for his age.

"He will be as great a king as both his grandfathers," Isabella told de Mortimer, a trifle smugly, as they supped together in her chambers in the royal palace. The court had returned to Paris shortly after the ceremony, and she had brought her son with her, pleading patience with Edward for his return. She had never really been allowed to know the boy before, and found unexpected pleasure in his company. De Mortimer was becoming bored with her endless chatter over Ned, but she failed to notice his sullen mood. While Emrys played old airs softly on his small harp, Roger sat by the hearth, his eyes resting on Isabella's animated face. He detested her pride in her son, for to him young Ned was merely a tool to be used until he had played the role de Mortimer intended for him.

"Lord help England if he be like your father, my love!" He laughed without mirth and it pleased him to see her flush with anger, rudely pushing away a dish of sugared chestnuts offered by a servant in her pique at his words.

"How can you say that, Roger? My father was a great king."

"To bring a curse upon his own house by destroying the power of the Templar knights and burning the Grand Master to death is far from showing greatness. It has always seemed to me to be more of a sign of excessive greed!" he said cruelly, wanting to strip her of her pride. "And from what I can see, the curse has certainly proven itself true—your three brothers all have sat on the throne of France. And where is there a male issue to follow Charles . . . the last of the Capets?" He emptied his goblet, deliberately turning it over so the remaining drops spattered the floor, staining the carpet. "Our first Edward was far wiser by allowing the Templars their lives."

"I thought you scoffed at curses—believing only in what life offers," Isabella cried, furious with him for having spoken of her family in so sneering a fashion. Obeying her sudden order of dismissal, the servants hurried from the chamber, glad to escape her unbridled temper. Roger looked at her coldly and rose, calling for his cloak. Emrys remained where he was, for he had seen this game played before.

Watching Roger reach for the mantle, which lay on a large coffer, the queen said evenly, "Walter Stapledon has returned to England to tell Edward of our relationship, and 'tis just a matter of time before he will demand my return."

Having told Roger the news she knew would keep him with her, Isabella sat back in her elaborately carved and gilded chair, the firelight casting a warm glow over her pale features. Her eyes did not leave him as he turned to face her.

"And what will you do?" Roger asked thickly.

"You dare ask?" she spat out scornfully. "I'll not return to England as long as the accursed Despensers are in power, and he knows it. And if needs be, I'll put it into writing." Her voice softened and she held out a hand to him. "*Mon coeur,* how can I fear Edward or those about him when I have you by my side. And we're not alone, for there's Richmond, Henry de Beaumont, and your friend Maltravers. Even the Bishop of Norwich, Lord Airmyn, holds as little love for Edward as we do."

" 'Tis true—and I sometimes forget that I'm not the

only man with a price on his head. Should I return to England now . . ." Roger threw his cloak down and knelt by Isabella's chair.

"When the time is right, we'll return together." She looked at de Mortimer, so obsessed with his destiny and daring to challenge the world in order to attain all that he desired. Together! A feeling of power surged through her. She had found a lover and companion in this wildly passionate man to share her life with. 'Twas more than she had ever dreamed of, and would never surrender it to anyone. "We must have patience, *gentil* Mortimer."

He drew her into his arms, feeling her body mold itself against his own, ready for his love.

"And then?" he asked, seeing her hunger for him darken the blue eyes. His mouth hovered above her own.

"And then we will gain a kingdom."

Emrys's hand lay on the silent harpstrings as he watched his master lift the queen into his arms and carry her into the bedchamber. A darkness fell over his spirit and he shivered. Thinking suddenly of Bleddyn, he was glad that the boy had refused to come. There was a madness in these two which frightened him more than their unbridled lust for each other. What could they be thinking of, to contemplate treason, though neither one had ever put voice to their folly. Wrapping himself in his cloak, he leaned his head against the warm stones of the hearth and willed his mind to empty itself of all thought. And as he slept, the darkness within him fed upon his fear, creeping into the innermost reaches of his soul.

" 'Tis an impossible situation which you've created by your scandalous behavior with the baron of Wigmore, and I'll countenance it no further."

"And I'll not go back to England, brother. My marriage is over, and 'tis widows' weeds I'll wear till the Despensers are defeated."

Charles sat in his council chamber beneath a brocaded canopy, the jeweled crown of France sparkling brightly with every movement of his head. The handsome features were cold and unreadable as he sat stiffly on his thronelike chair while inwardly seething with fury in the face of Isabella's defiance.

" 'Tis not for you to dictate your future state to me, Isa. I warned you when you first arrived at court that a scandal would not be tolerated, and believed your protestations of innocence."

"What harm can it do France if I refuse to leave my lover's side? All know that Roger cannot return, for Edward's threatened him with death—and 'twould be a living death for me, were I forced to part from him."

Isabella stood before her brother, eyes flashing their outrage at being flayed so by his words. Rising in anger, Charles towered over her, tall and imposing in his royal robes.

"You've said enough, sister! I know of the letter the bishop of Winchester took to England, and its contents. Because of your refusal to return either yourself or your son, and because of that loyal group of political exiles who now surround you, Edward claims I mean to invade his realm on your behalf."

" 'Tis not true, Charles—I can't believe Edward so naive." Isabella protested hotly, twisting a silk handkerchief in nervous hands.

"Not Edward, you fool, the Despensers!" Charles said scathingly. "Your husband writes long letters assuring us of their sincerity and honest service to the crown. He insists your life is in no danger, as you seem to think it is."

"But does not tender one word of assurance that matters will improve if I do return," she said bitterly, turning away from her brother to look out of a window. Between two towers she caught a glimpse of the Seine sparkling in the sunshine. The pressures on Charles were great. She had known that they would be, but she had trusted him, somehow believing that he would remain loyal to her.

"You believe Edward's protestations of innocence!" she said in a resigned tone and turned from the window to look at him, her face bleaker than he had ever seen it.

"Of course I don't—but there are consequences to my

421

inaction that I can't tolerate. My people in England are being harassed, put under arrest for no reason other than their nationality. There have been difficulties with the customs and the mails delayed. 'Tis a most unpleasant state of affairs." The king's tone softened. "Isa, I must think of France first. You should be able to see that for yourself. If you were to cease your affair . . ."

"Never, Charles! Don't even suggest it," she cried, horrified by his words. Give up Roger? 'Twas unthinkable!

"You're a royal whore who shames the name of Capet each time you couple with Wigmore."

Charles's voice was cold and flat as he returned to his seat. His sister remained by the window, angered by his words. She had seen the change in him, realizing that he would not be moved by any further emotional outbursts.

"Your husband has placed the entire matter into the hands of the pope." A scroll seemed to materialize in his hand. She could see the heavy seals appended to the crimson ribbons hanging from the parchment. "A communication arrived this morning from Avignon. 'Tis from Pope John, ordering me to turn my back on you and your lover. I have no choice but to obey."

Without uttering a further word to her, Charles terminated their interview, calling for servants to bring him wine. Soon the chamber began to fill with his advisers and members of the council who had been waiting outside. For a moment Isabella could not move, stunned by the suddenness of his decision. He had shorn her sense of security from her, allowing her no dignity and vilifying her cruelly. Angry and hurt, she drew herself up stiffly, stalking from the chamber with her head held high. Charles, surrounded by elegantly clad men, some of whom had grown old in the service of the royal household, pretended ignorance of his sister's departure, but was keenly aware of her. His shrewd eyes narrowed, pondering his next step. She would have to be dealt with swiftly, he decided morosely, and turned his attention elsewhere.

"You must leave at once, cousin, if you value your safety!"

The duke of Artois leaned over Isabella's sleeping form, speaking to her in an urgent whisper. He had burst into her chambers moments before, startling the ladies sleeping on pallets in the anteroom. The old woman, Claude, had followed him in, holding back the curtain as Artois shook Isabella's bare shoulder roughly.

"Sweet Jesù, *m'amie,* rouse yourself!"

Isabella opened her eyes reluctantly, focusing with difficulty on the pale, brooding face of her cousin, Robert. She saw that he was dressed for travel in hauberk and surcoat, his gauntlets tucked into his belt. Pushing her hair from her sleep-drugged face, Isabella shrank from the lantern he held in one hand, noticing that the other grasped the hilt of his sword.

"What do you want with me?" Fear tightened her throat and she could scarcely speak. Mother of heaven, he's been sent by Charles to slay me, she thought wildly. "Robert! Why are you here?"

"You must leave Paris at once. I've already sent word to your son to prepare for the journey." Artois sat down on the edge of her bed, relieved that she was listening to him. "Charles intends to turn you over to Edward, and all the other English exiles as well." He glanced at Claude, ordering her to begin packing the queen's things. "You must leave quickly. There's very little time."

Pushing back the covers, Isabella ignored her naked state, aware only that she must obey him, for Robert of Artois was her only friend at the French court. One of her ladies pulled a shift over her head, and as she struggled with it, she whispered, "Roger—I must warn Roger!"

Upset by her meeting with Charles, she had told Roger of the pope's intervention and her brother's decision to take no side in the matter. De Mortimer had exploded in violent rage, blaming her unjustly for having handled the situation badly. When she protested, seeking only comfort, he had refused to stay for supper, slamming the door loudly behind him. She had responded with a tantrum of her own, which had left her weeping with fear that he too had deserted her.

"He's coming, Isa. He was with me when I received the news, and has gone to collect his belongings. I've also alerted the others, telling them to meet us at the Porte St. Antoine at dawn. Go to Burgundy or the Netherlands. You'll be safe in either place. In the meantime, I'll speak to Charles on your behalf. Once you've removed yourself from France, he'll find it easier to forgive you."

The duke watched Mistress Claude fold Isabella's robes carefully into a large coffer. He deplored the size of her entourage, doubting that everyone could be ready in time. As if reading his thoughts, Isabella smilingly assured him that all would be in readiness sooner than he expected. Her heart sang . . . Roger would be with her! 'Twas all she had needed to know. She insisted upon packing her jewels personally, and as she sat before the gem casket, her mind trying to dwell on the future, her eyes stared at a golden pendant set with sapphires . . . the gift from Edward on the birth of their firstborn, and heir to the crown of England. Her hand closed over it, feeling the cold hardness of the stones. When she had left this chamber a maid preparing to become England's queen, she had longed for romance. Her mouth twisted wryly. Little had she known then that she would find it here, and though it cost her the friendship of her brother, she would hold to that love with every fiber of her being.

She shook her head, forcing herself to think of where they could go. There had to be a solution to her dilemma —of course . . . she suddenly recalled that the younger brother of the count of Hainault had often urged her to visit Valenciennes—assuring her that she would be most welcome. Sir John had seemed quite taken with her. Yes, Isabella decided—they would go to Hainault, at least for a while. She was smiling as she secured the lock on the heavy casket.

When de Mortimer, having slipped quietly through the postern gate, entered the queen's chamber, he found her waiting amidst her coffers, with only Claude beside her. Her women and young Edward had already joined the rest of her household assembling in the courtyard. The duke, in company with young Kent, had gone to arrange for their exit from the palace, Isabella told him with mounting excitement, and soon they would be far from the dour restrictions of her brother's court.

He fell to one knee before her, drawing his sword from its scabbard. Holding it up, he kissed the crest on its hilt and swore fealty to her and to the young prince.

"There will be no turning back from our journey," he told Isabella quietly.

"I committed my soul to you, *mon coeur*. 'Tis all I had to give. What else is left me?" and her eyes swam with sudden tears as Roger pressed her small white hand to his lips.

PART SEVEN
1326

Chapter 16

1326
Glairn

The rumors began slowly, drifting through the countryside—whispering first of the queen's refusal to return
from France with her eldest son and then of her flagrant
affair with the fugitive baron of Wigmore. Rumor followed
rumor, strengthened by Isabella's flight to Hainault, and
as summer gave way to autumn, it was said that she was
calling for loyal supporters to rally about the standard of
young Prince Edward. When rumor became fact, it did so
with astonishing swiftness, for late in September, the queen
landed in Suffolk with a force of knights and mercenary
soldiers from the low countries, Germany, and even so
distant a land as Bohemia. Flanked by her son and her
cousin, Edmund of Kent, Isabella was followed closely by
her generals, Roger de Mortimer and Sir John of Hainault.

In London, King Edward, safely behind the fortified
walls of the Tower, grew more and more frightened as he
heard accounts of the queen's advance through East
Anglia. Walton-on-Naze, Bury St. Edmunds, Cambridge,
Dunstable—all opened their gates to her army, swelled
each day by more of the gentry pledging themselves to her
banner.

Couriers galloped urgently along the high roads, sent
by a desperate king calling vainly for assistance from
barons believed loyal to the crown. Most refused to com-

mit themselves while secretly throwing their support to the queen. There were many who rejoiced that she was at long last taking a stand against her ineffectual husband on behalf of her son.

On a crisp, bright day in mid-October, with a late autumn sun glittering on helms, armor, and bridles, Lord Henry de Percy rode through the heavy gates of Glairn Castle at the head of a large troop of knights and mounted men-at-arms just two hours before the arrival of the royal messenger. Clad in full battledress, Sir Henry stood before the earl in Glairn's council chamber and announced that he was riding south to join the queen.

"Will you accompany me?" he asked, eagerness stamped on his blunt young face, the clear brown eyes awash with excitement.

Without replying, Kilburn offered his visitor a cup of claret and motioned him to take a seat at the council table littered with maps.

"I see you're trying to trace the queen's route," Sir Henry said, peering intently at a map of southern England.

Kilburn smiled, in spite of his own dubious reaction to the reports which were reaching Glairn each day.

"I must admit that my ignorance of what's happening is becoming unbearable. 'Tis like when the first Edward died and we heard naught but unsettling rumors of the new king—but you're too young to remember that!"

"But I do, my lord," Simon Jardine said, joining them at the table. "And a fair stir those rumors caused." He saw how young de Percy's presence seemed to disturb his lord, and with a sinking heart knew that Kilburn would deem it his duty to involve himself one way or another in what was happening. The days were long past when he had turned his back on England's troubles, caring only for his own lands. If only I were twenty years younger, the old man thought bitterly, looking angrily at his gnarled hands. His joints ached constantly from the damp, and old wounds had begun to make themselves felt again after all these years. Old age had crept upon him almost unnoticed, but he was not alone. With a feeling of sadness, he saw that even his lord's hair was silvered at the temples.

"I fear that if the tales are true, we face vengeful

times!" Kilburn said slowly, hoping to draw out the younger man's opinions.

" 'Tis said that Wigmore has totally ensnared the queen's passion, and if true, Edward should indeed be watchful." De Percy's voice was full of admiration, for he viewed the queen's actions as some daring adventure rather than fraught with political dangers. He leaned back in his chair, prepared to say more but for Thomas Fitzhugh's announcement that a royal messenger had just arrived with an urgent letter from the king. The men exchanged curious looks as Kilburn broke the royal seal on the square of folded parchment. His face was devoid of any expression as he quickly scanned its contents. It was exactly what he had feared—yet, what other choice did Edward have, save to beg his barons' fealty to the crown. He raised his eyes to the men seated about the table.

"Edward requests my support. It seems he has left London, intending to seek sanctuary in Bristol."

"The postern gate to Ireland," Sir Simon remarked dryly,

"He's fleeing for his life!" Thomas whispered, appalled at the news. "I fear for him, should he be captured by Lord de Mortimer."

"Wigmore would not dare harm the king! Though he's despised, folk would not tolerate any violence against him. He's still the annointed sovereign of the realm!" de Percy retorted in defense of de Mortimer.

"But there's his son, my lord de Percy," Kilburn said slowly. "All that is needed is for Edward to abdicate in favor of the young prince." He crumpled the king's message in his hand as everyone's attention focused on him. "I think 'tis other game they hunt now, and my fear is for the lives of any of us who have ever crossed them." He could not shake off his uneasiness that they were all in peril of their lives. If only Pembroke were still alive, he thought bitterly. Now was the time his talent for diplomacy and clear-minded sagacity would be most needed. Kilburn breathed in deeply, thrusting aside thoughts of his dead friend. There was no choice for him to make.

"Henry, I'll leave with you in two days' time, and we'll see for ourselves what course we must take."

Rising from his chair, he issued rapid orders to Sir Simon, while Thomas hurried out to begin the preparations for his lord's departure. Kilburn's spirits plummeted as he went in search of Gillian. It would be difficult to part from her in the face of de Mortimer's obviously growing power over the queen. De Mortimer! He fought the hatred which even the mention of that despised name evoked in him. A confrontation was inevitable, and Kilburn harbored few illusions as to his enemy's self-indulgent dispensing of justice.

Bristol

"The earl of Winchester is in our hands, *mon coeur!* Can you believe it?" Isabella was filled with a wild, exultant sense of victory. "All these years I've hated and feared Hugh Despenser—yet, when he stood before me, all I saw was an old man with but half his wits left to him." She laughed as she threw herself into de Mortimer's arms. "If he thinks to mock my triumph with his helplessness, 'twill do naught to save him!"

"My queen," de Mortimer admonished smoothly, his dark eyes glinting with a devilish light, "you forget that Lord Despenser should stand trial before he can be properly punished."

Isabella pulled his head down, and with her lips brushing his enticingly, murmured, "Then you needs must find the proper judges, *mon gentil* Mortimer."

" 'Tis what I plan to do!" he said, answering her kisses with his own. Holding her in his arms, he carried her to the bed. No more narrow camp beds or tiny cell-like quarters for him, Roger vowed with satisfaction as he laid Isabella on a coverlet of silken fur pelts. The bed was hung with richly embroidered velvet curtains which shimmered softly in the firelight, seeming to echo his thoughts. Her hair spread over the bed like a golden pillow, Isabella waited impatiently for him. Instead he stood over her, staring at the canopy with its royal arms, suddenly lost in some world of his own.

They had accomplished much in the month since

their landing on the soil of England. Bristol's citizens had welcomed them with hysterical joy, cheering the foreign knights as lustily as they did their English barons. So had it been in Gloucester—in the Great Hall of the castle, where they all had gathered to do homage to the queen and her son; he had been amazed at the many familiar arms emblazoned on surcoats of knights who, only a few years earlier, had sided with Edward against Thomas of Lancaster, Hereford, and himself. Isabella's cousin, Thomas Brotherton of Norfolk, had come forth immediately, joining his brother of Kent in support of the queen's cause. It must have been a bitter blow for Edward to find both of his half-brothers taking sides against him. And with what haste had Lancaster's brother, Henry, come down from the north to join them. Roger did not doubt that his action was prompted more from vengeance against those who had destroyed his brother rather than a belief in Isabella's ability to wrest the crown from Edward. Reasons did not matter, he told himself grimly, so long as they succeeded in what they had begun. So black was his look that Isabella grew anxious.

"*Mon coeur*—what thoughts trouble you to cause you to look so fearsome?" Her hands plucked at his sleeves. Returning to the present, he forced himself to smile at her.

"I was thinking of Gloucester and all who came to honor you." Roger felt her hands tug at his belt. Unclasping the gold links, he let it drop to the floor. "And of the declaration . . ."

Isabella's eyes sparkled, remembering how the Hall shook with the roars of outraged barons when a herald had read her accusations of Edward's grave errors and the harm done England's folk by their king, as well as listing the evil deeds committed by the Despensers. Was there a man present who had not been the target of their greed?

"But the best was my bounty of two thousand pounds for the head of Nephew Hugh. 'Twas fitting since Edward's value for yours was only half as much." Isabella smiled into Roger's black eyes—opaque and unreadable.

"I still think you should have arrested Glairn!"

"Nay, Roger, I've told you before—you'll not harm him!"

She struggled to sit up, her desire for him forgotten as she fought the memory of James Kilburn's lean, austere face, glimpsed suddenly amidst the assembled barons. 'Twas clear he had come with Henry de Percy, who wholeheartedly pledged his sword to her, but he himself did not come forward. Her throat had tightened painfully as she looked into the long hazel eyes burning with a strange fire beneath arched dark brows. And then he was gone, lost in the press of knights eager to be singled out for a word or gesture from her. Had she changed so much, she wondered, remembering the unspoken shock which crept into his face as he stared at her.

"Isabella—Glairn is your enemy and should be disposed of." De Mortimer, too, had seen Kilburn's face as he looked at the queen, and was surprised that she did not share his desire to rid themselves of the troublesome border lord once and for all.

"James Kilburn has never been my enemy and never will be." The words were sharp and imperious. Isabella's face was suddenly distorted with anger at his single-minded refusal to accept her decision. "I owe him my life and that of my son's. He and his lady are two of my most trusted friends and I'll not allow anything to happen to either of them."

"You're thinking with your heart," Roger said with derision, catching Isabella's hand as she sought to strike him. Her silk shift had ridden above her bare thighs and he felt the softness of her body through the thin cloth as he held her immobile against him with hands no longer gentle. Her breath was warm against his face as he met her cold, shrewd, and unblinking stare.

"And 'tis not your head you use when you think of either James or Gillian Kilburn, *mon coeur*. I'm not as great a fool as you believe." Her voice was sheer ice. "And what lies between Glairn and the young, helpless queen I was once is my secret and not to be shared by even you."

She had changed in the weeks since they had landed, Roger realized. While the passion for him still ran hot and undiminished, her father's nature was beginning to strongly assert itself. It fascinated him, for at times he imagined he held two women in his arms.

He kissed her, forcing her to lie back in his arms. The day had been long and strenuous for both of them. They were alone, he told her quietly, soothing her with his hands. The door of the bedchamber was closed against the castle and all that lay behind them. In answer to her unspoken question, he said, "I'll not bring it up again, my love—I promise," and closed her eyes with kisses which burned her skin with their touch while he masked the hatred still boiling inside of him.

Much later, lying against his long, hard body, she murmured sleepily, "What was it that Adam Orleton quoted when we heard him preach in Oxford?"

"I will put enmity between thee and the woman and between thy seed and her seed," Roger said softly, running a finger lightly over a silken cheek. He felt her smile in the darkness.

"Yes—'tis fitting. Bishop Orleton was ever our friend." She sighed. "Edward's seed . . . it has indeed undone him."

The man was old and scarce seemed aware of the reason all eyes were fixed upon him. His white hair was matted with dirt and sweat, for they had thrown him into the dungeon and chained him there. He looked about and saw a familiar face—nay, two. The fair hair and blue eyes of the Plantagenets. Edward? Impossible! Edward had escaped from Bristol with young Hugh before . . . before . . . he frowned, trying to remember. Ah, yes, Thomas Brotherton and his young brother, Edmund—but why were their looks so solemn? He stiffened with alarm as he caught sight of the tall dark man clad in black velvet. Sweet Jesu—'twas Roger de Mortimer! And the realization of where he was and the hopelessness of his plight broke over him in an icy deluge. Even Henry of Leicester sat before him as judge, anxious to send him to his doom.

The earl of Winchester barely heard the charges brought against him, read quickly and unemotionally by one of the royal clerks. Denied the right to answer, he sat contemplating his manacled hands as he was named a traitor to the realm, for had he not counseled the king to disinherit his lieges. The flat voice droned on. He was a robber of the land, having lined his pockets at the expense of his peers. When the death of Thomas of Lancaster was laid upon him, he felt Leicester's hatred about him.

Stoic of face and silent, Hugh Despenser, earl of Winchester, was sentenced with uncommon haste to hang on the common gallows in Bristol while Isabella watched triumphantly, sitting among those who had judged him guilty. For a second his red-rimmed eyes met hers, seeing no mercy in their cold depths, and he resigned himself to his fate.

That same day, amidst the excited shouts of Bristol's citizens, the life of that most hated man was ended, leaving his enemies with the bitter knowledge of a victory only half won.

Pen-yr-bryn

Jehan moved closer to the hearth as she felt the sudden cold seep through the stone walls, causing tapestries to move and candles to flare and snap in the draft. Outside a few early snowflakes had begun to drift over the turrets of the small castle. She lifted her head, not sure whether the sounds she heard were that of the drawbridge's shrieking chains or the eternally wailing wind—had a trumpet sounded as well? I'm becoming fanciful, she decided irritably. Resting her chin in one hand, she stared blindly at the drab little tapestry hung against a portion of the round wall of her tower chamber. Since Lady Olwen's death, there had scarce been anyone to talk to— even if there ever was anything worthwhile to talk about. With increasing frequency she found herself seeking the sanctuary of her small chamber in attempts to evade Sir Powys. In the face of his lady's death and de Mortimer's failure to provide further for her, the Welsh lord had insisted she assume the duties of chatelaine in order to earn her keep if she wished to remain at Pen-yr-bryn. He wished to have included the sharing of his bed as one of them, but had had little luck. In spite of her low spirits,

Jehan allowed herself a thin smile—a well-placed knee and sharp teeth which drew blood had made him a trifle wary of her. But her position in his household was a humiliating one. She was trapped, for there was no place she could go until Roger came for her. Everyone else believed he had deserted her, but she held fast to the conviction that he would come—no matter what tales were being told of his amorous entanglement with the queen.

"My lady," Bertha's low voice was insistent, "Sir Powys wishes your presence . . . at once!"

With a sigh, Jehan rose, instinctively smoothing away imaginary wrinkles from her simple, unadorned woolen tunic. In a few minutes, having descended the winding steps of the tower and walking quickly through a dismally cold, narrow passageway lighted by a single torch, she opened the wooden door to Sir Powys's small council chamber, feeling the welcoming warmth of several braziers and a roaring hearth on her chilled flesh.

"Ah, Lady Jehan!" Sir Powys's loud, rough voice grated on her ears as her gaze swept past him to rest curiously on the figure of a tall dark-haired man standing by the hearth, clad in hauberk and surcoat. She caught her breath as he turned to face her. He smiled and held out a hand to her. She could not move, nor take her eyes from him.

"We've an unexpected visitor, my lady, and one who has requested your presence." There was an air of smug satisfaction and propriety in Sir Powys's demeanor toward her which should have put Jehan on guard, but naught caught her attention save the man who suddenly stood before her, his lips brushing her hand. How warm they felt against her cold skin.

"Lady de Maudley, you're looking well. You never change." The low, musical voice made her head swim. Did he really find her unchanged? How could he tell, when her hair was hidden beneath the white wimple and her body encased in the shapeless woolen gown worn for warmth.

"My lord," she replied in appropriately demure tones, not daring to raise her eyes lest she reveal her joy to him. "We have been hearing of all that has happened since your return—'tis nigh impossible to comprehend."

De Mortimer laughed. Releasing her hand, he returned to the hearth. Sir Powys handed her a goblet of wine.

"A gift from our lord—'tis finer than the thin stuff we can offer," he told her quickly, glancing at the baron for a sign. When Roger did not respond, Powys added, "Lord de Mortimer·has been to Wigmore, Jehan, and thought to see to his Welsh properties."

"I can speak for myself," Roger said, a frown crossing his face at the Welshman's words. He sat down by the fire, leaving his host and Jehan to hover awkwardly before him. "'Tis but a short visit, for I must ride to Hereford tomorrow."

"To join the queen?" Jehan asked innocently, impulsively taking an unbidden seat opposite him. He smiled at her, his face blandly expressionless.

"Of course. She's most anxious to discover the whereabouts of the king. Leicester has gone to Glamorgan in the hope of finding some trace of him, and I thought perhaps some rumor may have reached Pen-yr-bryn."

"Nay, my lord, we've heard naught here," Powys replied. "Save that the elder Hugh Despenser has been executed."

"And his head sent to Winchester," Jehan added.

"Because he was its earl."

Did she imagine a cold detachment in Roger's dark eyes as they slowly roamed over her before turning his attention back to his host. Jehan looked from one man to the other, beginning to feel ill at ease. Despite Roger's arrogant treatment of Sir Powys, they seemed to share a bond which excluded her. Why was Roger acting so oddly—treating her with almost icy formality, as if she no longer interested him? Could he have drawn so far a distance from her? Her happiness began to falter in the face of his attitude.

She still had come no closer to fathoming the cause of his coldness as she sat beside him in the Great Hall several hours later, while platters heaped high with roasted meats and saffroned rice fragrant with the taste of raisins and almonds were served to the knights, retainers, and castle folk seated at the long tables. It seemed to Jehan that Roger's retinue far outnumbered the people from Pen-yr-bryn—another sign of his sudden importance. Vegetable fritters basted with the juices of the wild boar still turning on its spit, fresh trenchers of bread, and tiny skewered birds, golden with glazed honey, were placed before Sir Powys and his guests.

Jehan had taken great care with her appearance and knew she looked well in a fur-trimmed gown which had belonged to Lady Olwen, her face framed by a silk head-cloth. Yet, Roger paid scant heed to her. Beset by mounting apprehension, she found it difficult to swallow even the smallest morsel of food. Sipping slowly from a half-empty goblet, her green gaze sought out Bleddyn's tall, thin form, seated among his uncle's knights. He had lost the awkwardness of childhood, and there was a lithe leanness to him which reminded her increasingly of Roger. She had hoped that for tonight at least he would have shed the truculent expression he habitually wore, for it masked features exceedingly fine. At the moment he was sulking again, and she saw his strange eyes fixed unblinkingly on de Mortimer's flushed, arrogant face. She toyed idly with a piece of bread used as a sop, while Emrys's harp sounded faintly through the hall's din. Never too far from his master, he was kneeling near Roger's feet, seemingly only aware of his music until she caught him looking at her—so piercing and sad a look that her uneasiness returned.

"Bleddyn-bach!" Sir Powys bellowed good-naturedly down the long table. "Lord de Mortimer wishes to speak with you. *Yn wir!* You're honored by his attention!"

The boy's face drained of color as he slowly put down the cup he was drinking from. Sweet Jesu, Jehan prayed silently, please don't defy Roger. She knew that there had already been a fight when the boy refused to sit with his uncle's guest, preferring the company of his friends. Bleddyn rose, his young face turned toward the dais, and the Hall became quiet, sensing the tension which seemed to flow between de Mortimer and Sir Powys's nephew. Jehan caught her breath as she saw a familiar look of defiance leap into his eyes, but he must have thought better of it, for he presented himself at last to Roger. Although he sank to one knee, Bleddyn remained stubbornly silent.

It was a miracle that he was even at Pen-yr-bryn, Jehan thought, remembering the long weeks when he disappeared into the mountains without a trace. Were defiance, resentment, hatred, and that passionate desire for independence the only facets of his nature? No one was allowed within the wall which he had raised during the last days of Lady Olwen's illness. He had fled from home until after her funeral and though nearly two years had passed since her death, he never spoke of her. It was as if, for him, she had never existed.

Jehan sighed and stared moodily into her wine cup. Bleddyn was sixteen now—a man grown. There was naught that could be done with him. Besides, Jehan told herself, she had herself to think about. Since their short conversation earlier, she had begun to realize that Roger was indeed lost to her. It had been foolish to dream of being reunited with him when he returned to England. Isabella had won after all!

The sound of a chair overturning startled her, and she saw Powys advance on Bleddyn with a murderous look.

"You dare defy your lord? You, who've yet to win spurs but put on the airs of your betters. What possesses you to say such things to your liege lord?" He spluttered with rage while Roger sat back in his chair, his face pale and unreadable as the storm raged about him.

"I've said naught but the truth, Uncle. The baron of Wigmore gains power through robbery and murder. All know it, yet no one dares to say it. And I've told you before. You've sworn fealty to him—you! I never shall!"

Jehan could see that he was close to tears, frightened because he knew that he had gone too far in putting voice to his thoughts, probably placing his own life in jeopardy —yet he refused to retreat.

"Get out of my sight, Bleddyn ap Rhys, before you say more to imperil that handsome head," Roger said in a quiet, even tone, controlling his anger with difficulty. No one dared to speak to him so—the boy was impossible!

"Emrys, take this young ass to the well and pour cold water over him." He saw Jehan's alarmed face, her gaze lingering on the doorway through which Bleddyn had vanished.

"And you, my lady, I wish to see in my chambers—now!"

With an ungentle hand, he grasped her arm and forced her to accompany him from the Hall.

"Explain to me why Bleddyn chose to insult me before my people."

Roger's voice lashed out coldly as he strode restlessly about the chamber, anger whipping him into a towering fury.

"I would hardly listen to a private conversation, Roger—particularly a tender reunion such as we've all just witnessed!" she said spitefully.

"Are you telling me you didn't hear how he vilified me?" Roger was incredulous. "Then you're the only one at Pen-yr-bryn who didn't."

"He certainly must have told the truth, since I've yet to hear you deny a word of what he said," Jehan trembled as he stepped before her, his dark eyes stripping her soul bare.

"He despises me without having reason to. I've done naught to him save try to help him achieve a better place in life than that of being Pen-yr-bryn's lord."

" 'Tis not only you he's against, Roger. He's like that with everyone. I've yet to hear one gentle word from him. No one really knows him—he won't permit it. No one but the lady Olwen. I think she's the only one he ever loved." She could not keep the bitterness from her voice.

"So you've not done too well with him!" he snarled cuttingly. "Does he know who he is!"

Jehan shook her head. "I think 'tis one of the demons which pursue him. I believe he suspects who I am—he's no fool, and he does resemble me greatly. But other than that . . ." She frowned. Why was he blaming her for his own failure to win the boy over to his side?

"Still, he does not like me and never has." Roger laughed bleakly at her questioning look. "He's never hidden it from me. He defied me when he was a small child and takes every opportunity to remind me of it."

He seemed to wait for Jehan to give some sign of assurance that he was mistaken, but she said nothing. With an impatient gesture, he turned away from her. She realized with surprise that Bleddyn's hostility disturbed him more than he would openly admit. Why should this son's opinion matter so greatly to him? She stared at him, trying to understand him. Tomorrow he would be gone— gone to Hereford, to Isabella and the world he coveted above all else. Even now he seemed to have suddenly been able to banish Bleddyn from his mind, Jehan thought, watching him break the seal of a dispatch which had been given him in the Great Hall just as they were leaving.

" 'Tis not possible!" Roger shouted with glee as he held the message closer to the candlelight in order to read it over again. His face was triumphant and his voice shook with barely suppressed emotion. "Leicester has found both Edward and the younger Despenser. They were hiding in Neath Abbey, together with the king's chancellor, Robert Baldock, and a household clerk." He threw the dispatch on a coffer and grasped Jehan's shoulders, looking into her stunned face. "The king has been captured, Jehan, and Leicester is bringing them both to Hereford." The dark eyes gleamed with excitement. "He's mine, at last—and so is Nephew Hugh!"

De Mortimer's blood clamored and pulsed through his veins as the joy of victory washed over him. Never had he felt so alive. If he could only leave for Hereford immediately! His mind reeled with the news, and only when Jehan stirred in his arms did he realize that in his elation he had unconsciously drawn her close. He felt the familiar softness of her body molding itself against him and fire coursed through him, hot and demanding.

"Jehan . . ."

She heard the change in his voice and stiffened, trying to draw away from him.

"Nay, my lord . . . I told you years ago that I am no harlot to be used for your pleasure when there's no one else to ease your desire. Share your jubilation with your own people and, if you must, bed a scullery wench, but leave me be. Please—I beg you, don't awaken hopes that I deemed lost forever."

Blind to everything but his own needs, he did not see the tears begin to flood the slanted eyes and trickle slowly down the white face he lifted to his. Though his lips touched hers at first in a light, feathery kiss, the dark, insane magic which always sprang up between them began to weave its wild spell. His mouth covered hers in ever-deepening kisses until Jehan felt herself being drawn into the whirlpool of his overpowering passion, drowning her with emotions she had believed dead.

"Nay, Roger," she protested brokenly, vainly trying to gain control of her senses. In spite of the throbbing of her heart, she told herself that she meant nothing to him. "You've found another to share your dreams with."

"But she's not here, Jehan," Roger whispered. His hand ripped the silk covering from her head and the flaming tresses, released from their confinement, tumbled down her back. He breathed in the remembered fragrance of roses. "And never was there one such as you." His voice was hoarse with desire. He had forgotten how she felt in his arms, her small body instinctively fitting into his. His lips, hot and dry, were on her throat, moving slowly downward to the smooth swell of her breasts bared by his impatient hands. She arched back as his searching mouth closed over a nipple swollen and taut with the hunger for him she could no longer contain. As he lifted her in his arms and carried her up the few steps to his bedchamber her hands tore frantically at the fastenings of his tunic, trembling in their eagerness to touch his naked flesh. Isabella faded from his mind as he began to caress the sensual body offered so passionately to his savage craving. When she felt the familiar weight of his body on her own she was filled with the wild, mindless joy of knowing him a part of her again. All thoughts were blotted out save the love she still held for him despite his betrayals and desertions. In the blinding moment when Roger brought her once more to the crest of ecstatic fulfillment, she cried out, knowing that naught had changed for her.

"I'm taking Bleddyn with me this time."

The words hung quietly in the warm, love-drenched darkness which surrounded them, but Jehan paid them no heed. She murmured a soft endearment as she laid her cheek against his chest, listening to the slow, even breathing of his heart. He still needed her, she thought happily, wondering whether he would take her back to the manor house. Because of the queen it would not be possible for him to keep her with him. A fluid languor crept through her, and she nestled closer against him, wishing he could absorb her totally, so deeply did she love him.

"I've arranged for your marriage to Sir Powys—all the necessary documents have been signed. As I am his liege lord and yours, I've given my consent. 'Tis a pity I cannot be at the ceremony, but I'm leaving at dawn."

"Sir Powys?" Jehan murmured, wondering why Roger had mentioned the Welsh knight. Wed Sir Powys—her languor changed to cold shock as the impact of his words hit her. "Wed Sir Powys? I'll not!"

Her hands stopped caressing him and she sat up in bed, unable to believe the truth of his words. Strong fingers closed over her wrist, hurting her with their unloving hardness.

"You will, Jehan. You've no choice in the matter."

Roger drew back the curtain with his other hand, letting the firelight fall over them. It bathed Jehan's face with a reddish glow which masked the sudden, drained, sick look of her.

"Did I not promise you that you would be told when I was done with you," he said cruelly. " 'Tis now, Jehan. I have no further need of you and give you to Sir Powys. At least I can see that you are taken care of and will want for naught. He is a good man and will treat you well." His voice was calm and matter-of-fact as he told her that she no longer had a place in the life he had made for himself. He had attained nearly all that he had wanted, but would not jeopardize it with attachments belonging to his past life. Ignoring her lacerated pride and his debasing rejection of her love for him, de Mortimer continued to speak of his future life, boasting of the power he wielded over Isabella. Though Jehan's body still felt the lingering warmth of his possession, an icy fury was rising within her, routing all other feelings.

"You whoremongering bastard!"

She spat out the words and slapped him as hard as she could, satisfaction darting through her as she saw a dark flush suffuse his lean features.

"You used me yet again, knowing what your touch does to me. You've played me for the fool I am. Though you feel passion for me, it means naught to you. You use Isabella in the same way . . . 'twas only in her bed that your ambitions became victorious." Jehan's face was wet with tears as she raked her nails across the naked flesh she had touched with love so short a time before. "You use your body as wantonly as any harlot and are no better . . ."

Summoning all her strength, she managed to pull free of him and scrambled from the bed. Finding her gown crumpled on the floor she pulled it about her, hiding her nakedness from him. He did not move, the wounds of her assault rising in angry welts on his pale skin. His eyes, unreadable and black as obsidian, watched as she stumbled blindly from the chamber, slamming the door behind her.

Forgetting the small steps, Jehan fell down heavily, tangled in the thick folds of her gown. Sobbing wildly, she beat her hands against the floor until she was spent. Looking fearfully at the closed door to the bedchamber, she was relieved that Roger had not followed her. Choking on her tears, she sat up carefully, lest she had hurt herself in the fall, but the only pain she felt was in her heart.

"Lady Jehan!"

Hands steadied her as she slipped on the thin covering of snow which blanketed the battlements, and found herself looking into the startled green eyes of Bleddyn ap Rhys.

"Sweet Jesu, my lady, what's happened to give you so bleak a look?" For once his voice was devoid of the sneering tone he was fond of using when he addressed her.

Jehan took deep shuddering gulps of the cold night air in an attempt to quiet her shrieking nerves. She seemed unaware of the tangled mass of hair falling about a

445

robe obviously pulled on in great haste. One knee had begun to throb where she had fallen on it and her wrist was bruised from de Mortimer's hand. But all that was nothing compared to the unbearable agony of her wounded soul. Feeling the sharp sting of tears, she turned her face away from the fitful light cast by the flaring torch thrust into an iron holder near a tower entrance.

" 'Tis naught to concern you—I wanted some air . . ." She could not control her trembling and feared that he would see her tears. "What are you doing here? Shouldn't you have found your bed long ere now?"

"I couldn't sleep. When Lord de Mortimer leaves at first light, I too must leave. He has ordered me to attend Prince Edward. He claims that my place is to be with him." Bleddyn's young voice shook with anger. "He ordered me! The arrogance of him—to use folk as he wills with no thought to their wishes."

" 'Tis one of his talents," Jehan said bitterly.

The boy looked at her, surprised by her comment. All knew that de Mortimer had taken her to his chamber, none doubting the reason. He felt an odd rush of indignation at the thought.

"I despise him, Lady Jehan! I always have, for there is something in him which makes me want to defy him—to shake somehow that insufferable arrogance."

Jehan stared at the thin face gleaming eerily in the dim light and found herself shaken by his confession. The loathing in his voice had not escaped her, for it found a kindred spirit in her own heart. Her eyes narrowed in thought. Bleddyn! Could he be the key to the vengeance she desired above all else to wreak upon the man who had so cruelly betrayed her? 'Twould be an easy matter to fan the seemingly rootless animosity he now felt toward Roger into a deep-seated hatred. Listening to the boy speak bitterly of his resentment of Pen-yr-bryn's liege lord, she knew it could be done. There was time to nurture the seeds of his hatred, Jehan decided coldly. 'Twas best to move slowly and with care. She would marry Sir Powys. What other choice did she have? For a moment she faltered in her resolve, shuddering at the thought of having to give

446

herself to so physically repellent a man—to be touched by his large, heavy hands . . .

With a start she felt a mantle being wrapped warmly about her and realized that it was Bleddyn's.

"You're shivering, Lady Jehan—did Lord de Mortimer use you badly?" Bleddyn had never concerned himself over her before but he observed her struggle to keep from weeping. She was so distraught and seemed suddenly vulnerable as she leaned against the outer wall of the battlement, her breath a white mist in the chill darkness.

"Yes, Bleddyn, he did," Jehan said softly. "You were right—though I was too blind to see it. 'Tis over between us and has been long ere now, and I begin to understand your feelings toward him. He's an evil man." Her voice was disarmingly gentle as she put a small hand pleadingly on his arm. Never had she spoken so openly to him, and a vague desire to comfort her stirred in the boy's heart. Jehan watched his reaction to her pitiful disillusionment with veiled eyes. Oh yes—his hatred would grow red-hot . . . and then he could be used against his father.

Standing beside her son on the battlements of Pen-yr-bryn, she allowed him to console her awkwardly. Drying her eyes on a corner of his fur-lined mantle, Jehan beguiled him with the advice that he should study the baron's ways well, never allowing his dislike to falter, for that was the door to his freedom. In his innocence, Bleddyn marveled at the depth of her understanding, and felt ashamed. Perhaps he had misjudged her, this woman to whom he carried so close a likeness. There were moments when he was filled with the desire to know exactly what she was to him—and yet he feared the answer. When she shyly told him of her impending marriage to his uncle, he found to his amazement that the thought was far from displeasing. And what of Aunt Olwen? Nay, he thought, Aunt Olwen was dead and her loving memory buried deep within his heart—belonged to him alone.

At dawn Roger de Mortimer rode over the draw-bridge and down the causeway leading to the valley, banners fluttering in the wintery gusts while his herald's trumpets blared his departure from Pen-yr-bryn through the valley and the rocky slopes of the surrounding mountains. Bleddyn, astride his gray horse, rode sullenly beside Emrys, comforted by the discovery that he was not alone in his hatred of the Marcher baron. Jehan did not come down to the courtyard to bid them a good journey, nor had her presence been demanded.

Standing alone now where she had stood during the night with Bleddyn, Jehan observed the long cavalcade of riders wending its way down the twisted way, her eyes never leaving de Mortimer's tall figure until he was finally lost from view as the road turned southeastward. She lifted her face to the sky streaked pink and gold with the coming day. Buffeted by the wind sweeping down from the craggy heights and her cloak streaming out behind her, she called out softly, "I don't know how, Roger, but I swear to God and all the saints that your son will bring you down and see you dead. And I pray that you will know it before you die."

So did Jehan make the oath unto herself, and what had been passion and consuming love turned into cold, murderous hatred against the man who had torn her life into shreds and scattered the pieces about her feet.

Glairn

"Thank the Virgin you've returned safely!"

Gillian's voice was hoarse with relief when she saw the large black stallion trot slowly through Glairn's massive gate, followed by the other members of Jamie's party who had accompanied him south. It had been nearly two months since they had ridden off with Henry de Percy, and save for one short message that he had business in Sussex, they had heard nothing from the earl. Gillian stifled a cry as Jamie pushed back his hood, showing her a face white and hollow-eyed from exhaustion. Although it was already late, the courtyard was alive with grooms and retainers as the men slowly dismounted, speaking in weary tones as they stretched limbs cramped from hours of sitting a horse in the bone-chilling temperatures of late December.

Standing beside Kilburn's mount, Hal reached up to take the cloak-wrapped form the earl had carried before him on the saddle.

"'Tis Alianor Fitzalan, lovely," Jamie's quiet voice answered her unvoiced question. "I've brought her home." Heavily he stepped down from the destrier's back while Gillian looked at the pale, thin face of the sleeping child before ordering Hal to take her to the bedchamber shared by Margaret and Jennifer. Followed by the nurse who had come with them, the squire disappeared into the keep. Staring after them, Jamie's mouth twisted with suppressed anger and pain. He held out his arms, gathering Gillian to him.

"You're home, my darling—and Glairn stands secure to welcome you," Gillian murmured to him, feeling the tension in the body pressed tightly against hers. There was time to ask questions of him later. "Come, Jamie—'tis rest you need now above all else."

Together they mounted the steps beneath the huge banners of former battles, suspended from the high ceiling of the entry hall, and he touched the stones of Glairn as he had done so often, wondering anew at the ability of the castle to survive the turmoil which surrounded it.

When Gillian left him to see to the child's welfare, Jamie stood by the hearth, still fighting the bleak, sick feelings of helplessness which had threatened to devour him during the journey north. He scarce heard the clatter of his sword falling to the floor as he unbuckled the wide belt with almost nerveless fingers. A servant came to draw the travel-stained surcoat from him and another divested him of his hauberk and tunic, but he paid little attention to their ministrations. Hot water was poured into a large copper basin and he felt its comforting warmth as he began to wash. It would take more than soap and water to cleanse his soul of the filth and degradation he had witnessed in the weeks spent away from Glairn.

The chamber was almost in darkness, with only the hearth's glow shedding a dim light when Gillian returned. She found Jamie stretched out on the bed, his head resting on a bolster and his eyes staring blindly at the gathered folds of the velvet canopy. Leaning over him, Gillian searched his face with anxious eyes until he turned away, made uncomfortable by her scrutiny. How could he tell her of the revulsion he still felt as the scenes he had witnessed continued to haunt him.

The food which had been brought him remained untouched, nausea wracking him as he had stared at the platter of thin-sliced smoked ham, a generous slice of cold meat pie, and the wedge of yellow crumbly cheese set out upon a small table by the fire. Though he could not eat, he had consumed all of the wine, hoping that it would dull his senses. A second flagon sat on the floor beside the bed where he could reach it in order to refill the goblet he held in his hand.

Sitting on the edge of the bed, Gillian said quietly, "I've left Agnes to tend Alianor—she barely woke as we undressed her."

Jamie reached for her hand, holding it tightly to his cold cheek.

"Her nurse came with her, lovedy. Let her tend to the child's needs." He drained the goblet and let Gillian take it from him.

"Nay, the poor woman is exhausted and we laid a pallet close to Alianor's bed for her."

He did not answer and Gillian saw that his eyes were closed. Something dreadful had happened. She could feel it emanating from him, but until he was ready to tell her, she would have to wait. She lay beside him, and he moved close, seeking her comforting warmth.

"They're all dead, Gillian!" When he spoke, his voice was hollow with despair. "First the earl of Winchester—executed—beheaded in Bristol . . . and Edmund . . . Edmund was taken prisoner and brought to Hereford. I saw him just before his death."

"Oh sweet Jesu, Jamie—nay! Not Arundel!" Gillian's voice mirrored her shock.

"Aye, lovedy. He and Surrey were the only barons, other than the Despensers, who remained loyal to Edward and were with him when he fled London. They're all dead except de Warenne. His life was spared and in exchange, he's pledged his loyalty, for what it's worth, to the queen."

"But why?"

Gillian fell silent as Jamie rolled over and buried his face in her breasts, holding her to him with a desire to ward off the coldness of all the deaths that had pursued him north. Only with Gillian's pliant and fragrant softness in his arms could he speak of his last, agonizingly heart-breaking encounter with his friend, and he wondered aloud at the capriciousness of a fate that could destroy as warm-hearted and joyous a spirit such as Edmund Fitz-alan. When word reached him at his lodgings in Hereford that one of de Mortimer's supporters had captured Arundel and brought him to the queen, he had impulsively hastened to the castle. Gillian listened as he told her of petitioning Lord Carlton for permission to see Edmund, in spite of a vague fear that he might have risked his own life, but to which he had given little thought. Surprisingly, his request was granted and one of de Mortimer's men brought him to Edmund's cell with a curt warning that his visit could be but for a few minutes. He was appalled at the sight of his friend's bruised face, the blue eyes hidden by swollen eyelids, a wild growth of beard obscuring the once merry mouth. In answer to James's shocked look, Arundel rattled the chain which shackled him to the wall.

"As you can see, James, I've fallen on hard times," he said thickly, a flash of humor still evident. " 'Tis over for me . . . had I not remained with Edward, I might have survived."

"But you still have a chance to speak for yourself when you come to trial."

"Then you've not heard? I'm to be executed today—there's been no hearing and no trial. Just the order of death." Arundel spoke without hope, knowing there would be no miraculous deliverance.

"God's blood, Edmund, how can you resign yourself so easily to your doom?" Kilburn felt sick with suppressed rage.

"Should I weep with fear and beg for mercy, James? Nay, I'll not give de Mortimer that satisfaction." His voice sounded wistful. "Roger has all he wanted—and we laughed at his dreams!"

"Aye, but how long can he hold on to it, Edmund? Until the queen tires of him?"

"She'll not, my friend. Roger will see to that." Arundel's mouth twisted in a rueful smile. To James it seemed unbelievable that he would die without being given a chance to speak out for his life against his executioners.

"Is there naught that can be done for you? Perhaps I can go to the queen."

"Nay!" Edmund's voice was sharp. "Don't risk your life for me. Let Roger be satisfied with taking mine—'tis vengeance enough." Straining against his chain, he clutched James's arm, searching his face. "I do have a boon to ask of you."

"Anything, Edmund."

"Go to Sussex, to Arundel—Alianor is there. Take her north with you. My lady will agree to cede her to you." His voice faltered. "I can only hope that de Mortimer's hatred of me will not extend to my children, but I fear for them. My sons have already been seized. At least let this daughter—my last—be safe from his hatred. In a few years she will be of an age to wed your son. I pray that her life be a happy one and that she will remember me with love."

There were tears in Edmund's eyes and James's throat tightened painfully as he fought to remain calm. He embraced Arundel, feeling him tremble in spite of his brave words, and promised to do as he asked. Suddenly there was no more to be said between them. All the years of their friendship lay in their faces as they said farewell for the last time. Edmund's eyes had followed him through the cell's heavy door.

An hour later, James knelt in a dark corner of the small church near the castle where he had taken refuge for his grieving soul. Sounds filtered dimly through the thick stone walls as he listened to the excited shouts of the queen's men, together with those of de Mortimer's, as Arundel was beheaded. He tried to pray, while tears streamed down his cheeks and his heart raged in futile anger against Arundel's murderers.

"Had I left Hereford sooner I would not have seen Geoffrey."

All through the night Jamie had lain on the bed, reaching out for Gillian when his memories were more than he could bear. She listened quietly to his disjointed, rambling account of the nightmare world he had stepped into, smoothing back the unruly strands of hair from his face with a gentle hand. At times he seemed to drift into sleep and she waited for the husky voice to begin again.

"No one seemed to know what was happening. The countess feared for properties the Despensers had seized from Aymer's estate and sent Geoffrey to speak with the queen. The country is alive with wild rumors and 'tis difficult to know what is true. Poor Geoff—though he never got to see Isabella, he did arrive in time for the younger Despenser's execution." Jamie laughed mirthlessly, the sound harsh. "At least he was allowed a trial —a mockery of a trial actually, for Roger was determined that he would not escape with his life. He was dragged through the streets like some common criminal." He stumbled over the words and Gillian touched his face. His skin felt clammy and cold.

"No more, Jamie—'tis too much for you to remember," she begged him, her eyes dark in a face drained of color. Why was he torturing himself so?

"Nay, lovedy—I must or I shall lose my sanity. I can't carry these abominations in my mind, never speaking of them—'twould be too much to bear." He looked into her face, mirroring his own horror. "Geoff and I . . . we were there."

"But why? You've always loathed such public displays of violence, and Geoffrey—he must have been mad to go."

"It sickened us both, yet there was a certain fascination to see that mighty lord brought down. Roger ordered an enormously high platform erected so that all could see. It began to snow, yet no one seemed to feel the cold. He died bravely, I'll say that for him, but I've never seen such savagery in my life as when his still-warm body was drawn and quartered . . ." Jamie remembered the strangely sexual throbbing in his loins as he stood with Geoffrey among all those who had come to witness Hugh Despenser's degradation and seen the naked body stretched out as if on a pagan altar of sacrifice.

"Spare me, Jamie. 'Tis enough!" Turning away from him, Gillian rose and poured herself some wine. She drank it quickly and refilled it, trying to wash away the horror of his words. Her hand still shook as she emptied the goblet for a second time. Jamie had followed her, pouring the rest of the wine into his own goblet.

"The queen had his head sent to London and ordered the family arms struck from the rolls permanently. Roger and Isabella were both there to relish the scene." He sat down in his chair by the hearth, feeling suddenly light-headed. "The world's gone mad. London's citizens actually beheaded the bishop of Exeter as he sought sanctuary in St. Paul's. I was in the castle in Gloucester when his head was brought to the queen as some sort of trophy . . ." He shook his head at the memory of the cheers which shook the hall. "Blood lust has gripped all of them—and how Roger glories in it! Geoffrey thinks he exacts vengeance for his uncle of Chirk, for the old man died earlier this year in the Tower, still in chains."

"Nay, 'tis not for his uncle, but for himself alone. Everything Roger's done has been for his own ambitious greed. And he'll not content himself with ridding England of the Despensers."

"I wonder that he's not moved against me. He saw me in Gloucester." Jamie shuddered, remembering the look of cold hatred which had passed between them. But Isabella too had seen him, and smiled in greeting. "For the first time, I'm glad that Pembroke is dead. He'd have been sacrificed along with Arundel. 'Tis not meet these days to be known as a king's man."

Seeking warmth, Gillian knelt before the hearth, holding her hands close to the dying flames. A faint light was beginning to fall through the long windows.

"Where is the king?"

"At Kenilworth Castle in his cousin Leicester's keeping. For the moment he is safe."

"His life is already forfeit," Gillian said, her voice muffled by the veil of hair which hid her face from him.

"Why do you say that, lovedy? Once he agrees to his

abdication in favor of the young prince, Isabella and Roger will have what they're striving for. Parliament has been called in January to order it."

She spun around, her eyes gleaming feverishly in a face he could barely recognize as Gillian's.

"They're fools! I've seen it written on Roger's face—death is his sole companion in life; the death he brings to all those who oppose him. The king is a small matter to him now, but I fear that Roger will find Edward alive a threat to his own security. England cannot contain two kings—'tis too tempting for Roger's enemies."

"Gillian! What are you saying?" Jamie whispered as he came to her, drawing her into his arms. She frightened him when she spoke of things he could not see. Her eyes rested on his face, begging for his understanding of what she felt so strongly. In spite of their dreadful portent, he could see the truth in her words.

"Promise me that you will not involve yourself in this, my darling," she pleaded. "Young Edward will need true friends in the months to come, loyal to him and not to that unholy pair of vengeful murderers. He will have need of you."

And Jamie agreed, oddly relieved in the knowledge that his position would be that of observer. Gillian had said that de Mortimer lived with death as a companion—so Glairn would wait until that companion turned and claimed him, he decided grimly, taking a measure of comfort in that thought.

In the months that followed Kilburn's return to Glairn, Gillian's words would often come to his mind as they heard of the efforts made by the more moderate barons to restore order to a land torn apart by the dethroning of a king and the humiliation caused him by being forced to swear that all the charges against him were true. Between them, Isabella and Roger de Mortimer had shorn Edward of his friends, his honor, his children, and his crown.

On the 1st of February, 1327, his son was crowned Edward III in Westminster Abbey with great pomp and amidst much speculation. Though Isabella had been passed over as regent for the young king in favor of a council led by Henry Plantagenet, now the earl of Lancaster, such was the power of Roger de Mortimer that when she defied the council and assumed the reins of the regency, few dared stand in her way.

But there was still the deposed king to consider. Taken from the relative comfort of his confinement in Kenilworth, he heard the gates of Berkeley Castle, belonging to a son-in-law of de Mortimer, closed behind him with grim finality. Edward never saw the outside world again.

News of the former king's death quickly spread through the land, and Geoffrey Harron, on a rare visit to Glairn in early October, confirmed the ghastly tale of Edward's murder at the hands of his jailers. Though naught could be proven, Geoffrey had been told that terrifying screams resounded through the castle one night while servants cowered in their beds. The next morning, Edward was found dead in his cell, and while it was claimed his death was from natural causes, those who were allowed to view the body lying on the narrow pallet in the small, dreary cell where he had been confined, were horrified by the hideous expression of painful violence which the dead face wore, though there seemed to be no other visible marks on him. The manner of his death remained a mystery, giving rise to many wild, improbable rumors, which continued to be spoken of in quiet corners by responsible folk, that the baron of Wigmore, with the queen's consent, had ordered Edward's murder.

The king was dead—long live the king.

Chapter 17

1329
Glairn

"We'd not expected you for another week!"

Gillian moved out of her son Alain's embrace reluctantly and looked up into his smiling face as he greeted his father. When the door to the solar flew open, she had been startled, at first not recognizing the tall, slender figure until she saw the golden hawk on his red linen surcoat. Since the summons from Isabella two years earlier, Glairn had seen little of its heir, for he was a member of Edward's court, one of the young men of high birth who must surround the new king as the queen had insisted.

"So I thought myself, Mother, but Edward gave me leave to come while he stays with his queen at Woodstock."

"We hear that the young queen is quite beautiful," Jamie said with a smile, for he had seen Alain's face change as he mentioned Queen Philippa.

"She's like an angel!" It was obvious that he adored her.

"Lady Gillian's as beautiful as I remember," a fair-haired young man standing near Alain said quite seriously, his fine eyes fixed with concentration on her face. "She's not changed at all."

Gillian laughed delightedly. It was difficult to find the small page she remembered with such affection in the elegant young man with the handsome features who had greeted her earlier.

"I agree with you, Arthur." Jamie put his arm about her, knowing the truth of young d'Umfraville's compliment. Her eyes glowed with the happiness she felt at having Alain back, if only for a short while. For a moment he felt his years as the tall youths' vitality surrounded him. Already the atmosphere was charged with life, for Alain had brought several companions with him. Their high spirits would play havoc with castle discipline, he thought with amusement, remembering earlier times.

" 'Tis a pity Hugh's not here. He would have relished all the tales you have to tell. Lord de Percy is a severe taskmaster, but your brother seems to take to the martial arts exceedingly well," Jamie said, adding dryly, "which I can't say of my eldest son!"

"I'm afraid Sir Simon found me impossible! And yet, he taught me well." Alain laughed, pushing back a shining wing of bright hair from his animated face. "I've not seen Hugh since I left for court. Poor little brother—'tis not only my tales he'll miss!" He laughed again as Gillian looked disapprovingly from her son to his father.

" 'Twill be a busy time for all of us with little time for telling tales," she said firmly. "You've not come home to be idle. Preparations for the marriage are already under way and there's still much to be done."

"I doubt that Glairn will ever be the same," Jamie said irreverently. "Guests have already begun to arrive. Even Margaret and her husband are journeying from Essex to see you wed Alianor."

Gillian caught an oddly resigned expression in Alain's hazel eyes at the mention of his bride's name. She wondered how really anxious he was about the marriage, for he'd never paid the young maid much attention whenever he was at home, treating her more like a younger sister. She felt a stab of guilt. Was it fair to either of them to force them to wed? Alianor was a sweet and biddable girl, but Alain . . . Gillian looked thoughtfully at her eldest son, so like his father in looks, but so different in temperament.

"Mother, I've a wonderful surprise for you—there

will be some unexpected guests." His young voice trembled with excitement as he broke into her musing. She saw him exchange a nervous glance with Arthur. "We're to have the king here for the wedding, and his mother!"

Gillian went white and she felt Jamie's reassuring hand on hers.

"Isabella?" Her eyes darkened. "Isabella is coming here?"

"Aye—'twas she who proposed the visit. Edward is coming north shortly, as will Queen Isabella. She said she'd not seen you in years." The boy's voice faltered, for the distress on his mother's face was not what he had expected. "I thought you'd be pleased!"

"And the earl of March? Will he too be journeying to Glairn?"

"Gillian . . ." Jamie's voice was low but carried a warning tone. He saw Alain's bewilderment, but was more concerned for Gillian. He could feel her sudden trembling and knew the fear which gripped her.

"Mother, what is it?"

"Answer me, Alain—will Roger de Mortimer be with the queen?" All her joy had fled and she was consumed by cold dread.

"Nay, he's gone to Ludlow to hold his own court." Jamie caught a hint of bitterness in the boy's voice. "We hear he plans a splendid tournament and all who curry favor with him will be there." Barely seventeen, Jamie thought with regret, and he's already caught up in the politics of court life.

"But I vow Bleddyn ap Rhys will be with the king, though the earl desires his presence in Ludlow," Arthur volunteered. Both boys smirked, sharing in some private joke.

"Aye, he delights in defying the mighty earl every chance given him." Alain turned to his parents. " 'Tis a Welsh friend of ours who's much admired for his courage in preferring Edward's company to that of the queen's gentle Mortimer."

"Alain—'tis not meet to say too much." Arthur's handsome face darkened at his friend's rash words.

"At Glairn one can say what one wishes, Arthur, or have you forgotten?" Kilburn said.

"My lord—these days one must take care, for the very walls seem to listen." Arthur's voice was pitched low and he seemed uneasy.

"I think 'tis time I look for Alianor!" With a nervousness new to him, Alain rose and, in company with Arthur, hastened from the solar. As the door closed behind them, Jamie heard Alain's voice raised in anger. He stared at the closed door, puzzled by the behavior of both boys. 'Twas passing strange.

"They've moved beyond our world," Gillian murmured, feeling drained. Jamie's cheek rested on her hair as she relaxed against him with her eyes closed. The solar seemed strangely quiet.

"To live in constant fear of one man's power . . . will it ever end?" she asked, burying her face in his shoulder.

"Aye, sweetheart. And from what we've just heard, I think it has already begun."

Kilburn could not put Alain's words from his mind, wondering at the underlying current of animosity contained in the boy's voice and echoed by Arthur. Caught up in the bustle of preparations for the forthcoming wedding, he found no time to talk privately to his son. Alain, too, proved uncommonly elusive, for he had discovered that Alianor was quite changed from the plain little maid he remembered. Judging from the eagerness with which the youth agreed to each new plan, his father concluded that he must have decided marriage did not seem so unwelcome as it once had. It amused him to see how different Alain was from himself, for his son had inherited none of the shyness or sensitivity which had made his own youth so painful.

Since the royal visit would include hundreds of courtiers, followers, retainers, and guards, all part of the king's court, Glairn underwent a total cleaning, refurbishing, and decorating. The lord, his knights, and the increasing number of wedding guests finally were able to escape the tumult by hunting and hawking through its vast tracts of forests and meadowlands. Glairn's folk had only begun to venture into the forest in recent months and James found it good to hear the hunting horn echo again through the ancient trees. When the old truce with Scotland was broken during the tumultuous days of dead Edward's deposition, blood had flowed again on both sides of the border. Though peace had been restored through a treaty concluded by Roger de Mortimer and Robert Bruce, it was an uneasy one in which few border lords placed much faith.

"I didn't realize how much I loved Glairn till I was gone from it," Alain said, sitting on the sun-warmed rocks above the old cave. The hunting party was spread out all about the rocky ground for a well-earned rest. While game had been pursued with great vigor and enthusiasm, the hunters' only trophies were an aging stag, weary muscles, and ravenous appetites. The company made short work of the hampers of food and small barrels of wine and ale which retainers had brought out in the large wagons now drawn up beneath the trees.

Though his eyes rested on the servants busily clearing away the remains of the meal, James was unaware of the activity about him, for his mind dwelled on more private matters. Room would have to be made for the royal pair and their entourage, he thought gloomily, anger stirring in him that Isabella's pending visit had managed to ruin Gillian's happy anticipation of her son's wedding. Margaret's marriage to the Deveron heir had caused little stir, save that her presence was sorely missed by everyone at Glairn. And it disturbed him how evasive Alain had become since his return.

His arms encircling his drawn-up knees, Alain studied his father's somber face. From earliest memory, he had been wary of him, finding him a tall and forbidding figure, to be avoided if possible. Perhaps he had resented the strong bond of love which existed between his parents, for it had often wrested him from his mother's arms. And yet, had he not also found it a haven from his childhood fears? There was much he didn't understand about his father, but as he grew older he began to realize that James was a man capable of deep emotions and high principles which set him apart from his peers, forcing him to walk alone. There had been little chance for levity in his life, the boy thought, for most of it had been spent battling the Scots. Though he had not been able to speak of it, he was glad that his father had not taken part in the humiliating campaign young Edward had mounted against Robert Bruce. That unfortunate undertaking had brought the Black Douglas and the earl of Moray deep into Northumberland in pursuit of the English forces, including the Flemish knights brought over by Isabella. Alain's own dreams of glorious battles had been badly shattered by the inhuman conditions of a foraging army mired by its own weight and the final terrifying surprise attack upon the English camp by the Black Douglas himself, which had almost cost Edward his life. It had taken all of his strength of mind and pride to remain with his king rather than ride for home. Until he had heard that Glairn was safe, Alain had known no peace.

Thinking aloud, he said, " 'Twas a fortunate thing that the Black Douglas did not attempt to raid Glairn after his victory over Edward."

James shook his head grimly. "Our Scottish cousin has had sufficient warning to tread carefully on Kilburn land, my son—it has cost him many a clansman. But 'tis that accursed treaty I can't abide. It makes a mockery of all the years of battling to make peace on Scottish terms and not our own."

"Perhaps had it not been Roger de Mortimer who concluded the peace, the terms would have seemed less bitter," Alain said slowly, watching a bird circle over the treetops and suddenly disappear into the forest's depths.

"That's a rather shrewd observation for one of your tender years," James remarked with surprise. His son laughed, and there was a hint of his uncle Robert in the hazel eyes sparkling with amusement for a brief moment.

"Nay, Father—'tis not mine, but only what I've heard others say. And Edward violently opposed the marriage of his youngest sister to Bruce's heir. The boy is but four

462

years old—and England's enemy, no matter what the treaty claims. But March has a way with the queen, and Edward loves his mother."

James's gaze swept over the ground surrounding the rocks and saw most of the company sprawled out lazily in the warm spring afternoon, their cups emptied, relishing their total idleness. In contrast, Thomas Fitzhugh was engaged in a lively conversation with young Arthur d'Umfraville, whose fair hair gleamed silvery in the sunlight.

"You and Arthur spoke in unflattering terms of the earl of March the other day," James said in a low voice. "Is Roger hated by so many of his peers?"

"More each day, for as his power grows, so does his greed. I think there are many barons who would like to see him brought down, yet fear him. Particularly since the queen will hear no word spoken against him."

"Has Edward ever said aught of his feelings?" It was an unfair question to ask the boy, but James had to know. Alain frowned, pondering heavily on his reply and looked at his father with astonishment.

" 'Tis strange, for I would think he carries the most hatred—yet I realize now that he's said nothing. But then the king is surprisingly deep and keeps his own counsel. We're but six months apart in age and I feel he's years older. Lord de Mortimer would wish to keep him a child always, but the day will come when he'll not need his mother nor her lover."

To hear such a thought uttered so calmly by his son shocked Kilburn and made him uneasy. If a seventeen-year-old youth could see the truth, why then didn't Lancaster move against Roger—or was he too powerful to touch? James shivered in the sunshine, feeling as if a pall had been cast over the day. Alain rose, supple and graceful, and James was reminded of himself at that age. He was indeed his father's son in features and coloring. The short dark green tunic and hose fitted the tall slender body well, and his fingers unconsciously strayed toward the dagger he wore as he said, "Edward has bidden me accompany him to Amiens in June. He goes to swear fealty to the new French king." He hesitated, knowing that he

463

would cause his father pain, but it had to be said. "I will have to leave Alianor here. As a Fitzalan she'd not be welcome at court. Besides, 'tis well known how friendly you were with her father. 'Tis not Edward or his mother I fear, but March. There's so much hate in him."

James shook his head, tired suddenly of Isabella, Roger, and even the young king. Alain should not have to concern himself with such matters when he had a maid like Alianor Fitzalan to take as bride. Slapping the boy playfully on his back, he bade him forget Edward and court intrigues and teased him gently over the lovely girl he was to wed. James was pleased to see Alain blush. With Jennifer betrothed to a son of Lord de Laurensmere and a de Percy bride for Hugh, it would be good for Gillian to have Alianor to remain with them. Laughing together, James and Alain descended the rocks, and for the rest of the day were able to forget all but the pleasure of being alive.

The wedding had been a glorious success and the Great Hall still resounded loudly with the lighthearted merriment and gaiety which had been the mood of the entire day, beginning in Glairn's flower-bedecked chapel where the young bridal pair had spoken their vows before a white-haired and exceedingly frail Father Godfrey.

"How handsome your son looked," Isabella told Gillian as they sat together on the large dais. She raised a goblet brimming with sparkling claret to her lips and sipped it slowly, savoring its clean, rich taste. "Alain is a great favorite at court . . . Edward enjoys his company, for there's much humor and joy of life in him." The distracting sounds of music and boisterous laughter seemed to fade as the queen leaned toward Gillian and smiled. "But then I find all your children enchanting."

Isabella sighed with contentment. It was the first chance she had had to speak with her old friend, and it was so happy an occasion that she never noticed Gillian's silent withdrawal. She chattered on about her own children and the busy life she led, now that Ned needed her to guide him wisely in the matters of state which occupied so much of his time. Trying with difficulty to concentrate on Isabella's words, Gillian stared at her lovely face circled above by a narrow crown and framed by the pale hair caught in loosely woven gold net cases set with countless small diamonds which sparkled in the candlelight. Although the delicacy of the queen's features had blurred slightly, Gillian found her beauty more radiant and glowing than in her youth.

"I'm most fortunate in Philippa, too," Isabella was saying. "The count of Hainault was quite anxious for an alliance with England and he had three daughters to choose from. I must admit I was distressed when Ned chose the plainest and plumpest, but even then he was much taken with her." She laughed, remembering how he had refused to even consider the older two, knowing she would agree because of her desperate need for Hainault's support in her plans for conquest. "How surprised we were when Philippa arrived last year for the marriage in York as beautiful and charming a queen as I could have imagined for him. And Ned is truly devoted to her . . ."

It was amazing, Gillian thought, listening to Isabella's gay prattle, how she could block all the ugliness of her past deeds from her mind.

The Hall suddenly erupted with raucous, teasing laughter and lewd remarks were bantered about as Margaret came to take her sister-in-law by the hand, leading her from the Hall to the bridal chamber, soon to be followed by her young husband. There would be a great deal of lighthearted and ribald antics before the newlywed pair were finally left alone. Gillian shuddered as she saw Alianor's white, exhausted face beneath her circlet of delicately hued spring flowers. She still found it to be a horrendously barbaric custom, filled with cruelty, embarrassment, and humiliation.

"Your son's bride is a lovely girl . . . 'Tis truly a sweet and gentle face."

"Aye, Your Grace, our Alianor is a dear child. 'Tis a pity her father could not enjoy this day. We all would have been the richer for his presence." The words were out before she realized it, but Isabella's eyes held their surprise for only a moment.

465

"Her father? Ah yes, the earl of Arundel." She leaned comfortably back in her carved chair. "Well, *ma chère,* 'twas a mad time, and many mad things occurred. He always was a fool, though I freely admit he was executed in excessive haste. I can assure you that his properties and possessions have been well seen to by my dear Mortimer."

Gillian recoiled visibly at the mention of his name, but Isabella pretended not to notice, smiling sweetly.

"With all the holdings and land he's been granted and given by the crown, 'twas only fitting that he should be named an earl—and how gloriously he bears the title!"

"Given by himself, Majesty, and all know it. How can you be so blind?"

"Blind, Gillian? I'm not blind. 'Tis quite simple. I love him. I had always envied the love which existed between you and your lord, but 'twas only when I won the love of my gentle Mortimer that I truly understood your passion. Roger made me whole . . . I no longer have cause to feel ashamed for being a woman."

"But you don't know him—not as he really is," Gillian whispered, pleading with Isabella to understand. She knew that she risked the queen's anger in speaking as she did, yet she could not hold back her misgivings.

"No? Then you are naive, *ma chère.*" Isabella's eyes flashed with scorn. "He's helped me to attain what I desired most. My freedom from Edward! To me it mattered little how it was achieved, nor who fell from grace because of it. Now my son sits upon England's throne and he'll be a far better king than his father. And I hold the love of the most passionate and devoted man in the realm. The women Roger had before he became my lover mean naught to me . . . and neither does his wife, though he remains with her, for I am the one he loves, and together we are invincible."

"Oh, Majesty—'tis so wrong. Do you think Roger will remain satisfied with what he has? The king—your son—stands in his way. If you don't take care, he'll destroy him."

"He would not!" Isabella's voice rose angrily and Kilburn, in brief conversation with the young king, raised

466

startled eyes, seeing a stubborn look on Gillian's face.

"We've known each other for many years, and you've looked rightly upon me as a trusted friend. I'd not speak so, did I not fear for you."

"You need not fear for me, you poor innocent. There's naught Roger's done that I've not supported with all my heart." The queen was annoyed, for no one had ever dared speak to her so bluntly. "You'd best not speak too much of this lest something unpleasant befalls you." Her tone was threatening and the blue eyes wintery. "Roger is mine, and what he desires, he shall have, and there's no one to stand in our way. Your lord is still alive because I willed it so—I alone! Had I not, his head would have been sent to London with that of that swine Despenser." She spat out the words as Gillian listened, shaken and ashen-faced. "Think well on it, *ma chère amie,* for friendship too has its bounds. As you put your love for James Kilburn above all else—even though it cost the life of your husband—so do I place my love for Roger de Mortimer foremost in my heart."

For a moment Isabella stopped speaking, allowing the pounding of her heart to subside. She was furious with Gillian for having thrown her own guilt into her face. The countess had spoken to her as an equal and would be shown the error of her presumption.

"You, though the wife of an earl, are the daughter of a minor lord . . . and I am a king's daughter, my lady, and the sister of kings. My son is king of England, while by divine right he should also have been chosen successor to my brother Charles." Her face hardened . . . she could not forgive her brother's refusal, when he was dying in Vincennes, to name Edward heir to the throne of France, preferring to choose a de Valois cousin to succeed him. Edward was his own nephew—and a hereditary baron of France! Damn Charles, she thought angrily while Gillian watched the violent emotions alter Isabella's face. She realized that the elaborately bejeweled woman seated beside her, clad in her sumptuously royal robes, was a total stranger to her—the stranger she had sensed lurking in the spoiled, self-indulgent child-wife she had first met in York twenty years ago. The queen had become everything she had most feared in her, and Gillian was filled with revulsion.

"I need not explain my actions to you nor ask your approval of them." Isabella rose, showing Gillian the icy contempt she now held for her. Her ladies stood waiting for her, wondering at the cold anger which consumed her. "I believe that 'tis time I retire, as we must leave quite early tomorrow. And you need not accompany me," she said haughtily as Gillian called for servants to light their way to the queen's chamber.

"Your Grace, as you reminded me, I am the countess of Glairn and your hostess. As such, 'tis my duty to see you safely and comfortably settled." Gillian's head was held high and the large eyes glittered their angry defiance of the queen's cruel words. "But know that 'tis but a gesture of the most basic courtesy and hospitality."

The queen, followed by her ladies, swept grandly from the Great Hall, ignoring the sudden silence and respectful homage by the guests. Gillian, passing James's chair, lightly touched his shoulder. Staring at her in surprise, he saw the strained expression in her white face. Only one who knew her well would have noticed the slight quivering of the sensitive mouth. Silently Gillian led the way through Glairn's corridors, feeling sick at heart. Only once more did she address Isabella, as they stood outside the door to the bedchamber she and Jamie had ceded to the queen's use.

"We both know that what friendship there was is ended by what has just passed between us, and therefore I think it right that this be returned to you."

Isabella's hand closed over what Gillian gave her, and she watched the tall, slender figure melt into the dark shadows of the dimly lit corridor. She knew without looking that it was the gold ring with fleur-de-lis engraved on the narrow band and set with a small sapphire—her father's gift to her which she in turn had entrusted to Gillian, asking only for friendship in return. All these years it had been worn in good faith—it still was warm from Gillian's finger—and now? Isabella slipped it on her own finger and shrugged. The past was dead to her. Only fools clung to old, sentimental attachments. 'Twas the present and the future which had any true meaning.

"I wonder what took place between Gillian and the queen? Isabella looked absolutely furious."

Robert slipped into Alain's empty chair beside Kilburn as the pace of the festivities began to quicken once more. James shook his head in bewilderment.

"When Gillian passed by me, she was close to tears." His eyes narrowed with sudden worry. "God's blood, Robert—I fear she chose to criticize the queen's actions or even her relationship with Roger, presuming too much on Isabella's friendship. She was quite upset at the thought of Isabella's visit. Though I cautioned her to take care, I wasn't certain whether she would really heed me. Your sister can be exceedingly stubborn and willful."

"All too true! After all, she is a Harron!" Robert laughed, lifting his goblet in a silent toast to them all. "By the rood, Jamie, feast your eyes on young Jennifer being honored by a dance with the king."

Following Robert's gaze, James watched his youngest daughter as she was led through the rhythmic steps of a dance by her royal partner, his blue eyes sparkling with enjoyment. Jennifer blushed in confusion but was obviously delighted as he circled about her in tempo to the merry tune. There was a courtly grace and charm in his attitude toward her which would have fluttered the heart of a maid even older than the twelve-year-old girl.

Young Edward was a surprise, James admitted to himself. He supposed it was natural to seek out his sire's traits in him, but the boy's vitality, intelligence, and sensitive strength allayed any misgivings one might have. Already tall and well built, he promised to be exceedingly handsome, with none of the disturbing weakness of feature or manner which had marred his father.

That the king had captured the total loyalty of his courtiers was obvious, and while he laughed and joked with them, James noticed that not one was singled out for special favors.

"I see you observe our young king with interested

eyes, my lord," Master Brassard remarked, carefully lowering himself into a chair. He moved slowly these days, leaning on his cane. Where he had once been a tall and dignified man, the years now lay heavily upon his back. His hair and beard were white, but the dark eyes, smiling now, were still sharp and all-seeing. "Nearly seventeen years ago I brought him into the world and what a beautiful, healthy babe he was!"

"England's hopes lie heavily upon those young shoulders, Master Brassard." James's words echoed his thoughts. " 'Tis only to be wished that naught happens to him because of one man's overly active ambition."

"Sweet Jesu, Jamie—no politics today," Robert begged. "There's a wedding being celebrated and we should be joyous . . . though I confess that this morning in the chapel, I could not help but wish that Mistress Non had lived but one year longer to see her nursling wed."

"After Maddie's death, she lost all reason, Robbie. Today would have had little meaning to her."

"She was very old, my lord," the physician said with a sigh. "Naught could be done for her and she died quite happy in her state, for you and Lady Gillian were with her."

"My lord earl, I return your jewel to you, but only for a while."

The three men raised startled eyes to the young man who stood before them with Jennifer beside him. Her pretty face was flushed with excitement and the large hazel eyes lowered in shyness, for Edward still held her hand clasped in his. His clear blue gaze rested on Kilburn, finding a comforting strength in his lean, fine-featured face with its firm mouth and intelligent eyes.

"Perhaps you will allow us to have the pleasure of this young maid's presence—I believe that Queen Phillipa would enjoy her company for a certainty." When he spoke of his young wife, the king's face radiated such loving pride that the men were moved.

"Your Majesty, I would be honored to have my daughter wait upon the queen, but I must beg patience until the maid is of a less tender age." James saw a relieved look cross Jennifer's face and felt a pang of regret that he knew her so little, for she was the quietest and shyest of his children, and rarely in his company.

Releasing the girl's hand, Edward smiled as she returned to her place by Elizabeth Harron. He bowed to his host's request with understanding and left for the company of one of his friends. James saw that it was the young Welshman Alain had presented to him so eagerly, admired for his persistent and successful defiance of Roger de Mortimer. He watched as the youth laughed at one of the king's remarks, the flickering light of a candle accentuating the redness of the dark auburn hair lying straight and shining above his strange green eyes. There was something about him James found oddly familiar, though he knew they'd never met before. Seeing him stride down the hall beside Edward with a lithe, catlike tread, he felt he'd almost caught the troubling resemblance—but a resemblance to whom?

The following day, as he stood on the steps before the keep with Gillian at his side watching the king and the members of his court stream through the massive gate, the young man halted briefly before them. His head was bare and the spring breeze ruffled the thick hair, giving the pale young face a very boyish look. The glowing eyes beneath the dark winged eyebrows gazed warmly at the lord and his lady. Sitting his restless horse with easy grace, he saluted the earl with a show of sincere deference.

" 'Twas an honor, my lord. I pray that we may meet again."

James acknowledged the gesture politely and looked after him, still puzzled.

"Who was that, Jamie?" Gillian asked, feeling a vague uneasiness in his presence. "I don't recognize his family arms."

"A minor Welsh lordling named, I believe, Bleddyn ap Rhys. Alain considers him a good friend and one to be most admired."

"Why does he seem so familiar to me?"

"I don't know, lovedy, but I feel the same."

There was no chance to say more, and before Bleddyn had ridden across the drawbridge, he was erased from their minds, for their attention was caught by Isabella's tumultuous emergence from the keep. Though her response to James as he bent over her hand bidding her a good journey was warm and gracious, she pointedly ignored Gillian's presence. Only once, as she was lifted onto her white mare's back by her groom, did her cool gaze flick over her old friend and a faint flush reddened her cheeks. Surrounded by her ladies and pages, she too rode through the gate and soon was lost to sight.

Gillian had told Jamie of her conversation with Isabella and the ensuing quarrel. Though he could not in good conscience condemn her for having spoken so bluntly to the queen, what Isabella had inadvertently revealed to her of her relationship with Roger de Mortimer alarmed him more than the dissolution of their long friendship. He wondered whether the queen would truly sacrifice her son to hold the love of a man who had lost all sense of humanity.

"Did you notice, Jamie? She wore the ring," Gillian murmured as they moved into the flagged entry.

"Aye, lovely, I did." He sighed, wishing he could see into the future.

"The queen's as doomed as Roger is." Her words drifted softly through the empty hall, and she clutched her lord's arm. "No wonder she is called the she-wolf of France!"

" 'Tis a dreadful name." Jamie felt Gillian's distress, and pressed her hand. "Put it all from your mind. 'Tis over."

The faint sounds of the royal heralds' trumpets echoed over the castle's turrets and battlements as the king's procession reached the road leading to Newcastle, and they exchanged glances, denying his words.

Ludlow

Throwing her cloak, richly lined with fur, carelessly over a heavily carved chair, Jehan moved restlessly about the small chamber into which she had been ushered. It was obviously used for council meetings and gatherings, for a large table surrounded by several chairs stood near

472

the center of the scrubbed wooden floor. A servant, lighting candles in a round iron holder lowered over the table by heavy chains, stared at her with insolent admiration. Her attention caught by a sparkling glitter, she saw the familiar gem-encrusted golden goblets standing among others beside a wine flagon; they served only to revive memories best laid to rest.

What could Roger want of her, she wondered, for only the official summons brought by an equerry wearing the arms of the earl of March could have brought Jehan within such close reach of him. Ever since his nightmarish visit to Pen-yr-bryn three years ago, she had carefully avoided any contact with him.

While Isabella and her son toured the northern counties, the earl of March and his countess were holding their own court for all those barons and lords who professed loyalty to him. Damn parasites and men too frightened to challenge his power, Jehan muttered to herself, examining a gilded box delicately inlaid with carved pieces of ivory. Lifting its lid, she found it empty. Just like everything else connected with Roger, she thought.

Sir Powys had brought her to Ludlow for the splendid tournament which was to be held two days hence, and they had set up their small pavilion amidst all the others which had mushroomed into a bustling encampment on the gently sloping ground below the castle's hill. While Powys hastened to present himself to his liege lord, Jehan had been content to remain behind, dressing herself in as inconspicuous a manner as was possible for her visit to the Great Hall, where all would gather for the evening meal. And now she was here . . .

"My lady . . ."

Her green eyes flashed her scorn as the servant dared offer her wine in a plain silver goblet. Waving him away disdainfully, she felt angry at the nervousness which continued to grip her. A document lying on the table caught her eye and she bent over, trying to decipher the small, cramped writing.

"Jehan!"

She spun about guiltily, annoyed at Roger's silent entry, and hoped that he had not noticed her curiosity.

Curtsying low before the earl, she felt his hand on her arm, raising her up.

"My dear Lady Powys, you need not bow before me . . . we're quite alone, save for this oaf of a servant who dared serve you wine in a silver goblet!" Roger's voice was heavy with sarcasm as he handed her one of the golden goblets, ordering the servant to pour wine into it. Jehan looked at him with suspicion as he dismissed the servant, waiting for the door to close behind him before turning toward her.

"You see, Jehan, I've not forgotten."

"Neither have I, my lord—naught!"

He laughed, tilting up her face with his hand in order to gaze into the heart-shaped face—he found her little changed, and was amused to see the full mouth tremble under his scrutiny.

"I saw your husband today—he looks exceedingly well, Jehan, and so civilized with hair and beard neatly trimmed and a tunic of such costly cloth! I've ne'er seen him so handsome. I did right to wed you to him. He's quite besotted with you."

"Aren't you going to ask whether I'm besotted with him?" Jehan asked, jerking her head away from his grasp.

"We both know the answer to that, my dove—even if you won't admit it to yourself. There's only one you've ever really loved, and I doubt you've given your heart to anyone else." His black gaze mocked her, but she remained still, refusing to reply to his insolence. He motioned her to take a seat in one of the chairs by the table and sat down at its head. Waiting for Roger to speak she gazed at him in silence. Jehan was relieved to find that the hatred she held for him was still with her, and she saw him now as she never had before. Though still handsome, his face seemed to have subtly changed, the sharp, clean planes of cheek and jaw blurred and his features revealing a coarseness that was new to him. Even his body, covered by a long, lavishly embroidered tunic trimmed with marten, had lost some of its graceful suppleness. He emanated an unpleasant aura of hard cruelty which made her wary of him.

"You've done exceedingly well with Bleddyn—'tis of him I wish to speak."

"Bleddyn? He's a man now and goes his own way, my lord. I've done naught save tell him to take care." Her eyes widened innocently, but her pulses began to pound with contained excitement.

"He's become one of the ablest swordsmen at court, for all his youth, and no one can best him with lance or battle axe. 'Twas as proud a moment for me when he was given his spurs as when my sons attained knighthood on the day of Edward's coronation. He's mine at last! No one dares question my orders or defy me, save Bleddyn—but with what reckless arrogance and courage!" Roger laughed, admiring his bold defiance. "He was ordered to attend me here, and instead went north with the king. 'Tis good, for when he returns, he'll tell me all that of which I've no knowledge."

"I see you're much taken with him," Jehan said, watching Roger's smug face. "You seem so sure of his loyalty despite his wildness."

"He's very like me when I was his age—and Powys named him well, for he is indeed a wolf's cub," Roger boasted, failing to see the odd smile lurk in the corners of Jehan's mouth. "In order to bind him yet closer to me, I've granted him total sovereignty over Pen-yr-bryn. Powys will remain there for now, of course," he added hastily as Jehan rose in sudden alarm. "And the manor house near Shrewsbury with all its lands and rents."

"The one you gave to me?" she asked without thinking.

"Yes—why not? 'Tis mine to do with what I choose. There's another holding near Pen-yr-bryn that I've also ceded to him, and next year I'll request Edward to confer a baronetcy upon him." He glanced at the small, slender woman who stood staring at him. The slanted green eyes he still found so enchanting were glacial.

"You're very generous, my lord—and to a poor bastard at that."

Her cold expression did not change as she saw him redden. So he thinks Bleddyn is his! Oh, Roger, how little

475

you know your son, she thought with secret glee. He hates you more deeply than any of the great lords you despise so, but I've taught him well to dissemble. You've forgotten that my blood runs in his veins as well as yours.

"I crave a boon of you, Jehan . . . for Bleddyn." He beckoned to her and she approached him slowly as he picked up the document from the table. "Although 'tis not yet the proper time, I intend to acknowledge him as my natural son. He'll bear my name."

"Your name?" She went white at his words—sweet Virgin, it would destroy all she had worked for.

"My signature and seal are on this paper naming him my son." Roger held it out to her. "But since unfriendly eyes might chance to see it were I to keep it with my other papers, I ask that you keep it in your possession till such time as I deem right to name him mine."

Holy Mother of God! This can't be happening, Jehan thought wildly, feeling the smooth texture of the parchment between her shaking fingers. Can vengeance reap fruit so soon, she wondered, as the words Roger wanted to hear came glibly to her lips. Lady Olwen's impassioned plea echoed through her mind. Bleddyn must never be acknowledged by Roger, she vowed, even as they drank a toast to seal the pact between them. Dispassionately watching him empty his goblet, she suddenly knew that he would not be allowed the chance. Someday he would have to face his peers and account for all he'd done—in his rise to power he had gained many enemies. Had his arrogance made him so blind to every thought but his own that he could not see the danger in his actions? Jehan hardened herself against a sudden desire to turn back the time. Nay! 'Twould be for naught, she told herself sternly, wishing only to be gone from his presence.

"Jehan . . ."

She stiffened as his hand gripped her shoulder, drawing her toward him. His eyes bored into hers, dark and totally lacking in tenderness or gentler emotions.

"Nay, my lord." Jehan pressed both hands against his chest, struggling to escape him. "Roger, this is madness."

" 'Tis indeed madness, Jehan, when you're so close —within reach," he murmured as he captured her mouth

476

with his own, certain of his power over her. She remained stiff and unyielding in his arms, her lips refusing to open beneath his. Taken aback by her lack of response, he released her and was confronted by a demon.

"You filthy swine!" she hissed, her face distorted with outraged fury. "How dare you believe I'd let you touch me after you cast me off so cruelly. Did you think I could still feel love or passion for someone who's degenerated into the inhuman creature you've become? The power you have seized through your arrogant manipulations of those less vicious and unprincipled than you will be your undoing."

Roger's face had grown dark and mottled at her words. Without conscious thought, his hand lashed out, desiring to end her tirade. He had heard enough accusations from this woman. She had tried his patience over and over again through the years. Her face stinging from his blow, Jehan staggered back, clutching the edge of the table to keep from falling.

"What will you do now, my lord earl of March?" she asked contemptuously, trying desperately to keep her voice from betraying her fear of him, for she had not meant to go so far. "Arrest me as you do all those who refuse to do your bidding? When will it stop—when there are no lords left in England to defy you?" She held up a hand, as if to fend him off. "Nay, Roger, listen well to me. I'll keep my promise and hold the paper you've given me, for it concerns my son as well as yours. But for that favor, you'll leave me in peace."

Almost imperceptibly, he nodded his agreement. Jehan took a shuddering breath. Her knees shook as she picked up her cloak, not daring to look any longer at the man who stood so silently observing her with veiled eyes. She lifted the latch and the door slowly swung open. With every step she took she expected him to call out for guards to take her prisoner. Strangely, he allowed her to go as he had that night in Pen-yr-bryn. Leaning weakly against the cold wall outside the council chamber, she realized that she was weeping. The man she had loved all these years no longer existed, vanquished forever by the monstrous savage who still inhabited Roger's body. She had won this battle, but she could never chance another, she told herself as she fled down the corridors, seeking the safe anonymity of the crowded Great Hall.

All through the long hours of that feast, Roger de Mortimer sat beneath the elaborate canopy, totally absorbed in conversation with those lords about him. From where she sat, Jehan watched him eat and drink with great enjoyment while she but toyed with the food set before her. She had hidden herself well, finding the raucous merriment and mounting drunkenness a perfect cover for her agitated state. Seated as far from the dais as her social position allowed, she saw with distaste that Powys, deep in his cups, busily pounded his fists on the table in appreciation of all the activity about him, his fine new tunic stained with food and wine. He had not even noticed her absence from his side, she thought with a flash of wry humor. As she believed herself unobserved, she was also able to steal curious glances at the richly clad woman seated beside Roger. In all the years of her involvement with him, she had never seen his wife, knowing her only through her lord's eyes. Expecting a plain and colorless woman, she was startled by Joan de Mortimer's charm and dignity displayed to her guests. Tall and still slender despite the many children she had borne her husband, her pleasant, even features seemed a trifle cool and austere until she smiled, betraying the warmth and compassion of her true nature.

Jehan could not know that two pair of eyes rested on her own still figure, aware of the fear which still held her in its cold grip. Lady de Mortimer had long known of her existence, and it was with mixed emotions that she searched the crowded tables until she caught sight of the extraordinarily beautiful woman who had held her husband's passion for so long a time. 'Twas not necessary to ask her name nor anything about her. Seeing the piquant, sensual features and the vividness of her coloring, enhanced by the deep green of her well-cut velvet gown, she understood all too well, and it was as if Roger had thrust yet another knife into her heart.

Only Emrys, seated before the dais near the countess,

saw the secret, guilty exchange of glances between the two women. His hands tightened on the strings of his small harp until they bit sharply into his fingers. No one would ever know the bitter frustration which swept over him at his ability to see everything and yet be able to reach out to neither woman and comfort her.

PART EIGHT
1330

Chapter 18

1330
York

" 'Tis good to have your company again, Jamie, if only for a little while."

Master Porcher's voice was cracked and dry with age, but the smile on the wrinkled face could not deny his pleasure at seeing his nephew once more. He had aged as greatly as had Sir Simon, Master Brassard, and Father Godfrey, James thought sadly, looking at the wizened figure huddled in the large chair opposite him.

"Uncle, if you'd only agree to give up this house and move to Glairn—'twould please us all! 'Tis where you belong, you know, for no matter what you say, you are a Kilburn by birth," he told the merchant, worry over his frail condition plain in James's eyes. The warehouses, once filled with raw wool and bustling with workers and apprentices, had stood empty for almost five years, but the stubborn old man refused to leave the house he'd called home for most of his life.

"There's no denying I get lonely, lad, but that feeling passes, and I welcome the serenity of solitude." He sipped the hot broth a servant brought to him. "I've all I want here—servants to wait upon me, food to keep me from starving, enough gold to pay my creditors, and now and again a visitor to keep me informed of the outside world."

" 'Tis not enough, Uncle." James shook his head, but the old man was adamant. "Were I not going to Nottingham to this mysterious council March has called, I'd not have stopped by to see you! You know that in the past few years I've left Glairn but rarely. I've no wish to place my head in any snare de Mortimer would lay for me. 'Tis not that I fear him, but I'd be a fool to risk my life for the likes of Wigmore—or March, as he insists on being addressed." He rose to hold chilled fingers to the fire roaring in the huge hearth. "Besides, with the endless rain we've had since spring, the harvest is late and exceedingly sparse. And now I fear an early winter. 'Tis already damn cold for October." Slowly, he added, " 'Twill only add to our troubles."

"Aye, and the chill does not only portend the coming winter, I fear," Master Porcher said. "There are strange rumors abroad."

"I've agreed to go to Nottingham only because Alain sent me an urgent message. You're right. There's something afoot, though I don't know what it's about. When Henry de Percy left last week, he mentioned something about Lancaster trying to foment trouble. He's been bitter ever since Isabella usurped his power. And now that he's totally lost his eyesight, I hear tell 'tis all he dwells upon. Though I tend to side with him, I can see no solution for the moment, for the king is still very young."

"Aye, but from what I've heard, there's more than one plot afoot."

James looked at his uncle with interest, for the old man had always had a nose for the truth.

"Lancaster apparently is in league with Richard Bury."

"The Keeper of the Privy Seal?" James sounded surprised.

"Aye, the same."

"God's blood, Uncle, I can only hope there'll be no more bloodletting. There's been too much already."

The old man sighed. " 'Tis a sorry business to be sure. March grows more arrogant each day, and other than those we know oppose him openly, there's no one who can challenge his power."

"Nay, Uncle, you're wrong!"

James spun about in surprise at the sound of the familiar young voice. Alain stood in the doorway of the merchant's study, muffled in a long dark cloak. He threw back its hood as he greeted his father and great-uncle warmly.

"I'd hoped to find you here," he told his father. "We've just arrived from Nottingham . . . Edward and his queen are there together with his mother and March." His hazel eyes searched his father's face. "We need your counsel."

Listening to his son, Kilburn noticed that he had not come alone, for there were two others with him, equally wrapped beyond recognition. All were fully armed as if expecting to be waylaid at any moment. Their actions smacked of conspiracy, and he began to grow uneasy.

"I take it that 'tis the earl of March you've all come about," he said quietly, motioning them to take seats by the fire.

"Lord Kilburn—the situation becomes more serious each day and we fear for the king's life."

One of Alain's companions leaned forward earnestly and James recognized the young Welshman his son held in such high esteem. His lilting speech, accustomed to a different tongue, was difficult to follow, but the frustration and worry were patently clear.

"Edward is virtually de Mortimer's prisoner!"

Lionel Porcher stirred in his chair, looking from one anxious young face to the other. While a servant poured heated wine into cups for his unexpected visitors, he said with ill-concealed impatience, " 'Tis not unknown to most folk that March has grown so in power that his will is placed above the king's. Yet the queen mother belongs totally to him, and through her, her son as well."

"It grows worse, Uncle, for March has even taken to sitting while the king stands and walks before him for all the court to see. 'Tis maddening—both for Edward and those of us who care for him" Alain replied, holding the steaming cup between his cold hands.

The third young man, introduced as John de Molines, one of William de Montecute's knights, had said little, allowing his companions to speak for him. With a vehemence born of the anger boiling inside of him, he now let out a bitter cry.

"'Tis rumored that March covets the crown for himself . . . only Edward stands in his way."

"No rumor, John, but fact. We still reel from the trickery he used to lure the earl of Kent into his trap of committing what March deemed treason."

The words were spoken quietly, yet Bleddyn ap Rhys, more than any of the others, seemed to comprehend the deeper implications of what they unconsciously wished to be told. James looked at the pale, handsome face with growing respect. Kent had soon been disillusioned by Isabella's actions, and together with Lancaster, formed the chief opposition to any of de Mortimer's dealings. 'Twas common knowledge that he had believed the stories told him that Edward was not dead, but imprisoned in Corfe Castle. The fool, James thought, remembering how Kent had been accused of plotting to free his brother, his own unguarded words and incriminating letters used as weapons against him to find him guilty. But there was something to the conspiracy which troubled him.

"If Roger de Mortimer could arrest the king's uncle, try him before a supposed court of his peers, and execute him without any opposition from Edward, then the realm is indeed in dire straits," he said, voicing his doubts.

"The king was in Woodstock, Father, to be with Philippa for their son's birth." Alain's excuse was glib in his complete confidence of Edward's innocence.

"Be that as it may, if Roger's done it once, he can do it again."

"'Tis our belief as well, my lord," Bleddyn said, looking at his friends for support. They nodded and he took a deep breath. "Do you believe the climate right to take action against March?"

It was out—and the words hung in the tense atmosphere of the suddenly silent chamber. Only the crackling of the fire and de Moline's sudden nervous cough broke the stillness. Master Porcher blanched as his dark eyes stared with disbelief at the auburn-haired Welshman.

"Sweet Jesu, young sir . . . 'tis treason you speak!"

"Aye, 'tis that, Uncle, and yet, what else is left for them?"

James spoke calmly, belying his true state. He closed his eyes, trying to sort out the myriad images racing through his mind. They were right, of course. Roger would have to be eliminated. But only with the king's blessing, he cautioned them, when he finally agreed to their plan. Their faces glowed with triumph at his advice. Knowing him for a cautious man and sincere in his beliefs, they had hoped to have his approval. There were others in the plot, Alain confessed, revealing that a great deal of thought had already been given to it. Lord de Montecute was their leader, and it would be his responsibility to convince the king of the rightness of their action. John de Molines explained that Lord de Montecute had been to Avignon and spoken to the pope of Edward's situation and that, together with Sir Richard Bury, had begun to persuade the king to break de Mortimer's hold over him.

The three young men spent the remainder of the night discussing their plans with Kilburn and Master Porcher. The old man viewed it all dubiously. 'Twas too great a risk, for their lives would be forfeit should it go awry.

"We live in fear now," Alain retorted with spirit. "At least we will have tried." James could see that the adventure beckoned strongly to him.

"Best take care and avoid any foolishness," James told his son sternly. "Remember that Alianor is carrying your child. You risk both her life and the babe's if aught were to happen to you."

Alain sobered in the face of his father's warning. "If naught is done, what future would any Kilburn have with a de Mortimer upon the throne!"

James fell silent, realizing the truth of Alain's words, and knew that all were now committed beyond the point of caution. It was decided that they would return to Nottingham immediately and that the earl would follow within the next few days. By then, they would have either triumphed or failed.

With Master Porcher beside him, wrapped warmly in a great fur cape, James watched quietly as Alain and his two comrades stood in the large courtyard beside their saddled horses, preparing to mount. Had the question of the Welshman's disturbing familiarity been in his mind, it had disappeared in the face of his quiet determination and high-minded intelligence. It was obvious that, in spite of a certain wildness of spirit, he had the ability to make such young men as Alain and de Molines listen to him. An unfamiliar grimness was reflected in the taut young faces, illuminated by the growing brightness of early morning. Even the grumbling of the gatekeeper, resentful at having been awakened at such an ungodly hour, did not relieve the tension. Unbarred, the heavy doors swung open, and the three horsemen rode out into the narrow street.

James saluted each of them silently as they passed him, his heart heavy with the knowledge that the future lay within their hands now, and not his.

Nottingham

The air felt cold and damp as the small group of men slowly made their way through the narrow tunnel with only the feeble light from a small lantern to guide them. It reflected on the slimy wetness of the walls as the sound of dripping water reached their ears. Treading carefully, their mailed feet still slid on the slippery, mud-covered floor, while they had to bend over to avoid the low ceiling .

" 'Tis like a tomb in here," one of the younger men said, and was answered by a nervous laugh.

"Quiet, young sirs!" came the terse order of their guide, Robert de Heland. "There's no way of knowing how far voices carry in the tunnel. At this point we've passed beneath the castle walls and should begin to ascend." True to his words, they could see where the ground sloped gently upward. The passageway twisted and turned so often that they had long ago lost their bearings.

Alain felt for his sword, making sure that it sat loosely in its scabbard, and wondered if his companions' hearts were pounding as loudly as his own. He sneaked a glance at Bleddyn, walking silently beside him, but his face showed no trace of fear or apprehension. The dim outlines of his brother-in-law's younger brothers, Humphrey and William de Bohun, could be seen directly in front of them, while a faint clanking noise from behind betrayed the presence of the others taking part. It had been a stroke of luck that Lord de Heland still remembered the underground passages. Alain found it difficult to concentrate on what lay ahead of them, certain only that Edward was waiting for them once they emerged from the tunnel within the castle fortifications. It had been quite a victory to persuade the king finally to move against de Mortimer, but William de Montecute, the most outspoken of the group, had prevailed. What had at last made Edward agree was the simple fact that if he did not strike first, he would himself be struck down.

"Do you think de Mortimer suspects trouble?" he whispered to his companion.

" 'Tis quite possible, for he's more closely guarded than ever," Bleddyn replied, moving closer. "The queen as well, for few have seen her these past weeks." His voice trembled with excitement and his hands itched to use the sword which hung so impatiently at his side.

The tunnel was becoming drier as they alternately crawled and walked along the passageway which now led straight upward, even allowing for a few steps to be cut into the rock. Calling a halt, de Heland waited for the others to catch up, de Montecute and John de Molines flanking him.

"If I recall correctly, there should be an artery from this main tunnel a few yards farther on which leads to the keep where the queen's apartments are." His voice was so low they strained to catch his words. Robert de Heland had altered little since being replaced as constable of Nottingham Castle after the fall of Berwick, save for some added weight and a small beard which gave the pleasant features a sharp look. Although he continued to serve the crown, his dislike for Isabella had not lessened through the years and it had not been difficult to persuade him to enter into their plot.

"What if March is not with the queen?" one of the young men, Robert Ufford, asked.

"Oh, he'll be there," Bleddyn said, a bitter taste flooding his mouth at the thought of de Mortimer with the queen.

" 'Tis not the queen we're after," de Montecute cautioned, and started forward, the others following. In a few minutes they came out of the narrow passage to find themselves at the foot of the stone staircase in the keep. With a sense of relief, Alain saw Edward's drawn face peering at them as he sat on the stairs, waiting for them. He was alone.

Warning that de Mortimer had posted guards before the chamber, he silently led them up the winding stairs, stepping into a small corridor which ended at a low wooden door set into the castle's thick stone wall beneath a Norman archway.

The young men looked at one another with mounting excitement and drew their swords.

Roger looked up with astonishment and a strangled oath as, with a tremendous crash, the door burst open and the chamber was suddenly alive with armed men. His companions, with whom he was sharing a final cup of wine before retiring, sprang to their feet, their swords already in their hands. Sword met sword before his startled eyes while the cries of both friends and enemies rang through the small room. His own sword was snatched from his hand before he had a chance to use it.

Emrys, trying desperately to reach his lord's side in the wild melee, was paralyzed with shock at the sight of Bleddyn's face, blazing with unmasked loathing as he laid hold of de Mortimer's sword arm, twisting it roughly behind his back, while John de Molines grasped the other.

"Father!"

The cry was anguished, and Roger saw William de Bohun's gauntleted hand fell his younger son as he ran blindly into the chamber, fumbling for the dagger at his waist.

"Geoffrey!" He looked at the inert figure crumpled

on the floor. "If you've killed my son . . ." he shouted, trying vainly to escape his captors.

"Nay, he's but stunned, de Mortimer. You'd best look to yourself," de Bohun called, swinging his sword in wide arcs over his head. John Neville de Hornbie gave a triumphant shout as Sir Hugh Trumpington slowly sank to his knees with an amazed look on his face. His sword clattered to the floor as blood suddenly streamed from a deep sword thrust in his side. Realizing the household steward was dying, Alain dragged his body out into the corridor, leaving a trail of blood in its wake. Rising to his feet, he found himself by the king, whose eyes questioned him mutely. He scarcely had time to shake his head when a scream pierced the sounds of battle, followed by another and another.

Isabella stood in the doorway to her bedchamber, disheveled hair tumbling over her bare shoulders, her eyes wide with fright as she gazed at the wild scene confronting her. Like a wildcat, she leaped at de Montecute, vainly clutching at his sword, but he shook her off.

"Sweet Jesu, nay—oh, God, oh, God, nay!" she cried, beating Bleddyn with both fists before turning to Roger, tears streaming down her cheeks. Weeping hysterically, she threw her arms about his neck, pressing herself tightly against him. Roger still fought fiercely to loosen the grip on his arms, but now Isabella hampered him, knowing only that he was in grave danger.

"Stop this outrageous fighting at once," he roared. "And release me! Now!" His wild face was like that of a trapped, spitting animal caught in a snare, the features distorted, lips drawn back in a feral snarl. "How dare you raise your swords against me? The castle is mine. I swear you'll pay for this with your lives!"

Isabella raised her head and looked into his face, hardly knowing him. Still clinging to him, she turned to glare at Roger's attackers.

"Please, dear sirs—take care. 'Tis your queen who orders you to stop this madness," she called out in a tone at once pleading and imperious, but no one listened to her. They had obeyed her last command.

491

Busily binding the arms of Simon de Beresford and John Deveril, who had finally been subdued, the young men avoided her gaze. Dragged to their feet, the prisoners followed Geoffrey de Mortimer, who had already been carried from the chamber.

William de Montecute pulled Isabella roughly away from de Mortimer, and met black eyes burning with impotent rage.

"My lord de Mortimer, I place you under arrest in the name of our king." His voice was hoarse with triumph. "And 'tis not your castle—'tis the king's."

At his words, Roger began to struggle once more, and as the hold on his arms tightened cruelly, he looked around at his captors. Unexpected pain coursed through him as he caught the naked hatred in Bleddyn's green eyes.

"You Judas!" he spat. "Christ's wounds, I'd not have thought it of you!" His face drained of all color and he turned his head away from the force of Bleddyn's black emotion. "May you rot in hell!" he growled.

"You'll get there first, my fine lord," Bleddyn muttered in his ear, the taste of victory incredibly sweet.

"Bel filz!" Isabella's voice called out suddenly as she fell to her knees. *"Bel filz!* I beg you . . . spare my *gentil* Mortimer!" Over and over she entreated her son to spare her lover, sensing instinctively that Edward was present, even though he had not shown himself. The young men stared at her in shocked pity, uncomfortable in the presence of a woman suddenly stripped of her royal divinity. She was completely unaware of their attention, her overpowering fear for Roger's life the only reality left to her. She knelt near the door, barefoot, naked arms outstretched, and her face wet with tears. Her shift clung to her, outlining the swell of breasts and rich roundness of hips and belly no longer hidden by her curtain of hair.

"Sweet Mother of God!" Humphrey de Bohun softly voiced the appalled reaction of them all. Alain's gaze followed the others and shared their horrified shame. The thin silk cloth of her shift revealed what the voluminous skirts of her gowns had hidden. The queen mother was pregnant!

"You filthy vermin!" One of the knights struck de Mortimer in the face. Before de Montecute could stop him, another had kicked him in the groin, and Roger grimaced from the sudden agonizing pain. With a great effort, he remained upright, refusing to give his enemies the satisfaction of having to hold him up.

"That's enough!" de Montecute said shortly.

Uncertain of how the queen should be treated, he cast about for advice, but no one seemed to know. His eyes fell on Emrys whose face was twisted with emotion. The Welshman was lost, bereft of master and a world he had known all his life. Standing by de Mortimer, he had resigned himself to death.

"You, harper, go and find some of the queen's women to care for her."

Emrys scuttled out to do de Montecute's bidding, his face hidden from de Mortimer and his mind holding the image of Bleddyn's hate.

Isabella still lay sobbing on the floor, unaware of them, knowing only the blinding anguish of having de Mortimer torn from her arms. There was little enough any of them could do to stem her grief, Alain thought, as he left the chamber behind Emrys. The corridor was filled with de Mortimer's guards who had already laid down their arms. Placing the castle's keys, which he had discovered in Isabella's bedchamber, in Edward's hand, Alain was rewarded by a fleeting smile which crossed the white, strained face.

It took four men to drag the snarling, struggling earl of March from the chamber, his arms tightly bound behind his back. Edward in the corridor, his face once more cold and expressionless as he faced his mortal enemy. The light from the chamber fell upon the narrow crown circling his brow, its points glinting and sparkling, seeming to mock the tall, black-haired lord brought low before him.

"Lock him in the dungeon."

The order was curt and spoken in a voice which would not tolerate any challenge. For a moment he glanced into the chamber, his eyes resting on the weeping, prostrate figure of his mother, but he showed no emotion.

His friends, less two who had lost their lives, stood about him, their bloodied swords sheathed, watching him. The blue eyes warmed slowly as he held out his hands to thank them, and they rejoiced in the knowledge that he had thrown off the hated yoke of regency. At eighteeen, Edward had truly become their king.

The journey to London began the following day, with the king, surrounded by his close companions, riding at the head of the large company. From the first sounds of the trumpets heralding Edward's emergence from the castle, the streets leading to the high road erupted with the roar of folk who had been gathering since the early hours of morning. Word of de Mortimer's arrest had spread swiftly, and the joyous clamor of the crowd turned to angry shouts and jeers at his appearance. The sight of the pale, unbowed figure of the hated lord, his hands manacled before him, drove them into a frenzy of virulent hatred, and his guards were hard put to dodge stones, mud, and rotting vegetables aimed at their prisoner. Several times the earl's mount shied in fright, pulling at the lead rein held by a captain of the royal guards, while de Mortimer's hands clung to the pommel of his high-cantled saddle to keep from being unhorsed. It seemed to Kilburn, who watched the procession from the tiny window in his chamber at an inn outside the city walls, that all the high-born lords who had come to Nottingham for the council meeting were unaware of mingling with folk of lesser birth in their eagerness to catch a glimpse of that despised man in chains. Henry of Lancaster, though sightless, must have insisted upon being present for the occasion. With grim amusement, James saw him stand at the roadside amid the crowd and shout with glee as de Mortimer rode past, obviously having been told that fact by one of his retainers who led him carefully away from the press of humanity a few minutes later. Isabella was not traveling with the king and it was rumored that she would follow a few hours later in company with the young queen. Kilburn knew from speaking with an elated Alain earlier that morning that she too was heavily guarded, although not under arrest. She had gone quite mad with grief, Alain whispered as he broke his fast with his father, and no one had been able to stop her hysterical weeping. Only some of the young knights who had taken part in last night's escapade would accompany the two queens on their journey. Isabella too was being taken to London, but no one believed she would be held in the Tower.

So burning with the desire to share the excitement of de Mortimer's capture with his father, Alain did not seem to find anything strange in James's taciturn reaction to the news of Isabella's pregnancy. 'Twas not to be spoken of, he said, finishing his broth with relish, and there was already great speculation as to what the king would do with his mother once her lover was disposed of. As he was leaving, Alain hesitated and then turned a puzzled face to his father. 'Twas odd, but of their group, only Bleddyn did not rejoice at the king's triumph, and behaved as if some great personal wrong had been avenged. When Edward had told them in the first heady moments of victory that he would grant a boon to any who asked, the Welsh knight had requested that he remain within sight of de Mortimer until his imprisonment in the Tower. With an embarrassed laugh, Alain admitted that he had suddenly become a stranger to his friends. James listened quietly to his son without commenting on his confidences. Bidding him a safe journey, he watched as the tall, long-legged youth mounted his black destrier and clattered out of the inn yard into the October sunshine. But Alain's words remained with him, and he had later sought out Bleddyn from among Edward's knights as they rode past, and recognized the wild, hate-ridden exultation on the young man's face, for it mirrored his own.

As the prisoner was transported by way of Loughborough and Leicester, the large crowds lining the way of the royal procession southward showed unbridled joy at the sight of a fettered de Mortimer. On the 27th of October, the prisoner was delivered to the Tower while Edward issued a proclamation to his people that the government and rule of the realm now lay safely in his own hands.

The Great Hall at Westminster was crowded with nearly every magnate and lord of England, all fulfilling their obligations to attend the meeting of Parliament which had been called for November 26th. The mood was somber, yet the air crackled with excitement as Edward, resplendent in a royal mantle of red velvet, heavily embroidered with gold, and the state crown resting on his blond head, took his rightful place on the dais for the first time without the presence of either the Council of Regents or the queen mother and her lover. In a firm, controlled voice, he ordered that the charges against de Mortimer be read to all who were assembled. The prisoner, pale, gaunt, and still in chains, stood facing his accuser, while the curious eyes of his judges rested on the tall, straight figure whose will refused to submit to the blow fate had dealt him.

"These are the treasons, felonies, and misdeeds done to our lord the king and to his people by Roger de Mortimer and others of his brood."

The voice of the royal clerk rang through the Hall so all could hear, and the long parchment roll held in his hand trembled with nervousness, for it was a momentous occasion.

While he was being charged with usurping the royal power and government of the realm over the estate of the king, de Mortimer's gaze swept contemptuously over the assembled lords. He caught looks of triumph on some of their faces, particularly blind Lancaster, who had become so violent a foe. There had been a time, a very short time ago, when these self-same lords had fallen over themselves to do his bidding. Two-faced bastards, he thought maliciously, to sit in judgment upon me! John de Warenne, aware of Roger's piercing gaze, refused to look at him, preferring to examine the gold chain about his neck.

"He had procured the death of the king's father, Lord Edward of Caernarvon . . ."

"He had contrived the death of Edmund of Kent . . ."

The king's uncle, Thomas of Norfolk, met Roger's eyes unexpectedly as the charge was read and the accusation in his glance caused Roger to look away first. His knowledge of Kent's innocence was the one fact he had admitted to during the endless hours of interrogation in the Tower. Damn! he thought bitterly, young Edward had neatly shafted him by denying him the right to speak in his own defense or enter a plea refuting the charges.

Sitting beneath the banner bearing the golden hawk of Glairn, James Kilburn listened to the clerk's voice read the words which caused Roger de Mortimer's ambitious scheming and greedy accumulation of power and wealth through murder and theft to suddenly take on eerie substance in the charged atmosphere of the hall. Every baron present could find a score to settle with him because of his disregard of the rights of others to challenge his actions. 'Twas why they had all come! Even I came to see him brought to his knees, James admitted to himself, finding the sight of Roger in chains strangely gratifying. It was amazing how fear fled in the face of an enemy disarmed. The Hall was uncomfortably damp, in spite of the torches and many braziers standing along its great length. James saw Roger shift his feet on the stone floor, swept clear of rushes, obviously cold and hard against his leather-shod feet.

"He had sown discord between the king's father and his queen, Isabella . . ."

So that was it! Roger was jolted by a sickening anger. He knew then why Edward had forbidden him to speak. 'Twas to protect his mother! He had indeed been delivered into the hands of a jackal! How clever the young king had been, never challenging his power as long as he himself had not had the strength to take that power from him. Isabella was right—there was naught of his father in him, but a great deal of both grandfathers. Roger shook his head—how stupidly blind he had been! But those thoughts fled abruptly, and his face grew taut and drained as he heard the clerk charge all those present to pass judgment on him, proclaiming that he was truly guilty of all the stated crimes.

To spare Isabella he would be made to bear the total burden of guilt for all the foul deeds laid at his feet, and there was naught to alter his fate. So must the Despensers have felt, he thought in a rare moment of introspection. He had not allowed them to speak in their defense either.

Their fates had already been preordained as he was certain his was. He brought his dark eyes to rest at last on the fair, handsome features of the young king as he quietly watched his clerk roll up the parchment. There was no triumph in the blue eyes, or satisfaction—only that purposeful, intense expression that had slowly come upon him since the birth of his son . . . his heir now, Roger thought grimly. The next king!

His judgment was swift and unanimous, requested of and responded to by every member present. Deemed traitor and enemy to the king and realm, the earls, barons, and peers, as judges of Parliament, awarded and adjudged that he should be drawn and hanged, such judgment to be executed and performed on the first Thursday following the first day of Parliament, it being the eve of St. Andrew's. Four days—'twas all that was left him. Better they had slain him where he stood, he wished angrily.

But no matter what his thoughts were, while the judgment was being given, proclaimed loudly for all to hear, Roger's face remained blank before his peers, though the muscles in his jaw tightened. When he was finally removed from the Hall, he walked with a steady, firm step, refusing to show any fear or even anger.

Observing de Mortimer's departure with reluctant admiration at the other's strength, James tried to quell the exultant feeling of vengeance which was beginning to rise once more within him. The cold hatred which he had harbored for so long against the Marcher baron clamored and called for release, and while he would not be the executioner, he felt a satisfaction that de Mortimer, so sure of his destiny, had been vanquished.

The heavy wooden door swung open with difficulty and the rush of air caused the short, thick candle sitting in its simple iron holder on the low, badly scarred wooden table to gutter wildly, plunging the small cell into momentary darkness before renewing its light. It was bone-chilling cold, for no brazier had been provided, but the man who slowly rose from the narrow cot seemed impervious to it. His dark eyes glittered as they swept over the tall, cloaked figure hesitating for a moment in the doorway before finally stepping into the cell.

"How delightful of you to call!" The familiar voice with its unmistakable timbre was heavily laced with sarcasm. "I didn't know whether you had received my message, or if you would even come."

"Emrys brought it to me—he still waits outside the Tower's main gate, hoping for a miracle! I've told him 'tis futile, but I doubt he even heard me."

"He's always been my creature and will stay so." Roger shrugged with indifference.

"You asked to see me. I have come, though with great reluctance, for I've no wish to speak with you," Kilburn said coldly. "What is it you want of me?"

He had never before been in the dungeon of the Tower, and the insidious dampness and unbelievable stench of forgotten humanity sickened him. His face was expressionless as he fought a growing revulsion and unconscious fear of his surroundings. Even as he spoke, he could hear the regular dripping of water as it slowly trickled down the walls to the stone floor sparsely covered by moldering straw. As he approached the prisoner, his soul recoiled at the sight of Roger's white face. The coarseness which had marred his handsomeness and had still been evident at his trial was erased from his features. Had he retained the marks of his cruelty and debauchery, James could have held on to his hatred, but this man was almost the Roger of his young years when his ambitions were still dreams and not yet reality. For a brief moment, pity stirred within him, but it was quickly stifled.

Roger stared intently into his visitor's face, perhaps himself searching for some sign of the younger Kilburn who had been his friend so long ago. He ran a hand through hair still dark and untouched by gray.

"So it's come to this!" he said cynically. "I wondered whether your curiosity was sufficient to your responding to my request! How confident you looked at the trial, sitting among your fellow peers judging me. Did it give you satisfaction, James, to order my death?" There was a sneer in his voice which he refused to hide. "How you all have brought me low!"

"You brought yourself low, Roger, through your arrogance and pride of self. Did you think yourself so omnipotent that no one could touch you?"

"Whatever opinion I held of myself is unimportant, for you and your friends have managed to destroy me." Roger's face twisted with bitterness and anger. For a moment, his eyes gazed beyond James, fixed on the light falling through the small barred opening in the door. "Do you think me such a dolt that I was unaware of the king being turned against me?"

"Only in the last months, Roger, for you went too far! It was to save his life and the crown he wears." James's eyes suddenly burned with outrage. "You would have seen him dead in order to set yourself upon the throne!"

Roger was taken aback at James's vehement accusation. "I never said I wanted him dead! Nor committed one deed to jeopardize his life." He was defensive, anxious to prove Kilburn wrong.

"God's blood, man—you have been judged guilty of the foulest deeds, been branded a traitor and murderer, and still dare to hold to your claim of high-mindedness? You—the self-proclaimed earl of March!" James was furious.

"And what of Isabella, my lord? Naught's been laid at her threshold!" Roger spat out, stung by Kilburn's words.

James shook his head in wonder. "You are incredible! I'm sure 'twas not difficult for you to hold her in thrall. She cannot be totally blamed for her passion. She deserved to taste love, poor little queen." His face hardened. "But never with such as you! Had you left things alone, perhaps all might have been different, but you wanted everything. I know that she carries your child—and have you thought what will come of that?"

De Mortimer began to laugh, his eyes black and wild.

"What does it matter to me now? You still see her as she was in Tynemouth, you idealistic fool! 'Tis not for naught she's called a she-wolf. Did you think 'twas all done without her knowledge?"

"Nay, you're wrong. I know all too well what she has become, but 'tis over for you both. Yet she must live on with the knowledge of her sins and there's not a grain of pity for her in you. You've lived with deceit for so long, you can no longer distinguish between any emotions."

How righteous James sounds, de Mortimer thought, swirling the dregs of the sour wine he had left in the bottom of a forgotten cup. Now he can feel himself vindicated! Forcing back his irritation at the other's attitude with difficulty, he said bluntly, "James, I want you to intercede with the king. If I must die, allow me the courtesy of beheading . . . the thought of hanging is unacceptable to me."

Kilburn stared at him, scarce believing his ears.

"I'll not! You are not a member of the royal family to be accorded such consideration, and even if you were, I still would do aught to ease your death. You've stolen the lives of too many decent men. I owe you nothing, Roger . . . the debts owed are on your side alone."

Pointing a finger at James, Roger laughed, his face flushed with anger.

"You stiff-necked bastard! Had it not been for Isabella, you would have climbed the scaffold with that fool Arundel. Your high-minded, principled kind is the undoing of this realm. Had I had my way, you would be long dead." His voice lashed out at James, trying to provoke a display of angry hatred from the cool, unshakable earl.

"So she has said herself, and 'tis a debt owed to her," James said, realizing with surprise that his desire for revenge was gone. What was left for Roger now but the gallows and the executioner's knife? Revenge was meaningless in the face of death.

"If you wish to regard it as such, do—there's little we've ever agreed on, save one thing." De Mortimer's voice sank down to a soft whisper. James looked at him warily as he came close and said with a leer, "Your lady's bed was indeed worth your lack of ambition, my old friend. 'Twas only when I bedded her myself that I understood."

Kilburn went white, but de Mortimer, watching his reaction closely, was not finished.

"She has always been a woman who draws men with

her slumbering, elusive sensuality, and I had long ago promised myself to have her."

" 'Tis enough, Roger—you've scarred her for life by what you did to her." James's voice shook and he spoke with difficulty, for he felt as if he were choking. De Mortimer smiled darkly, and Kilburn knew that the demon which inhabited his soul was still there, for he lurked in the depths of the dark eyes.

"So Gillian told you I forced her! Perhaps she struggled against me at first, but not for long. She was starved for love and her body soon opened to me . . ."

He staggered back as Kilburn struck him in the face, his eyes blazing green with raging hatred. Before Roger was able to fully regain his balance, James had grasped him by the front of his tunic, his face wild, demented by the taunting words.

"We'll not see each other again, friend James, but I leave with you the knowledge that we both have possessed your lady and that I too have tasted the sweetness of her skin and the softness . . ."

He had no chance to complete his remorseless baiting of the furious man, for Kilburn, desperately striving to control his desire to kill him, said tightly, "No more, de Mortimer—you've succeeded in your endeavor to awaken my hatred again, but what good will it do you tomorrow, when your life is brought to an end while James Kilburn, who is everything you despise, lives on, to feel the sun, breathe the air, know the changes of seasons, and still have the love and passion of a woman who is his alone?"

"Well said, James," de Mortimer murmured as he loosened the other's hold. Moving away, he began to laugh again. "Consider it my legacy to you—the memory of my possession of your lady." And he continued to laugh as James stared at him, his anger ebbing in the unhappy presence of the doomed man.

"Gillian was right. She saw death in your face when you first came to Glairn. She said you would destroy yourself and all who believed in you, for death was your true destiny." Pale and shaken, he walked to the door and called for the guard. It was time to leave Roger to his fate.

But the sound of de Mortimer's mocking laughter pursued him through the dark stone corridors of the Tower.

De Mortimer watched James leave, and when the door closed behind him, he sank down on his cot, suddenly drained of the demonic amusement which had driven him on. So it was death that had terrified Gillian when she looked into his face! He pushed his hair back and saw that his hand was trembling. Sweet Jesu—death was all that was left to him now, he realized, and he began to sweat, in spite of the cold. He had gambled everything, sacrificed not only the lives of others, but his own as well in the glorious ambitious dream of his youth. His children would inherit his misfortunes and reap his follies, but not for long, he assured himself, for Edward was not so implacable an enemy as to hold the sin of one man against another. He clenched his hands and rose, moving like a caged animal about the small cell. As his world came crashing down about him, the sight of Bleddyn's pale face and glittering green eyes beneath the gleaming auburn hair as he attended Edward during the trial returned to haunt him. His father's trial! What pure hatred had been reflected in those features so like Jehan's. And then he knew what she had done to him—oh, the clever, vengeful bitch! She had waited to exact her revenge through her own son! Roger stopped by the table and stared into the candle's flame, the words of Bishop Orleton in Oxford suddenly flooding his mind—"I will put enmity between thee and the woman and between thy seed and her seed." Though it had been said for another purpose, how apt it was when turned against him!

A man's life is indeed a plaything of God, he thought, seeing the irony of his own existence . . . and found that it meant nothing.

"Was the meeting with Roger so dreadful?" Gillian asked anxiously, sitting beside Jamie on the broad settle by the hearth. He had returned to the Pembroke Palace in Flete Street several hours earlier to find her with Lady Mary in the solar. Both women had voiced concern over his look of bleak devastation and insisted that he take his ease by the fire until some color returned to his face.

While he hastily downed a cup of heated ale, he told them of his confrontation with de Mortimer, wisely omitting the bitter ending. They were shocked by de Mortimer's lack of remorse, and Lady Mary voiced relief that his death would put an end to the misery endured by so many he had deemed enemies.

When they had bidden the countess good night and retired to their chamber, Jamie could find little rest, but was thankful to have Gillian beside him. He was pleased that she had been able to leave Westminster Palace so soon after bringing Jennifer to Queen Philippa's court, for he wanted only to return to Glairn as soon as possible.

Feeling her gentle hand on the side of his face, he caught it in his own and kissed it.

"Aye, 'twas difficult, for I found that although my hatred was gone, his still ran hot. He's lost everything while I've held to what's mine." Jamie gathered her into his arms and she leaned contentedly against him, her long dark plait falling over her shoulder. He lifted the thick braid, feeling its silken softness ripple through his fingers.

"You've changed so little, lovedy," he murmured with an expression akin to wonder, breathing in the sweet scent of her. Gillian smiled, relieved that his mind had turned from Roger.

"I only know I've changed when I see Alain so tall and your image as I first remember you." She frowned and said with a sigh, "Yet, I'm afraid he's not the constant man his father is. I saw him today at the palace—he thought himself unobserved—with his arm about one of the pretty maids Queen Philippa brought with her from Hainault. They seemed quite engrossed with each other."

Jamie laughed. "Don't dwell on it. He's young and high-spirited, and I fear a trifle greedy for life. Let his desires run their course, and he'll settle down. Once Alianor has her child, he'll find his roots. There's nothing so sobers a man as the birth of a son."

" 'Tis simple for you to think so, my darling—but Alain is not at all like you."

He had hoped to lighten her mood but saw that she was still reflective, her dark blue eyes blindly contemplating the long narrow windows of the bedchamber.

"All his friends seem to be as irresponsible as he has become, particularly that young Welsh knight," she said with great disapproval. "Alain said he's been granted permission to return to Wales after Twelfth Night. Perhaps 'tis best for Alain, because there's an unsettling wildness to him which makes me uneasy. I've seen it before, but where?"

"You're much too fanciful, sweetheart, and look for ghosts where there aren't any." Jamie tilted her face up, noticing the shadows still lurking in her eyes. "But 'tis not Alain's behavior which disturbs you the most, is it? Tell me now, so you can lay your fears to rest."

"I tried to see Isabella today, but was told that the king has forbidden anyone to visit her in her apartments. Even the young queen has been told to stay away. Though I said naught, as you bade me, I felt it was to hide her pregnant state, though 'tis rumored that she's lost her mind and recognizes no one, while weeping bitterly and calling for Roger. 'Tis so dreadful for her, no matter what she's done." She shivered and nestled closer to Jamie. "If she is truly mad, 'tis for the best, for she'll not even know when he is executed. At least she can be spared that."

" 'Twas of her own doing, lovedy," Jamie told her quietly. "She alone is to blame for what has happened to her. She placed her love in a man who used her shamelessly, and would have had her share his guilt, were it not for her son's protection. If it will ease your sadness, be comforted that she has her memories of a Roger she alone knew and loved. I think 'tis what she holds fast to in some corner of her soul." He saw tears sparkle on the long dark lashes.

"Alain is to accompany her to Castle Rising in Norfolk, when she's fit to travel; 'tis where she's to live, at least for the present time." Her mouth quivered. "He had hoped to be home with us for Yule, but 'tis not possible now."

Jamie was suddenly sated with the dark passions and sins of both Isabella and her lover.

"How is Queen Philippa?"

"A lovely young girl, exceedingly fair and so warm and kind to Jennifer. She recognized her shyness at once

505

and soon had her smiling and eating comfits. I think our young maid will be happy waiting upon her. There's much laughter in her." Gillian's face cleared as she spoke of the queen.

"I'm glad, sweetheart. 'Tis time for more gaiety and happiness in all of our lives." He turned her to him and kissed her until she began to tremble, forgetting everything but Jamie's lips on hers.

Jamie woke with a start, gripped by a strange restlessness. In the dim light filtering through the bed curtains he saw that Gillian was sleeping quietly, her cheek resting on her hand. Slipping from the bed, he noticed that although the sun had just begun to rise, someone had already lit the hearth, for there was a pleasant warmth to the small chamber. He walked to the window, peering out at the new day, and saw what had disturbed his sleep. Hastily pulling on a woolen tunic and soft leather boots, he seized his cloak and hurriedly strode from the chamber.

When he reached the courtyard, a guard moved away from a small open door set into the still-barred gate, so that he could look out into the street. Muffled drums heralded the passing of a condemned prisoner being taken to the Elms, the place of execution on the bank of the Tyburn, a small stream emptying into the Thames. Jamie saw with surprise that the street was filled with people already abroad at this early hour. Four Tower guards wearing the king's badges rode by, followed by Roger de Mortimer, ashen-faced and clad in a plain black tunic with no family arms to identify him. Though the air was chill, he wore no cloak and was bare-headed, his dark hair falling lankly to his shoulders. Mounted on an aged, spavined horse without a saddle, he clutched with bound hands the animal's mane while his booted feet were tied beneath its belly. The executioner rode behind him, a tall, broad-shouldered man whose face was hidden beneath a black hood. The tools of his profession, a broadaxe and several long, sheathed knives, hung from the saddle horn. With a start, Jamie saw that Bleddyn ap Rhys was among those accompanying Roger to the Elms, and wondered again at the hatred which possessed him so passionately, although there was no sign of it in the drawn, brooding young face.

As Roger passed the gate, his eyes, which had been staring so fixedly before him, suddenly met Jamie's gaze. For a moment the red-rimmed eyes glowed with their old fire and the dark head inclined slightly in a last farewell. Then he was gone, and the street began to empty of its spectators.

" 'Twill be a fine execution, good sir," the guard said, locking the door behind the grim-faced, somber-eyed lord. His small eyes twinkled beneath heavy black eyebrows, and he smiled broadly. "I hear that many of the members of the court will view it. The king has even ordered the earl's body to hang on the gallows for two days—what's left of it."

The guard's coarse laughter followed Jamie as he returned to the bedchamber, his stomach lurching as he forced the image of Roger's face from his mind. 'Twas over, and he refused to dwell any further upon how costly the Marcher's dream had been. No more, Jamie vowed as he sat down quietly on the bed. Gillian stirred in her sleep and he gazed at her face, turned toward him, her long lashes lying like dusky shadows on the still softly rounded cheeks while the red, sensuous mouth curved in a slight smile. It always amazed him that he never tired of looking at her beloved features framed by the dark cloud of hair. He was overcome by such a surge of love for her that he closed his eyes for a moment, shaken by the intensity of his emotions. He roused her gently, kissing the soft mouth until it opened beneath his.

"Gillian," he said in a low voice, tender with the feeling she stirred in him. " 'Tis time we return north, sweetheart."

She was in his arms, her cheek pressed to his.

"Oh, Jamie, yes . . . please take me home," Gillian whispered, tears burning her eyes for the pain she felt within him. He pulled her head back to look into her face. His hazel eyes were filled with love. Holding her close, he felt her heart and soul merge with his own. They were one, as they had always been.

"You've been mine from the moment my hand

touched yours so long ago, lovedy. I loved you then, and my love has grown each day we've been together," he said with wonder. "But never have I loved you as much as now, Gillian. Now," he murmured against the mouth lifted blindly to his, "and always."

Jehan did not feel the cold penetrating the mantle which swathed her small figure as she leaned against the rough stone parapet of Pen-yr-Bryn's highest tower. Looking at the wind-driven dark clouds spilling over the stark rocky crags, she found an answering wildness in her heart. She had rejoiced with Bleddyn in their shared triumph when he brought her the news of Roger de Mortimer's death, and yet, the feeling of exultation that revenge should have brought did not come. The overpowering hatred that had sustained her during the last years fled in the face of the reaped fruit of the seed she had planted and nurtured with such care in her son. In its stead there was the agonizing realization that in helping to destroy Roger she had destroyed her own soul, leaving her with naught but a wrenching, aching loss which would never lessen throughout all the years remaining to her. Tears streaming down her cheeks, she sank slowly to the tower's floor and hid her white, grief-stricken face in her arms.

Epilogue

The countess of March, dry-eyed and with a face etched as from marble, ordered that her lord's remains be removed from Coventry where the good friars had taken his body, and brought back to the Welsh Marches which had bred him.

For her the anguish of the many separations, the silent, painful knowledge of his countless infidelities, and the ultimate humiliation of having to lose him to Queen Isabella were at an end. She ordered masses read for his soul, and the voices of the chanting monks rose to the vaulted stone ceiling of the chapel in the Austin Priory at Wigmore. A bronze lamp with its unquenchable light hung suspended above the tomb to which his restless, endlessly dissatisfied spirit had finally brought him. But with darkness, the monks retired, deserting the chapel, and Roger de Mortimer lay in his eternal prison, all that was left to him of the great holdings, lands, treasures, and power he had attained in life, unmourned and forgotten by all save those who remembered his arrogance, ambition, cruel savagery, and greed.

Emrys had remained with his master even beyond death, and sat alone in the chapel through the night, surrounded by the tiny, flickering flames of the votive candles. Staring blindly at the figure of Christ writhing in perpetual agony on the cross above the silent altar, his fingers moved softly over his harp. It was a lament which had no place in that hallowed corner of Christianity, for it was drawn from a time when pagan darkness had obscured the world, though even then, men had wept for their dead.

As the first rays of the cold winter sun crept over the stark, sleeping land, Emrys set his face toward the west, toward the darkness which had not yet received the day. His harp slung behind him, he sat on the small gray horse with naught but a sack holding his meagre possessions which hung from the saddle beside a small shield bearing his lord's arms. His strange green eyes still glittering with the tears which had come unbidden as he mourned, the harper realized that there was but one place left for him to go—into the mountain fastness of Wales, to seek out the son his lord had secretly loved above all his others. Bleddyn ap Rhys, honored by the young king for his fidelity to the crown, would never know his true identity and it was better so.

For a while, the small hooded figure of the harper could be seen on the narrow king's road slowly climbing upward toward the dark, brooding Welsh hills.

He turned his back forever on what was past, knowing that before him lay a new beginning with his master's son. And his heart began to sing within him, for he was going home.

THE END

ROMANCE ... PASSION ... INTRIGUE
FROM WARNER BOOKS

CARESS AND CONQUER
by Donna Comeaux Zide   (82-949, $2.25)

Was she the mistress of a pirate as she claimed when first they met? Or the favorite of the King of France? Was she a woman capable of deep love—or only of high adventure. She was Cat Devlan, a violet-eyed, copper-haired beauty bent on vengeance and a living challenge to Ryan Nicholls. She was a woman to CARESS AND CONQUER.

SAVAGE IN SILK
by Donna Comeaux Zide   (81-878, $2.50)

Born of violence, surrendered to the lust of evil men, forged to travel and suffer the world over, Mariah's only sanctuary lay in the love on one man. And nothing—neither distance nor war nor the danger of a wild continent—would keep her from him! A runaway bestseller, SAVAGE IN SILK is a page-turner that moves like lightning, covering territory from the mountains of the Blackfoot Indians to the post dwellings of London aristocracy.

LOST SPLENDOR
by Donna Comeaux Zide   (91-274, $2.50)

Jenny would find sorrow in Spain, torment in Montana, intrigue in Caracas, misery in the Venezuelan jungles before the passion she was predestined to know became reality in a make-believe land of LOST SPLENDOR. Many men would entangle their hands in her long black hair; many men would gaze into her deep blue eyes and caress her silken body in lust or love. But someday she would meet that man ... and someday that love would be hers ...

RAKEHELL DYNASTY
by Michael William Scott   (96-201, $3.25)

From the first time he saw the ship in full sail like a winged bird against the sky, Jonathan Rakehell knew the clipper held his destiny. First he must persuade his New England family that the future of their shipping business lay in this amazingly fast vessel. He must build a clipper ship, sail it, and in proving its worth, prove his own. The grand saga of the great clipper ships and of the men who built them to conquer the seas and challenge the world!

PULSE-RACING, PASSIONATE, ADVENTURE-FILLED FICTION

CASABLANCA INTRIGUE
by Clarissa Ross   (91-027, $2.50)

Morocco, 1890. Beautiful Gale Cormier is on her honeymoon. Her husband is talking to a dark man in a red fez . . . at least, he was a moment ago. Now she is alone as a curious crowd moves in upon her . . . examining . . . begging . . . menacing . . .

CARESS AND CONQUER
by Donna Comeaux Zide   (82-949, $2.25)

She was Cat Devlan, a violet-eyed, copper-haired beauty bent on vengeance. She was a living challenge to Ryan Nicholls, but was she the mistress of a pirate as she claimed when they first met? Or the favorite of the King of France? . . . and a Murderess?

LIBERTY TAVERN
by Thomas Fleming   (91-220, $2.50)

The American Revolution is love and hate, a beautiful woman, flogged for loving a Royalist. It is a young idealist who murders in the cause of liberty. "A big historical novel with a bracing climate of political sophistication."
—*New York Times Book Review*